WarCraft

The Sunwell Trilogy

Volume 1

Dragon Hunt

Written by
Richard A. Knaak

Illustrated by
Jae-Hwan Kim

KAPLAN

TOKYOPOP®

HAMBURG // LONDON // LOS ANGELES // TOKYO

History of the World of Warcraft

It is indeterminate exactly how the universe began, but it is clear that the Titans—a race of powerful, metal-skinned gods from the distant reaches of the cosmos—explored the newborn universe and made it their mission to bring stability to the various worlds and ensure a safe future for the beings that would follow in their footsteps.

As part of their inexorable, far-sighted plan to end the chaos and disseminate order, the Titans shaped the worlds by raising mighty mountains, dredging out vast seas, breathing skies and raging atmospheres into being, and empowering primitive races to maintain their reshaped, plentiful new worlds.

Ruled by an elite sect known as the Pantheon, the Titans brought a utilitarian order to the clutter of a hundred million worlds scattered throughout the Great Dark Beyond during the first ages of creation. The benevolent Pantheon assigned their greatest warrior, Sargeras, to be the first line of defense against the extra-dimensional demonic beings of the Twisting Nether who sought only to destroy the life and energy of the flourishing universe. Sargeras was more than powerful enough to defeat any and all threats he faced...except one.

Unfortunately for the Pantheon, the Titans inability to conceive of evil or wickedness in any form worked against Sargeras. After countless millennia of witnessing the atrocities of the demonic beings he fought, Sargeras eventually fell into a state of deep turmoil, despair, and madness.

Sargeras lost all faith in his mission and the Titans' vision of an ordered universe. It wasn't long before he came to believe that the concept of

INDETERMINATE

\in de TER mi net\ (adj.): vague, unknown, imprecise

Samuel looked forward to leaving school to face the *indeterminate* obstacles of the real world.

DISTANT

\DIS tent\ (adj.): separate, far apart

Mary sounded very *distant* on the telephone, so her mother worried that she might be sick.

INEXORABLE

\in EK sur uh bul\ (adj.): inflexible, unyielding

Undeterred by their opponents' efforts, the invading hordes kept trudging forward, like an *inexorable* force of nature.

DISSEMINATE

\dih SEM uh nayt\ (v.): to spread far and wide

The wire service *disseminates* information so rapidly that events seem to get reported before they happen.

PLENTIFUL

\PLEN tee ful\ (adj.): abundant

After this year's *plentiful* harvest, the farmers were sure they could feed the entire country.

UTILITARIAN

\yoo til ih TAYR ee un\ (adj.): efficient, functional, useful

I have no doubt that these *utilitarian* solutions to the budget problems will be employed immediately.

CLUTTERED

\KLUT erd\ (adj.): messy, disorderly

Jeffrey could no longer manage working in such a *cluttered* environment, so he spent half the day cleaning up the mess around his office.

BENEVOLENT

\bu NEV uh lint\ (adj.): friendly and helpful

Ben and Eve volunteer at the shelter, which is typical of their *benevolent* nature.

FLOURISH

\FLUR ish\ (v.): prosper, thrive

While one immigrant family had a hard time and was unable to survive in their new country, the second family *flourished* in their new home.

TURMOIL

\TUR moyl\ (n.): state of extreme confusion or agitation

In the *turmoil* of the fire drill, Jackie had forgotten where she left her wallet and cell phone.

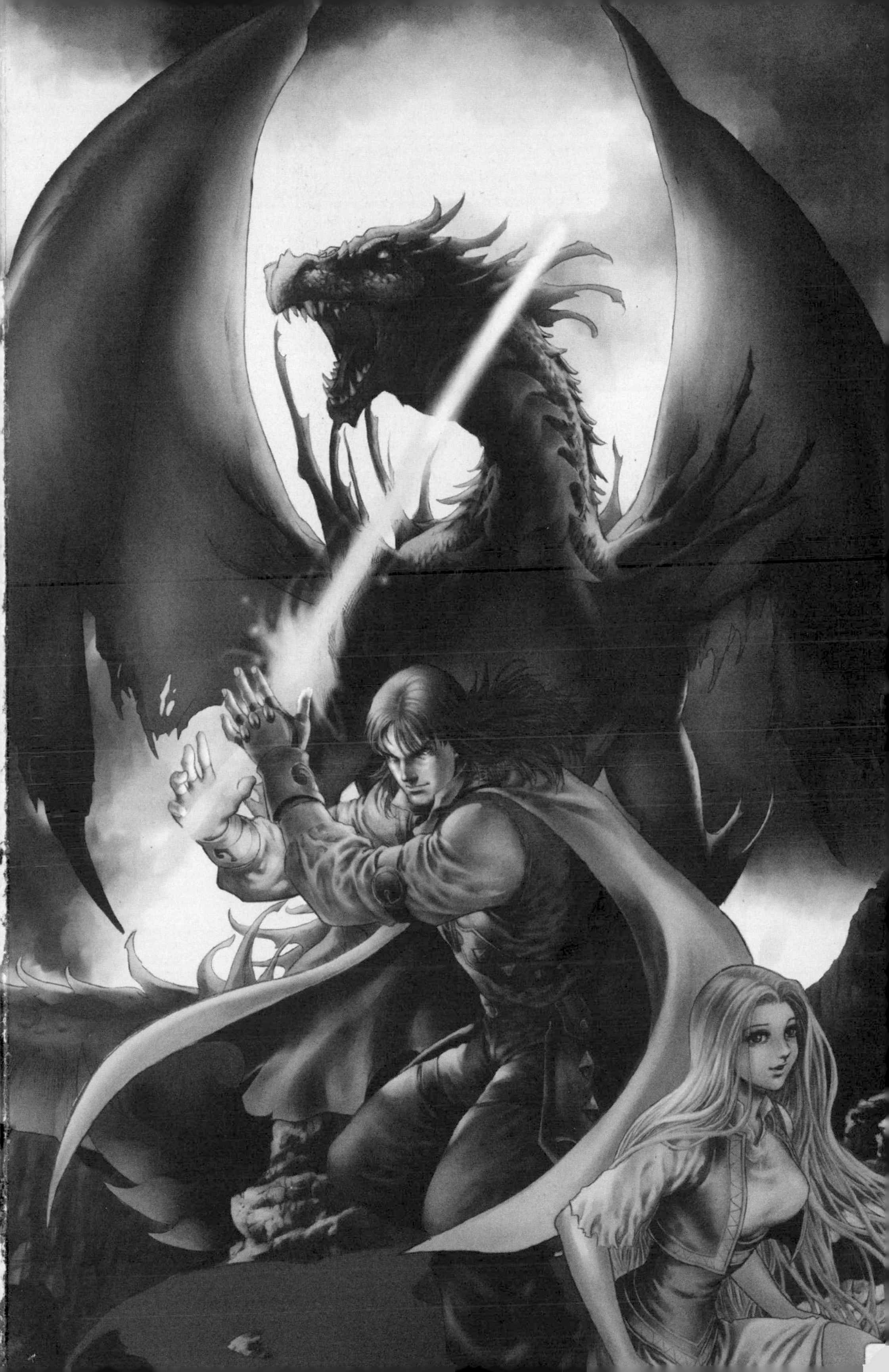

Warcraft®: The Sunwell Trilogy™ Vol. 1

Written by Richard Knaak

Illustrated by Jae-Hwan Kim

Cover Artist - Jae-Hwan Kim
Kaplan Edition Writer - Sheryl Gordon
Production Artists - James Lee, James Dashiell and Mike Estacio
Artist Liason - Eddie Yu and Studio Ice
Additional Design - Louis Csontos
Cover Designers - Raymond Makowski and Louis Csontos
Editors - Lillian Diaz-Przybyl and Mark Paniccia

Editorial Director, Kaplan Publishing - Jennifer Farthing
Project Editor, Kaplan Publishing - Eric Titner
Production Editor, Kaplan Publishing - Fred Urfer

Digital Imaging Manager - Chris Buford
Pre-Production Supervisor - Erika Terriquez
Art Director - Anne Marie Horne
Production Manager - Elisabeth Brizzi
Managing Editor - Vy Nguyen
VP of Production - Ron Klamert
Editor-in-Chief - Rob Tokar
Publisher - Mike Kiley
President and C.O.O. - John Parker
C.E.O. and Chief Creative Officer - Stuart Levy

Special thanks to Chris Metzen, Lisa Pearce, CoryJones, Brian Hsieh and Elaine Di Iorio for their effort, energy, and enthusiasm.

Published by Kaplan Publishing, a division of Kaplan, Inc.
1 Liberty Plaza, 24th Floor
New York, NY 10006

A TOKYOPOP® Manga

TOKYOPOP and are trademarks or registered trademarks of TOKYOPOP Inc.

TOKYOPOP Inc.
5900 Wilshire Blvd. Suite 2000
Los Angeles, CA 90036

E-mail: info@TOKYOPOP.com
Come visit us online at www.TOKYOPOP.com

ISBN-13: 978-1-4277-5495-0
ISBN-10: 1-4277-5495-0

First printing: July 2007

10 9 8 7 6 5 4 3 2 1

Printed in the USA

Kaplan Publishing books are available at special quantity discounts to use for sales promotions, employee premiums, or educational purposes. Please email our Special Sales Department to order or for more information at kaplanpublishing@kaplan.com, or write to Kaplan Publishing, 1 Liberty Plaza, 24th Floor, NY, NY, 10006.

order itself was folly, and that chaos and <u>turpitude</u> were the only fundamental absolutes within the dark, lonely universe. Believing that the Titans themselves were responsible for creation's failure, Sargeras resolved to form an unstoppable army that would undo the Titans' works throughout the universe and set the physical universe aflame.

Even Sargeras' <u>enormous</u> form became distorted from the corruption that plagued his once-noble heart. Fire <u>blazed</u> through his eyes, hair, and beard, and his metallic bronze skin split open to reveal an endless furnace of blistering hate.

In his <u>wrath</u>, Sargeras <u>mandated</u> that the <u>vile</u> demons he'd previously imprisoned be freed. These <u>cunning</u> creatures bowed before the dark Titan's immeasurable rage and offered to serve him in whatever malicious ways they could. From the ranks of the powerful Eredar, Sargeras picked two champions to command his demonic army of destruction. Kil'jaeden the Deceiver was chosen to seek out the most sinister races in the universe and recruit them into Sargeras' ranks. The second champion, Archimonde the Defiler, was chosen to lead Sargeras' vast armies into battle against any who might resist the <u>merciless</u> Titan's will.

Once Sargeras saw that his armies were amassed and ready to follow his every command, he launched his raging forces into the vastness of the Great Dark. He referred to his <u>extensive</u> army as the Burning Legion. To this date, it is still unclear how many worlds they ravaged on their Burning Crusade across the universe.

Unaware of Sargeras' mission to undo their countless works, the Titans continued to move from world to world, shaping and ordering each planet as they saw fit. Along their journey, they happened upon a small world whose inhabitants would later name Azeroth.

TURPITUDE

\TUR pi tood\ (n.): inherent vileness, foulness, depravity

The utter *turpitude* of his offenses ensured an immediate dismissal.

ENORMOUS

\ee NOR muss\ (adj.): very great in size or degree

The *enormous* sculpture of the elephant dwarfed the delighted children.

BLAZE

\BLAYZ\ (v.): shine brightly, flare up suddenly

The fire *blazed* through the night, providing heat and light to the campers as they slept.

WRATH

\RATH\ (n.): forceful anger

Hillary feared her father's *wrath* when she told him that she wrecked his car.

MERCILESS

\MER see less\ (adj.): without pity

The *merciless* dictator imprisoned an entire village for yelling at him when he rode through their town.

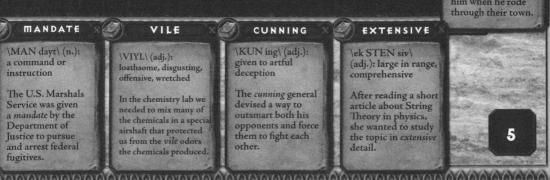

MANDATE

\MAN dayt\ (n.): a command or instruction

The U.S. Marshals Service was given a *mandate* by the Department of Justice to pursue and arrest federal fugitives.

VILE

\VIYL\ (adj.): loathsome, disgusting, offensive, wretched

In the chemistry lab we needed to mix many of the chemicals in a special airshaft that protected us from the *vile* odors the chemicals produced.

CUNNING

\KUN ing\ (adj.): given to artful deception

The *cunning* general devised a way to outsmart both his opponents and force them to fight each other.

EXTENSIVE

\ek STEN siv\ (adj.): large in range, comprehensive

After reading a short article about String Theory in physics, she wanted to study the topic in *extensive* detail.

For many ages, the Titans moved and shaped Azeroth, until at last there remained a <u>utopia</u> for all. At the continent's center, the Titans crafted a lake <u>resplendent</u> with energies. The lake, which they named the Well of Eternity, was to be the fount of life for the world. Its potent energies would nurture the bones of the world and empower life to take root in the land's rich soil. Over time, plants, trees, monsters, and creatures of every kind began to thrive on the primordial continent. As twilight fell on the final day of their labors, the Titans named the continent Kalimdor: "land of eternal starlight."

Satisfied that they had brought order to the small world and that their work was done, the Titans prepared to leave Azeroth. However, before they departed, they charged the greatest species of the world—the dragon—with the task of watching over Kalimdor, lest any force should threaten its perfect <u>tranquility.</u> In that age, there were many dragonflights, yet there were five groups that held dominion over their brethren. It was these five flights that the Titans chose to shepherd the budding world. The greatest members of the Pantheon imbued a portion of their power upon each of the flights' leaders. These chosen majestic dragons became known as the Great Aspects, or the Dragon Aspects.

Empowered by the Pantheon, the Five Aspects were charged with the world's defense in the Titans' absence. With the dragons prepared to safeguard their creation, the Titans left Azeroth behind forever. Unfortunately, it was only a matter of time before Sargeras learned of the newborn world's existence.

In time, a primitive tribe of nocturnal humanoids <u>warily</u> made their way to the edges of the mesmerizing enchanted lake. Drawn by the Well's strange energies, the wild, nomadic humanoids built crude homes upon its tranquil shores. Over time, the Well's cosmic power affected the tribe, making them strong, wise, and virtually immortal. The tribe adopted the name Kaldorei, which in their native tongue meant "children of the stars." To celebrate their budding society, the

UTOPIA

\yoo TOH pee uh\
(n.): perfect place

Wilson's idea of *utopia* was a beautiful, sunny beach on a tropical island.

RESPLENDENT

\ri SPLEN dent\
(adj.): splendid, brilliant, dazzling

The bride looked *resplendent* in her long train and sparkling tiara.

TRANQUIL

\TRAN kwil\ (adj.): peaceful, calm, composed

The ship's captain looked over at the *tranquil* sea, motionless in the sun's setting sky.

WARY

\WAYR ee\ (adj.): careful, cautious

The dog was *wary* of Bola at first, only gradually letting its guard down and wagging its tail when Bola came home at night.

Kaldorei constructed great structures and temples that <u>flanked</u> the lake.

The Kaldorei—or night elves, as they would later be known—worshipped the moon goddess, Elune, and believed that she slept within the Well's shimmering depths during the daylight hours. The early night elf priests and seers studied the Well with an insatiable curiosity, driven to uncover its untold secrets and power.

As the seemingly endless ages passed, the night elves' civilization expanded and Azshara, the night elves' beautiful and gifted queen, built an immense palace on the Well's shore that housed her favored servants within its bejeweled halls. Her servants, whom she called the Quel'dorei or "Highborne," doted on her every command and believed themselves to be greater than the rest of their brethren.

Sharing the priests' curiosity towards the Well of Eternity, Azshara ordered the Highborne to plumb its <u>complex</u> secrets and reveal its true purpose in the world. The Highborne buried themselves in their work and studied the Well ceaselessly. In time, they developed the ability to manipulate and control the Well's cosmic <u>resources</u>. As their experiments progressed, the Highborne found that they could use their newfound powers to either create or destroy at their leisure. The heedless Highborne had stumbled upon primitive magic and they devoted themselves to its mastery.

The Highborne's <u>reckless</u> use of magic sent ripples of energy spiraling out from the Well of Eternity and into the Great Dark Beyond, where they were felt by Sargeras, the Great Enemy of all life. Spying the primordial world of Azeroth and sensing the limitless energies of the Well of Eternity, Sargeras resolved to destroy the fledgling world and claim its energies as his own.

Gathering his vast Burning Legion, Sargeras made his way towards the unsuspecting world of Azeroth. The Legion was comprised of

FLANK

\FLANK\ (v.): to put on the sides of

The gardener had planted shrubs that *flanked* the steps and walkway.

COMPLEX

\kom PLEKS\ (adj.): intricate, complicated

Critics hailed J.R.R. Tolkien for creating a *complex* and complete world within the framework of a popular novel.

RESOURCE

\REE sors\ (n.): something that can be used

While we'd like to be able to help our neighbors construct a new barn, we just don't have the *resources* to spare.

RECKLESS

\REK lis\ (adj.): careless, rash

Gary's license was revoked for *reckless* driving; the police caught him speeding through traffic at twice the speed limit.

a million screaming demons, all ripped from the far corners of the universe, and the demons hungered for conquest.

Corrupted by the magic they wielded, Queen Azshara and the Highborne opened a colossal, swirling portal within the depths of the Well of Eternity for Sargeras and his forces. The warrior-demons of the Burning Legion stormed into the world through the Well of Eternity, leaving only ash and sorrow in their wake. Though the intrepid Kaldorei warriors rushed to defend their ancient homeland, they were forced to give ground, inch by inch, before the fury of the Legion's onslaught.

When the dragons, led by the great red leviathan, Alexstrasza, sent their mighty flights to engage the demons and their infernal masters, all-out warfare erupted. As the melee raged across the burning fields of Kalimdor, a terrible turn of events unfolded for the dragons. The details of the event have been lost to time, but it is known that Neltharion, the Dragon Aspect of the Earth, went mad during a critical engagement against the Burning Legion. In his madness, he began to split apart, and the flame and rage that erupted from his very core ignited his dark hide. Renaming himself Deathwing, the burning dragon turned on his brethren and drove the five dragonflights from the field of battle.

Deathwing's sudden betrayal was a watershed from which the five dragonflights could not recover. Wounded and shocked, Alexstrasza and the other noble dragons were forced to abandon their mortal allies.

Hatching a desperate plot to destroy the Well of Eternity, a band of Kaldorei freedom fighters clashed with the Highborne at the Well's edge. The ensuing battle threw the Highborne's carefully concocted spellwork into chaos, destabilizing the vortex within the Well and igniting a horrific chain of events that forever sundered

COLOSSAL

\kuh LOS al\ (adj.): immense, enormous

Joseph made a *colossal* error by skipping school; he failed the final and was forced to retake the course.

INTREPID

\in TREP id\ (adj.): fearless

The *intrepid* explorer entered the ominous-looking cave without a moment's hesitation.

MELEE

\ma LAY\ (n.): tumultuous free-for-all

The hunted fugitive managed to evade his captors in the *melee* of the St. Patrick's Day parade.

WATERSHED

\WOT er shed\ (n.): critical turning point

The invention of sound in movies was a *watershed* in the development of modern cinema.

CONCOCT

\kon KOKT\ (v.): to devise, using skill and intelligence

When pressed for an excuse for his weeklong absence, Richard *concocted* a story so outrageous that his teacher knew he was lying.

the world. A massive explosion from the Well shattered the earth and blotted out the skies.

As the aftershocks from the Well's implosion rattled the bones of the world, the seas rushed in to fill the gaping wound left in the earth. Nearly eighty percent of Kalimdor's landmass had been blasted apart, leaving only a handful of separate continents surrounding the new, raging sea. At the center of the new sea, where the Well of Eternity once stood, was a tumultuous storm of tidal fury and chaotic energies. This terrible scar, known as the Maelstrom, would never cease its furious spinning. It would remain a constant reminder of the terrible <u>calamity</u> that befell the once peaceful world. The utopian era had been <u>eliminated</u> forever.

The few night elves that survived the horrific explosion rallied together on <u>crudely</u> made rafts and slowly made their way to the only landmass in sight. As they journeyed in silence, they surveyed the wreckage of their world and realized that their passions had wrought the destruction all around them. Though Sargeras and his Legion had been ripped from the world by the Well's destruction, the <u>contrite</u> Kaldorei were left to ponder the terrible cost of victory.

Despite the devastation, there were many Highborne who survived the cataclysm—and who wanted to continue using magic. One had even stolen some waters of the Well of Eternity and created a new Well in the new homeland of the night elves. Unable to come to terms, the Highborne, or Quel'dorei, as Azshara had named them in ages past, set out on their own, eventually making their way to the eastern land men would call Lordaeron. They built their own magical kingdom, Quel'Thalas, and <u>rebuffed</u> the night elves' precepts of moon worship and nocturnal activity. Forever after, they would embrace the sun and be known only as the "high elves."

CALAMITY

\ka LAM uh tee\ (n.): disaster, catastrophe

Last year's formal dance was a *calamity*; the band was an hour late and the food was spoiled.

ELIMINATE

\ee LIM uh nayt\ (v.): get rid of; remove

One of television's first reality shows placed a group of strangers on an island and forced them to *eliminate* a contestant each week until there was only one person left.

CRUDE

\KROOD\ (adj.): unrefined, natural; blunt, offensive

After two months of ignoring Billy's *crude* remarks, Denise summoned the courage to ask him to stop.

CONTRITE

\kon TRYT\ (adj.): deeply sorrowful and repentant for a wrong

While Max appeared *contrite* before the court and even shed tears, the judge showed no leniency at the sentencing.

REBUFF

\re BUFF\ (v.): to bluntly reject

The princess coldly *rebuffed* her suitor's marriage proposal, turning her back on him and walking away.

Effectively cut off from the life-giving energies of the Well of Eternity, the high elves discovered that they were no longer immortal and no longer possessed immunity from the elements. They also shrank somewhat in height, and their skin lost its characteristic violet hue. But despite these hardships, they encountered many wondrous creatures that had never been seen in Kalimdor... including humans.

IMMUNITY

\im MYOO ni tee\ (n.): invulnerability, exemption

Many countries offer diplomats from other countries *immunity* from the law to prevent them from unfair prosecution.

Over the course of the next several thousand years, the high elves developed their society and made alliances with their neighboring human communities. To mask their magic from extra-dimensional threats, the elves had constructed a series of monolithic Runestones at various points around Quel'Thalas. However, the humans, who had learned their magic from the elves, were not so cautious. The sinister agents of the Burning Legion, who had been banished when the Well of Eternity collapsed, were lured back into the world by the heedless spell casting of the human magicians of the city of Dalaran.

COMPREHENSIVE

\kom pree HEN siv\ (adj.): very large in scope

The class was duly impressed by the guest lecturer's *comprehensive* knowledge of popular music.

Under Sargeras' comprehensive orders, the calculating demon-lord Kil'jaeden plotted the Burning Legion's second invasion of Azeroth. Kil'jaeden surmised that he needed a new force to weaken Azeroth's defenses before the Legion even set foot upon the world. If the mortal races, such as the night elves and dragons, were forced to contend with a new threat, they would be too weak to pose any real resistance when the Legion's true invasion arrived.

Kil'jaeden discovered the lush world of Draenor floating serenely within the Great Dark Beyond. Home to the shamanistic, clan-based orcs, Draenor was as idyllic as it was vast. Kil'jaeden knew that the noble orc clans had great potential to serve the Burning Legion if they could be cultivated properly.

CALCULATING

\KAL kyu lay ting\ (adj.): shrewd, crafty

The *calculating* lawyer put the mother of his client on the witness stand in order to garner sympathy.

SERENE

\se REEN\ (adj.): calm; peaceful

The beach at the island club was *serene* and beautiful as we sat watching the sunset.

Kil'jaeden enthralled the <u>venerable</u> orc shaman, Ner'zhul, in much the same way that Sargeras brought Queen Azshara under his control in ages past, and the demon spread battle lust and savagery throughout the orc clans. Before long, the spiritual race was transformed into a bloodthirsty people.

Consumed with the curse of this new bloodlust, the orcs became the Burning Legion's greatest weapon. With the aid of a corrupted human mage, a Dark Portal was opened between Draenor and Azeroth, igniting an all-consuming war between the orcs and the humans. Though the human knights of Azeroth had allies in the high elves, the dwarves, and other species, the army of orcish ogres was <u>reinforced</u> by strong alliances of their own with trolls, goblins, and other sinister creatures. The warring utterly devastated many human cities, and it seemed the orcs were poised to win the war, but internal <u>discord</u> among the orcs slowly began to weaken their front.

Seizing the opportunity, the humans retook their world and even fought the orcs in Draenor, though many heroic humans lost their lives when Draenor tore itself apart.

Though Ner'zhul was one of the many orcs who escaped Draenor's destruction, the orc shaman's body was torn apart by demons and his spirit was held helpless in stasis by Kil'jaeden. Recklessly agreeing to serve the demon, Ner'zhul's spirit was placed within a specially crafted block of diamond-hard ice gathered from the far reaches of the Twisting Nether. Though his spirit was growing <u>stagnant</u> within the frozen cask, he felt his consciousness expand ten thousand-fold. Warped by the demon's chaotic powers, Ner'zhul became a spectral being who possessed powers that could not be <u>fathomed</u>. At that moment, the orc known as Ner'zhul was shattered forever, and the Lich King was born.

VENERABLE

\VEN er a bul\ (adj.): respected because of age

All the villagers sought the *venerable* old woman's advice whenever they had a problem.

REINFORCE

\ree in FORSS\ (v.): strengthen

Linda *reinforced* her argument by quoting several authoritative sources that all agree with her.

DISCORD

\DIS kord\ (n.): lack of agreement; inharmonious combination

The *discord* emanating from the classroom was unbearable, as none of the students knew how to play their musical instruments.

STAGNANT

\STAG nent\ (adj.): immobile, stale

That *stagnant* pond is a perfect breeding ground for mosquitoes; we should drain it.

FATHOM

\FAH thom\ (v.): comprehend, penetrate the meaning of

Andrea couldn't *fathom* how a person could cheat on a test; every instinct told her it was wrong.

The Lich King was to spread a plague of death and terror across Azeroth that would snuff out human civilization forever. All those who died from the dreaded plague would arise as the undead, and their spirits would be bound to Ner'zhul's iron will forever.

Though the Lich King fought for the total eradication of humankind, the wealthy and prestigious archmage, Kel'Thuzad, left the city of Dalaran to serve the evil creature. As the ranks of the undead swept across Lordaeron, King Terenas' only son, Prince Arthas, took up the fight against the Scourge. Arthas succeeded in killing Kel'Thuzad, but even so, the undead ranks seemingly could not be diminished; their numbers swelled with every human soldier that fell defending the land. Frustrated and stymied by this unstoppable enemy, Arthas took increasingly extreme steps to conquer them. Finally Arthas' comrades warned him that he was losing his hold on humanity.

DIMINISH

\di MIN ish\ (v.): to make smaller

Despite all the advances in modern medicine, doctors have been unable to *diminish* people's susceptibility to many diseases.

Arthas' fear and resolve proved to be his ultimate undoing. Believing that it would save his people, he took up the cursed runeblade, Frostmourne. Though the sword did grant him unfathomable power, it also stole his soul and transformed him into the greatest of the Lich King's death knights. With his soul cast aside and his sanity shattered, Arthas led the Scourge against his own kingdom. Ultimately, the ruthless Arthas murdered his own father, King Terenas, and crushed Lordaeron under the Lich King's iron heel.

Soon after Arthas and his army of the dead swept across the land, Kel'Thuzad was resurrected, and not one living elf remained in Quel'Thalas. The glorious homeland of the high elves, which had stood for more than nine thousand years, was no more. Arthas subsequently led the Scourge south to Dalaran, and then to Kalimdor.

EXTREME

\ek STREEM\ (adj.): very intense, of the greatest severity

When the army officer discovered that his unit was getting lazy, he took *extreme* measures to get them back into shape, instituting mandatory weight training and early morning runs.

RUTHLESS

\ROOTH less\ (adj.): merciless, compassionless

The Terminator was a perfectly *ruthless* killer, not possessing any emotions or compassion for its victims.

At Kalimdor, the night elves braced themselves and fought a resolute battle against the Burning Legion to the bitter end. Allied with human and the orcs (now freed of their savage bloodlust), the night elves severed the Legion's anchor to the Well of Eternity. Unable to draw power from the Well itself, the Burning Legion began to crumble under the combined might of the mortal armies.

By this time, the undead Scourge had essentially transformed Lordaeron and Quel'Thalas into the toxic Plaguelands. The high elves grieved for the loss of their homeland and in honor of their fallen people decided to rename themselves "blood elves."

Meanwhile, half of the undead forces were in engaged in machinations to stage a coup to gain control over the undead empire. Eventually, the banshee Sylvanas Windrunner and her rebel undead—known as the Forsaken—claimed the ruined capital city of Lordaeron as their own and vowed to drive the Scourge and Kel'Thuzad from the land.

Though weakened, Arthas outmaneuvered the enemy forces that were closing in on the Lich King. Commanding Ner'Zhul's unimaginably powerful helm, Arthas and Ner'zhul's spirits fused into a single mighty being—the new Lich King—and Arthas became one of the most powerful entities the world had ever known.

Currently Arthas, the new and immortal Lich King, resides in Northrend; he is rumored to be rebuilding the citadel of Icecrown. His trusted lieutenant, Kel'Thuzad, commands the Scourge in the Plaguelands. Sylvanas and her rebel Forsaken hold only the Tirisfal Glades, a small portion of the war-torn kingdom, while the humans, orcs, and night elves are trying to rebuild their societies on Kalimdor.

RESOLUTE ✕

\REZ uh loot\ (adj.): determined; with a clear purpose

Louise was *resolute*; she would get into medical school no matter what.

MACHINATION ✕

\mak uh NAY shun\ (n.): crafty scheme; covert plot

When the public learned of the politician's *machinations*, they immediately called for his resignation.

After what seemed like ages of bloody conflict, the world appeared to have finally found peace. The war against the feral orcs had come to a definitive conclusion, and the remnants of the Horde had been rounded into enclaves and kept under guard.

But just as the lands were starting to be rebuilt and lives were beginning to be repaired, a monstrous evil had been resurrected. The demonic army of the Burning Legion had integrated with the ghoulish Undead Scourge, and together they swept over human and orc realms alike, forcing old enemies to converge in unity.

Yet, not until the coming of the mysterious Night Elves and after the sacrifice of countless lives was the Burning Legion demolished. Nearly all of the elven kingdom of Quel'Thalas and the human kingdom of Lordaeron lay in ruins; turned into the foul Plaguelands by the Scourge..

Now, as an unsteady serenity exists between living and Undead, elements of both sides seek out that which will decisively tip the scales in their favor.

Thus it is that a young blue dragon wings his way toward what little remains of southern Lordaeron...

CONFLICT

\KON flikt\ (n.): a clash, a battle

The *conflict* between Debbie and Gerry heightened as the former friends began to insult each other publicly.

FERAL

\FER ul\ (adj.): wild, brutish

After living with gorillas for several years, Diane Fossey seemed *feral* to her more civilized contemporaries.

REMNANT

\REM nent\ (n.): something left over, surviving trace

Although most of the food was devoured before he arrived at the party, Mike managed to grab some of the *remnants* before the end.

CONVERGENCE

kun VER jinss\ (n.): the state of separate elements joining or coming together

No one in the quiet neighborhood could have predicted the mass *convergence* of artists, writers, and musicians, and the birth of a miniature renaissance.

INTEGRATE

\IN tih grayt\ (v.): to incorporate, unite

When we learned of the new computer capabilities, we tried to find a way to *integrate* the new technology into our course.

DEMOLISH

\de MOL ish\ (v.): destroy, damage severely

Before starting construction on the new skyscraper, workers will have to *demolish* the old buildings that still sit on the site.

DECISIVE

\de SIY siv\ (adj.): conclusive; capable of determining outcome

The defeat of the Spanish Armada was a *decisive* battle in history as it marked England's ascendance as a naval power, and thereby as a world power.

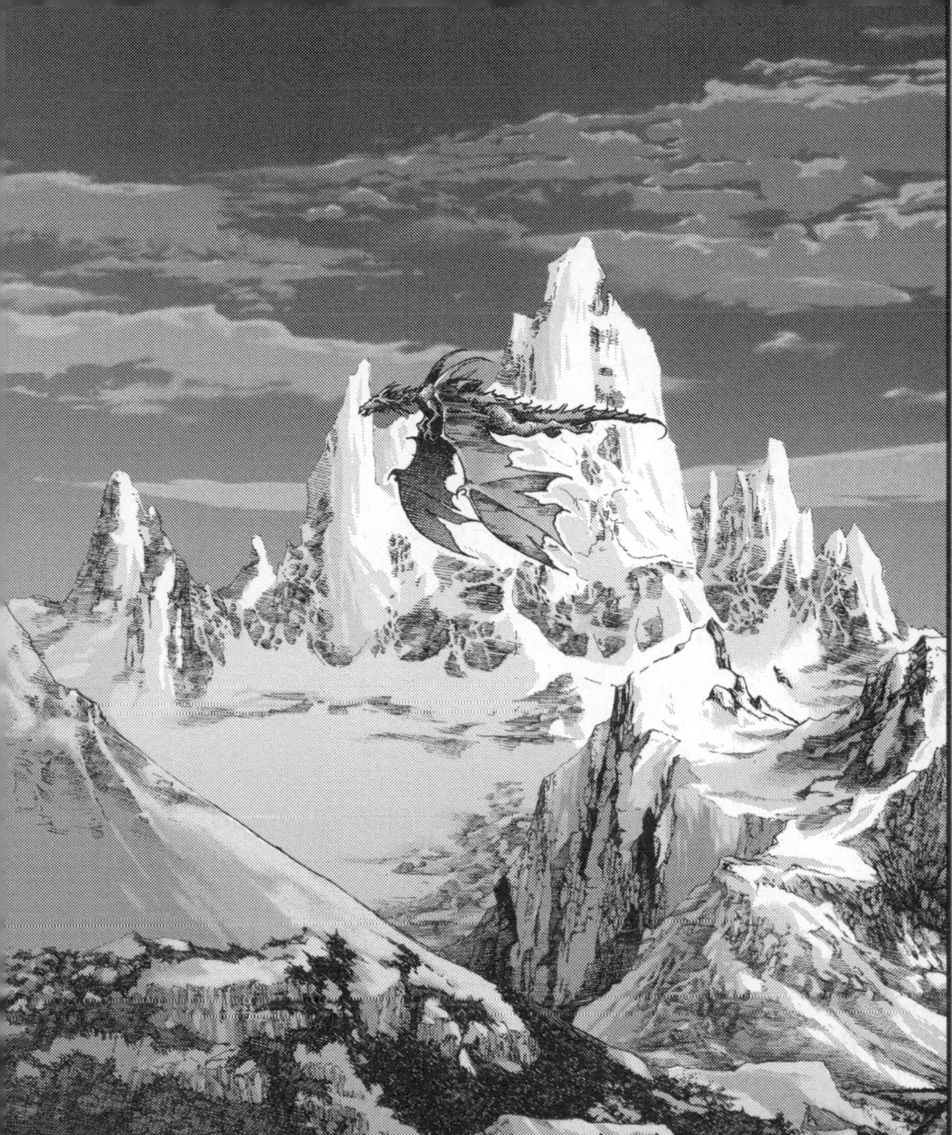

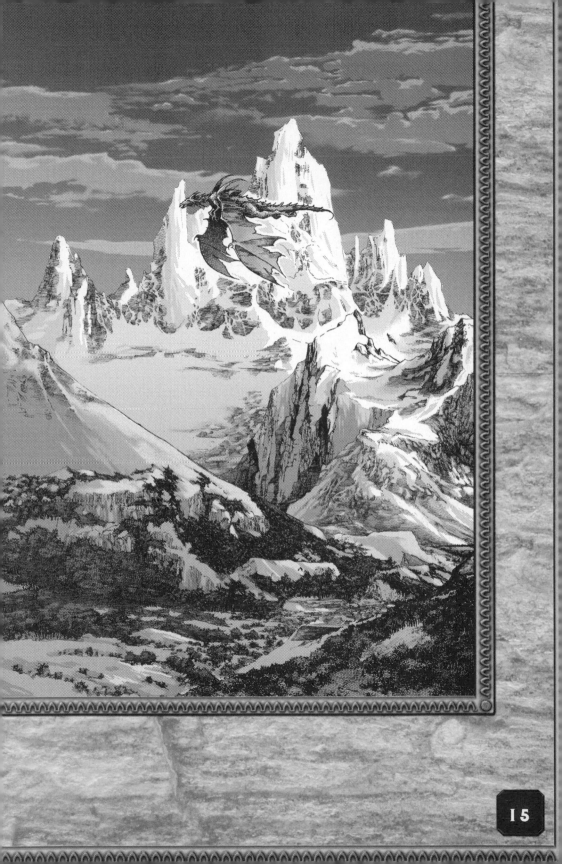

WarCraft
The Sunwell Trilogy

Dragon Hunt

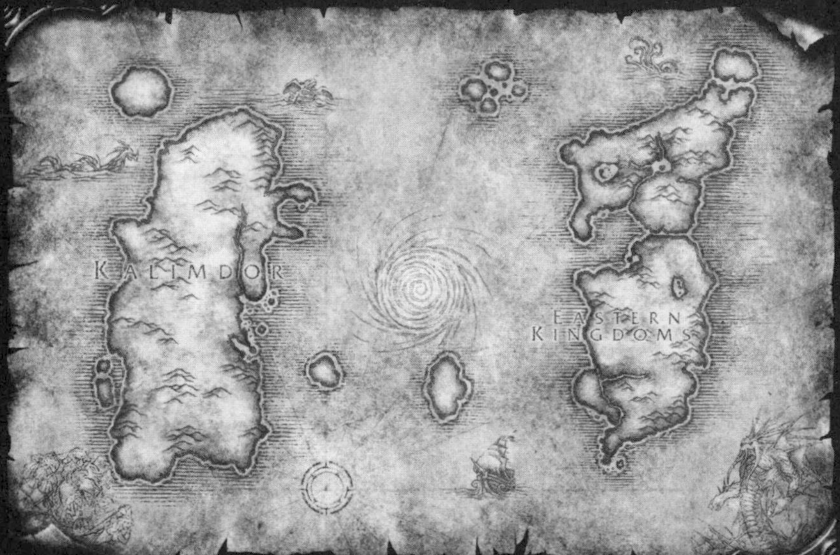
KALIMDOR
EASTERN KINGDOMS

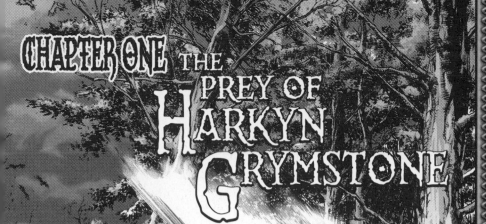

CHAPTER ONE THE PREY OF HARKYN GRYMSTONE

NOW!

FWOOOM

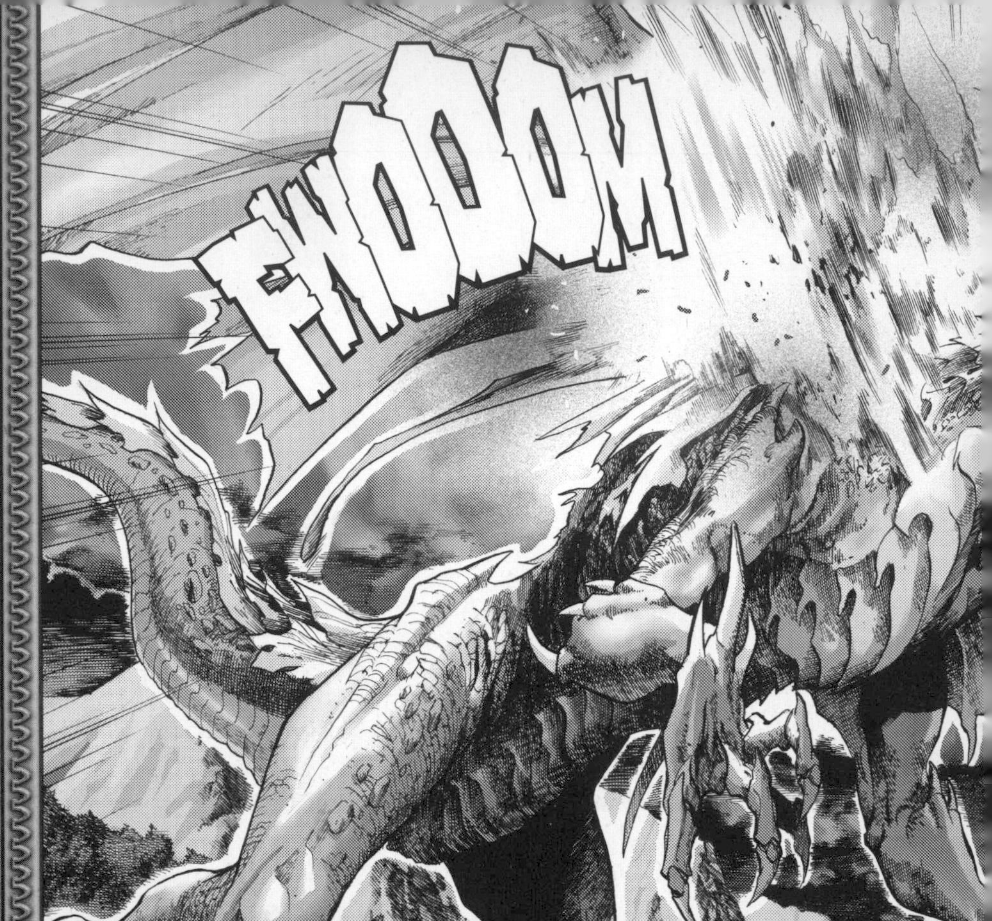
FWOOOM

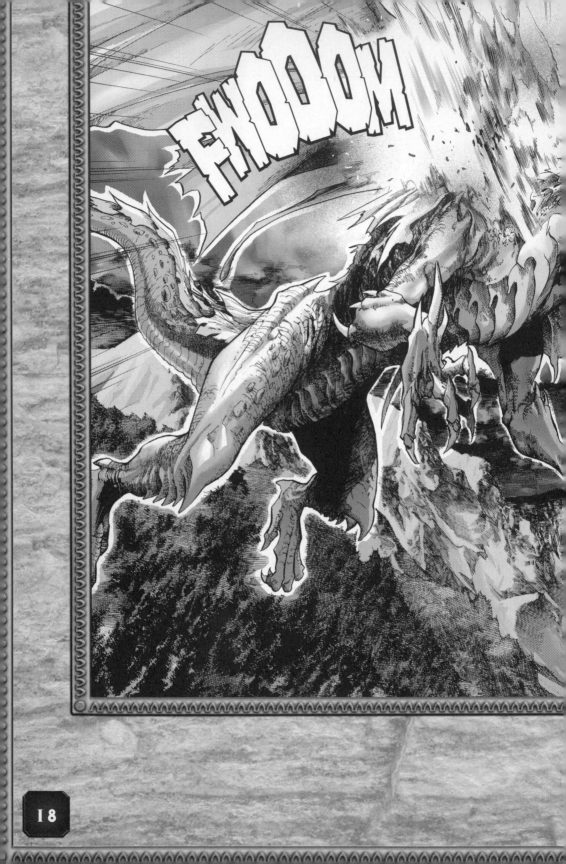

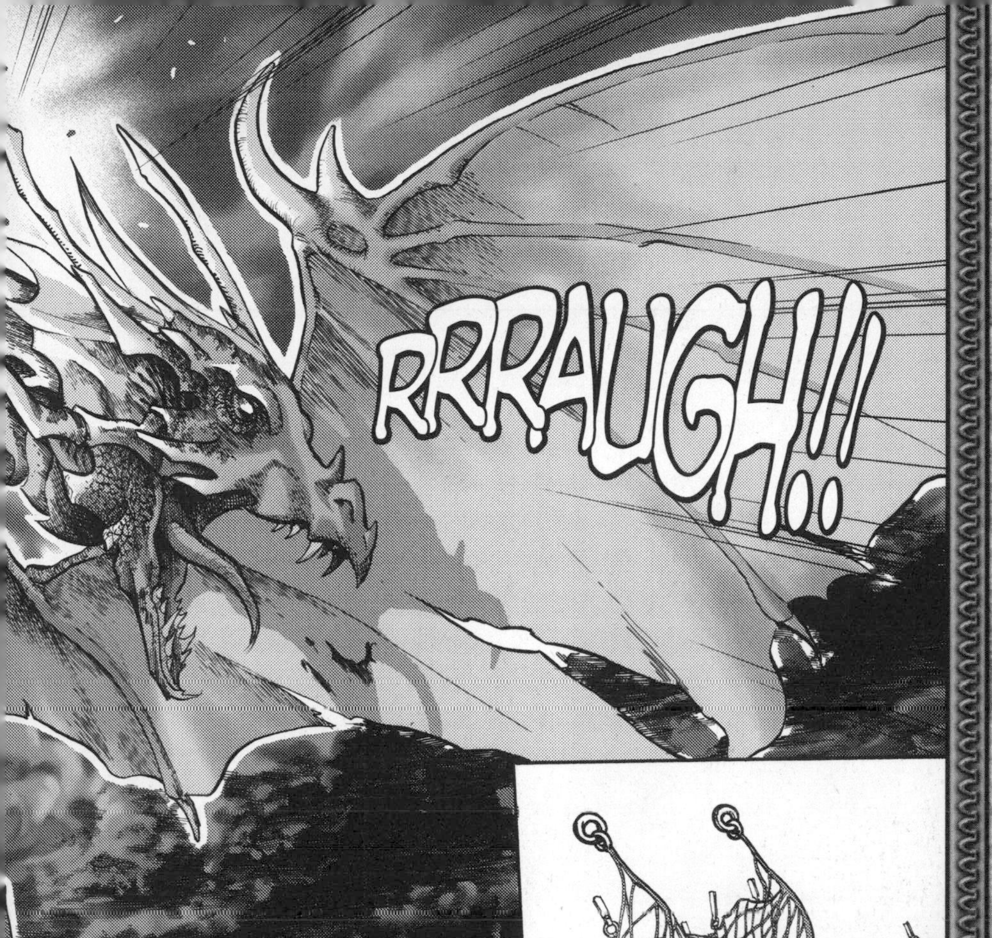
RRRAUGH!!
BWAM

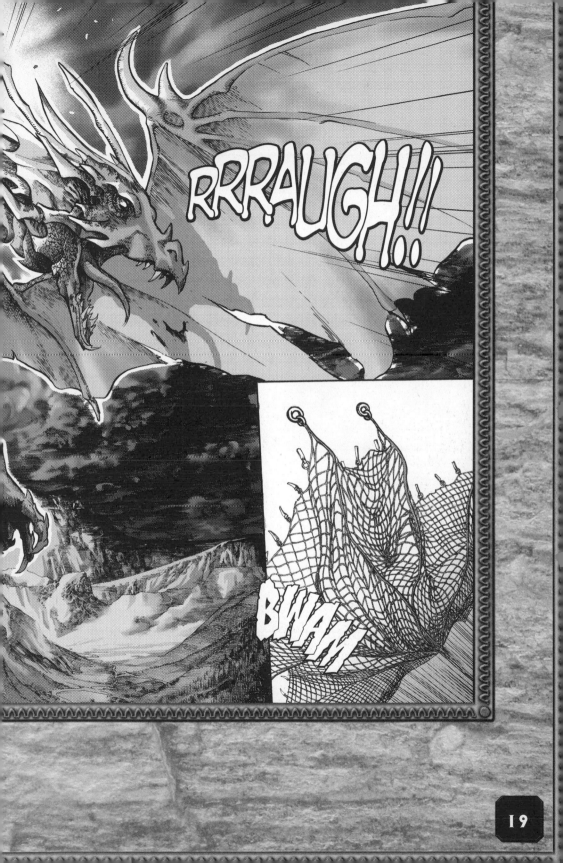

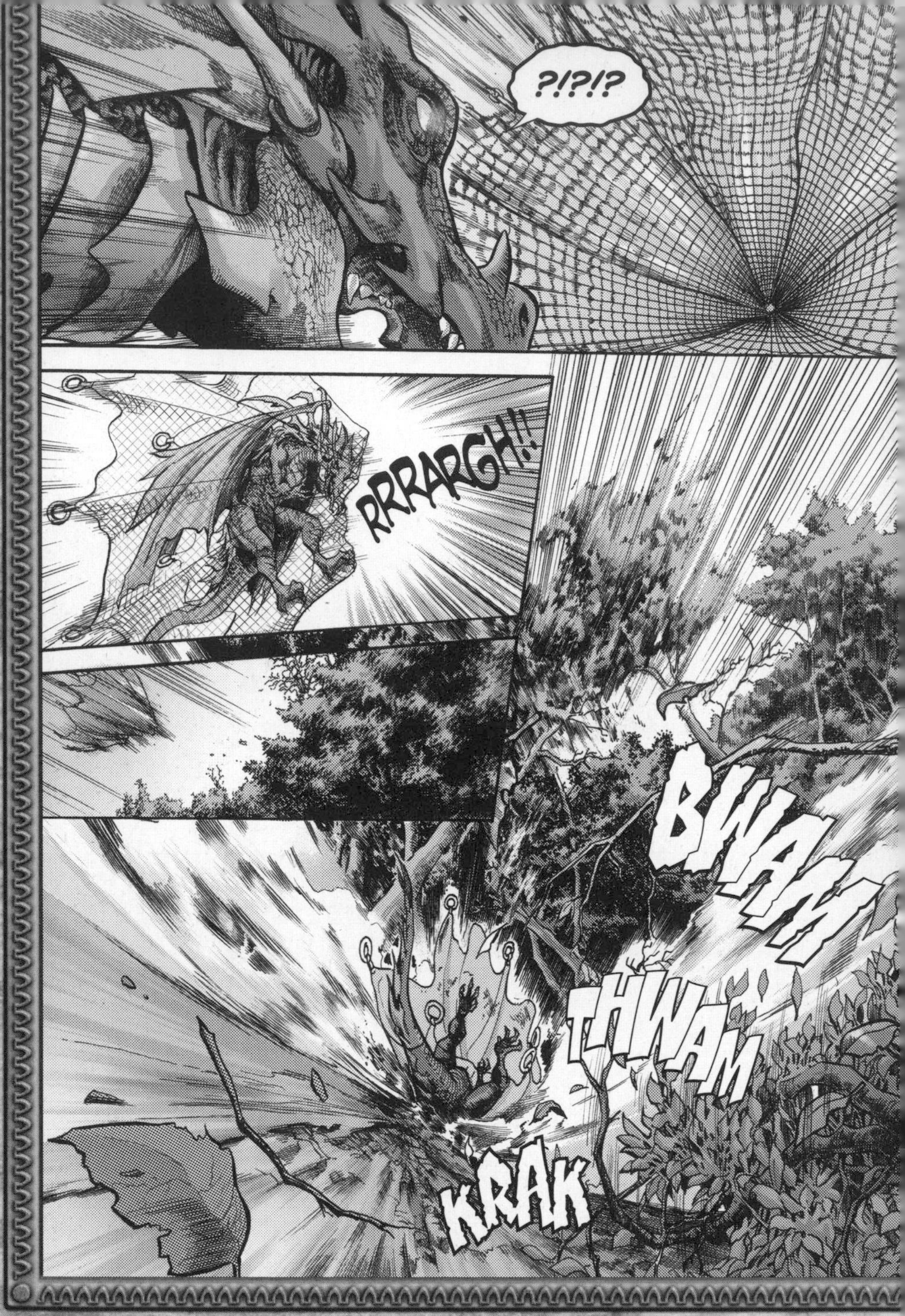
?!?!?
RRRARGH!!
BWAM
THWAM
KRAK

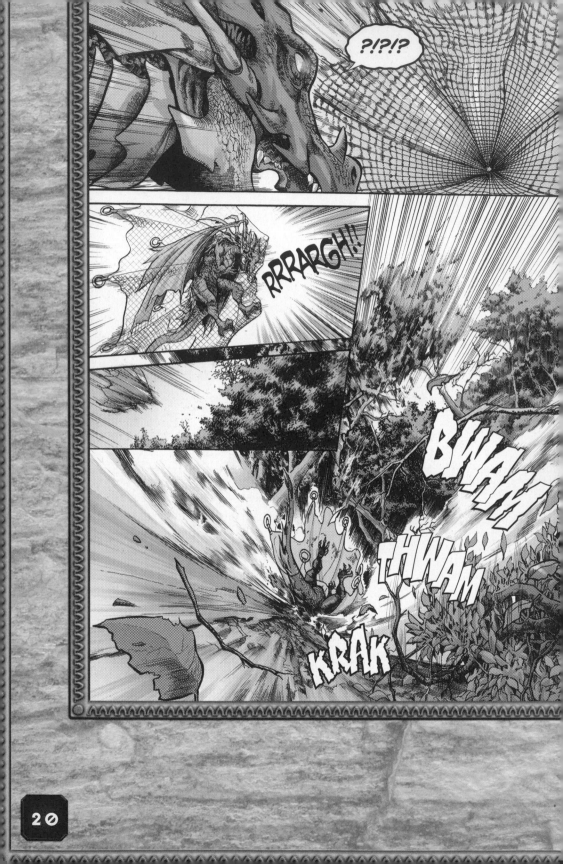

HE'S DOWN...

THERE WAS A <u>FLAW</u> IN OUR AIM! THE SHOT WAS OFF-CENTER! HE'S LIKELY ALIVE...

LET'S MAKE CERTAIN IT WON'T BE FOR LONG.

FLAW

\FLAW\ (n.): imperfection, defect

Because there was a *flaw* in the system, programmers had to rewrite the entire application.

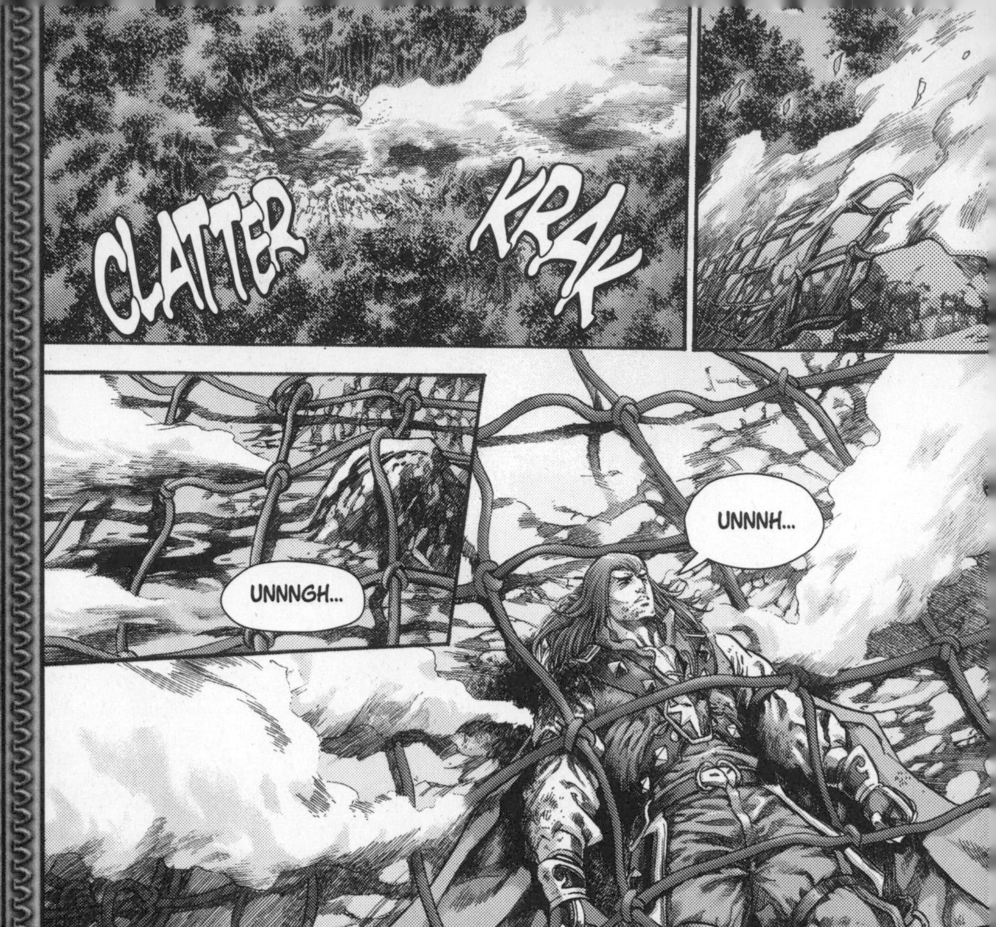
CLATTER
KRAK
UNNNGH...
UNNNH...

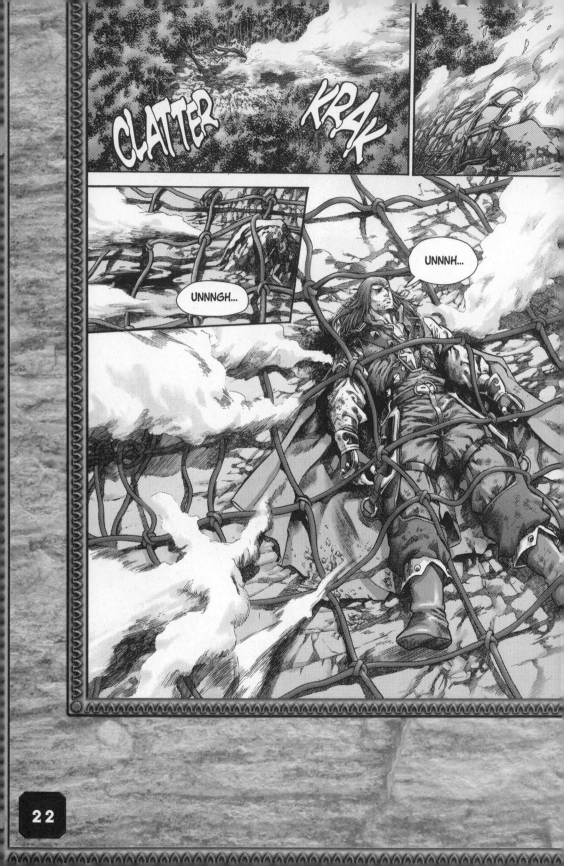

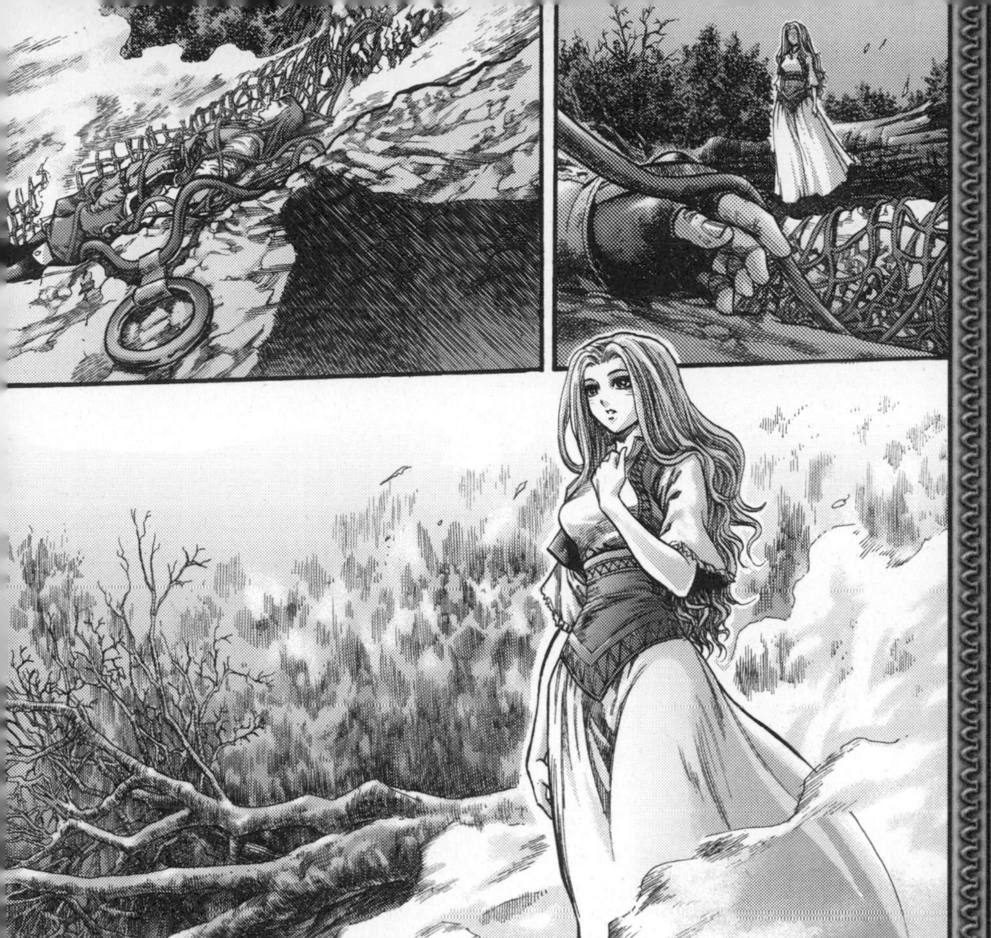
NNNGH...

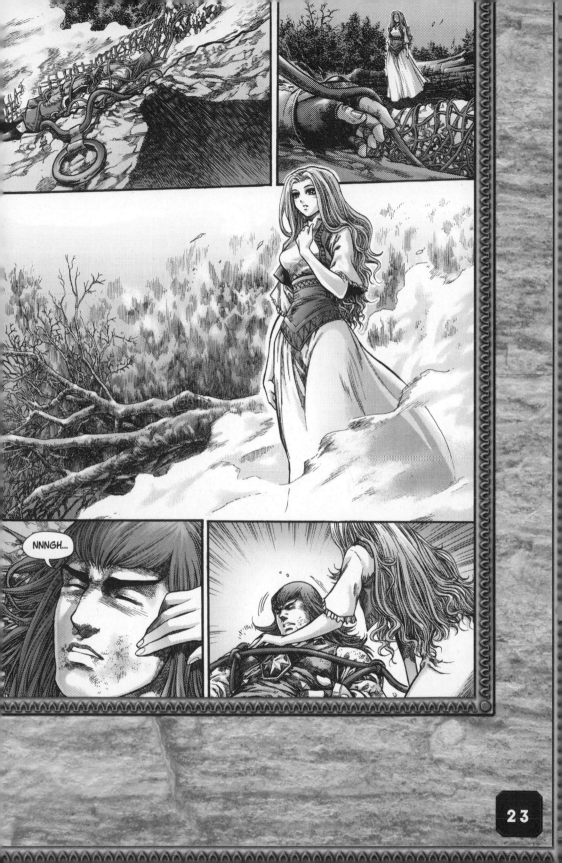

WHO--?
HUSH, DON'T MOVE. YOU'LL ONLY EXACERBATE YOUR INJURIES...
...YOU ARE BADLY HURT.
I M-MUST FLEE...AND YOU MUST, TOO. NEITHER OF US IS SAFE HERE...
IT'S INEVITABLE... THEY'LL COME BACK TO SEE...IF THEY SUCCEEDED.
UNNGH
L-LEAVE ME!
NO!

EXACERBATE

\ig ZAS ur bayt\ (v.): to aggravate, intensify the bad qualities of

It is unwise to take aspirin to relieve heartburn; instead of providing relief, the drug will only *exacerbate* the problem.

FLEE

\FLEE\ (v.): to run away from, escape

Many of the first immigrants to North America were *fleeing* religious persecution in their home countries.

INEVITABLE

\in ev ih tuh bul \ (adj.): certain, unavoidable

With an active effort to cut costs and raise productivity, bankruptcy is far from *inevitable*.

MY HOME IS ONLY A SHORT DISTANCE. YOU'LL FIND ASYLUM THERE.

YOU ARE VERY NAÏVE. MY PRESENCE WILL ONLY ENDANGER YOU! DON'T JEOPARDIZE YOURSELF!

THAT WON'T DISCOURAGE ME. I CANNOT LEAVE YOU HERE. YOU ARE HURT . . . WE WILL MOVE ON TOGETHER.

YOU DON'T EVEN KNOW ME...

BUT...

...YOU ARE A DRAGON...

IS THAT INACCURATE?

?!?!?

ASYLUM

\uh SY lum\ (n.): a place offering protection and safety

Many of the immigrants to the United States in the early part of the twentieth century sought *asylum* from government persecution.

NAÏVE

\niy EEV\ (adj): lacking experience and understanding

Although the newly elected politician was very *naïve* about political maneuvering in Washington, it only took her a few weeks to learn the tricks of Congress.

DISCOURAGE

\dis KUR ij\ (v.): dishearten, deprive of hope or spirit

Despite five hours of frustrating study for her exam, Athena refused to let the struggle *discourage* her, as she committed to keep working.

INACCURATE

\in AK yur it\ (adj.): mistaken, incorrect

Jean's guesses at Lois's age were completely *inaccurate*, so Lois finally told her the truth.

25

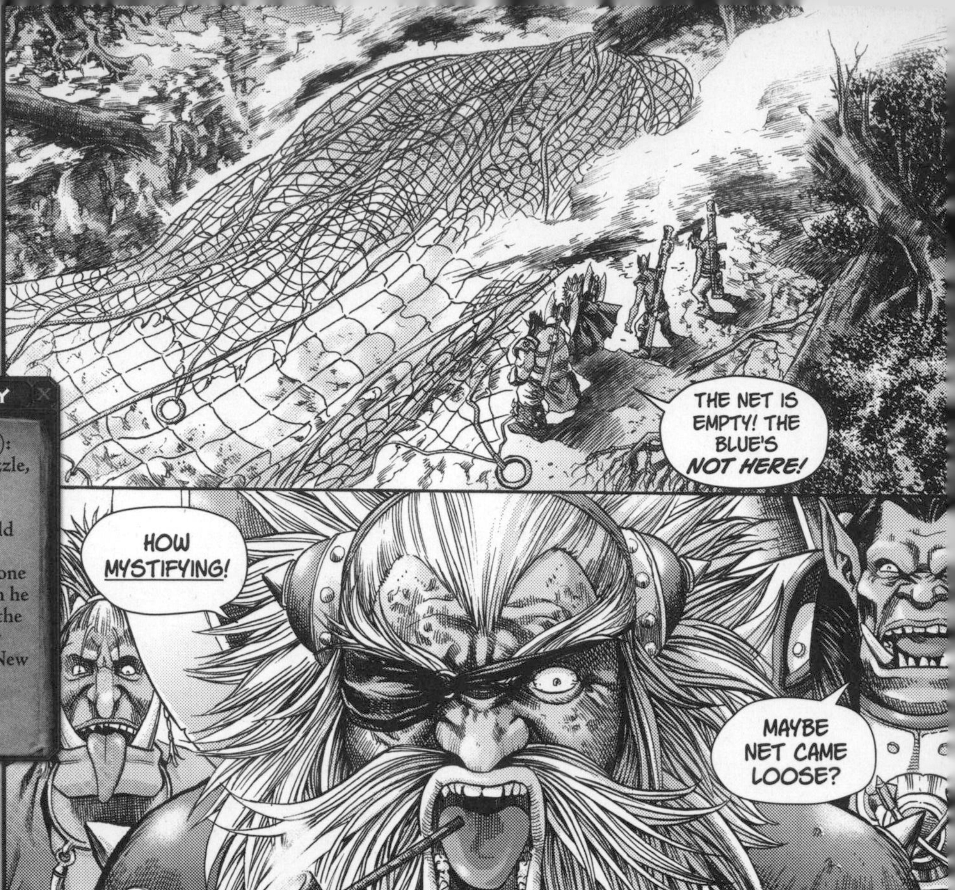
THE NET IS EMPTY! THE BLUE'S *NOT HERE!*
HOW MYSTIFYING!
MAYBE NET CAME LOOSE?
WHAT'S THIS? A BLOOD TRAIL!
BUT SMALLER CREATURE...
NO DRAGON FLESH? VOLL WANTS TO DEVOUR DRAGON FLESH! VOLL HUNGERS...
YOU GLUTTON! VOLL ALWAYS HUNGERS!

MYSTIFY

\MIST ih fiy\ (v.): to confuse or puzzle, to make obscure

David Copperfield *mystified* his audience during one magic show when he seemingly made the Statue of Liberty disappear from New York Harbor.

DEVOUR

\di VOWR\ (v.): eat greedily, consume

Robert was so hungry after his bike race that he *devoured* an entire pizza.

GLUTTON

\GLUT in\ (n.): person who eats and drinks excessively

Only a *glutton* could order dessert after such a rich meal.

IT'S GOT TO LEAD US TO THE BLUE! HE WON'T ELUDE US!
FORTUNATELY, OUR BENEFACTOR'S GIVEN US THE MEANS TO SEE IF FOLLOWING THIS TRAIL WILL BE ADVANTAGEOUS!
THERE! YOU SEE, GROTH? IT GLOWS WHEN I HOLD IT IN THE SAME DIRECTION!
SNEE! VOLL! WE MUST SPRINT!! THE PREY'S NOT FAR AHEAD!

ELUDE

\ee LOOD\ (v.): evade, escape

The gang responsible for the bank robbery was finally caught last Wednesday after *eluding* the police for several months.

BENEFACTOR

\BEN eh fak tur\ (n.): someone who helps others financially

Throughout most of Great Expectations, Pip speculates about the identity of the mysterious *benefactor* that paid for his schooling.

ADVANTAGEOUS

\ADD van TAY jus\ (adj.): favorable, useful

Derek found his Spanish-speaking skills to be *advantageous* in his travels to Mexico.

SPRINT

\SPRINT\ (v.): dash, run quick for short distances

When Peter realized that his package had arrived, he *sprinted* across the lawn to the front door.

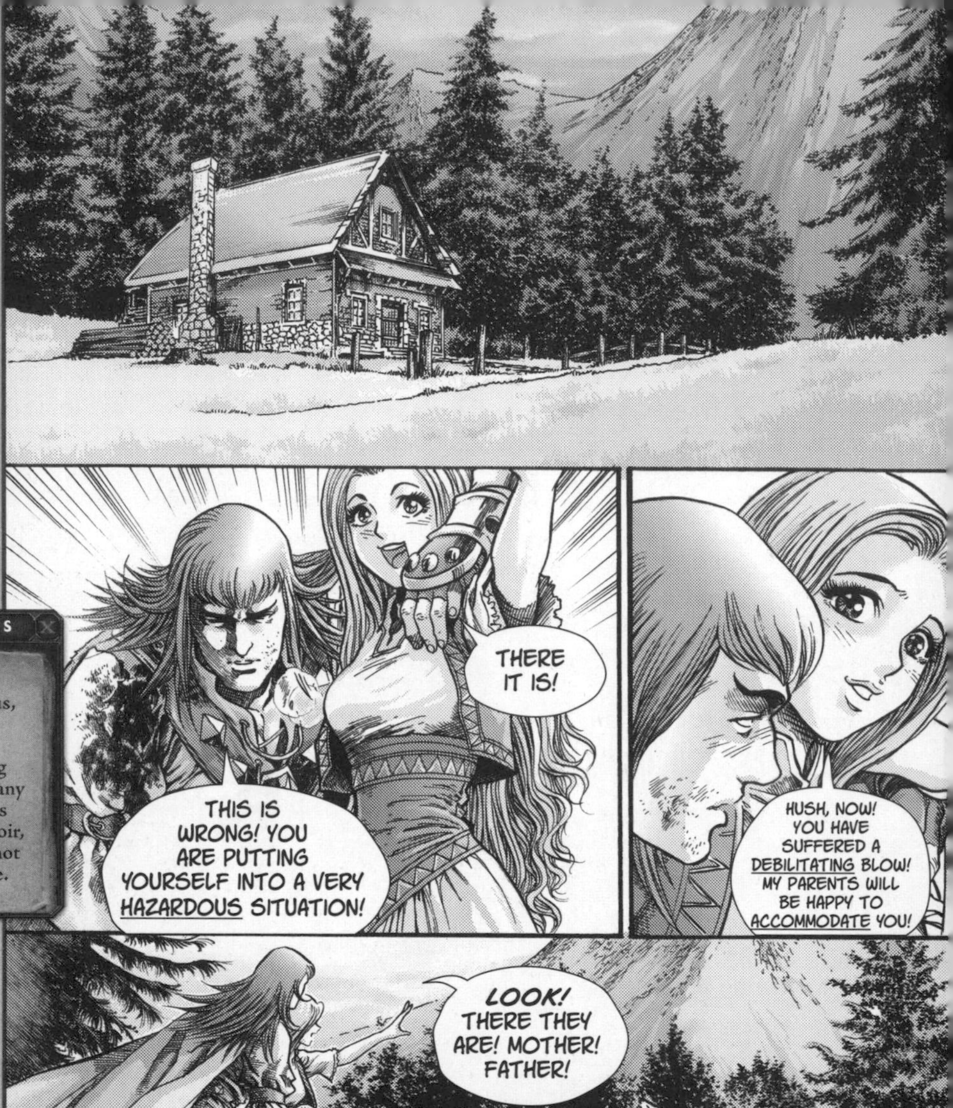
THERE IT IS!
THIS IS WRONG! YOU ARE PUTTING YOURSELF INTO A VERY HAZARDOUS SITUATION!
HUSH, NOW! YOU HAVE SUFFERED A DEBILITATING BLOW! MY PARENTS WILL BE HAPPY TO ACCOMMODATE YOU!
LOOK! THERE THEY ARE! MOTHER! FATHER!

HAZARDOUS

\HAZ er duss\ (adj.): dangerous, risky, perilous

Though filtering has removed many *hazardous* toxins from the reservoir, the water may not yet be drinkable.

DEBILITATING

\dee BIL uh tay ting\ (adj.): impairing the strength or energy

The company's relocation was *debilitating* to its employees; they lost all will to work in their new environment.

ACCOMMODATE

\uh KOM uh dayt\ (v.): to do a favor for; provide for

The restaurant enjoyed a reputation for excellent customer service, since the manager was always willing to *accommodate* special requests.

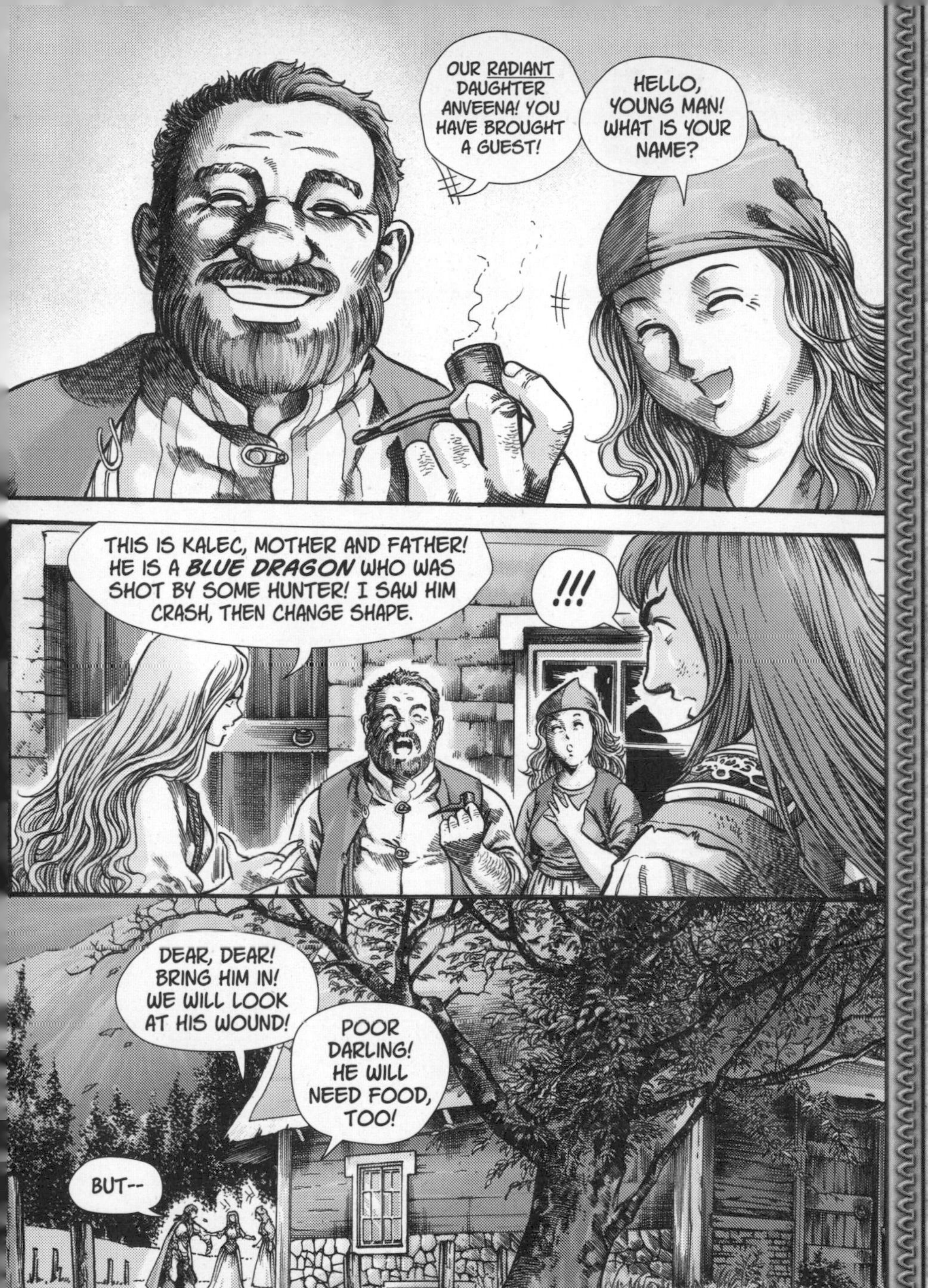
OUR RADIANT DAUGHTER ANVEENA! YOU HAVE BROUGHT A GUEST!
HELLO, YOUNG MAN! WHAT IS YOUR NAME?
THIS IS KALEC, MOTHER AND FATHER! HE IS A BLUE DRAGON WHO WAS SHOT BY SOME HUNTER! I SAW HIM CRASH, THEN CHANGE SHAPE.
!!!
DEAR, DEAR! BRING HIM IN! WE WILL LOOK AT HIS WOUND!
POOR DARLING! HE WILL NEED FOOD, TOO!
BUT--

RADIANT

\RAY dee unt\ (adj.): glowing, beaming; emitting heat

Christopher looked back and smiled at his *radiant* bride as she walked down the aisle.

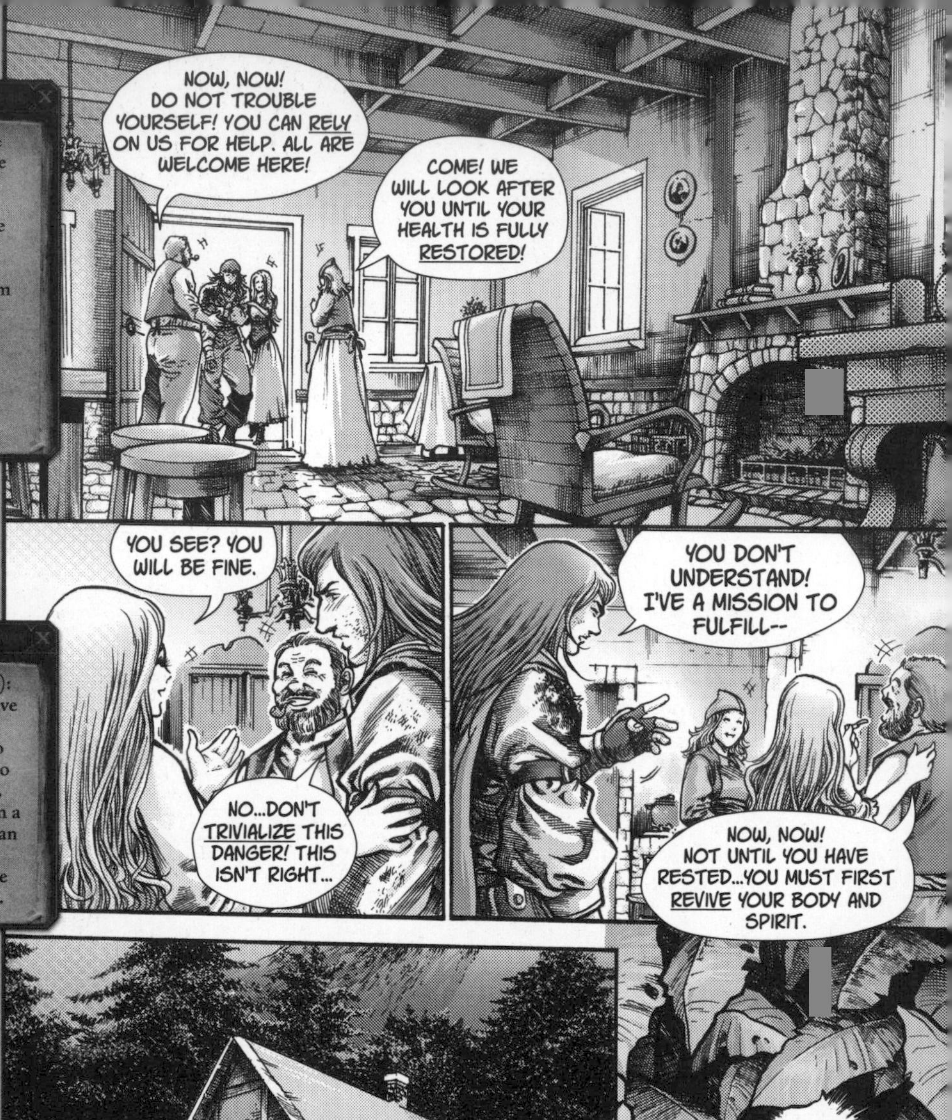
NOW, NOW! DO NOT TROUBLE YOURSELF! YOU CAN RELY ON US FOR HELP. ALL ARE WELCOME HERE!
COME! WE WILL LOOK AFTER YOU UNTIL YOUR HEALTH IS FULLY RESTORED!
YOU SEE? YOU WILL BE FINE.
NO...DON'T TRIVIALIZE THIS DANGER! THIS ISN'T RIGHT...
YOU DON'T UNDERSTAND! I'VE A MISSION TO FULFILL--
NOW, NOW! NOT UNTIL YOU HAVE RESTED...YOU MUST FIRST REVIVE YOUR BODY AND SPIRIT.

RELY

\re LIY\ (v.): be dependant, have confidence

The Delta Force *relied* on the intelligence supplied to them by satellite, and were forced to pull back when they lost their connection.

RESTORE

\reh STOR\ (v.): reestablish; revive

In an attempt to *restore* the city to its former glory, the mayor began a campaign to clean up the streets and attract more upscale citizens.

TRIVIALIZE

\TRIV ee uh liyz\ (v.): cause to appear insignificant

Rather than grant the legitimacy of her opponent's claims, the politician *trivialized* the question with a quick joke.

REVIVE

\reh VIYV\ (v.): resuscitate, bring back to life; restore to use

The competent acting troupe *revived* interest in the theater among neighborhood residents.

WE FOLLOW *TWO*. ONE LIGHTER THAN OTHER. A *FEMALE*, MAYBE...

I DON'T CARE WHO THEY ARE... WE JUST WANT THAT DRAGON. WE'LL BE GENEROUSLY <u>REMUNERATED</u> FOR ITS HEAD...FOR *ANY* DRAGON'S HEAD.

OF COURSE AS FAR AS I'M CONCERNED, THE MONEY JUST <u>AUGMENTS</u> THE EXTRAVAGANT HONORS WE'LL RECEIVE...

REMUNERATION

\ri myoon eh RAY shun\ (n.): pay or reward for work, trouble, etc.

You can't expect people to do this kind of boring work without some form of *remuneration*.

AUGMENT

\awg MENT\ (v.): to expand, extend

Ben looked to *augment* his salary by applying for extra overtime hours.

EXTRAVAGANT

\ek STRAV uh gent\ (adj.): lavish; unreasonably high, exorbitant

Among other *extravagant* demands, the hotel guest insisted upon bathing in natural spring water.

THE NIGHTMARES STILL _ROUSE_ ME FROM MY SLEEP, GROTH...

...THE BEAST... THE BLOOD... MY FAMILY...

...*EXTERMINATED*... AND MY OWN BODY TORN TO RIBBONS, LEFT TO DIE.

BUT I DIDN'T DIE... AND I SWORE I'D HUNT DOWN THAT DRAGON--

ROUSE

\ROWZ\ (v.): provoke, excite, stir

After noticing their listless play in the previous game, the cheerleaders were determined to *rouse* the basketball team to play harder in tonight's game.

EXTERMINATE

\ek STUR mu nayt\ (v.): destroy completely, annihilate

When the office manager noticed that the building was infested with vermin, he hired an expert to *exterminate* them.

--ANY DRAGON! AND NOW THAT OUR BENEFACTOR HAS GIVEN US THE MEANS...

...I WON'T LET ANYONE THWART US!

THWART

\THWART\ (v.): to block or prevent from happening; frustrate

After the tricky winds *thwarted* his attempts to throw the bag into the box, the chimp retired to the back of his cage in frustration.

33

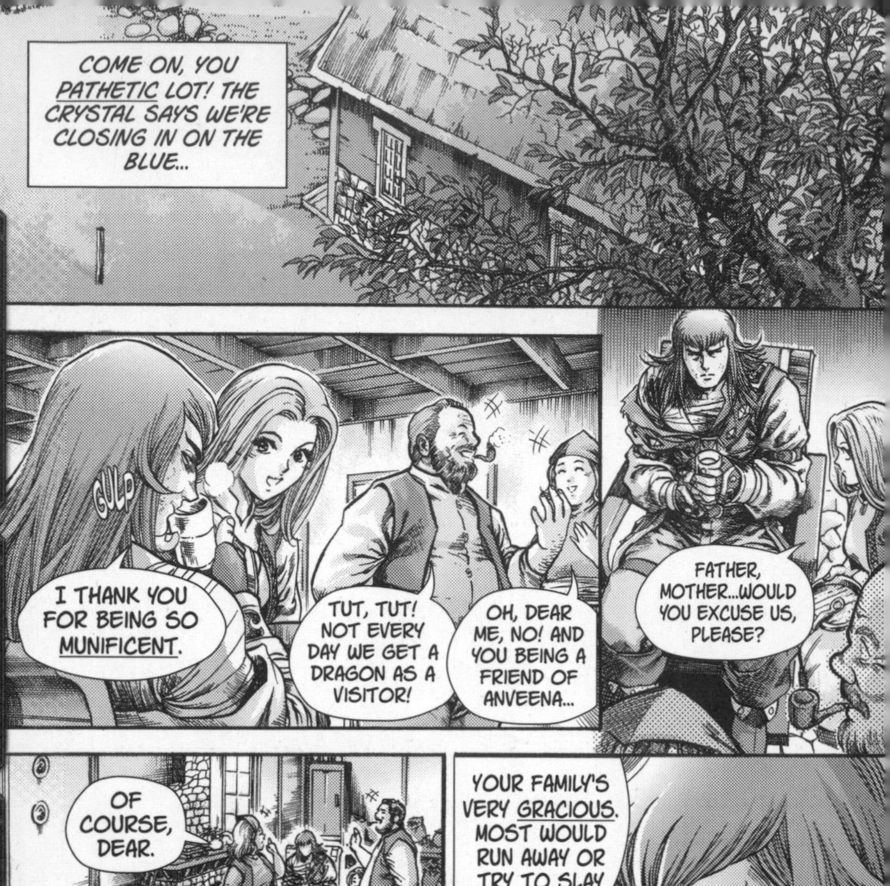
COME ON, YOU PATHETIC LOT! THE CRYSTAL SAYS WE'RE CLOSING IN ON THE BLUE...
GULP
I THANK YOU FOR BEING SO MUNIFICENT.
TUT, TUT! NOT EVERY DAY WE GET A DRAGON AS A VISITOR!
OH, DEAR ME, NO! AND YOU BEING A FRIEND OF ANVEENA...
FATHER, MOTHER...WOULD YOU EXCUSE US, PLEASE?
OF COURSE, DEAR.
WE'VE GOT OUR WORK TO DO.
YOUR FAMILY'S VERY GRACIOUS. MOST WOULD RUN AWAY OR TRY TO SLAY ME.
HOW HEINOUS! BUT WHY?
SIMPLE FEAR, MOSTLY. DRAGONS CAN BE EXTREMELY FORMIDABLE CREATURES. MOST DRAGONS WATCH OVER THE LESSER RACES, BUT SOME, ESPECIALLY THE BLACK DRAGONS, ARE RANCOROUS TOWARD ALL BUT THEMSELVES.

PATHETIC

\puh THET ik\ (adj.): arousing scornful pity

The judges could not believe that anyone would submit such a *pathetic* exhibit and were forced to reject the artist from the competition.

MUNIFICENT

\myoo NIF ih sint\ (adj.): generous

The *munificent* millionaire donated ten million dollars to the hospital.

GRACIOUS

\GRAY shus\ (adj.): kind, compassionate, warm-hearted

Ms. Kirchick proved to be a *gracious* host, welcoming her guests warmly and offering them tea and cookies.

HEINOUS

\HAY nes\ (adj.): shocking, wicked, terrible

The *heinous* crime shocked even the most seasoned officers on the force.

FORMIDABLE

\FOR mid uh bul\ (adj.): arousing fear or dread; inspiring awe or wonder; difficult to undertake

Realizing that she faced a *formidable* task, Barbara took a deep breath and began to clean her room.

RANCOROUS

\Rank o russ\ (adj.): bitter, hateful

Herbert was so *rancorous* that he could think of nothing but taking revenge on those who had humiliated him.

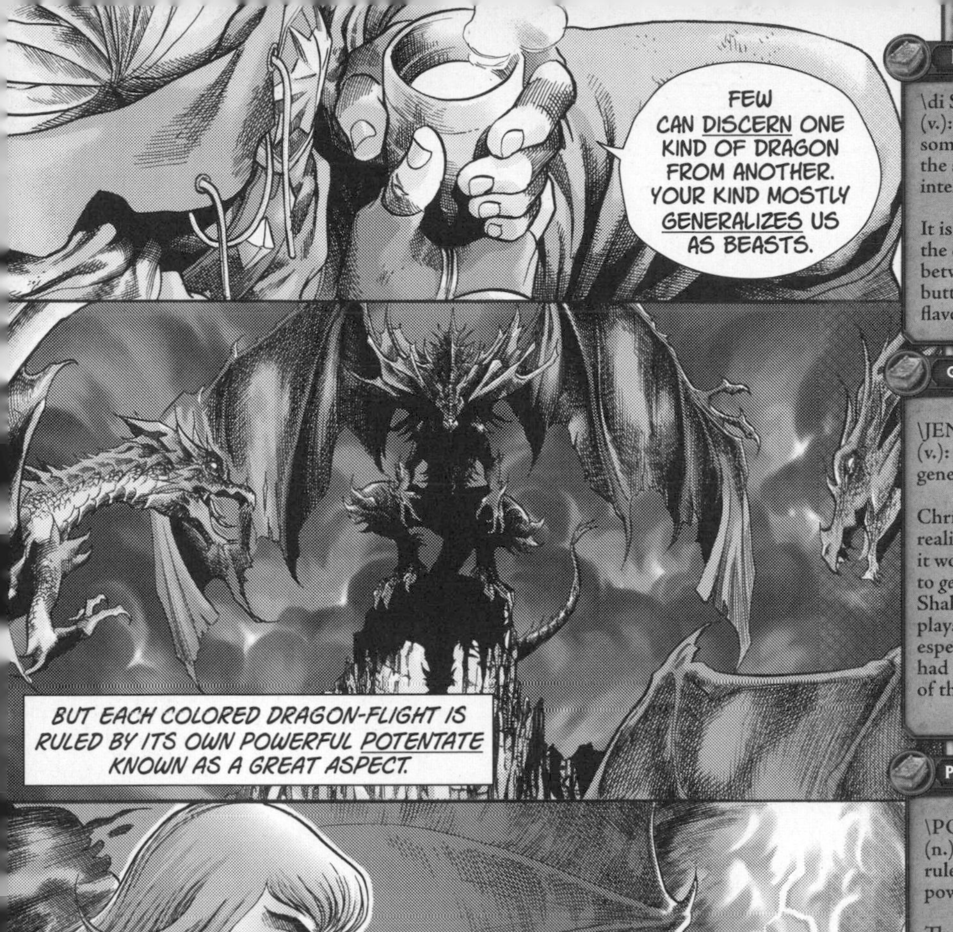
FEW CAN DISCERN ONE KIND OF DRAGON FROM ANOTHER. YOUR KIND MOSTLY GENERALIZES US AS BEASTS.
BUT EACH COLORED DRAGON-FLIGHT IS RULED BY ITS OWN POWERFUL POTENTATE KNOWN AS A GREAT ASPECT.
MY LORD IS MALYGOS THE BLUE, AND MAGIC IS HIS DOMAIN. THERE ARE ONLY A HANDFUL OF US. THE DREAD BLACK, DEATHWING, BETRAYED MY MASTER LONG AGO, AND IN THE PROCESS ERADICATED NEARLY ALL OF US.

DISCERN

\di SURN\ (v.): to perceive something using the senses or intellect

It is easy to *discern* the difference between real butter and butter-flavored topping.

GENERALIZE

\JEN er uh liyz\ (v.): reduce to a general form

Christopher didn't realize how foolish it would appear to *generalize* all Shakespeare plays as "boring," especially since he had read only one of the Bard's works.

POTENTATE

\POH tn tayt\ (n.): monarch or ruler with great power

The consul was a much kinder person before he assumed the role of *potentate*.

BETRAY

\be TRAY\ (v.): to be false or disloyal to

Unable to withstand the power of the dark side of the force, Darth Vader *betrayed* his teacher's confidence.

ERADICATE

\ih RAD ih kayt\ (v.): to erase or wipe out

It is unlikely that poverty will ever be completely *eradicated* in this country, though the general standard of living has significantly improved in recent decades.

ACCELERATE

\ak SEL uh rayt\ (v.): to cause to develop or progress more quickly

Professor Kinget stopped answering questions during the lecture so he could *accelerate* the pace of the class.

DIVULGE

\di VULJ\ (v.): to make known

Pat was fired for *divulging* company secrets to competitors.

SUMMARY

\SUM uh ree\ (n.): shortened version; abstract

The movie proved to be so complicated that the director had one of the characters give a *summary* of events to explain the story.

AMPLIFY

\AM pleh fy\ (v.): increase, intensify

We will need to *amplify* the music at the wedding so that everyone can dance.

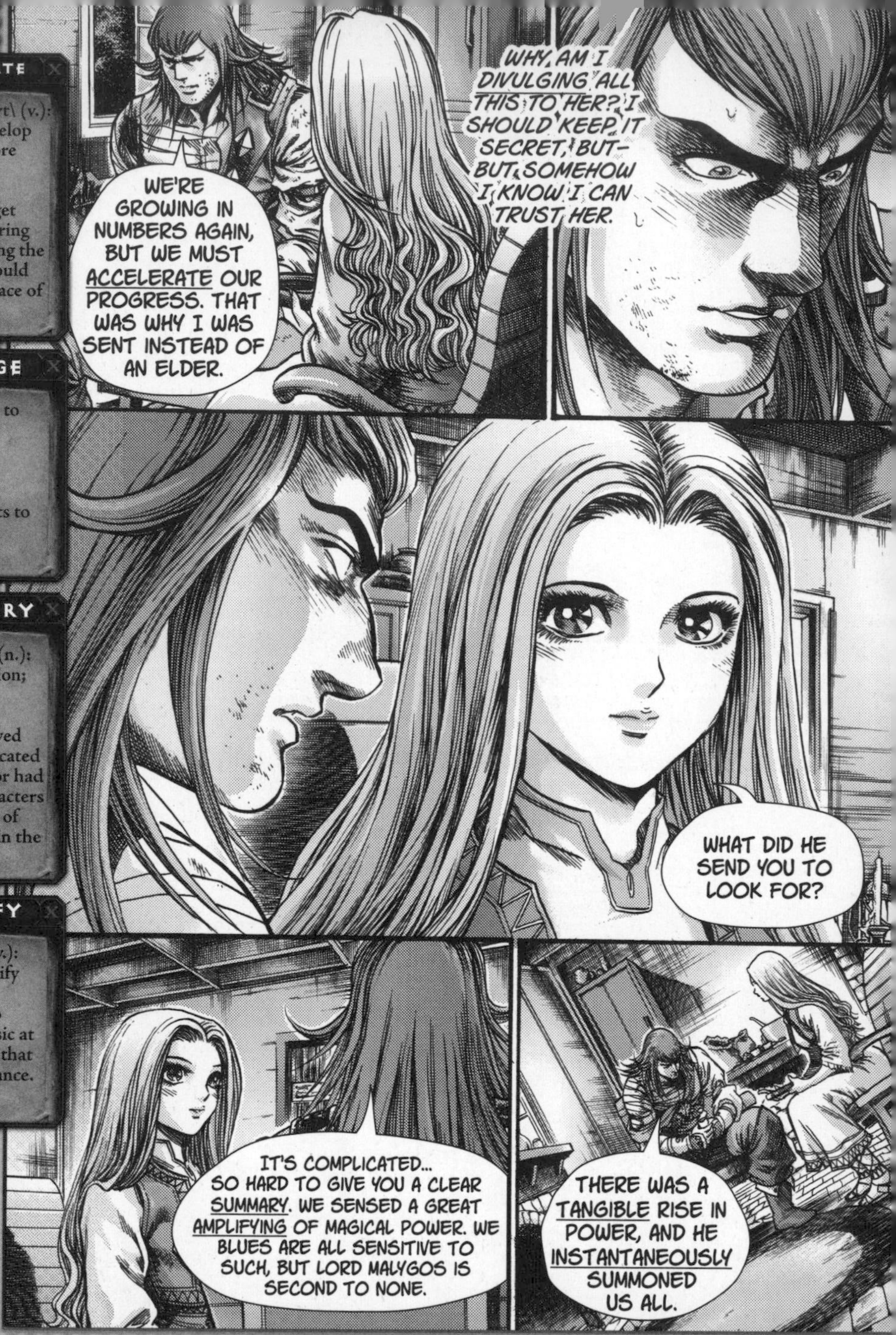

WE'RE GROWING IN NUMBERS AGAIN, BUT WE MUST ACCELERATE OUR PROGRESS. THAT WAS WHY I WAS SENT INSTEAD OF AN ELDER.
WHY, AM I DIVULGING ALL THIS TO HER? I SHOULD KEEP IT SECRET, BUT-- BUT SOMEHOW I KNOW I CAN TRUST HER.
WHAT DID HE SEND YOU TO LOOK FOR?
IT'S COMPLICATED... SO HARD TO GIVE YOU A CLEAR SUMMARY. WE SENSED A GREAT AMPLIFYING OF MAGICAL POWER. WE BLUES ARE ALL SENSITIVE TO SUCH, BUT LORD MALYGOS IS SECOND TO NONE.
THERE WAS A TANGIBLE RISE IN POWER, AND HE INSTANTANEOUSLY SUMMONED US ALL.

TANGIBLE

\TAN ji bul\ (adj.): able to be sensed, perceptible, measurable

The storming of the castle didn't bring the soldiers *tangible* rewards, but it brought them great honor.

INSTANTANEOUS

\in sten TAY nee us\ (adj.): immediate, without delay

The new computer system was designed to offer *instantaneous* feedback to the user's questions.

DO YOU KNOW ANYTHING OF THE ELVEN KINGDOM OF QUEL'THALAS?

DESTROYED BY THE UNDEAD SCOURGE WITH THE AID OF *TREACHERY* FROM WITHIN?

YES, WE KNOW QUEL'THALAS WELL!

THAT'S WHERE WE CAME FROM!

YOU? HUMANS? BUT THE ELVES ARE *PARANOID* ABOUT OUTSIDERS! THAT'S WHAT MADE IT SO TERRIBLE WHEN ONE OF THEIR OWN BETRAYED THEM!

TREACHERY

\TRECH uh ree\ (n.): willful betrayal of trust

When the president's own advisor turned against him in the revolution, it was the ultimate act of *treachery*.

PARANOID

\PAR uh noyd\ (adj.): exhibiting extreme mistrust of others

Leonard was very *paranoid* about losing his credit card, so he frequently checked his wallet as he walked down the street.

37

IT WAS THEIR STRONG CONVICTION THAT NONE OF THEIR OWN COULD BE _PERSUADED_ BY THE LICH KING'S POWER...BUT ONE WAS.

SURREPTITIOUSLY, HE TRIED TO STEAL FOR THE UNDEAD SCOURGE THE VERY SOURCE OF THE ELVES' POWER...THE _TALISMAN_ WHICH ALONE HAD PROTECTED THEM FROM THE HORRORS OF THE LICH KING.

THE SUNWELL...

PERSUASIVE

\pir SWAY siv\ (adj.): convincing

Because she was such a _persuasive_ negotiator, companies hired her to represent them in high-profile meetings.

SURREPTITIOUS

\sir up TISH iss\ (adj.): secret, stealthy

In order to achieve revenge on his former boss, George made some _surreptitious_ changes to the agenda for the meeting.

TALISMAN

\TAL iss man\ (n.): magic object that offers supernatural protection

The shop was selling _talismans_ that were rumored to protect the owner from car accidents.

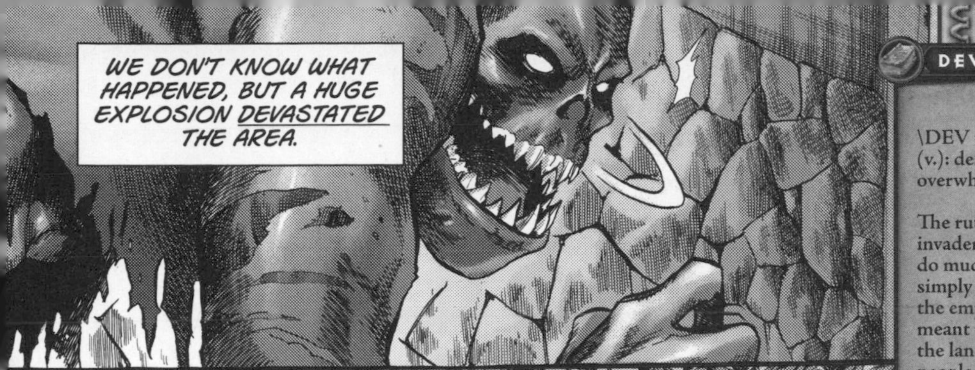
WE DON'T KNOW WHAT HAPPENED, BUT A HUGE EXPLOSION DEVASTATED THE AREA.

DEVASTATE

\DEV uh stayt\ (v.): destroy; overwhelm, stun

The ruthless invaders sought to do much more than simply intimidate the empire; they meant to *devastate* the land and its people.

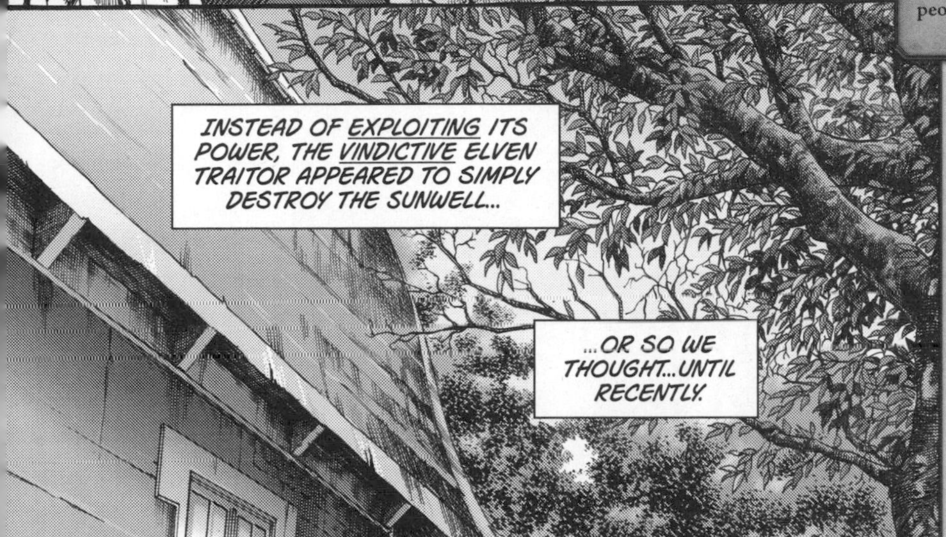
INSTEAD OF EXPLOITING ITS POWER, THE VINDICTIVE ELVEN TRAITOR APPEARED TO SIMPLY DESTROY THE SUNWELL...
...OR SO WE THOUGHT...UNTIL RECENTLY.

EXPLOIT

\ek SPLOYT\ (v.): take advantage of

The brilliant tactician studied his enemy's methods to discover a weakness that he could easily *exploit* in battle.

VINDICTIVE

\vin DIK tiv\ (adj.): spiteful, vengeful, unforgiving

After her husband left her for a young model, the *vindictive* ex-wife plotted to destroy their relationship.

THE BEAST'S SOMEWHERE NEAR HERE! SURROUND THAT COTTAGE!

THOSE INSIDE BETTER NOT BE <u>LOATH</u> TO TELL US WHERE IT'S HIDING...

...IF THEY WANT TO LIVE!

LOATH

\LOHTH\ (adj.): reluctant, unwilling

Jimmy was *loath* to visit the post office because he knew he would have to wait on line for hours.

CHAPTER TWO PURSUED

...OR SO WE THOUGHT...UNTIL RECENTLY...

PROXIMITY

\prok SIM ih tee\
(n.): nearness

Tim was careful to put the glass out of reach, since the toddler loved to yank down objects in her *proximity*.

THE EMANATIONS CAME FROM SOMEWHERE IN PROXIMITY TO THIS AREA. I WAS SEARCHING FOR THEIR SOURCE WHEN I WAS ATTACKED.

I HAVE NO IDEA WHO IS CULPABLE FOR ATTACKING ME, BUT THEY MUST BE AFTER THE SAME THING I AM...

...I'VE GOT TO SALVAGE IT BEFORE THEY--

CULPABLE

\KUL puh bull\ (adj.): guilty, responsible for wrong

The CEO is *culpable* for the company's bankruptcy, as the beginning of his new initiatives marked the end of profits.

SALVAGE

\SAL vij\ (v.): to recover, save from loss

Historians have been attempting to *salvage* the remains of the Titanic for years, but attempts to raise the ship to the surface have failed.

KLAK KLAK KLAK
NO! AN INTRUDER! IT'S—UNGGH—TOO LATE! OUR ADVERSARIES ARE HERE!
IF I LEFT, M-MAYBE THEY'D FOLLOW ME!
B-BUT I DON'T S-SEE ANOTHER WAY OUT--
HERE! ARE YOU AGILE ENOUGH TO CLIMB DOWN THROUGH THIS? COME, I WILL HELP YOU!
I DON'T RECALL--
SQUEEEEK
NEVER MIND...

INTRUDER

\in TROO der\ (n.): a trespasser

My uncle just bought a new watchdog to chase away any *intruders*.

ADVERSARY

\ADD ver SEH ree\ (n.): opponent, enemy

Joan and her *adversary* each won two fencing matches.

AGILE

\AH jel\ (adj.): well coordinated, nimble

The *agile* monkey leapt onto the table and snatched the boy's banana away in the blink of an eye.

RECALL

\re KAWL\ (v.): remember; cancel, revoke; to take back

When the car company realized that its latest model was unsafe, it was forced to *recall* fifty thousand automobiles.

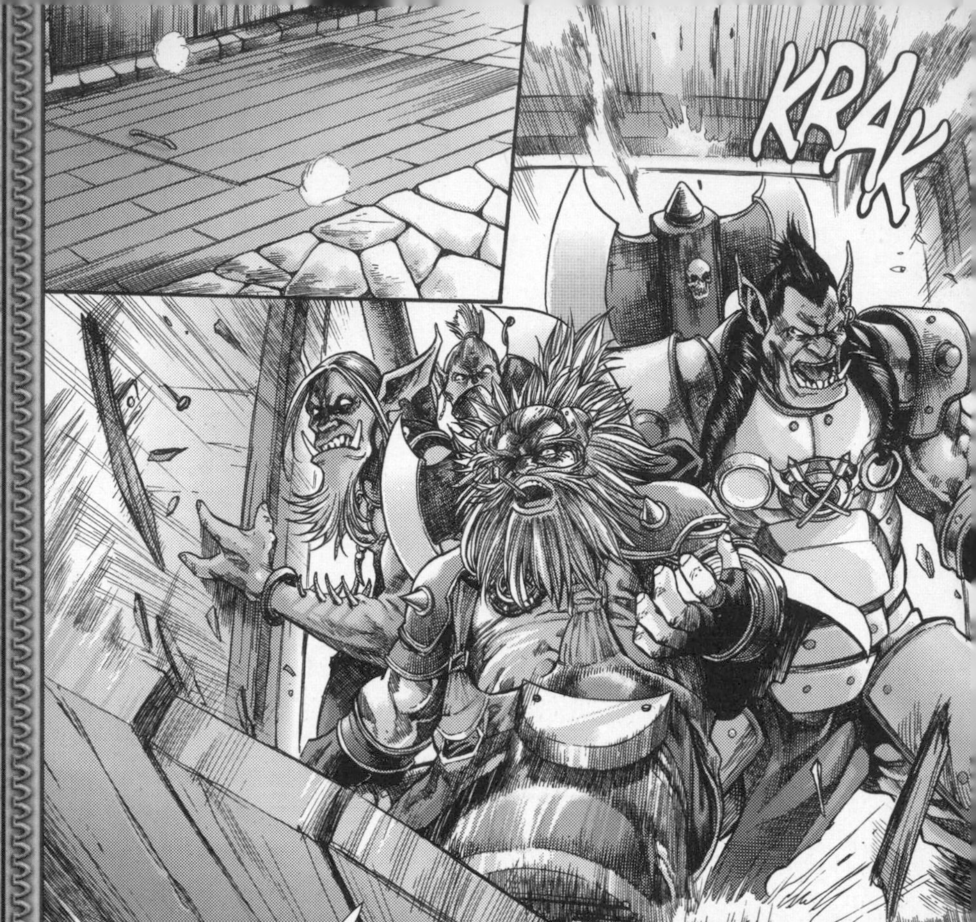
KRAK
DO NOT MOVE! ANY DEFIANT FOOL WHO DARES NOT HEED MY WORDS WILL SUFFER!
I KNOW THERE'S A DRAGON ABOUT, AND YOU MUST TELL ME WHERE HE IS!
CRASH

DEFIANT

\de FIY ant\ (adj.): boldly resisting

The *defiant* soldier ignored the general's orders.

HEED

\HEED\ (v.): pay attention to

Laura didn't *heed* her mother's advice and went outside without a coat.

GRRR...

YOU ARE BEGINNING TO AGITATE ME! DID YOU HEAR ME?!? DRAGON!! I'M HUNTING A DRAGON! WHERE IS IT?

AGITATE

\AH ji tayt\ (v.): upset, disturb

Peter always cleans up his dorm room so it doesn't *agitate* his mother when she visits him.

47

ENCHANT

\en CHANT\ (v.): attract and delight

Lorna was dazzled by her first visit to the Museum of Modern Art; the brilliant colors and bold paintings *enchanted* her.

EXHAUST

\eg ZOST\ (v.): to wear out; use up completely

The day at the beach *exhausted* all of Nico's energy, so she chose not to join her friends at the movie that evening.

GIBBERING

\JIB uh ring\ (v.): prattling unintelligibly

Cathy can't understand a word her friends say when they get excited; they start *gibbering* at incredible speeds.

BUFFOONERY

\bu FOO ner ee\ (n.): acting like a clown or fool

Jimmy's *buffoonery* had gotten him thrown out of class more often than any other student.

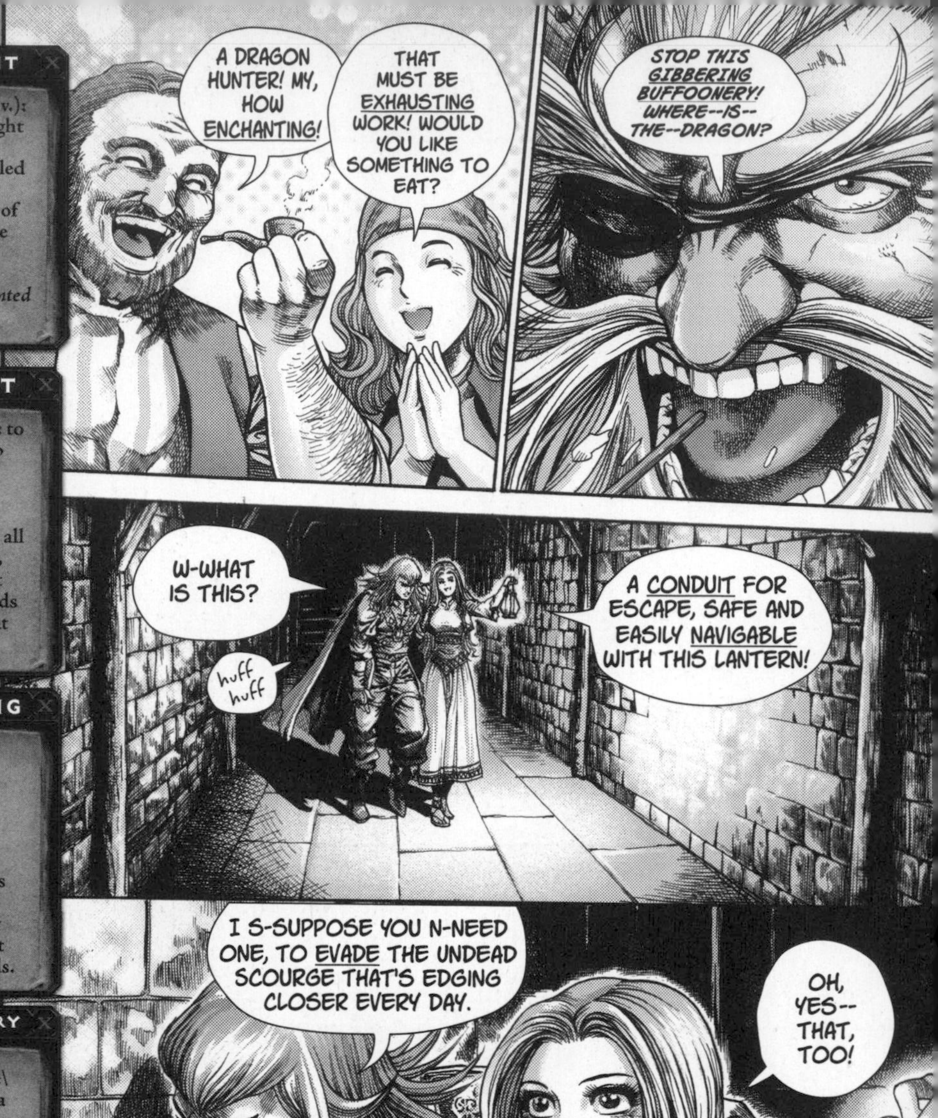
A DRAGON HUNTER! MY, HOW ENCHANTING!
THAT MUST BE EXHAUSTING WORK! WOULD YOU LIKE SOMETHING TO EAT?
STOP THIS GIBBERING BUFFOONERY! WHERE--IS--THE--DRAGON?
W-WHAT IS THIS?
huff huff
A CONDUIT FOR ESCAPE, SAFE AND EASILY NAVIGABLE WITH THIS LANTERN!
I S-SUPPOSE YOU N-NEED ONE, TO EVADE THE UNDEAD SCOURGE THAT'S EDGING CLOSER EVERY DAY.
OH, YES--THAT, TOO!

CONDUIT

\KON doo it\ (n.): tube, pipe, or similar passage

The *conduit* carried excess rainwater down to the ocean, preventing flooding.

EVADE

\ee VAYD\ (v.): to avoid, dodge

He *evaded* answering my question by pretending not to hear me and changing the subject.

NAVIGABLE

\NAV ih gu bul\ (adj.): sufficient for vessels to pass through

Although the water around Cape Horn is *navigable*, it is such a dangerous and expensive journey that most boats must sail through the Panama Canal to cross the Americas.

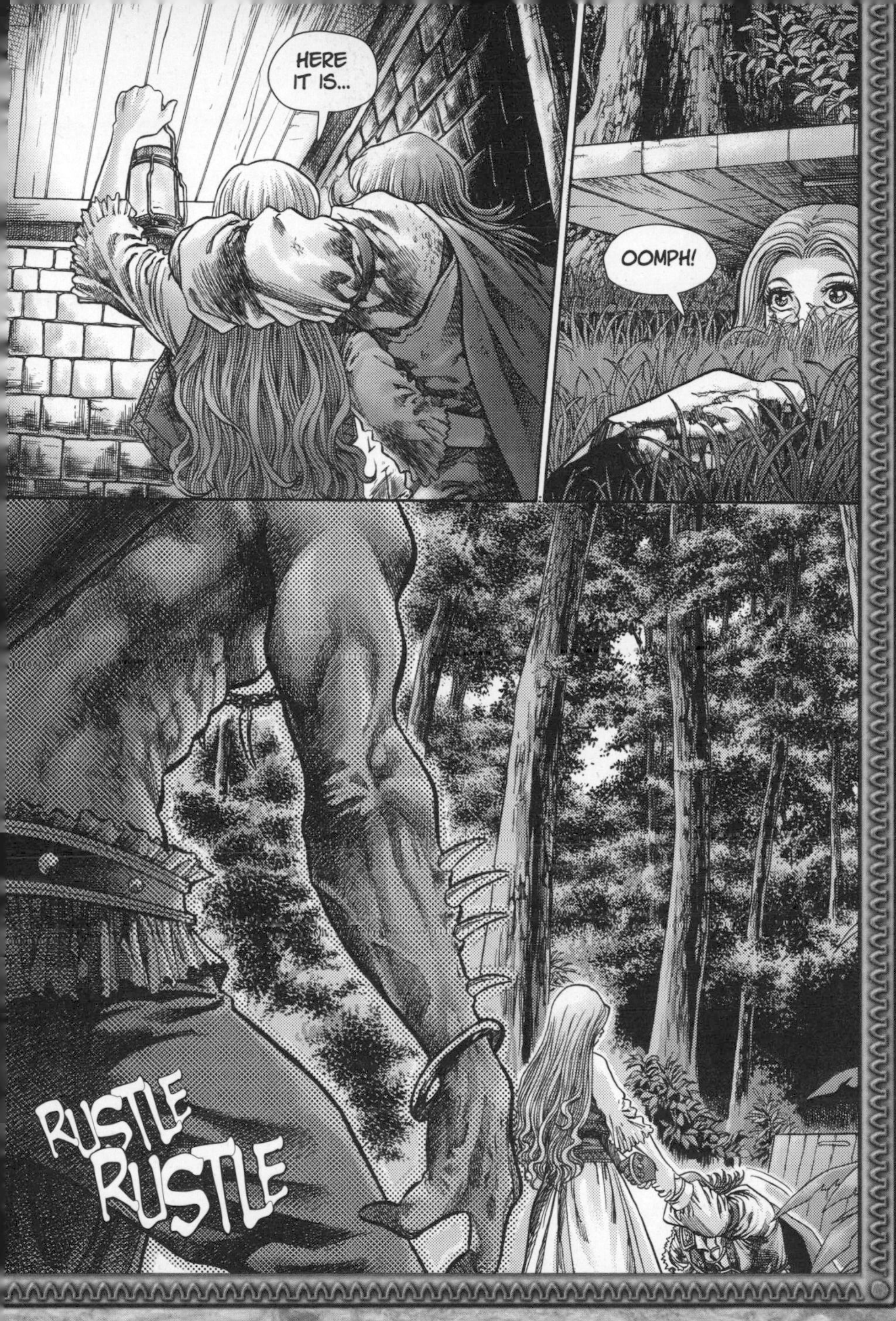
HERE IT IS...
OOMPH!
RUSTLE RUSTLE

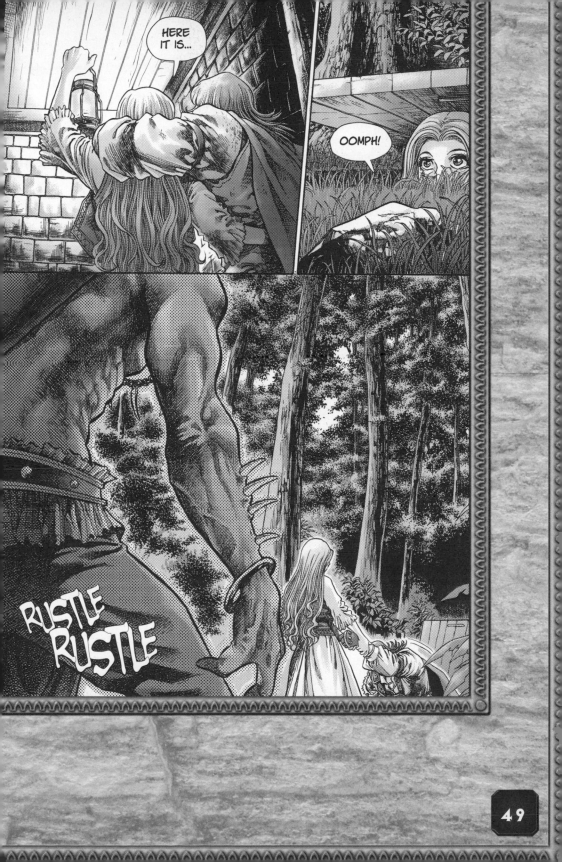

SCAMPER

\SKAMP er\ (v.): run off quickly

Peter Rabbit *scampered* out of Farmer McGregor's garden when he realized the old man had returned home.

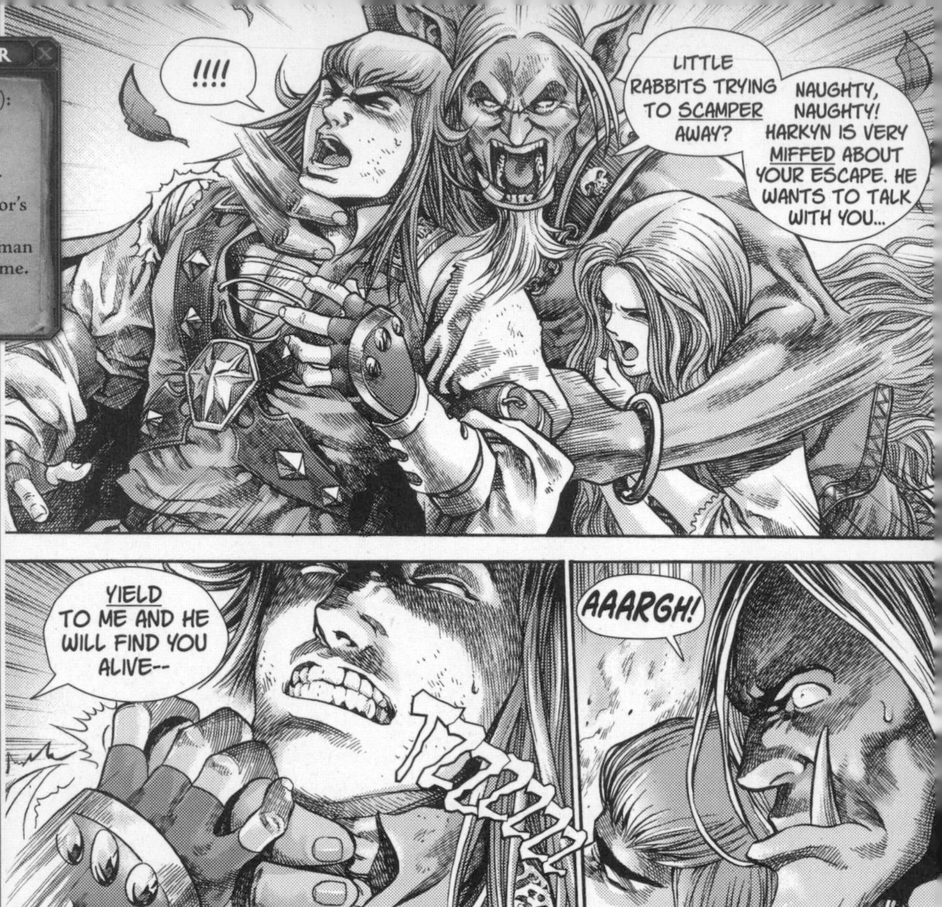
!!!!
LITTLE RABBITS TRYING TO SCAMPER AWAY?
NAUGHTY, NAUGHTY! HARKYN IS VERY MIFFED ABOUT YOUR ESCAPE. HE WANTS TO TALK WITH YOU...
YIELD TO ME AND HE WILL FIND YOU ALIVE--
AAARGH!
URGH!
GO, ANVEENA!
NO! NOT WITHOUT YOU!

MIFFED

\MIFT\ (adj.): offended, annoyed

Roger was *miffed* at his company's refusal to employ his son.

YIELD

\YEELD\ (v.): surrender, concede; be productive

Despite my initial pessimism about it, our staff meeting *yielded* a number of constructive suggestions.

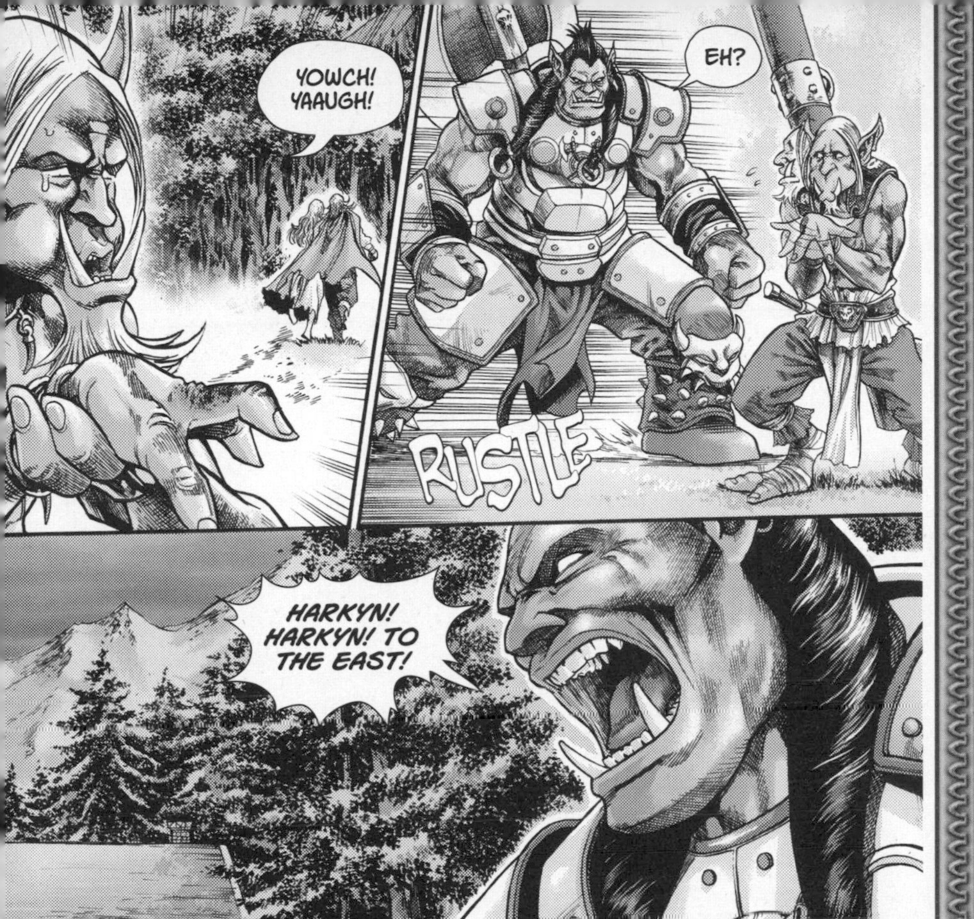
YOWCH! YAAUGH!
EH?
RUSTLE
HARKYN! HARKYN! TO THE EAST!
NO, I DON'T WANT ANY FOOD! ENOUGH PROCRASTINATING! I WANT--
SOME TEA?
AHH!

PROCRASTINATE

\pro KRAS tih nayt\ (v.): to push off doing work

Zack tried to *procrastinate* as long as possible, but knew that he would have to hand in his assignment eventually.

EAST?! THE DRAGON LIES EAST, TOO!

STOP SOCIALIZING! SPIT THAT OUT AND FOLLOW ME!

PTUU!

DO COME AND VISIT AGAIN...

CLATTER CLATTER

I HEAR THEM! TH-THEY'RE IN PURSUIT OF US! ANVEENA! GO! YOU HAVE BEEN VERY SOLICITOUS, BUT THIS ISN'T YOUR PROBLEM--

HUSH! WE WILL BE ALL RIGHT!

SOCIALIZE

\so shu LIYZ\ (v.): take part in group activities

Reggie felt that it was more important to finish his homework than to go out and *socialize* with his friends.

PURSUIT

\pur SOOT\ (n.): the act of chasing or striving

While the *pursuit* of happiness is a basic right afforded to citizens in this country, the law limits it when one person's rights interfere with the well-being of others.

SOLICITOUS

\su LIS ih tus\ (adj.): concerned, attentive; eager

The *solicitous* young waiter stood at the table the entire meal, waiting to receive another order.

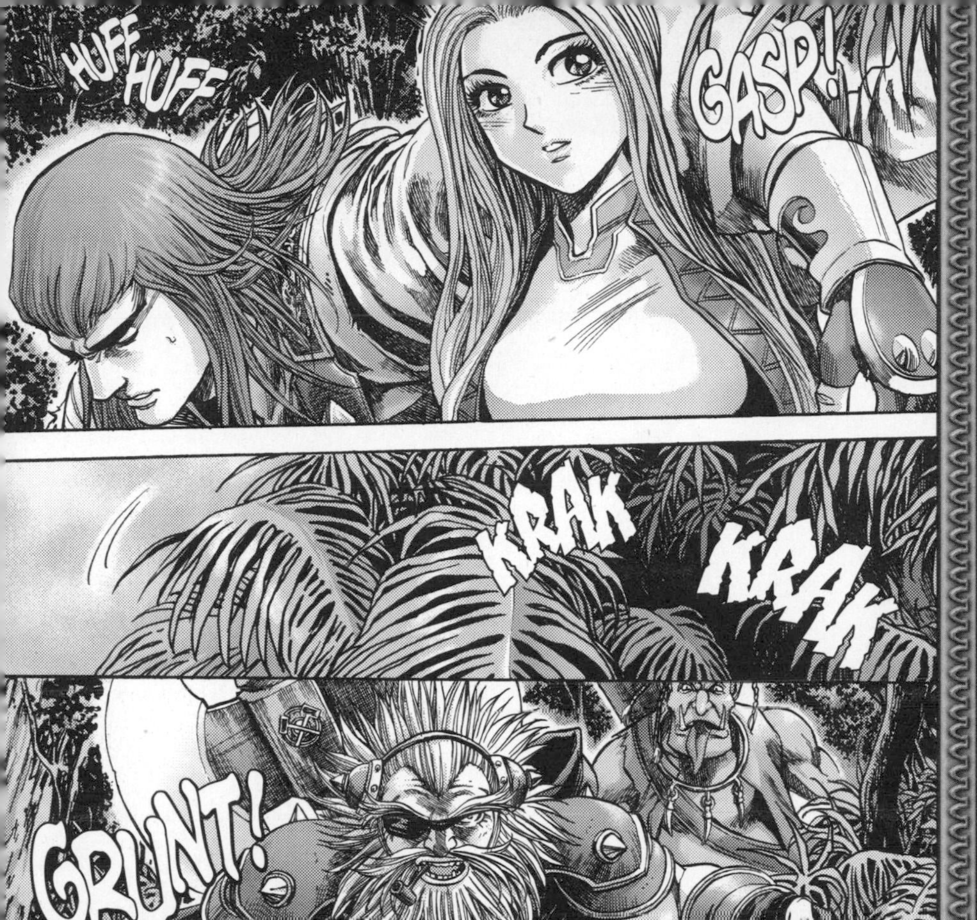
GASP!
HUFF HUFF
KRAK
KRAK
GRUNT!

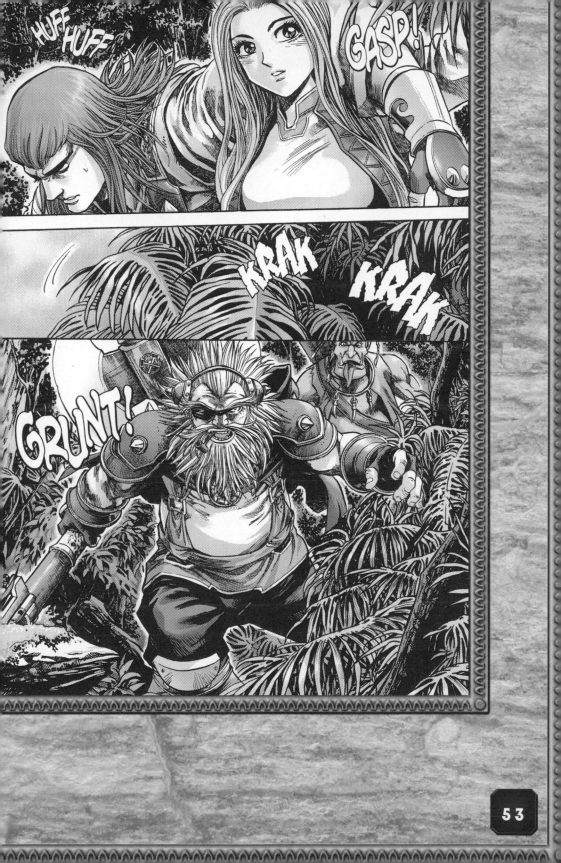

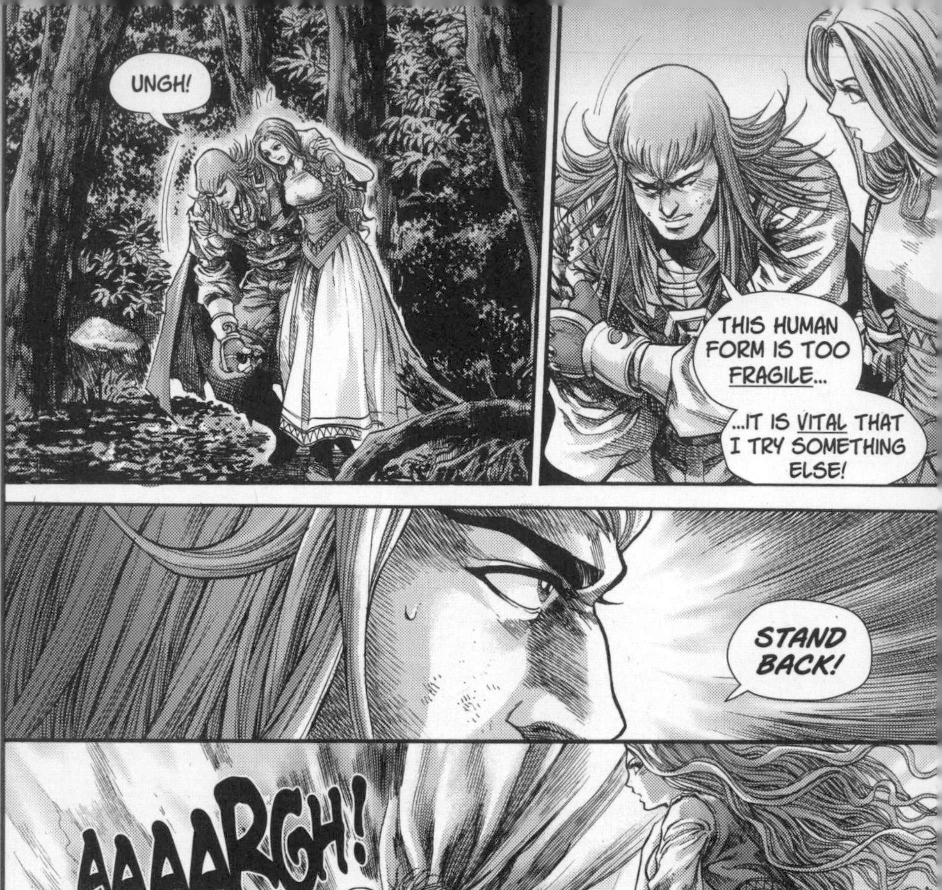
UNGH!
THIS HUMAN FORM IS TOO FRAGILE...
...IT IS VITAL THAT I TRY SOMETHING ELSE!
STAND BACK!
AAAARGH!
TZZZZZZZ

FRAGILE

\FRAJ il\ (adj.): delicate, frail

Mr. Thompson didn't trust his servants with the *fragile* vase and insisted on cleaning it himself.

VITAL

\VIY tul\ (adj.): urgently necessary, critical

The nurse sat with the patient, checking her heart rate and blood pressure until all the *vital* signs were back to normal.

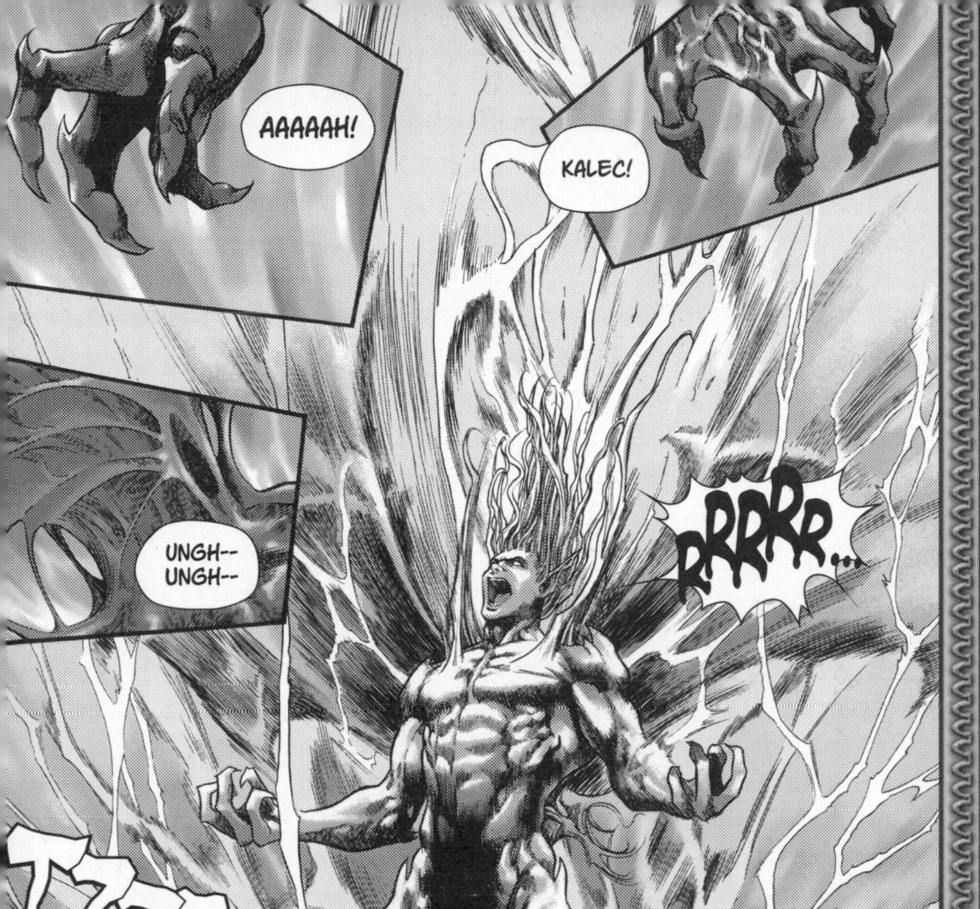
AAAAAH!
KALEC!
UNGH-- UNGH--
RRRRR...
TZZZZZZZ

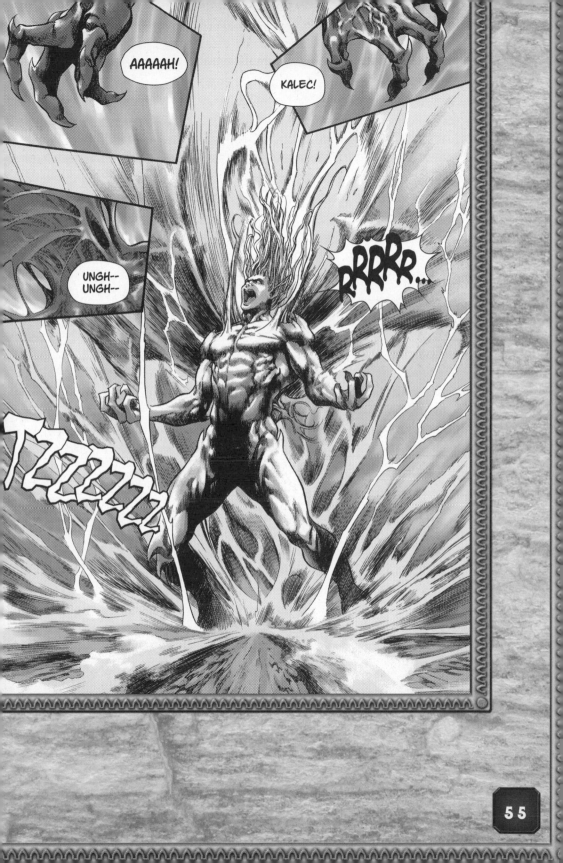

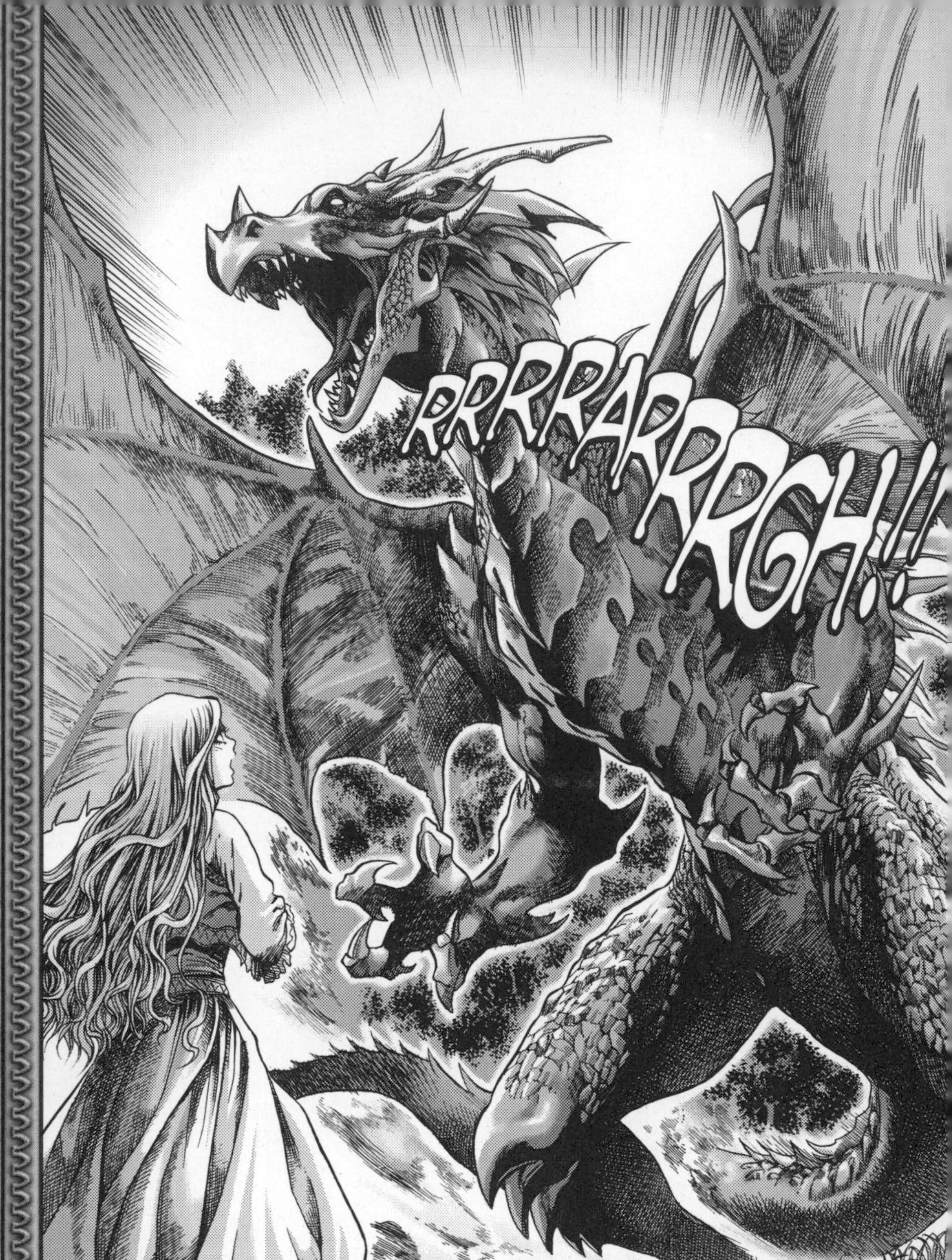
RRRRARRRRGH!!

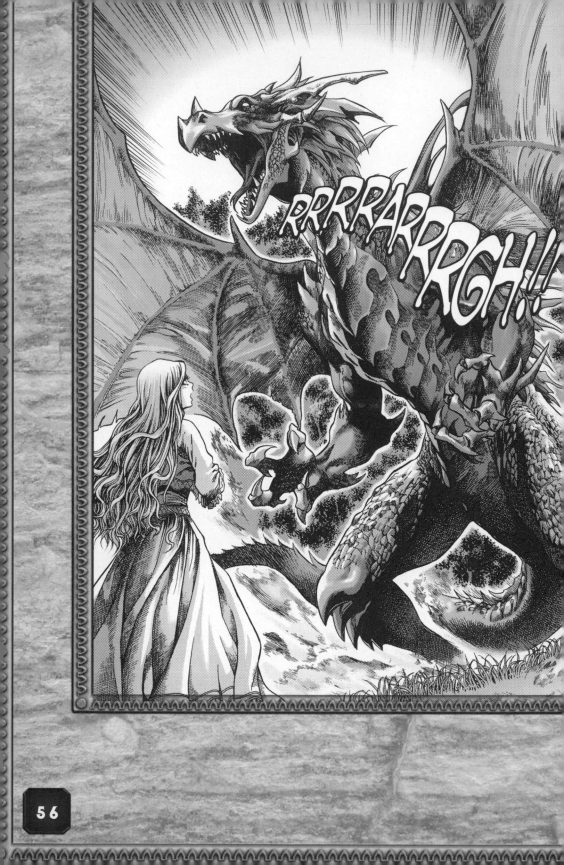

THE BLUE!!

YOUR TRUST IS PARAMOUNT TO OUR SURVIVAL. BELIEVE IN ME...

SWOOOSH

PARAMOUNT

\PAR uh mownt\ (adj.): supreme, dominant, primary

It is of *paramount* importance that we make it back to camp before the storm hits.

57

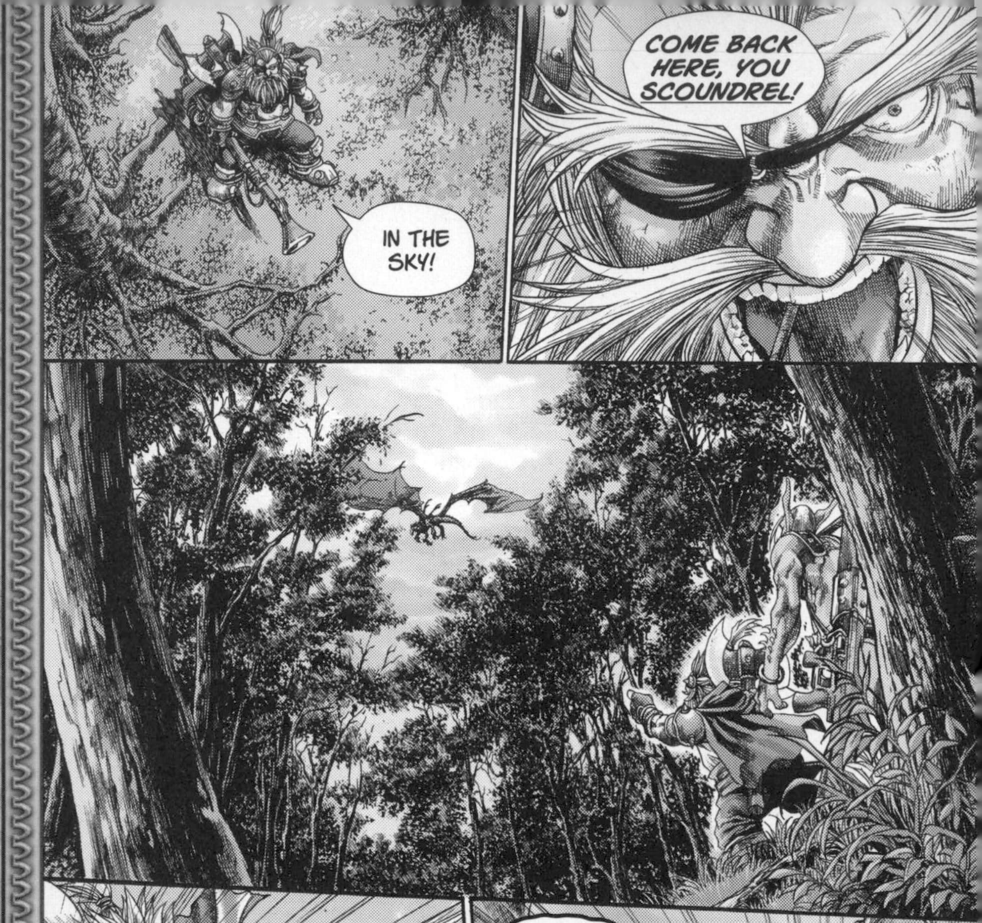
IN THE SKY!
COME BACK HERE, YOU SCOUNDREL!
THWAM
RRRAUGH!
BWAM
BWAM
AIEEE!

SCOUNDREL

\SKOWN drul\ (n.): villain, rogue

George the Pirate was the meanest *scoundrel* ever to roam the seas.

BLAST!!

UNGH--

KALEC! YOU MUST PERSEVERE!

I-I CAN'T PROPEL US ANY FARTHER... HAVE-HAVE TO LAND AGAIN!

H-HOLD TIGHT!

PERSEVERE ✕

\pir suh VEER\ (v.): to refuse to stop, regardless of difficulty

Gail *persevered* and trekked through three feet of snow to visit her sick uncle.

PROPEL ✕

\pro PEL\ (v.): to cause to move forward

"Our new ideas will *propel* this company into the next century," the executive promised.

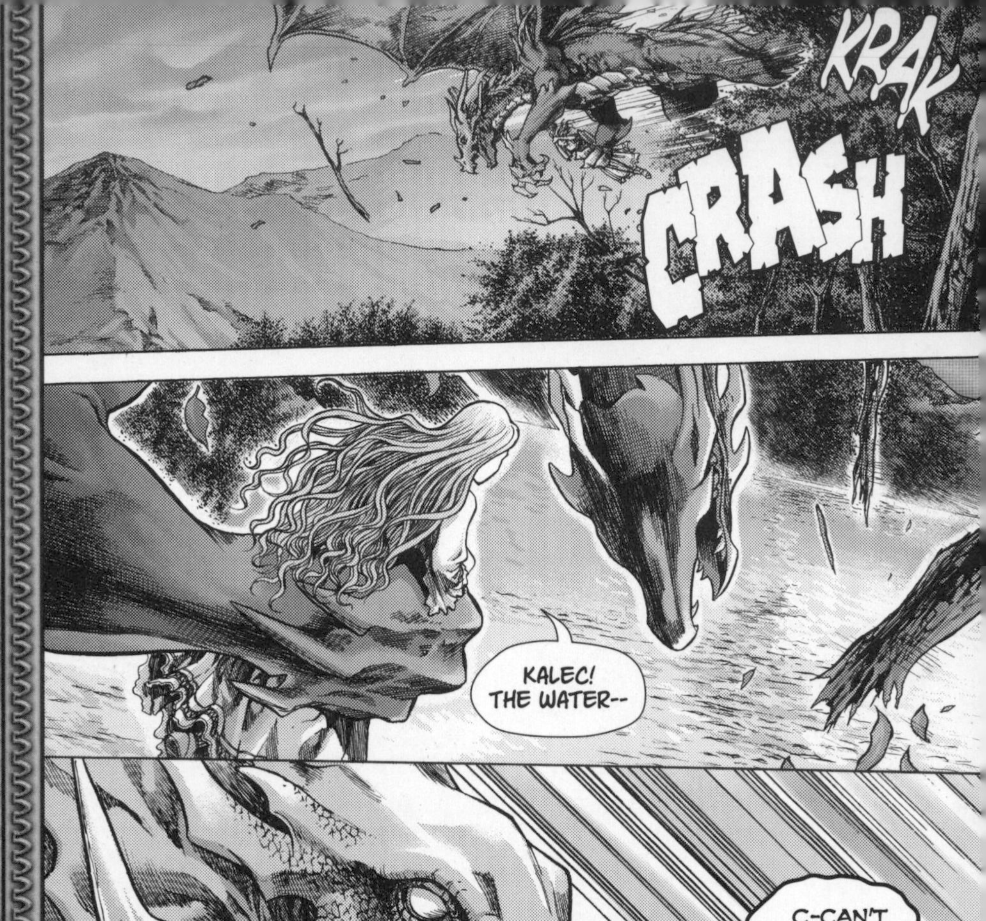
KRAK
CRASH
KALEC! THE WATER--
C-CAN'T STOP MYSELF!

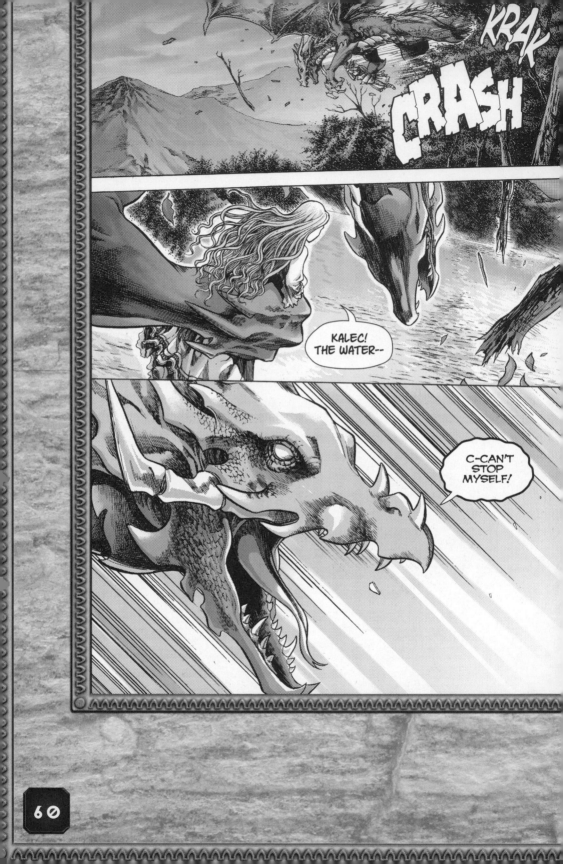

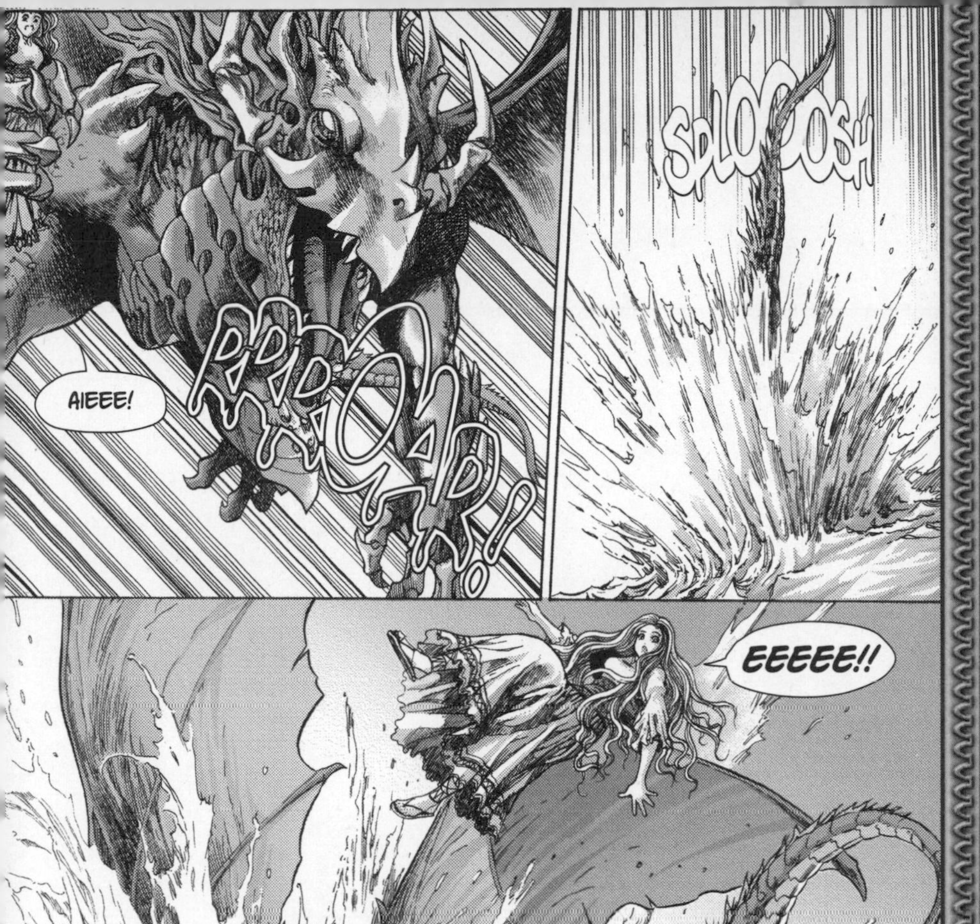

AIEEE!
RRROARR!
SPLOOOSH
EEEEE!!

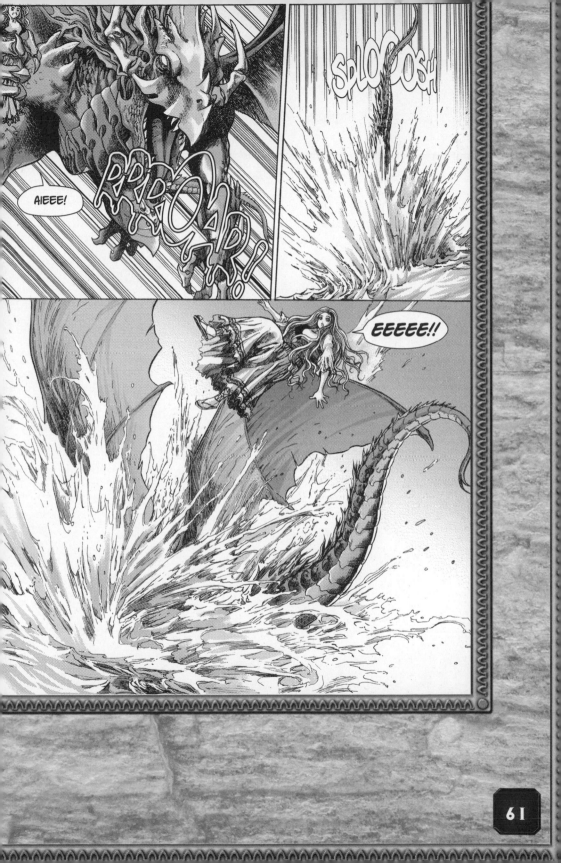

YOU *HIT* THE DRAGON?
I DON'T KNOW! WE'LL NEED TO VERIFY. I THINK I SHOOK HIM UP, THOUGH!
I THINK HE'S IN THE LAKE OVER THERE, BUT IT'S BARRICADED BY THAT PINE GROVE!
THOUGHT I HEARD A SPLASH, BUT WHAT--
EH?
?!!?
WOOOSH
WHA-? THE CRYSTAL BEWILDERS ME. IS IT DEFECTIVE? IT'S POINTING NORTH NOW!
BUT THE LAKE--

VERIFY

\VER ih fiy\ (v.): substantiate, confirm

Before we can go any further with the experiment, we need to *verify* that the results we've obtained are in fact accurate.

BARRICADE

\BAR ih kayd\ (n.): obstacle, barrier

During the French Revolution, students set up *barricades* in Paris to keep the army from moving through the streets.

GROVE

\GROHV\ (n.): a group of trees

Mark sat in the apple *grove*, surrounded by tall trees, and mulled over the week's events.

BEWILDER

\be WILL der\ (v.): to confuse or puzzle

The class found themselves *bewildered* by Professor Yasmeet's lecture on advanced photonics.

DEFECTIVE

\dee FEK tiv\ (adj.): faulty

After the second blackout in the building, the superintendent realized that the electrical grid was *defective* and needed to be replaced.

THAT WAS THE DRAGON OVER US! THE CRYSTAL'S JUDGMENT HAS NEVER BEEN *FALLACIOUS*. WE MUST HEAD NORTH....

MAKES MORE SENSE THAN A LAKE!

UNNNH...

FALLACIOUS

\fu LAY shuss\ (adj.): wrong, unsound, illogical

We now know that the statement "the Earth is flat" is *fallacious*.

63

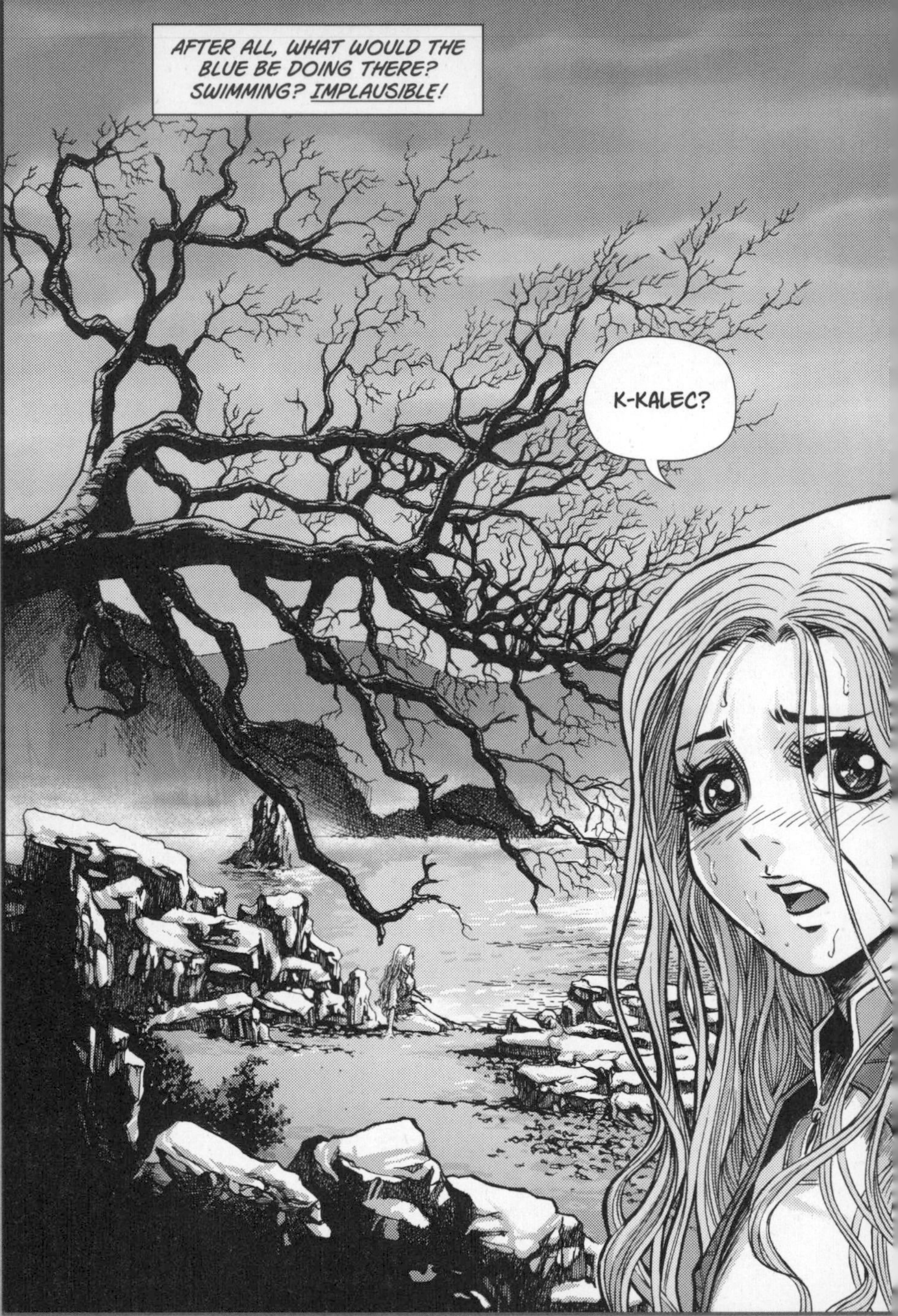
AFTER ALL, WHAT WOULD THE BLUE BE DOING THERE? SWIMMING? IMPLAUSIBLE!
K-KALEC?

IMPLAUSIBLE

\im PLAWS uh bul\ (adj.): improbable, inconceivable

A skeptical man by nature, Max found his neighbor's claim that he'd seen a UFO highly *implausible*.

CHAPTER THREE
DAR'KHAN

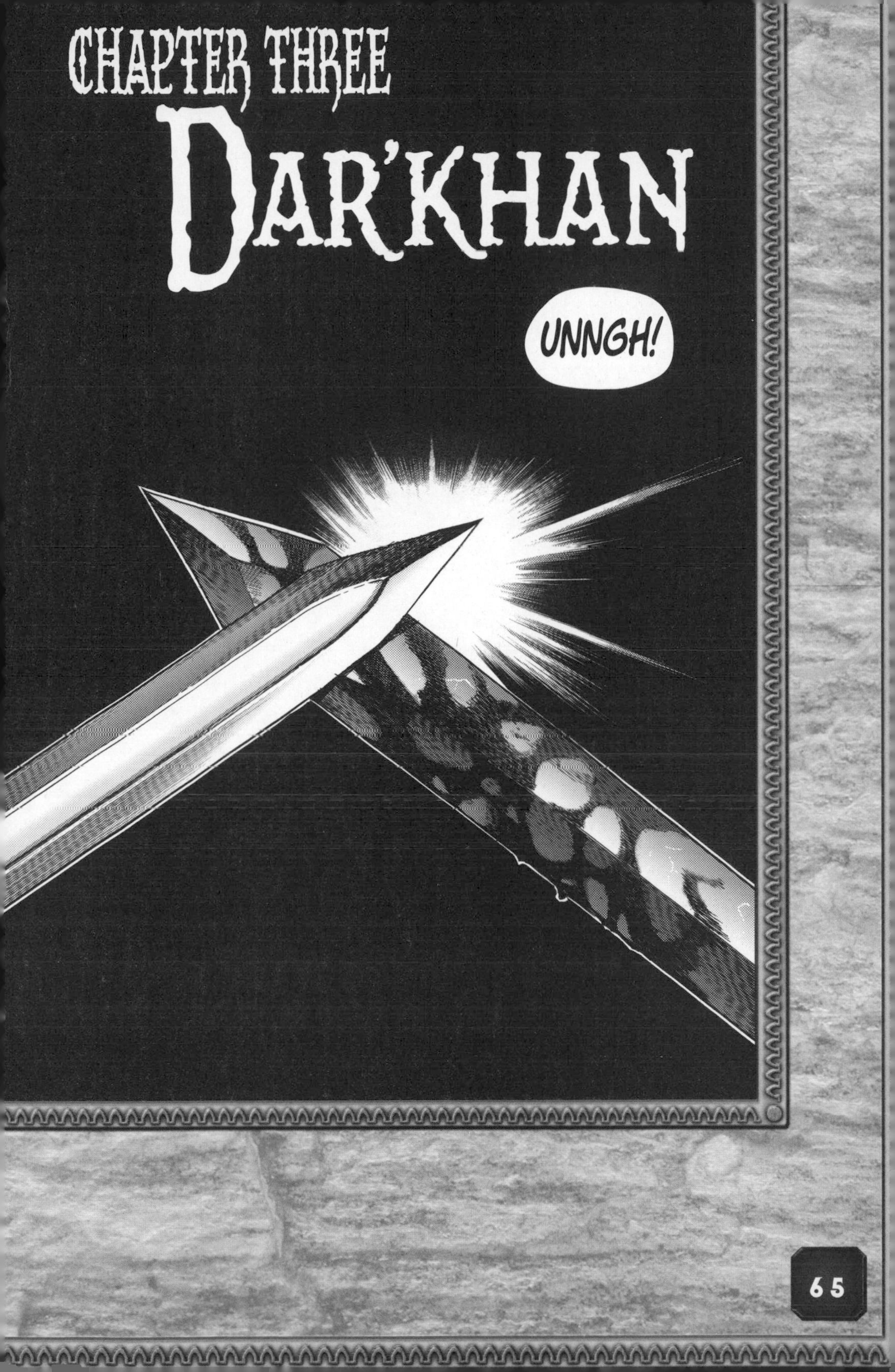
UNNGH!

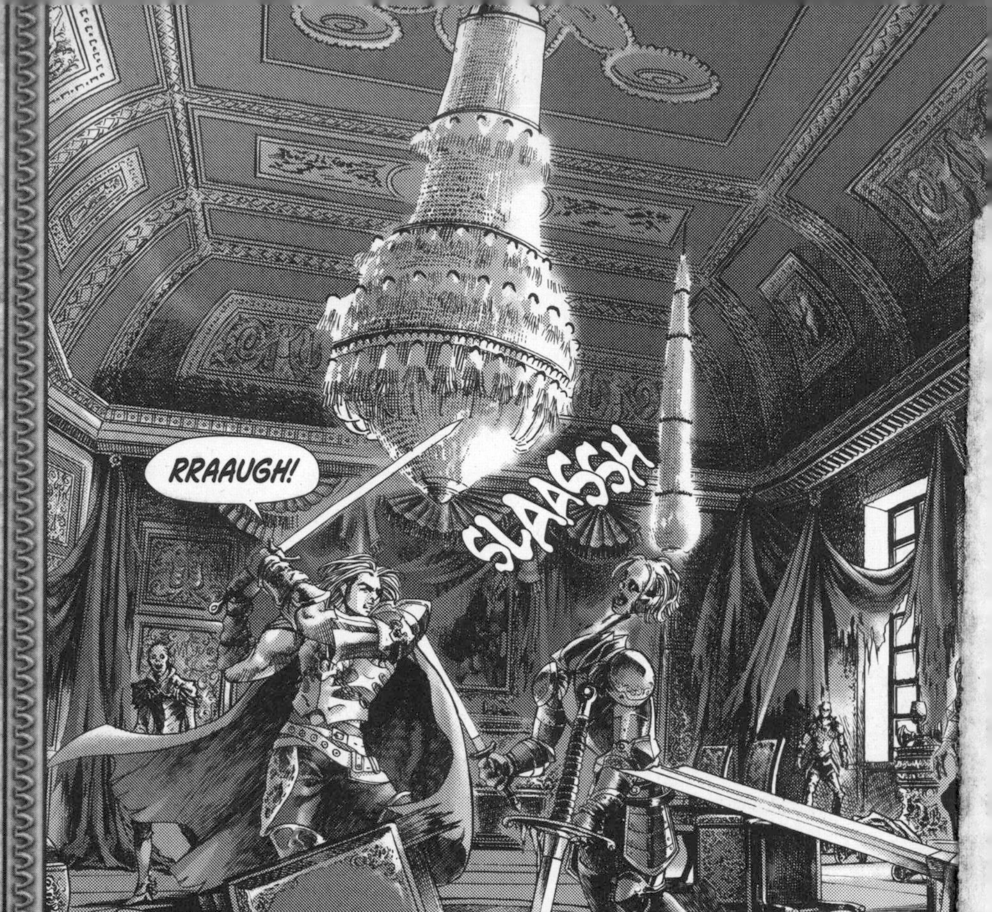
RRAAUGH!
SLASSH

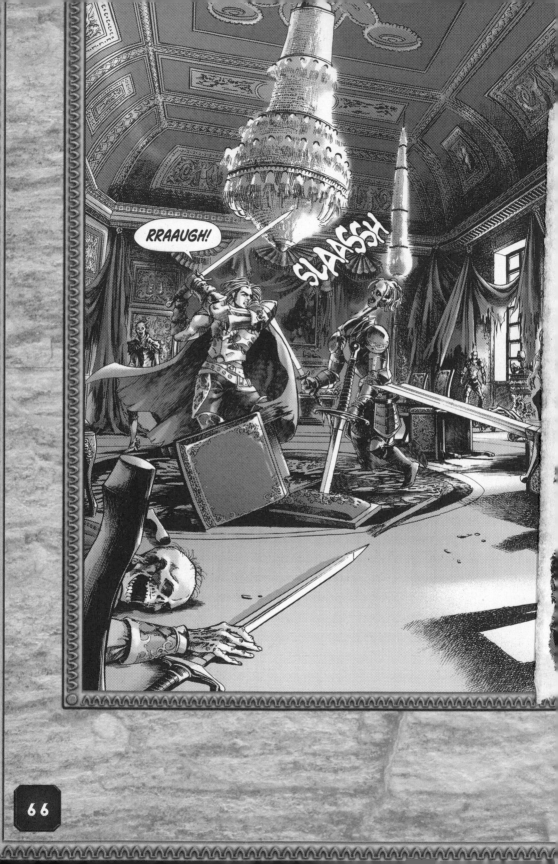

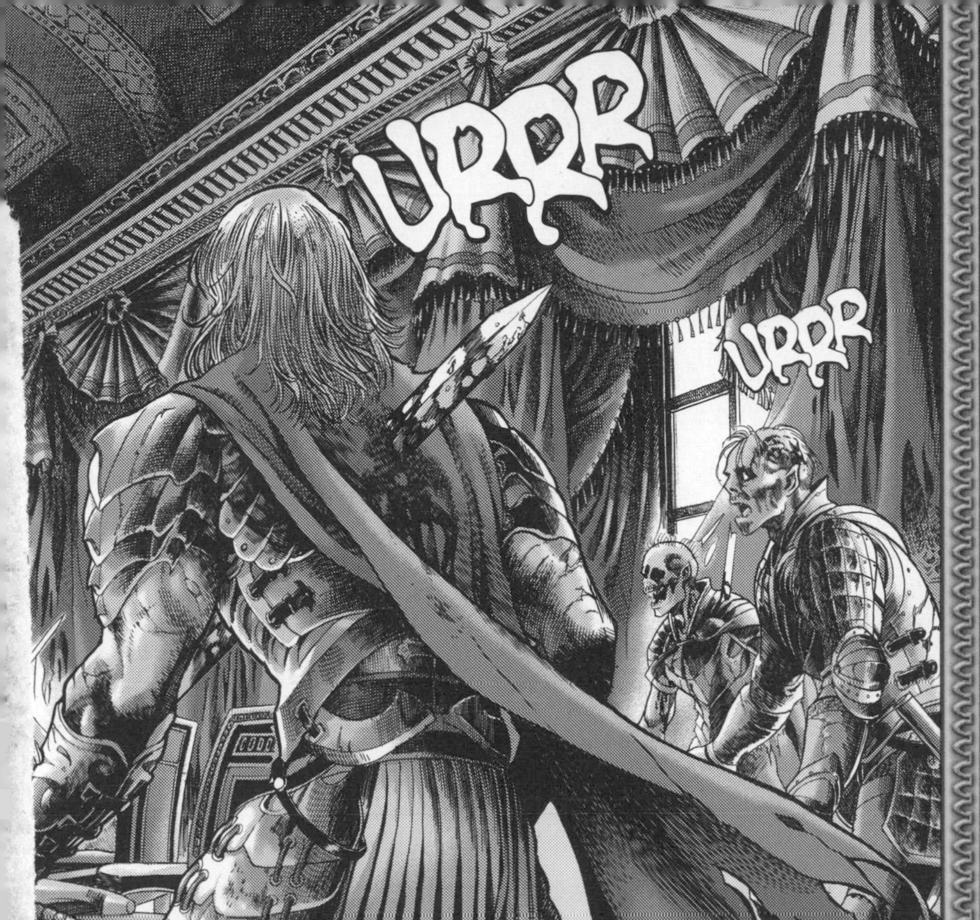
URRR
URRR

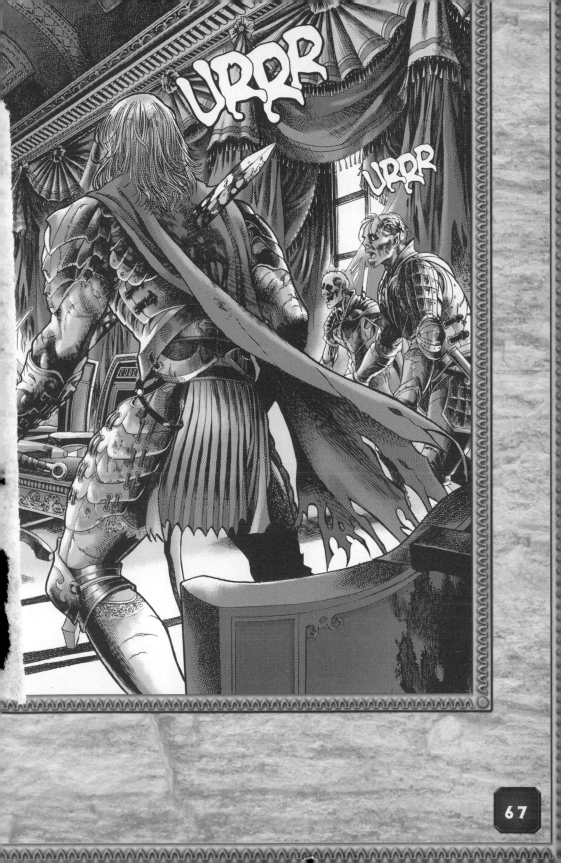

WHY DO YOU PERSIST, JORAD MACE?
CLANK
URRR
YOU WILL HARASS ME NO MORE!
UNGH!
YOU SWORE YOUR LIFE TO ME...
URRR
...NOW I SIMPLY WANT YOU TO REVERE ME IN DEATH, TOO.

PERSISTENCE

\pir SIS tuns\ (n.): the act, state, or quality of not giving up

Jamie's *persistence* at getting the petition signed amazed everyone on the team.

HARASS

\hu RASS\ (v.): irritate, torment

Susan wondered whether the department store was trying to *harass* her since, despite her repeated pleas, it kept sending her catalogue after catalogue.

REVERE

\ri VEER\ (v.): to worship, regard with awe

All the nuns in the convent *revered* their wise Mother Superior.

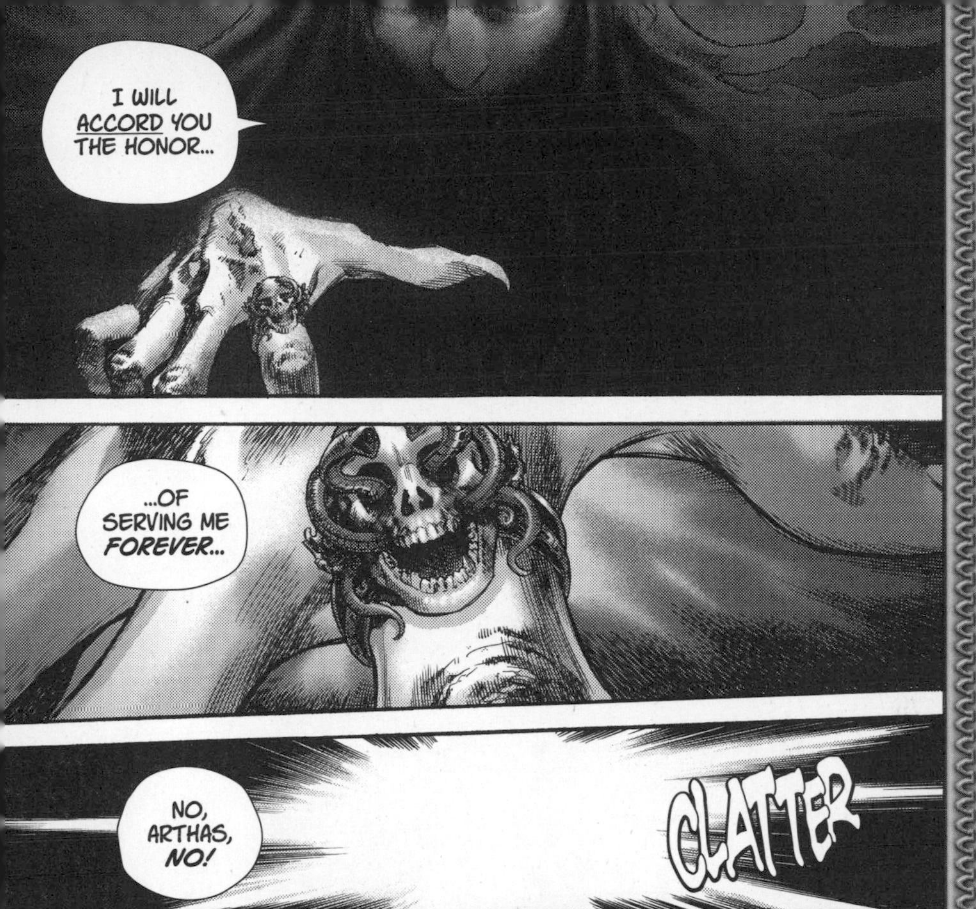
I WILL ACCORD YOU THE HONOR...
...OF SERVING ME FOREVER...
NO, ARTHAS, NO!
CLATTER
NO...

ACCORD

uh KORD\ (v.): to bestow upon

Congress will *accord* him the Medal of Honor for his bravery in World War II.

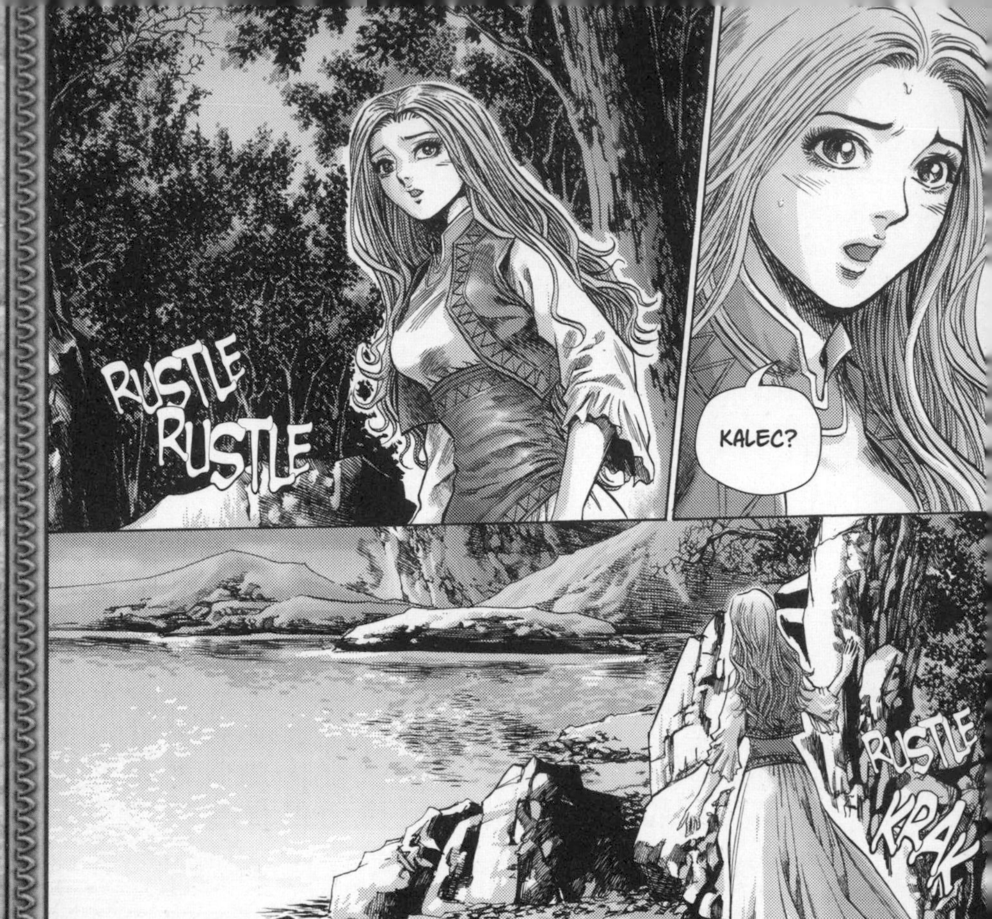
RUSTLE RUSTLE
KALEC?
RUSTLE
KRAK
KALEC?
OH... KALEC....

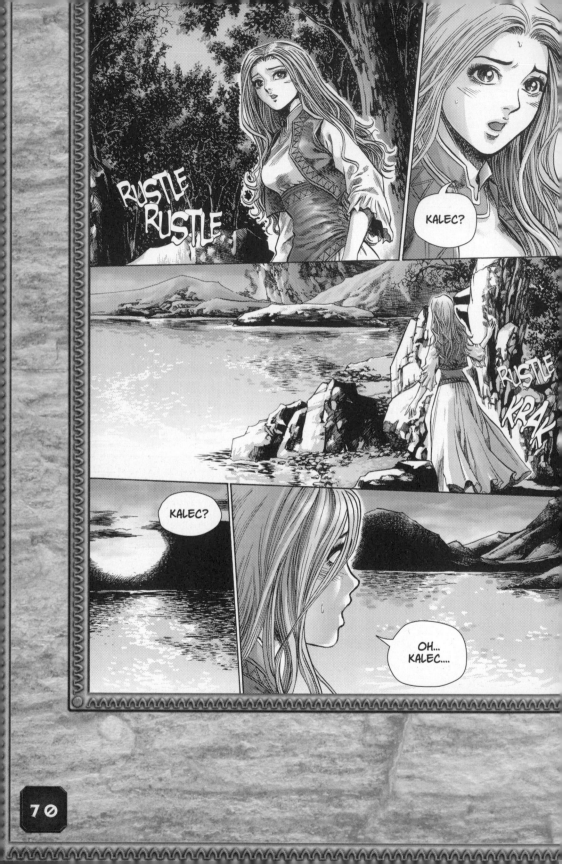

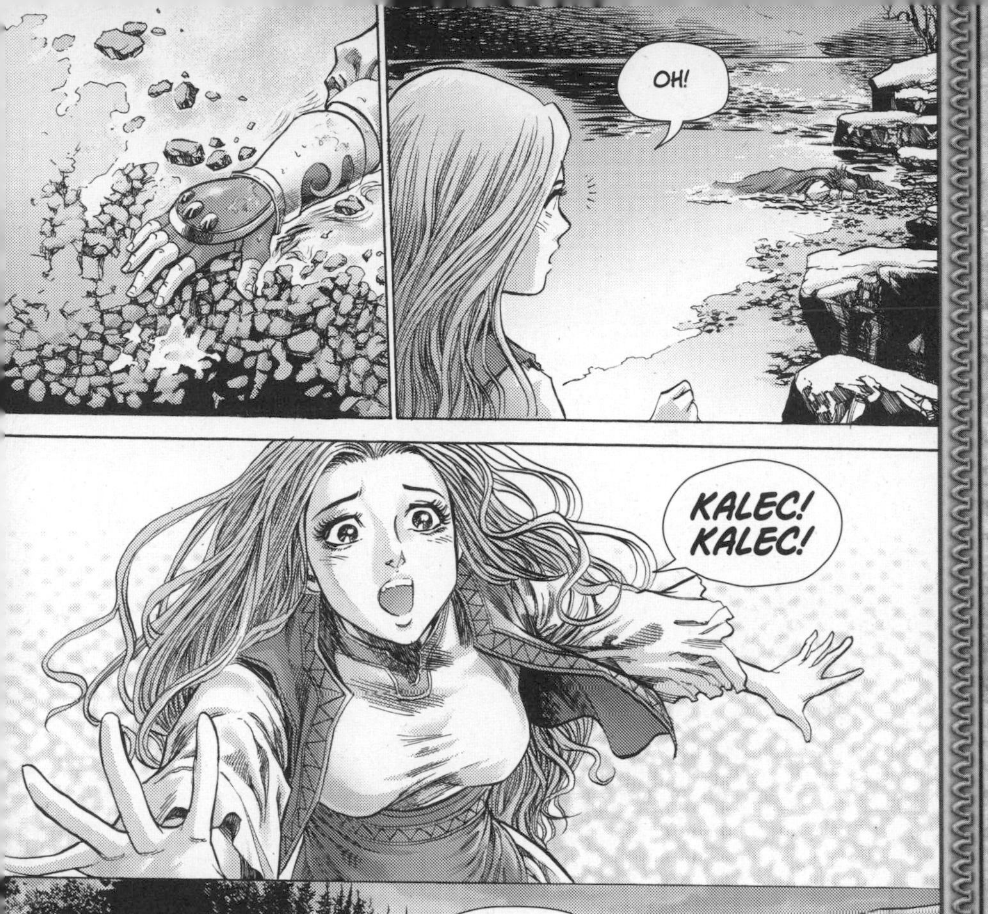
OH!
KALEC! KALEC!
KALEC! PLEASE BE ALIVE!

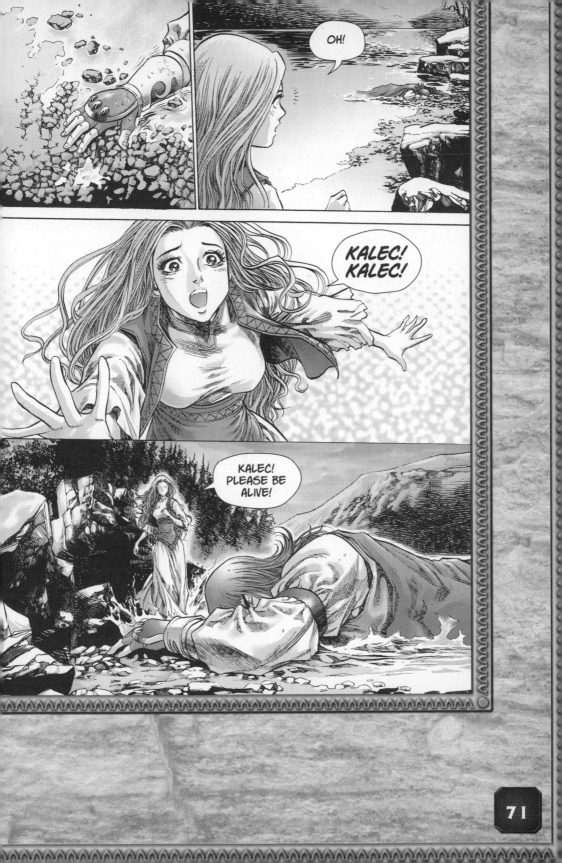

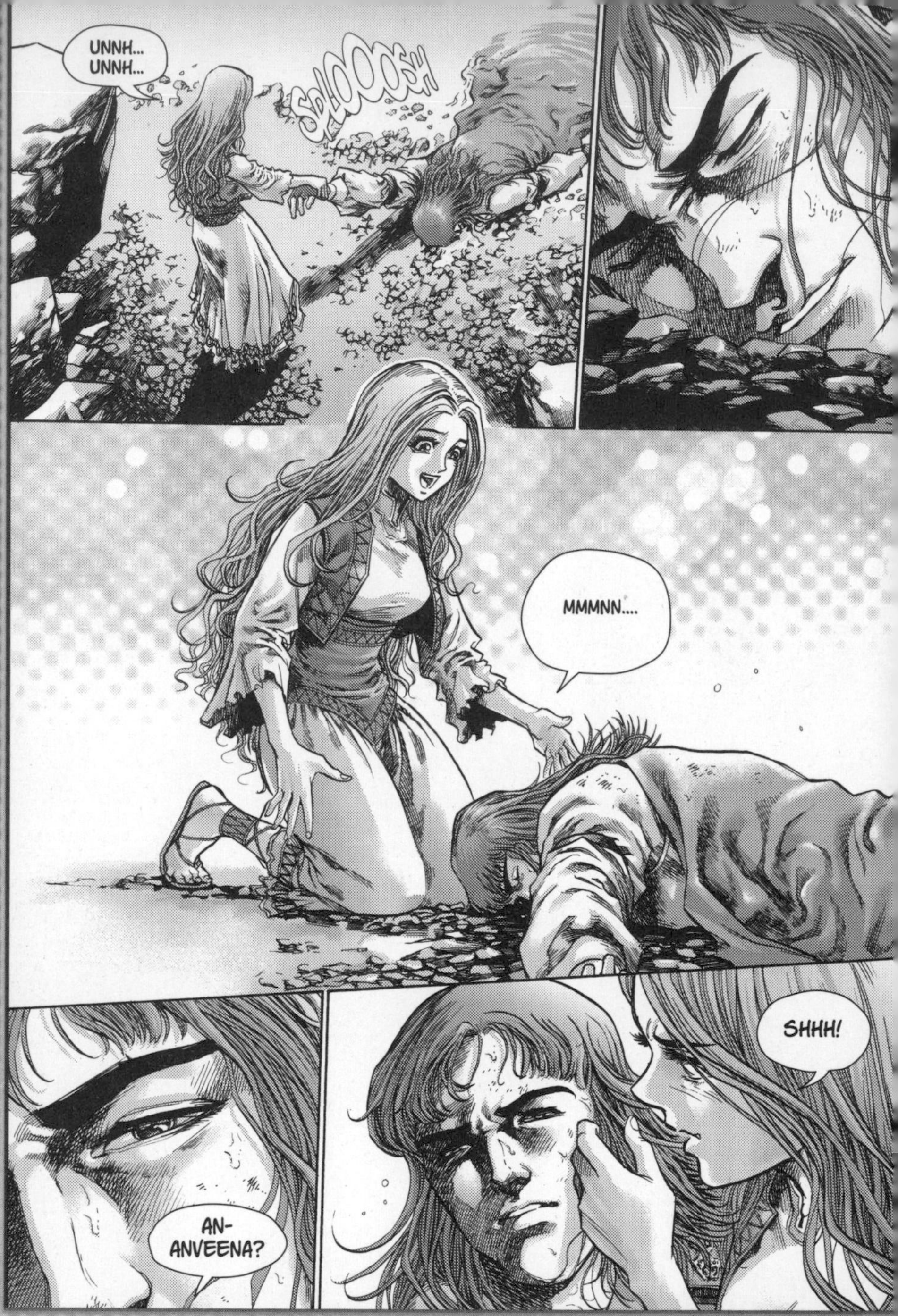
UNNH... UNNH...
SPLOOOSH!
MMMNN....
AN-ANVEENA?
SHHH!

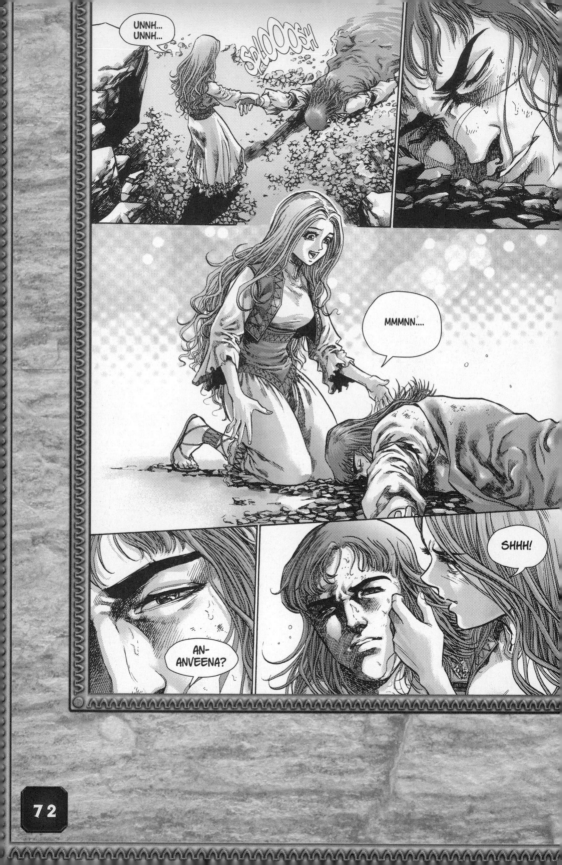

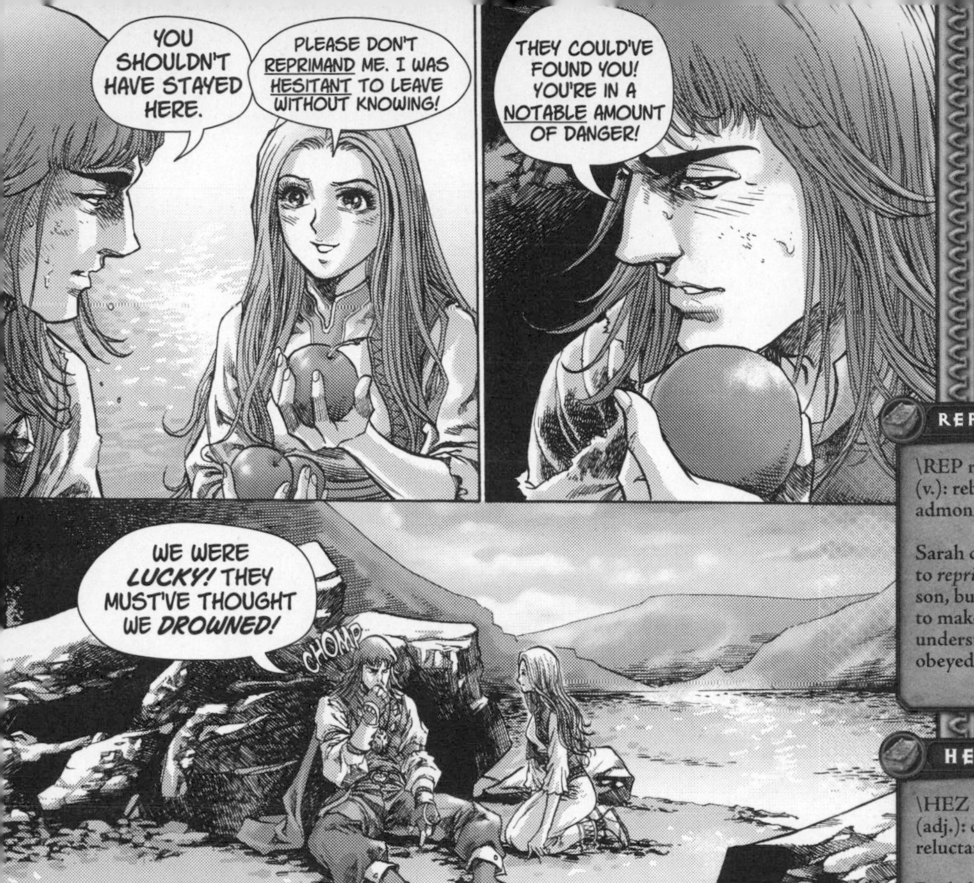
YOU SHOULDN'T HAVE STAYED HERE.
PLEASE DON'T REPRIMAND ME. I WAS HESITANT TO LEAVE WITHOUT KNOWING!
THEY COULD'VE FOUND YOU! YOU'RE IN A NOTABLE AMOUNT OF DANGER!
WE WERE LUCKY! THEY MUST'VE THOUGHT WE DROWNED!
CHOMP
I'M FLABBERGASTED THAT WE DIDN'T! I DON'T UNDERSTAND THAT...
...OR WHAT THE CATALYST WAS THAT CHANGED ME BACK AGAIN!

REPRIMAND

\REP ruh mand\ (v.): rebuke, admonish

Sarah didn't want to *reprimand* her son, but she needed to make sure he understood and obeyed her rules.

HESITANT

\HEZ ih tent\ (adj.): doubtful, reluctant

Rachelle was *hesitant* to give her credit information over the phone, preferring to pay by check.

NOTABLE

\NO tu bul\ (adj.): remarkable, worthy of notice

Sean didn't bother explaining the rules of the game again because no *notable* changes had been made since the last game.

FLABBERGASTED

\FLAB ur gas tid\ (v.): astounded, surprise

The sight under her pillow *flabbergasted* the young girl; where she had left a tooth, she found a dollar in its place.

CATALYST

\KAT uh list\ (n.): something that causes change

The imposition of harsh taxes was the *catalyst* that finally brought on a full-scale revolution.

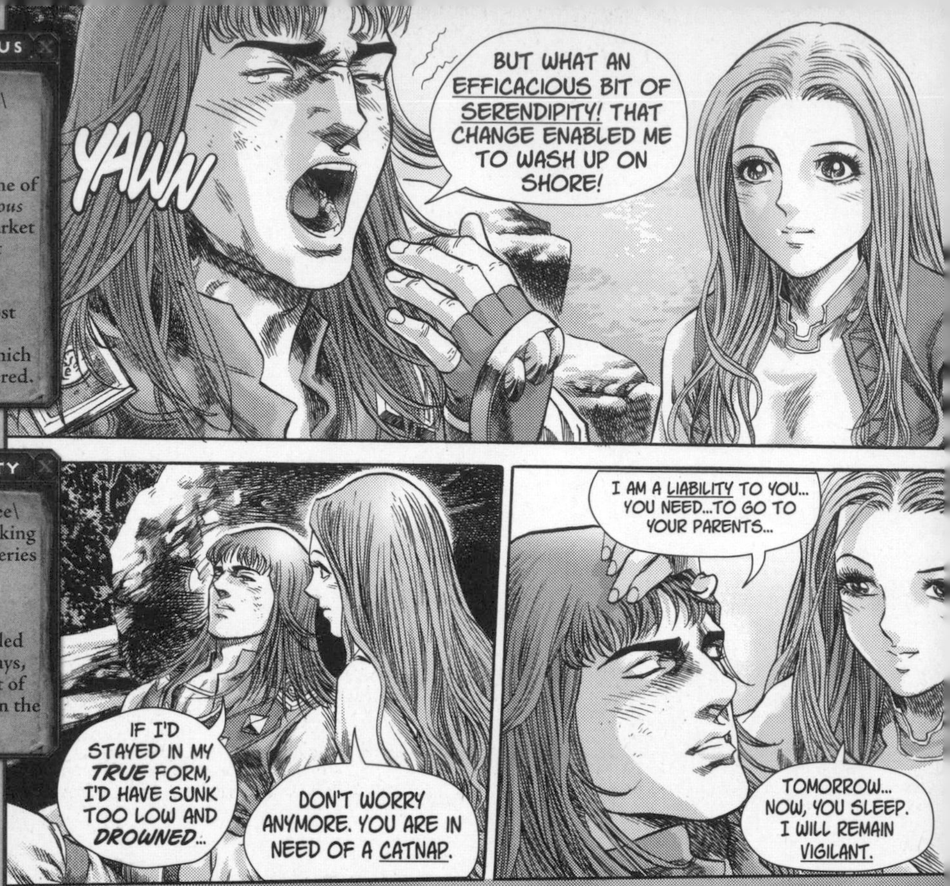
YAWN
BUT WHAT AN EFFICACIOUS BIT OF SERENDIPITY! THAT CHANGE ENABLED ME TO WASH UP ON SHORE!
IF I'D STAYED IN MY TRUE FORM, I'D HAVE SUNK TOO LOW AND DROWNED...
DON'T WORRY ANYMORE. YOU ARE IN NEED OF A CATNAP.
I AM A LIABILITY TO YOU... YOU NEED...TO GO TO YOUR PARENTS...
TOMORROW... NOW, YOU SLEEP. I WILL REMAIN VIGILANT.
ZZZZZ

EFFICACIOUS

\ef ih KAY shus\ (adj.): effective, efficient

Penicillin was one of the most *efficacious* drugs on the market when it was first introduced; the drug completely eliminated almost all bacterial infections for which it was administered.

SERENDIPITY

\se ren DIP ih tee\ (n.): habit of making fortunate discoveries by chance

Rosemary's *serendipity* revealed itself in many ways, such as her habit of finding money on the street.

CATNAP

\KAT nap\ (n.): short, light sleep

Since she had twenty minutes before her next appointment, Cheryl decided to take a *catnap* in her office.

LIABILITY

\liy uh BIL uh tee\ (n.): handicap, something holding one back

Although some businesses consider it a *liability* to be situated close to a competitor, many industries believe that they will attract more customers if they stay together.

VIGILANT

\VIJ uh lent\ (adj.): attentive, watchful

Our community members must remain *vigilant* if we are to discover the identities of the vandals.

SH-SHOULDN'T BE LONG NOW. I CAN WALK THE REST OF THE WAY.

I WOULD BE REMISS IN MY FRIENDSHIP TO LEAVE YOU NOW!

Tweet Tweet

RUSTLE

YOUR KINDNESS IS UNPARALLELED, ANVEENA, BUT I DON'T WANT TO ENTANGLE YOU ANY FURTHER IN MY MESS!

YOU NEED TO RUN HOME! LET YOUR PARENTS KNOW YOU'RE--

REMISS ✕

\ri MISS\ (adj.): negligent or careless about a job

Jon was fired for being *remiss* in his duties; the company hired him to write articles, not to surf the Internet.

UNPARALLELED ✕

\un PAR uh leld\ (adj.): unequaled;

To many, Michael Jordan was an *unparalleled* athlete who redefined basketball stardom.

ENTANGLE ✕

\en TANG ul\ (v.): to complicate, entwine into confusing mass, involve in

Minnie regretted *entangling* herself in the poorly-organized project.

PRUDENT

\PROOD int\ (adj.): careful, cautious

You should be *prudent* when giving out your personal information online – only use protected websites so your information will not be stolen.

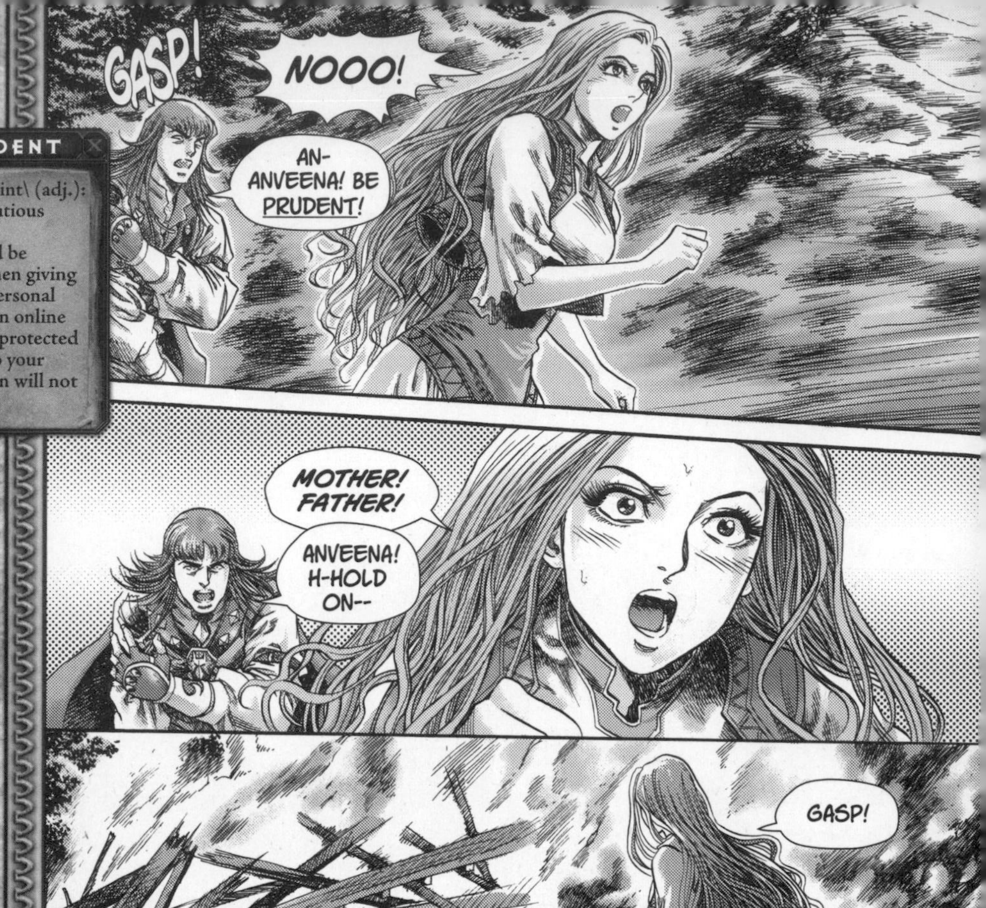

GASP!
NOOO!
AN- ANVEENA! BE PRUDENT!
MOTHER! FATHER!
ANVEENA! H-HOLD ON--
GASP!

NO...
NO...NO...

M-MOTHER...
FATHER...
I CAN'T FIND
THEM...

THOSE
NEFARIOUS
MONSTERS!
WHY?

HUH?

RUSTLE

NEFARIOUS

\ni FAHR ee uss\ (adj.): vicious, evil

The *nefarious* villain would stop at no act
of cruelty to get what he wanted.

77

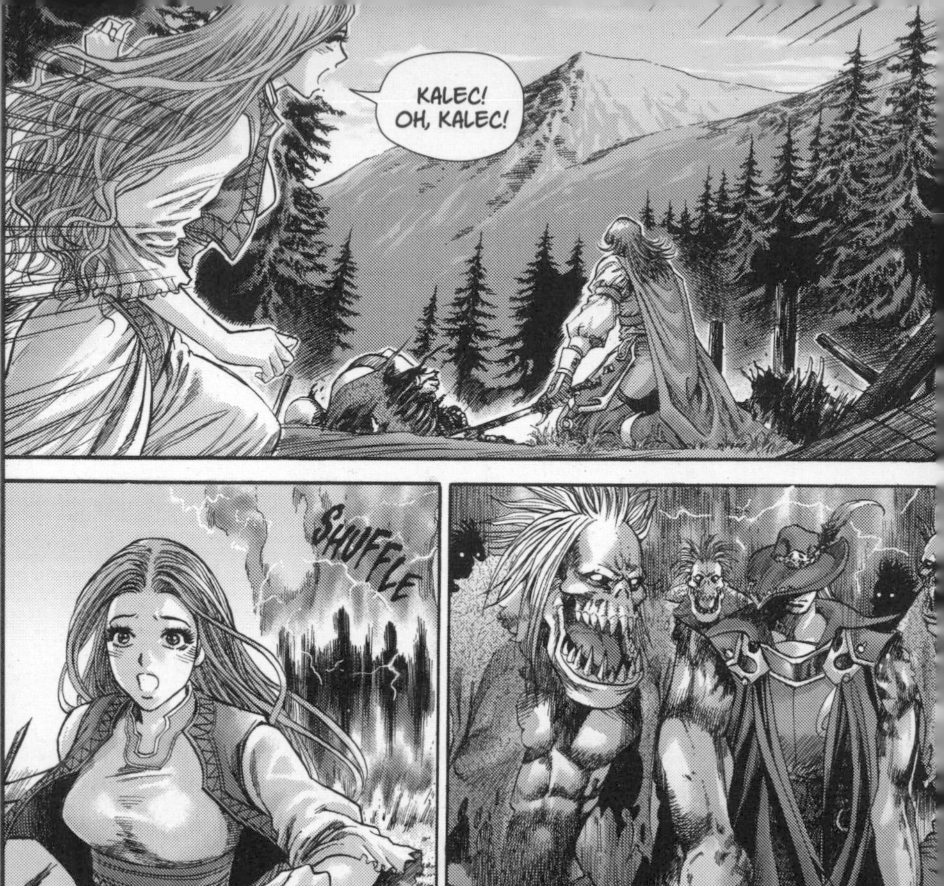
KALEC!
OH, KALEC!
SHUFFLE
!!!
ANVEENA!
L-LOOK OUT
BEHIND YOU!

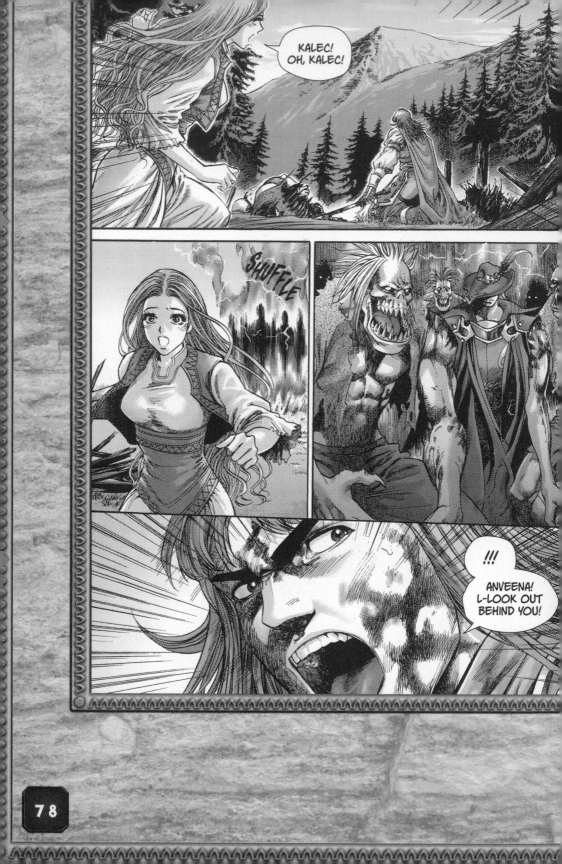

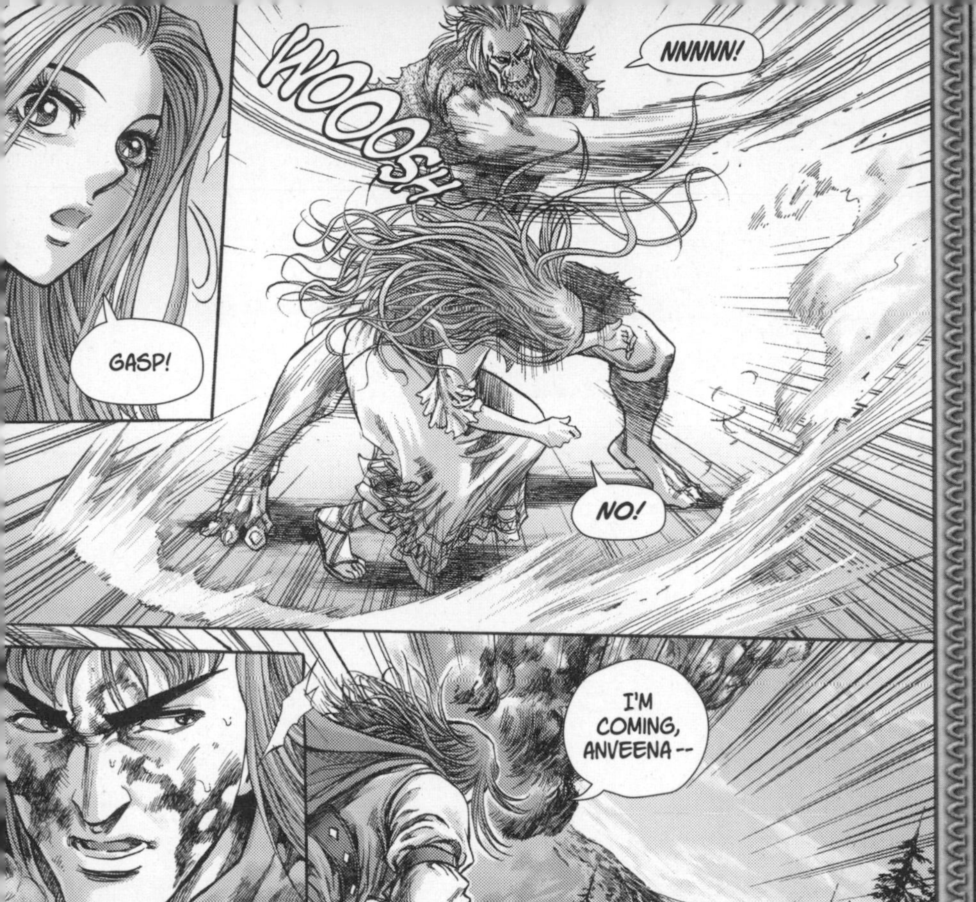
GASP!
WOOOSH
NNNNN!
NO!
I'M COMING, ANVEENA --

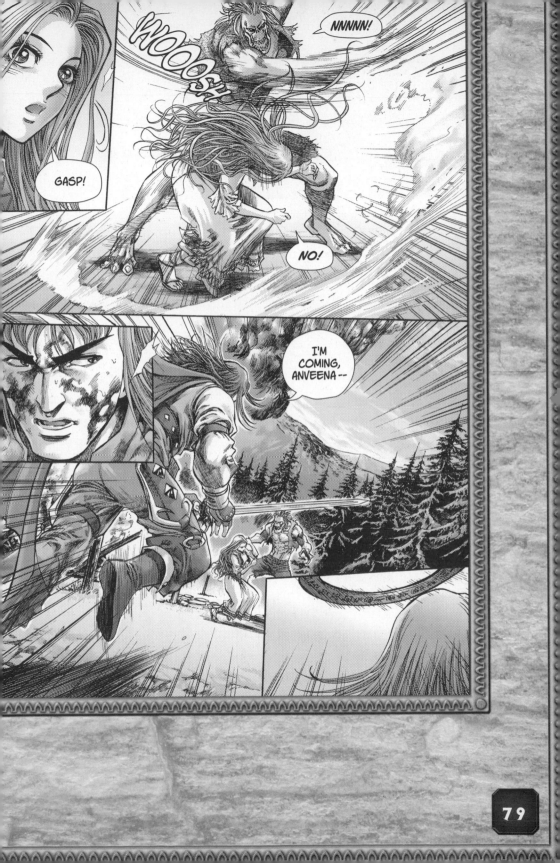

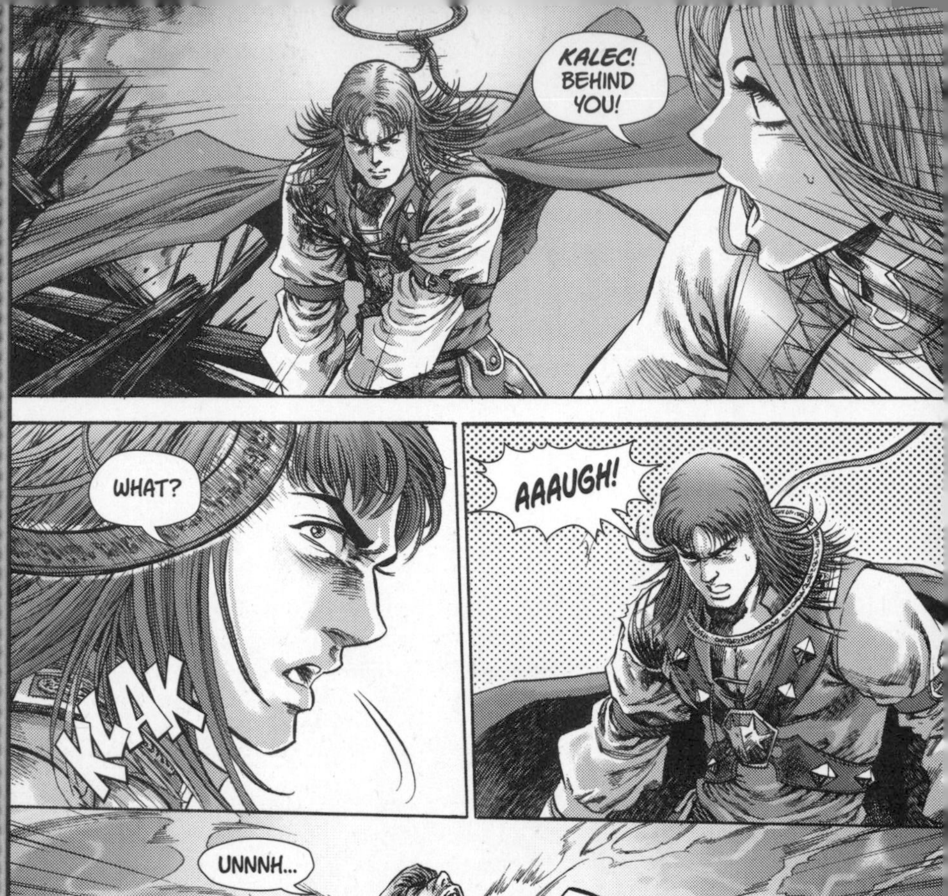
KALEC! BEHIND YOU!
WHAT?
KLAK
AAAUGH!
UNNNH...

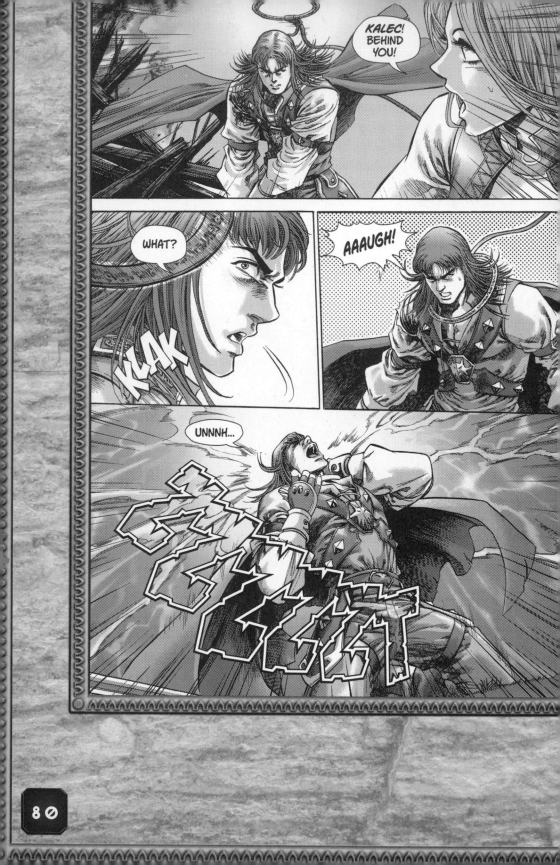

!!!

CLIK

THE MORE YOU STRUGGLE, THE MORE YOU WILL **ENHANCE** THE RING'S TIGHTNESS, LITTLE HUMAN. IF I WERE YOU, I WOULD REMAIN **COMPOSED**.

YOU ARE **IMPOTENT** AGAINST ITS POWERS...

ENHANCE ✕

\in HANSS\ (v.): to improve, bring to a greater level of intensity

They can sure use a hand in *enhancing* the quality of the food in the cafeteria.

COMPOSED ✕

\kom POS d\ (adj.): serene, calm

Friends noticed the valedictorian's *composed* appearance as he walked confidently up to the podium to address the crowd.

IMPOTENT ✕

\IMP uh tent\ (adj.): powerless, ineffective, lacking strength

Though initially optimistic about his ability to reform the organization, the new president eventually realized he was *impotent* against such fundamental flaws in structure.

81

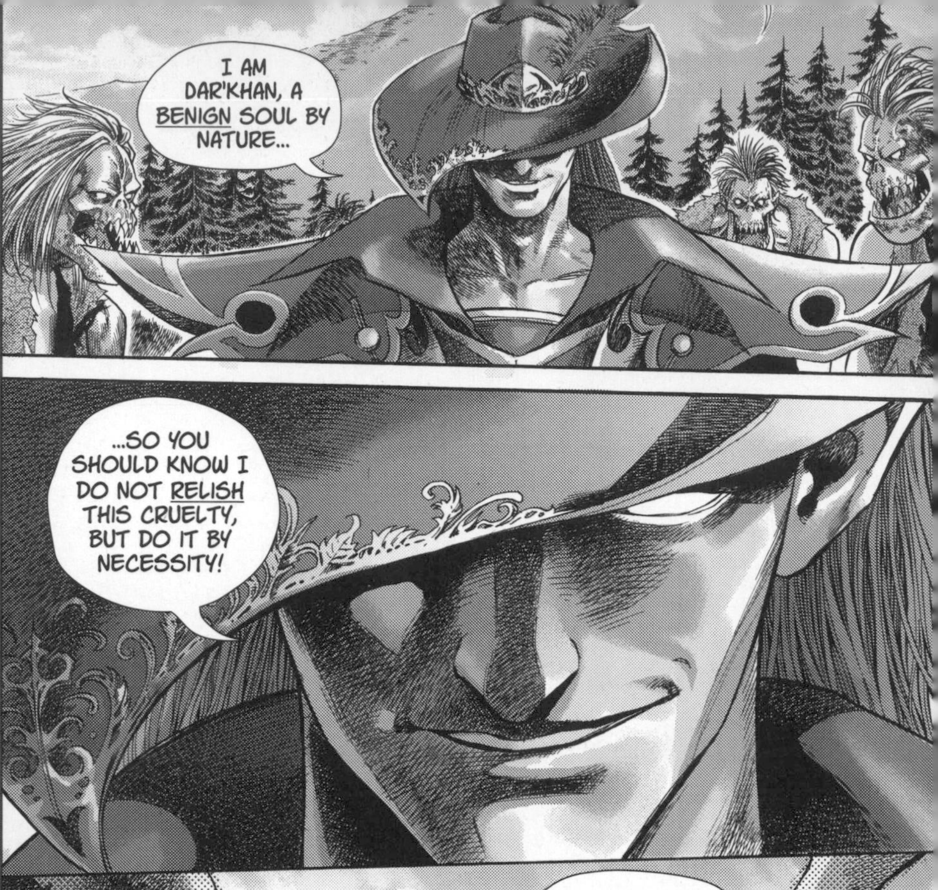
I AM DAR'KHAN, A BENIGN SOUL BY NATURE...
...SO YOU SHOULD KNOW I DO NOT RELISH THIS CRUELTY, BUT DO IT BY NECESSITY!
I AM SEARCHING FOR SOMETHING I HAVE LOST...

BENIGN

\bi NIYN\ (adj.): gentle, harmless

Although many children in the neighborhood feared the old dog, he was actually quite *benign*.

RELISH

REH lish\ (v.): to enjoy greatly

Cameron *relished* the tasty sandwich, but he didn't like the pickle that came with it.

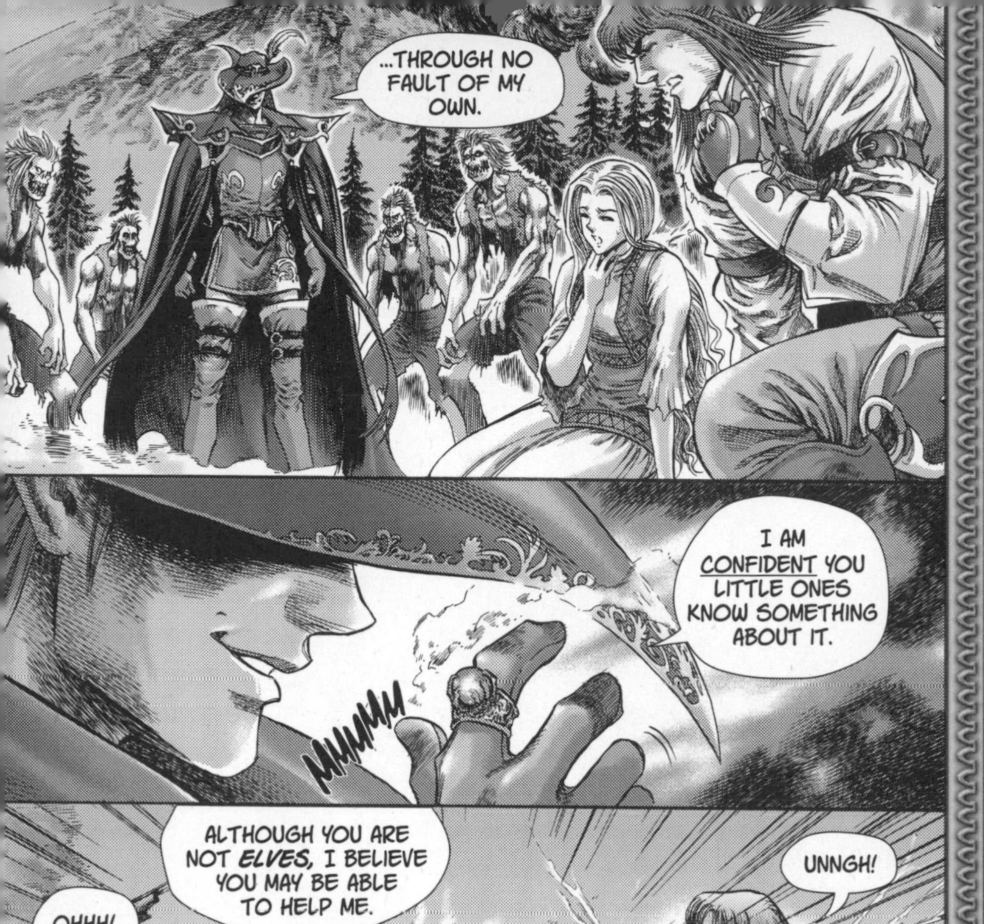
...THROUGH NO FAULT OF MY OWN.
I AM CONFIDENT YOU LITTLE ONES KNOW SOMETHING ABOUT IT.
ALTHOUGH YOU ARE NOT *ELVES,* I BELIEVE YOU MAY BE ABLE TO HELP ME.
OHHH!
UNNGH!

CONFIDENT

\KON fi dent\ (adj.): self-assured

Confident that she was going to ace the exam, Cynthia strode into class with a broad smile across her face.

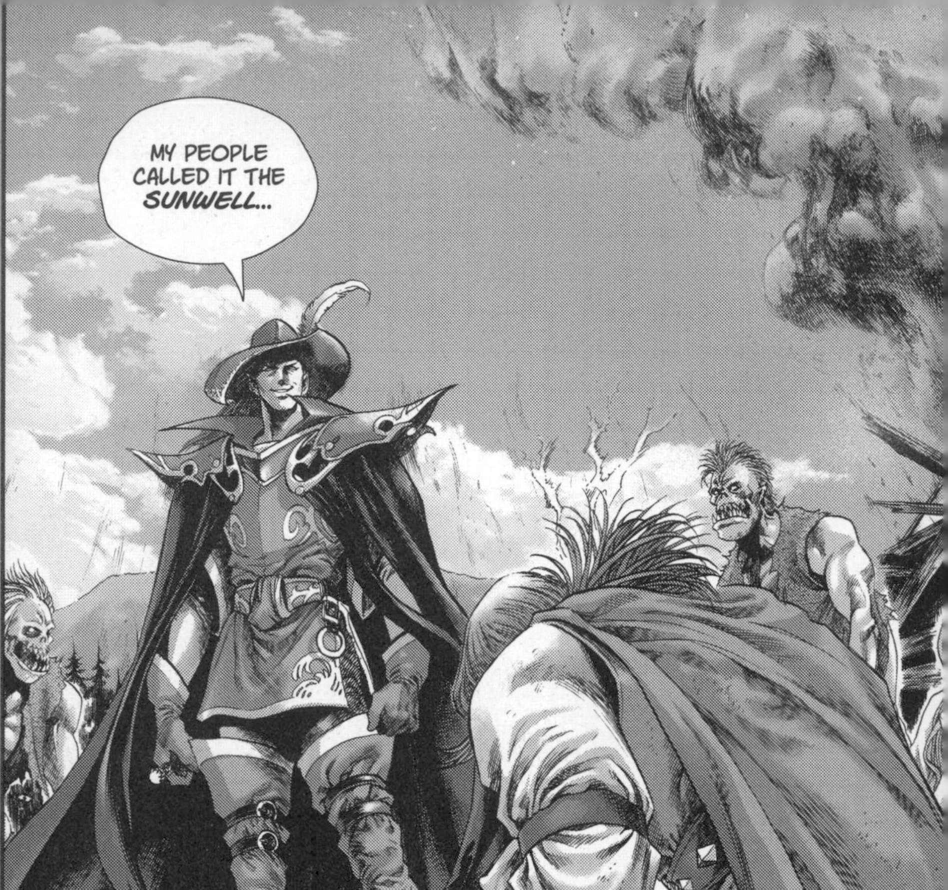
MY PEOPLE CALLED IT THE SUNWELL...

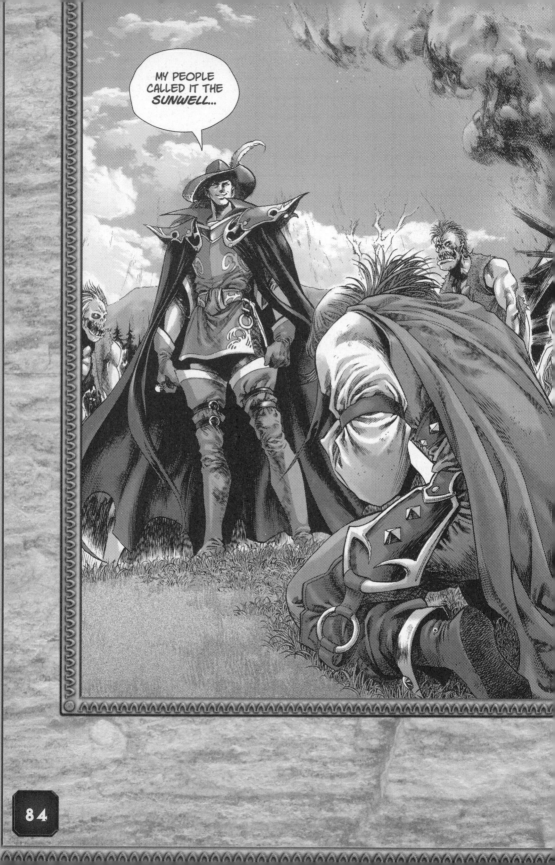

Chapter Four

Legacy of the Sunwell

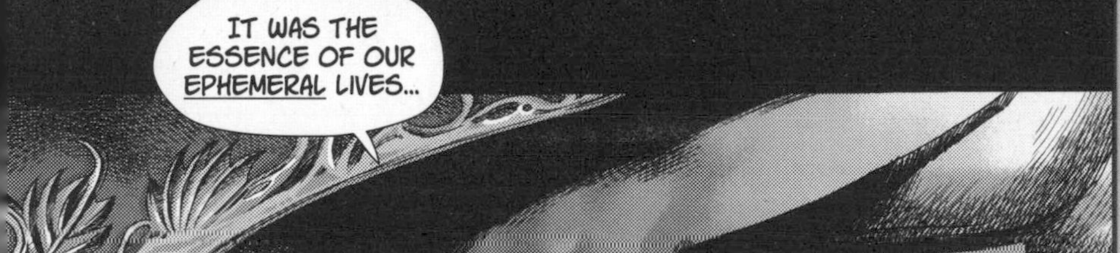
IT WAS THE ESSENCE OF OUR EPHEMERAL LIVES...

EPHEMERAL

\i FEM er il\ (adj.): momentary, transient, fleeting

The lives of mayflies seem *ephemeral* to us, since their average lifespan is a matter of hours.

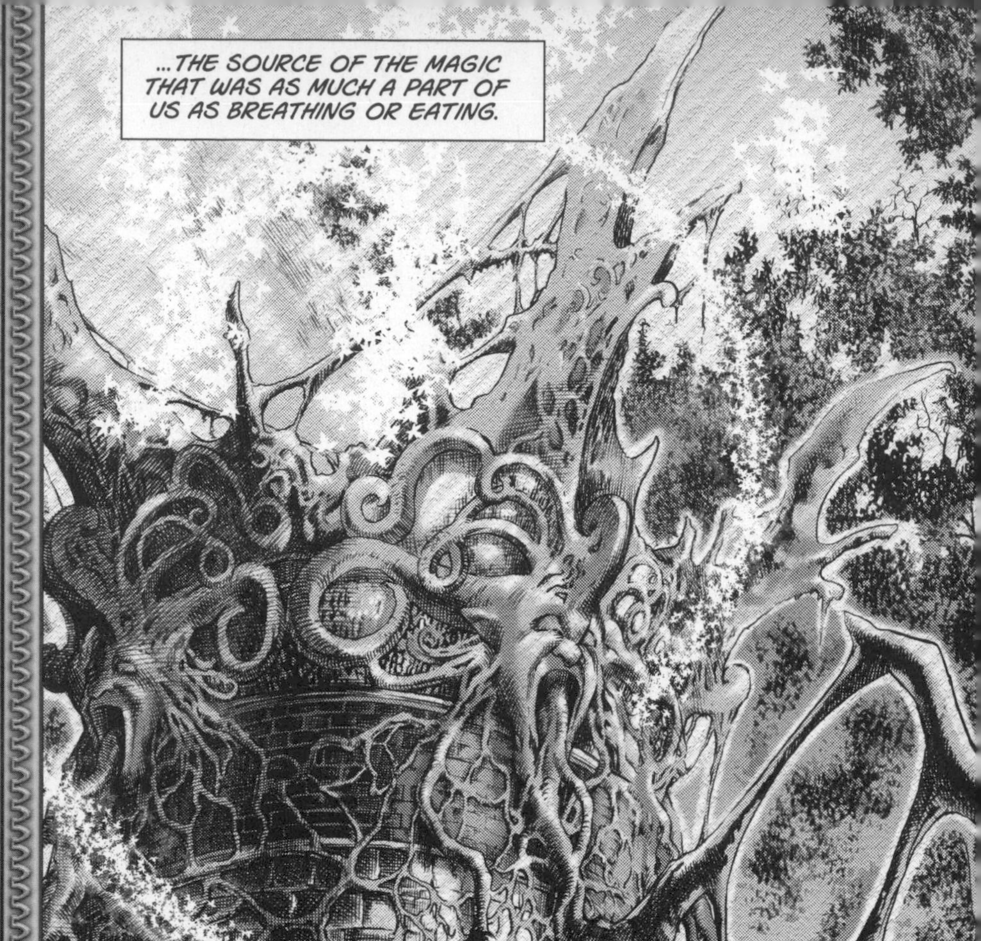
...THE SOURCE OF THE MAGIC THAT WAS AS MUCH A PART OF US AS BREATHING OR EATING.

WE BUILT OUR CITIES...

...USING OUR DESIRES AS _PROTOTYPES_...

...AND SO OUR LIVES _ENCOMPASSED_ WHATEVER WE DESIRED.

PROTOTYPE ✕

\PRO to tiyp\ (n.): early, typical example

When designing a computer, engineers will first build a *prototype* to test the efficiency of their design.

ENCOMPASS ✕

\en COM pass\ (v.): to constitute, include, encircle

The syllabus for Professor Grumman's upcoming course will *encompass* all American political history, from Teddy Roosevelt to FDR.

BUT FOR ALL THE _PROSPERITY_ CREATED THROUGH THE SUNWELL....

...THE REWARD FOR *MY* PART IN IT WAS *NOTHING.*

SO I BEGAN SEEKING COMPENSATION FOR MY GOOD WORK.

WHICH IS A _CONTROVERSIAL NOTION,_ FOR ELVEN FOLK, YOU MUST UNDERSTAND.

PROSPERITY

\pross PER ih tee\ (n.): wealth or success

While some people have achieved wealth in life, the pursuit of *prosperity* can mean sacrificing enjoyment and leisure.

COMPENSATE

\KOMP en sayt\ (v.): to repay or reimburse

The moving company *compensated* me for the broken furniture.

CONTROVERSIAL

\kon tro VER shul\ (adj.): producing or marked by heated dispute

Many people are very upset by the *controversial* increase in gasoline taxes that he government has authorized.

NOTION

\NO shin\ (n.): idea or conception

Mandatory school uniforms is a *notion* that has been tossed back and forth in governments, but has never been implemented on a national scale in the United States.

89

ENDORSE

\en DORSS\ (v.): to give approval to, sanction

The politician refused to *endorse* any group that wouldn't grant equal rights to all people.

SOLITARY

\SOL ih ter ee\ (adj.): alone; remote, secluded

I love going up to the mountains in the autumn to live in my *solitary* cabin in the woods.

CLANDESTINE

\klan DES tin\ (adj.): secretive, concealed for a darker purpose

The double agent paid many *clandestine* visits to the president's office in the dead of the night.

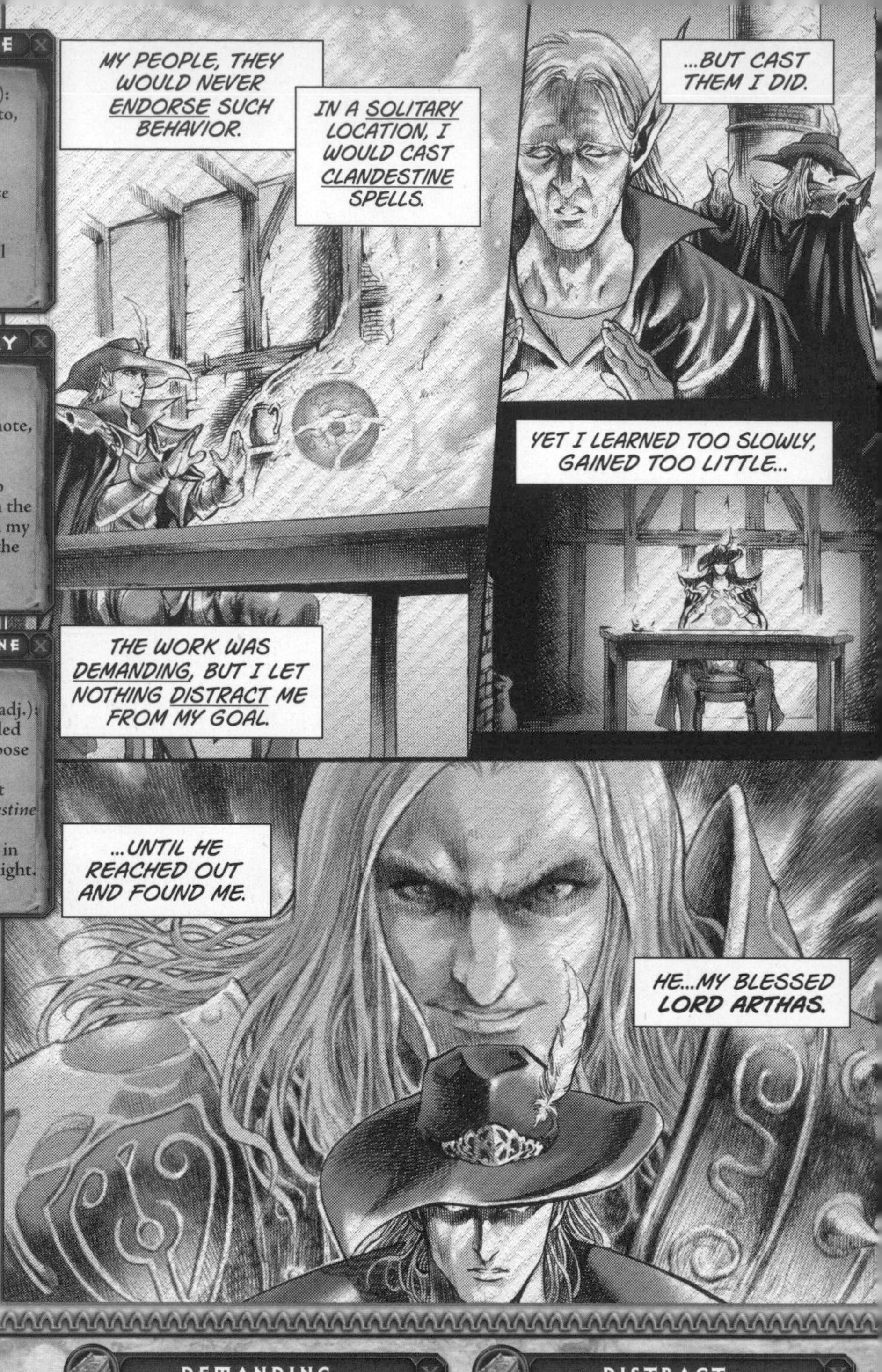
MY PEOPLE, THEY WOULD NEVER ENDORSE SUCH BEHAVIOR.
IN A SOLITARY LOCATION, I WOULD CAST CLANDESTINE SPELLS.
...BUT CAST THEM I DID.
YET I LEARNED TOO SLOWLY, GAINED TOO LITTLE...
THE WORK WAS DEMANDING, BUT I LET NOTHING DISTRACT ME FROM MY GOAL.
...UNTIL HE REACHED OUT AND FOUND ME.
HE...MY BLESSED LORD ARTHAS.

DEMANDING

\de MAN ding\ (adj.): requiring much effort and attention

Joe had to quit his part-time job in order to keep up with his *demanding* schedule at school.

DISTRACT

\dis TRAKT\ (v.): to cause to lose focus, to divert attention

Some students find that listening to music can *distract* them, so they prefer to study in silence.

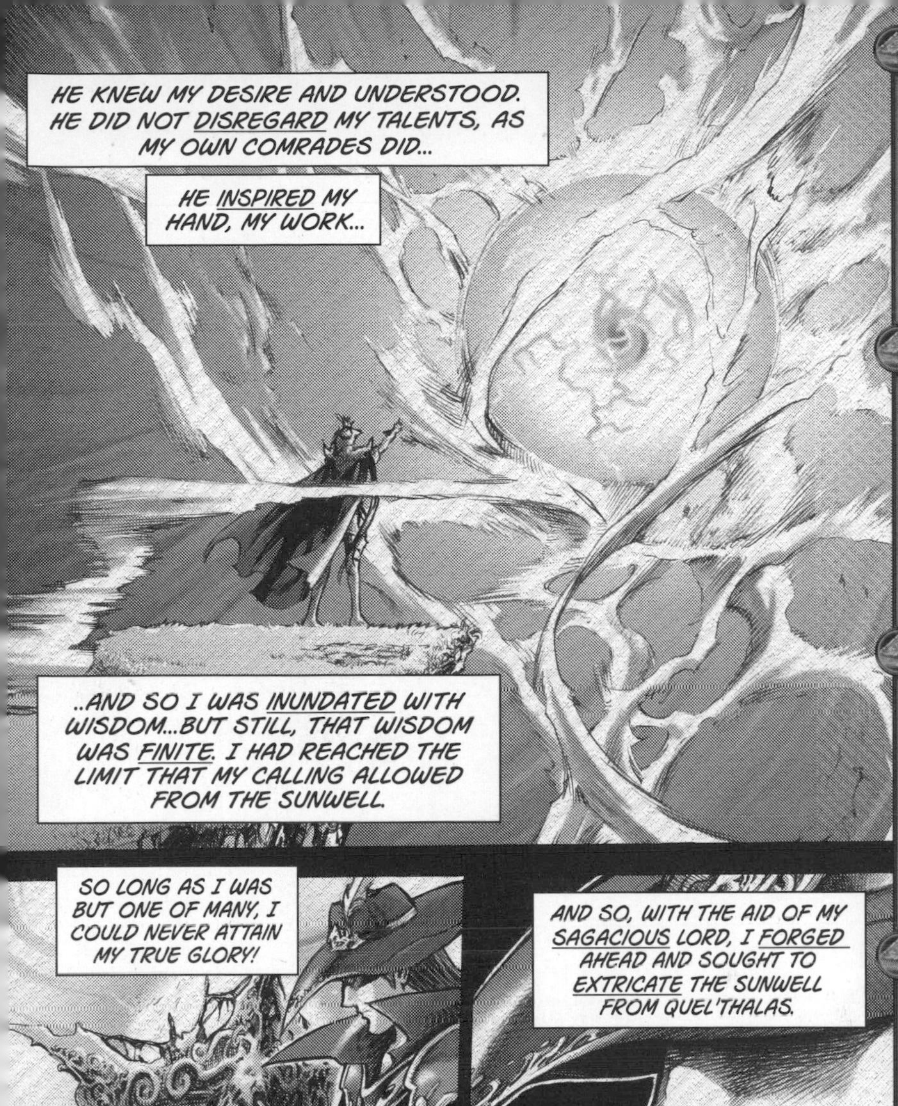
HE KNEW MY DESIRE AND UNDERSTOOD. HE DID NOT DISREGARD MY TALENTS, AS MY OWN COMRADES DID...
HE INSPIRED MY HAND, MY WORK...
..AND SO I WAS INUNDATED WITH WISDOM...BUT STILL, THAT WISDOM WAS FINITE. I HAD REACHED THE LIMIT THAT MY CALLING ALLOWED FROM THE SUNWELL.
SO LONG AS I WAS BUT ONE OF MANY, I COULD NEVER ATTAIN MY TRUE GLORY!
AND SO, WITH THE AID OF MY SAGACIOUS LORD, I FORGED AHEAD AND SOUGHT TO EXTRICATE THE SUNWELL FROM QUEL'THALAS.

DISREGARD

\dis rih GARD\ (v.): ignore

The building manager knew that people were going to *disregard* the "Do Not Enter" sign, so he put a security guard in front of the broken elevator.

INSPIRE

\in SPIYR\ (v.): motivate, affect

Classical poets claimed to have a muse that *inspired* them to write great works of art.

INUNDATE

\IN un dayt\ (v.): to cover with water, to overwhelm

After the press *inundated* her with requests for interviews, the author withdrew to the tranquility of her summer cottage.

FINITE

\FIY niyt\ (adj.): having bounds, limited

Because there are only a *finite* number of hiding places in the small warehouse, the police were sure they would find the crook eventually.

SAGACIOUS

\su GAY shiss\ (adj.): wise, shrewd

Owls have a reputation for being *sagacious*, perhaps because of their big eyes that resemble glasses.

FORGE

\FORJ\ (v.): to advance gradually but steadily

Despite her intense workload, Sharon *forged* ahead and graduated at the top of her class.

EXTRICATE

\EK stri kayt\(v.): to free from, disentangle

The fly was unable to *extricate* itself from the spider's web.

LEGION

\LEE jun\ (n.): a great number, a multitude

Legions of tourists, many with children, travel to Disney World during every month of the year.

OVERPOWERING

\oh ver POW er ing\ (adj.): overwhelming

Although the foolish man prattled on senselessly, Sandra held back an *overpowering* urge to quiet him down.

STURDY

\STUR dee\ (adj.): firm, well built, stout

The contractor decided that the girders already in place were *sturdy* enough to support the rest of the house.

BEQUEATH

\bi KWEETH\ (v.): pass on, hand down

Fred thought that his grandmother was penniless, and so was shocked when she *bequeathed* to him a beautiful gold watch.

IMPLEMENT

\IMP luh ment\ (v.): carry out, put into effect

Deciding on an appropriate course of action is often the easy part; the hard part is actually *implementing* it.

ARTHAS' GLORIOUS LEGIONS ATTACKED QUEL'THALAS, OVERPOWERING ITS ONCE STURDY DEFENSES WITH MY AID.

MEANWHILE, HE HAD BEQUEATHED TO ME THE SPELL OF UNBINDING AND BINDING...

...AND STEELED MY NERVE WHEN I IMPLEMENTED THE INTRICATE PLAN.

THE VIOLENCE TRIGGERED BY MY PLOY WAS REGRETTABLE...

...BUT SOME FUNDAMENTAL SACRIFICES MUST BE MADE FOR THE GREATER GOOD, YOU UNDERSTAND.

INTRICATE

\IN tri kit\ (adj.): elaborate, complex

The designer, though best-known for her *intricate* designs, was likewise capable of a simpler approach when appropriate to the project.

PLOY

\PLOY\ (n.): maneuver, plan

To catch the con artist, the detective developed a *ploy* whereby the criminal himself would admit his guilt to witnesses.

TRIGGER

\TRIG er\ (v.): to set off, initiate

Unbeknownst to Homer, his remark about catered lunch *triggered* a wholesale reformation of the company's human resources program.

FUNDAMENTAL

\fun da MEN tul\ (adj.): basic, essential

One of the *fundamental* tenets of the Declaration of Independence is that all men are created equal.

MY PEOPLE, OF COURSE, FOUND MY ACTIONS HIGHLY UNETHICAL.

BUT I NO LONGER HAD TO TOLERATE THEIR DISAPPROVAL.

THE PRECIOUS SUNWELL WAS NOW OURS...

UNETHICAL

\un ETH ih kul\ (adj.): not conforming to approved behavior; immoral

Rogers was summoned to a disciplinary meeting to discuss his multiple instances of *unethical* behavior this past week.

TOLERATE

\TOL uh rayt\ (v.): to endure, permit; to respect others

Peter was unable to *tolerate* the noise from below any longer, so he went downstairs to ask his neighbor not to play the drums at four in the morning.

PRECIOUS

\PRESH us\ (adj.): valuable; beloved

Although Michelle had a lot of expensive jewelry, the copper bracelet that belonged to her grandmother was her most *precious* possession.

I COULD FEEL MY BLESSED LORD ARTHAS *URGING* ME ON!

I EVEN SENSED HIM USING HIS OWN MAGIC TO *ACQUIRE* THE SUNWELL'S POWER...

...BETTER ENABLING ME TO *ABSORB* ALL OF IT, OF COURSE.

URGE

URJ\ (v.): to impel, to exhort, spur to action

Principal Slater gave a passionate speech *urging* all students to take their schoolwork seriously.

ACQUIRE

\ah KWIYR\ (v.): to gain possession of

After this weekend's movie marathon, Lenora *acquired* a taste for Italian movies; she now wants to see all of them.

ABSORB

\ab ZORB\ (v.): to soak up, consume; to occupy completely

Jason completely forgot to watch the baseball game, as he was too *absorbed* in his studies.

BUT THERE WERE THOSE WHO *BALKED* AT ALLOWING ME MY DUE!

THEY DARED TO *UNDERMINE* ME, AND CAST THEIR OWN SPELL IN THE MIDST OF MY GLORY!

THEY DARED TO TAKE MY SUNWELL FROM ME!

ALREADY FEELING LIKE AN *OUTCAST* FROM SOCIETY, I FOUGHT THEM, MY BLESSED LORD AIDING ME WITH HIS *GARGANTUAN* STRENGTH...

BALK

\BAWK\ (v.): to refuse, shirk; prevent

The horse *balked* at jumping over the high fence and instead threw his rider off.

UNDERMINE

\un der MIYN\ (v.): to sabotage, thwart

Rumors of his infidelities *undermined* the star's marriage, which eventually ended in divorce.

OUTCAST

\OWT kast\ (n.): someone rejected from a society

The *outcast* decided that the only way to rejoin the group was to give in to their demands.

GARGANTUAN

\gar GAN shoo in\ (adj.): giant, tremendous

Cleaning a teenager's room can often be a *gargantuan* task.

...AND THEN, SOMETHING WENT TERRIBLY WRONG.

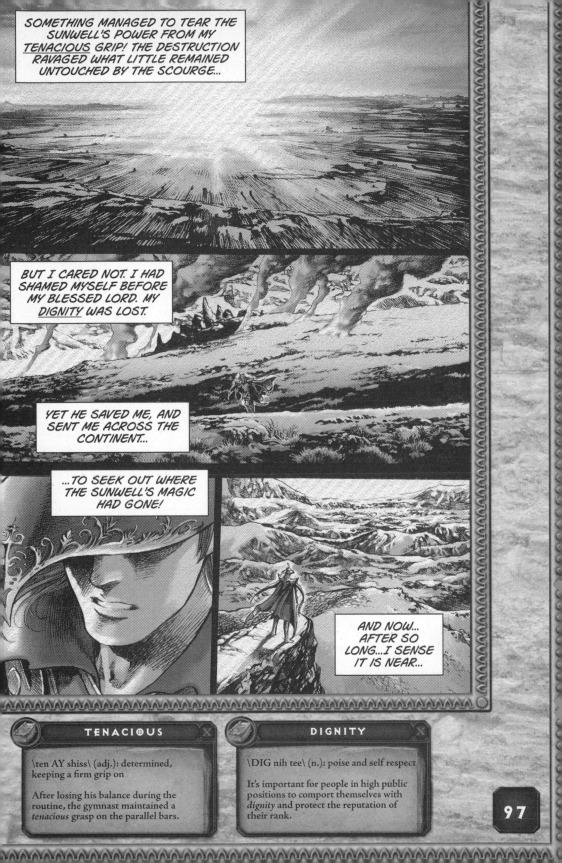

SOMETHING MANAGED TO TEAR THE SUNWELL'S POWER FROM MY _TENACIOUS_ GRIP! THE DESTRUCTION RAVAGED WHAT LITTLE REMAINED UNTOUCHED BY THE SCOURGE...

BUT I CARED NOT. I HAD SHAMED MYSELF BEFORE MY BLESSED LORD. MY _DIGNITY_ WAS LOST.

YET HE SAVED ME, AND SENT ME ACROSS THE CONTINENT...

...TO SEEK OUT WHERE THE SUNWELL'S MAGIC HAD GONE!

AND NOW... AFTER SO LONG...I SENSE IT IS NEAR...

TENACIOUS

\ten AY shiss\ (adj.): determined, keeping a firm grip on

After losing his balance during the routine, the gymnast maintained a _tenacious_ grasp on the parallel bars.

DIGNITY

\DIG nih tee\ (n.): poise and self respect

It's important for people in high public positions to comport themselves with _dignity_ and protect the reputation of their rank.

YOU NEED ONLY TO CONVEY TO ME WHERE IT IS.
THEN WHAT? YOU'LL LIBERATE US?.
WHY, NO!
BUT AS CONSOLATION, I WILL ALLEVIATE ANY PAIN YOU MAY FEEL UPON DEATH...
OH!

CONVEY

\kon VAY\ (v.): to transport; to make known

The goal of the game is to *convey* a phrase to your teammates without using words.

LIBERATE

\LIB uh rayt\ (v.): emancipate, set free

The politician promised to *liberate* individuals unjustly imprisoned during the current administration's tenure.

CONSOLATION

\kon so LAY shun\ (n.): the act of providing comfort or solace

The vast inheritance offered little *consolation* to the grief-stricken widow.

ALLEVIATE

\ah LEE vee ayt\ (v.): to relieve, improve partially

This medicine will help to *alleviate* the pain.

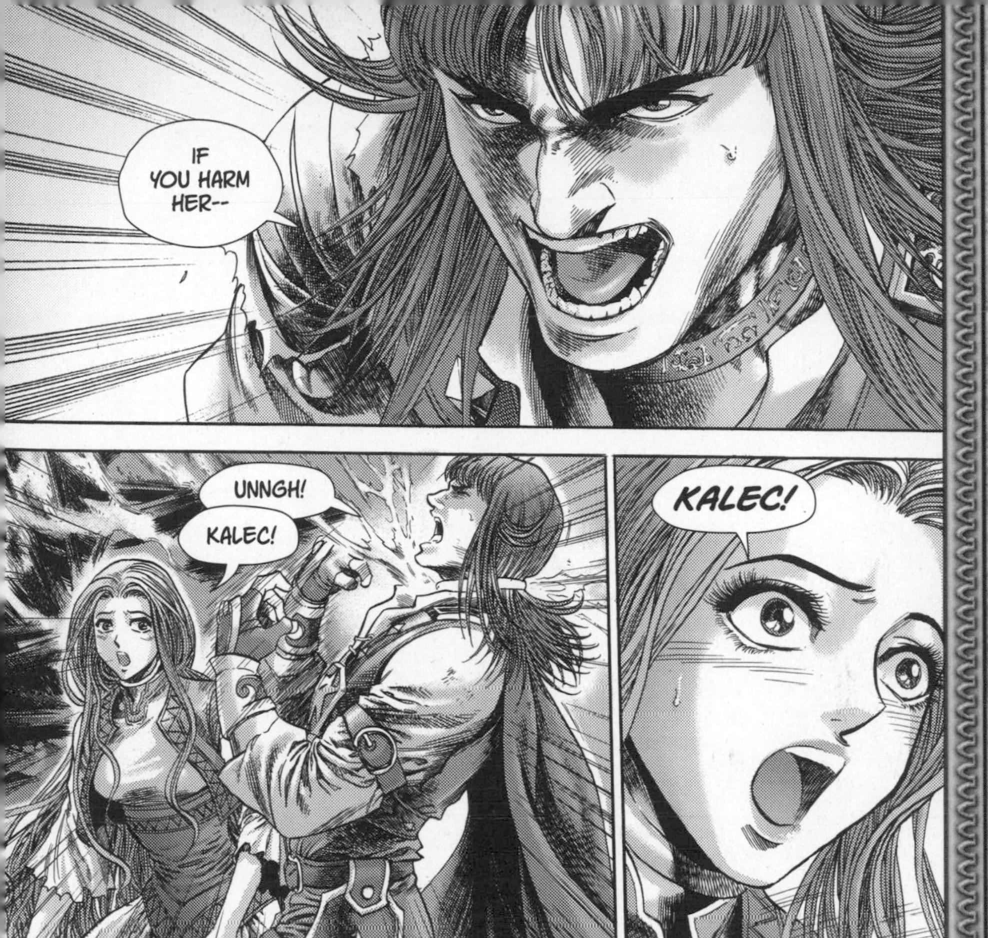
IF YOU HARM HER--
UNNGH!
KALEC!
KALEC!
STOP THIS! I WILL NOT LET IT HAPPEN!
BUT, MY DEAR LITTLE ONE, WHAT COULD YOU POSSIBLY-- HMM?

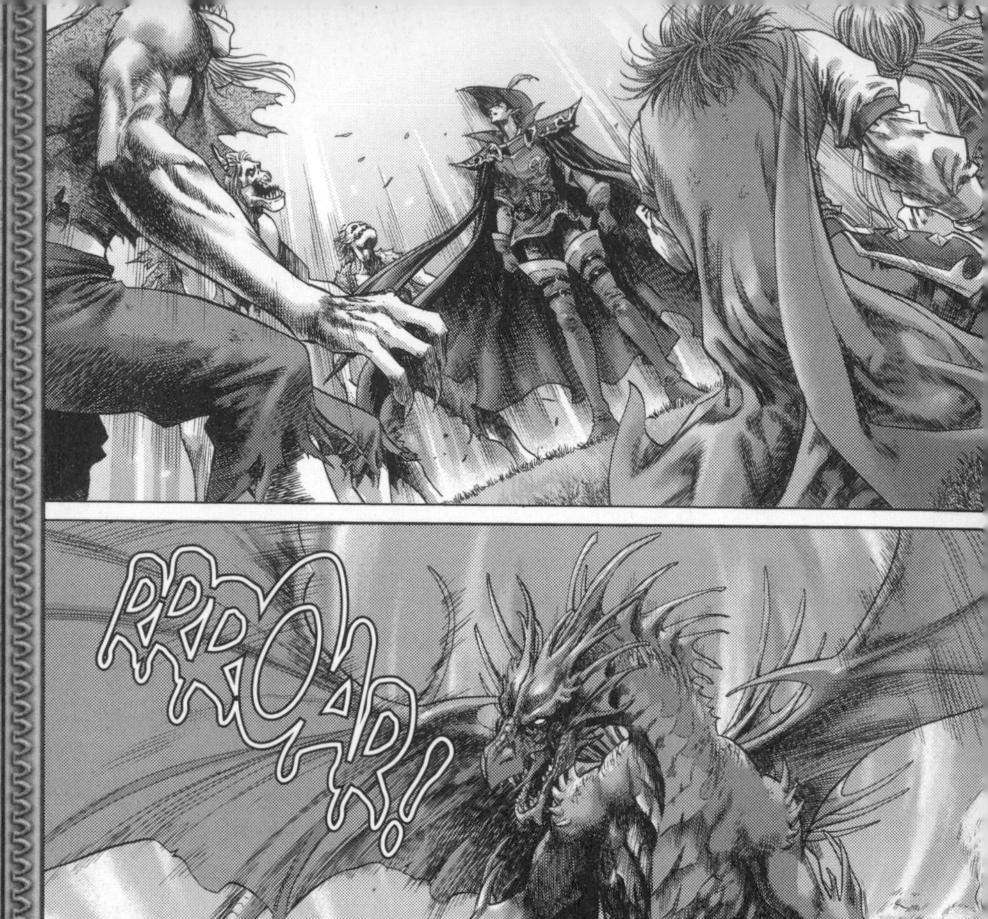
RRROAR!
WOOOSH

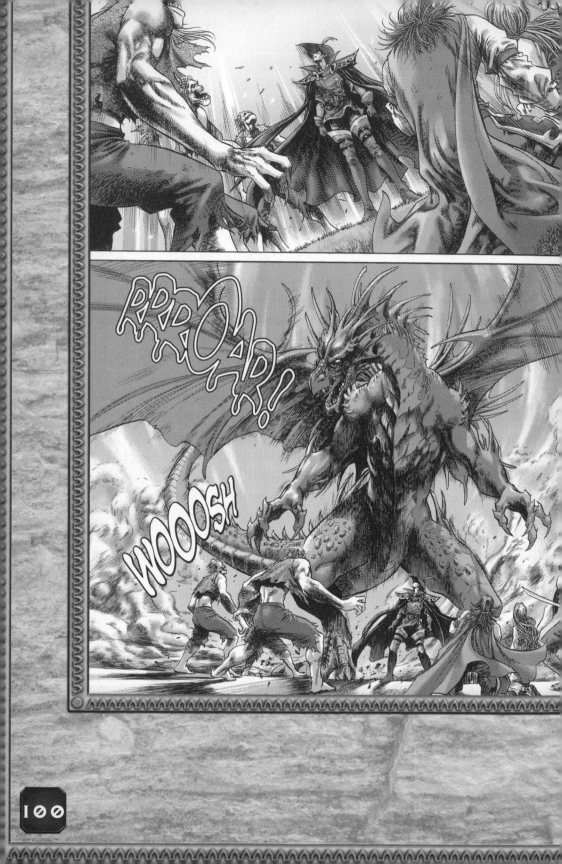

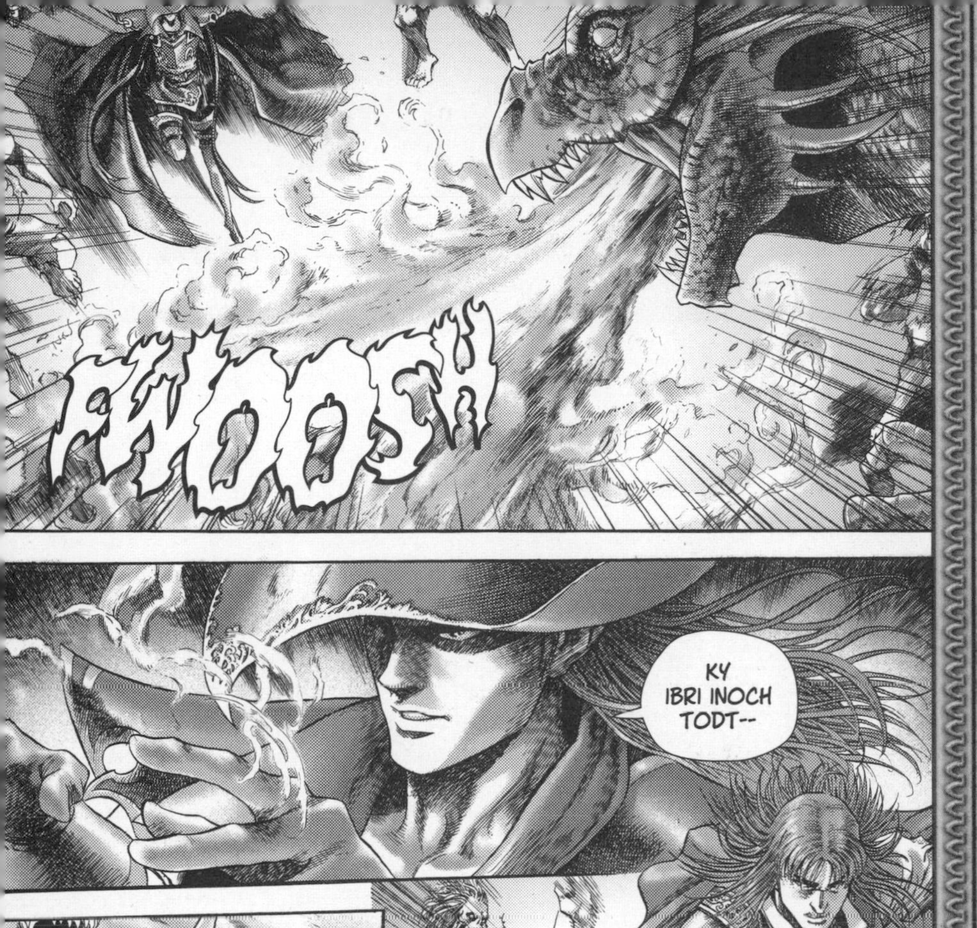
FWOOSH
KY IBRI INOCH TODT--
SNATCH

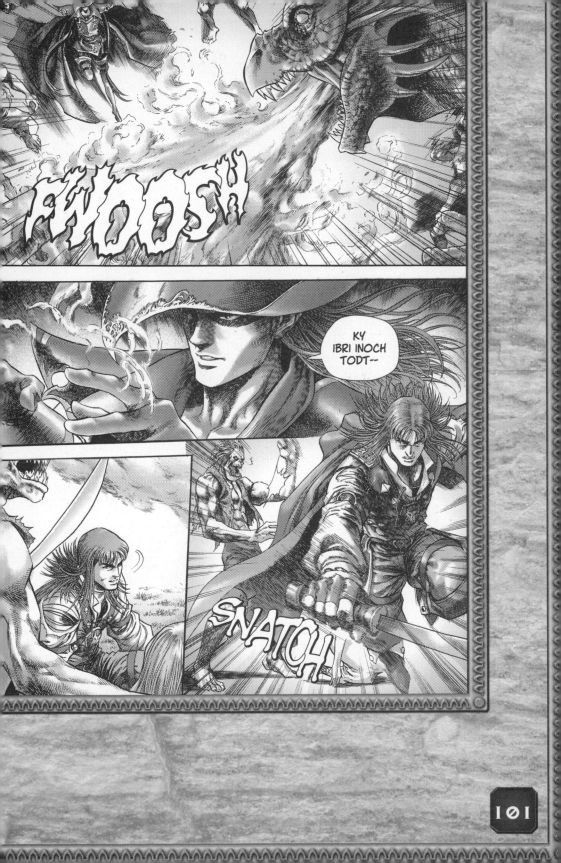

VEROT!
KRAK!
RRRAUGH!!!

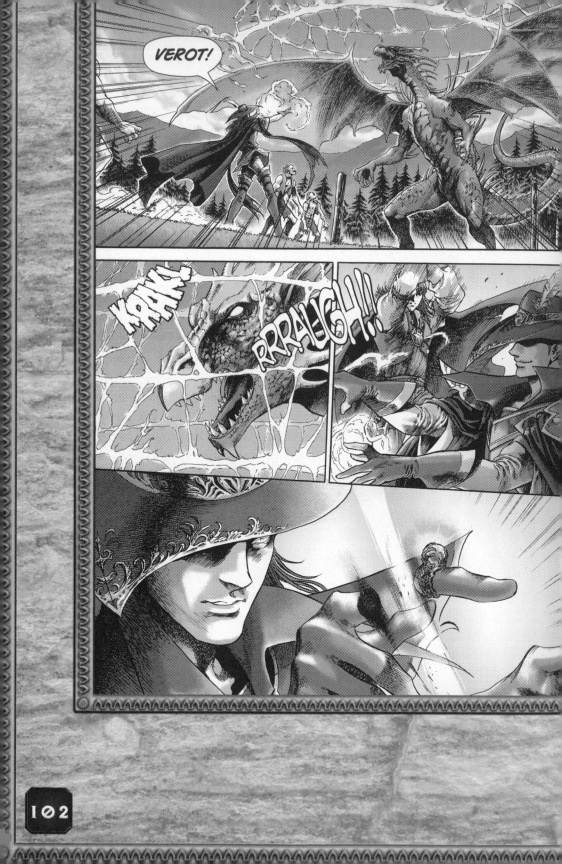

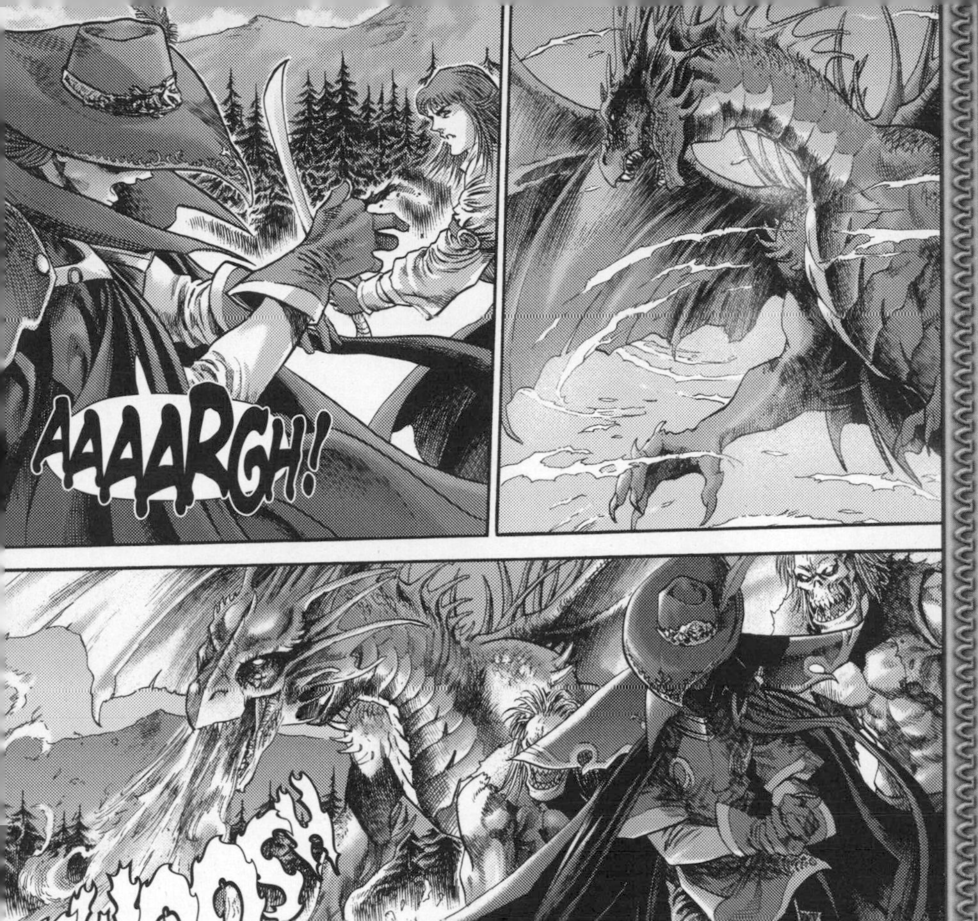
AAAARGH!
FWOOSH

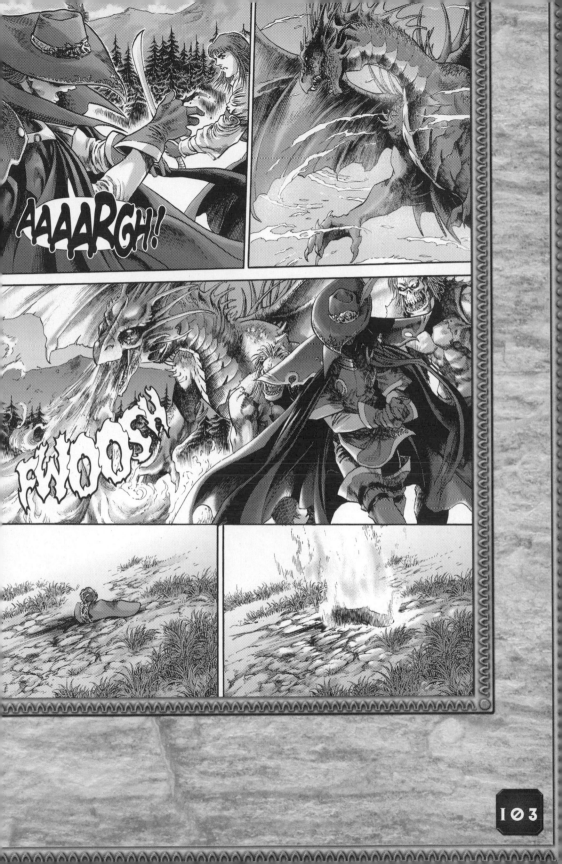

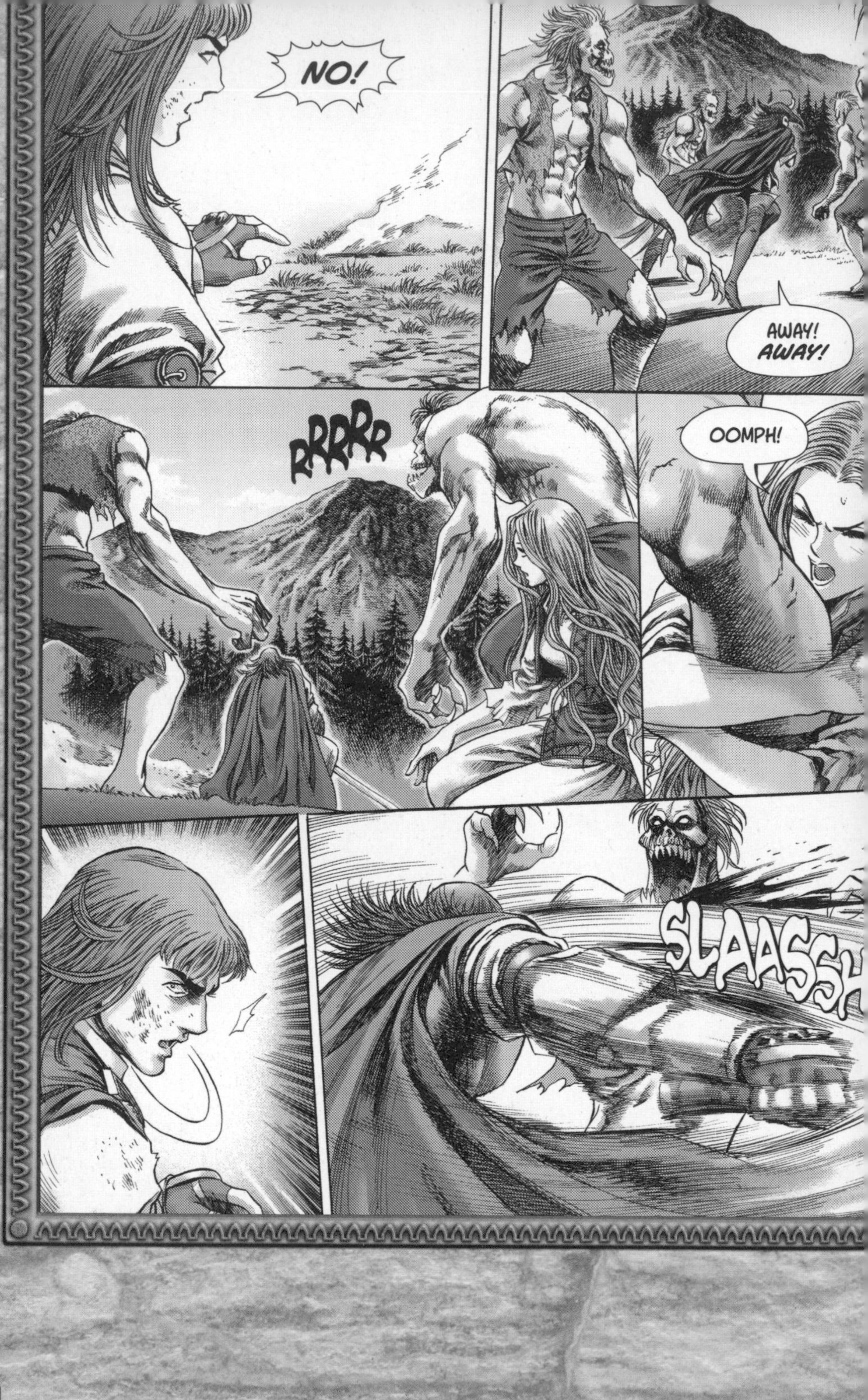
NO!
AWAY! AWAY!
RRRRR
OOMPH!
SLAASSH

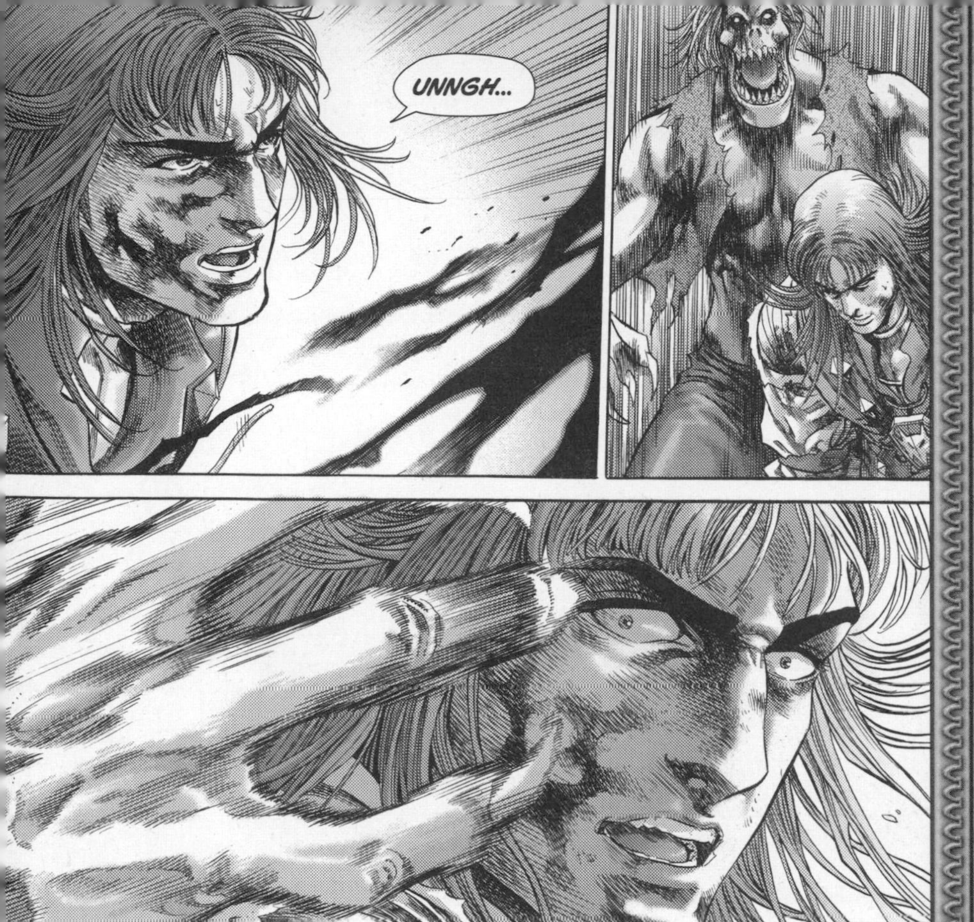
UNNGH...
F-WOOOM

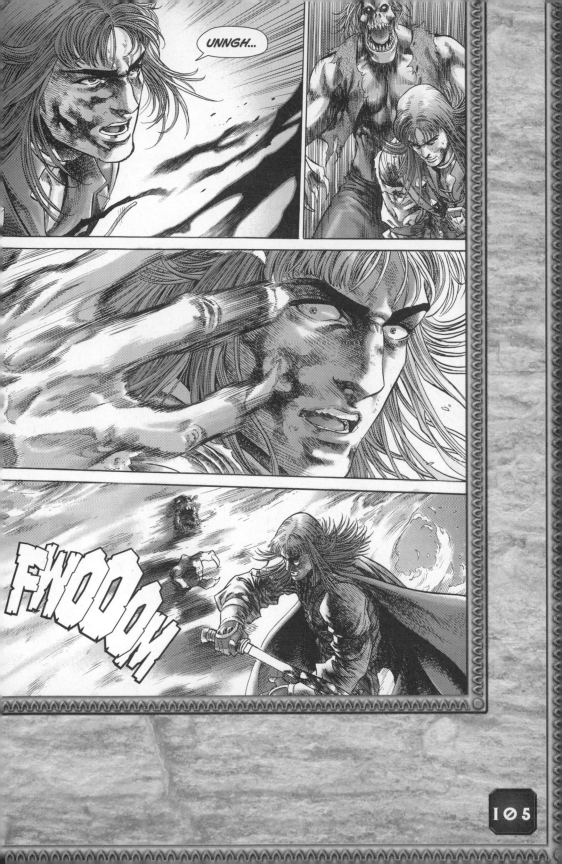

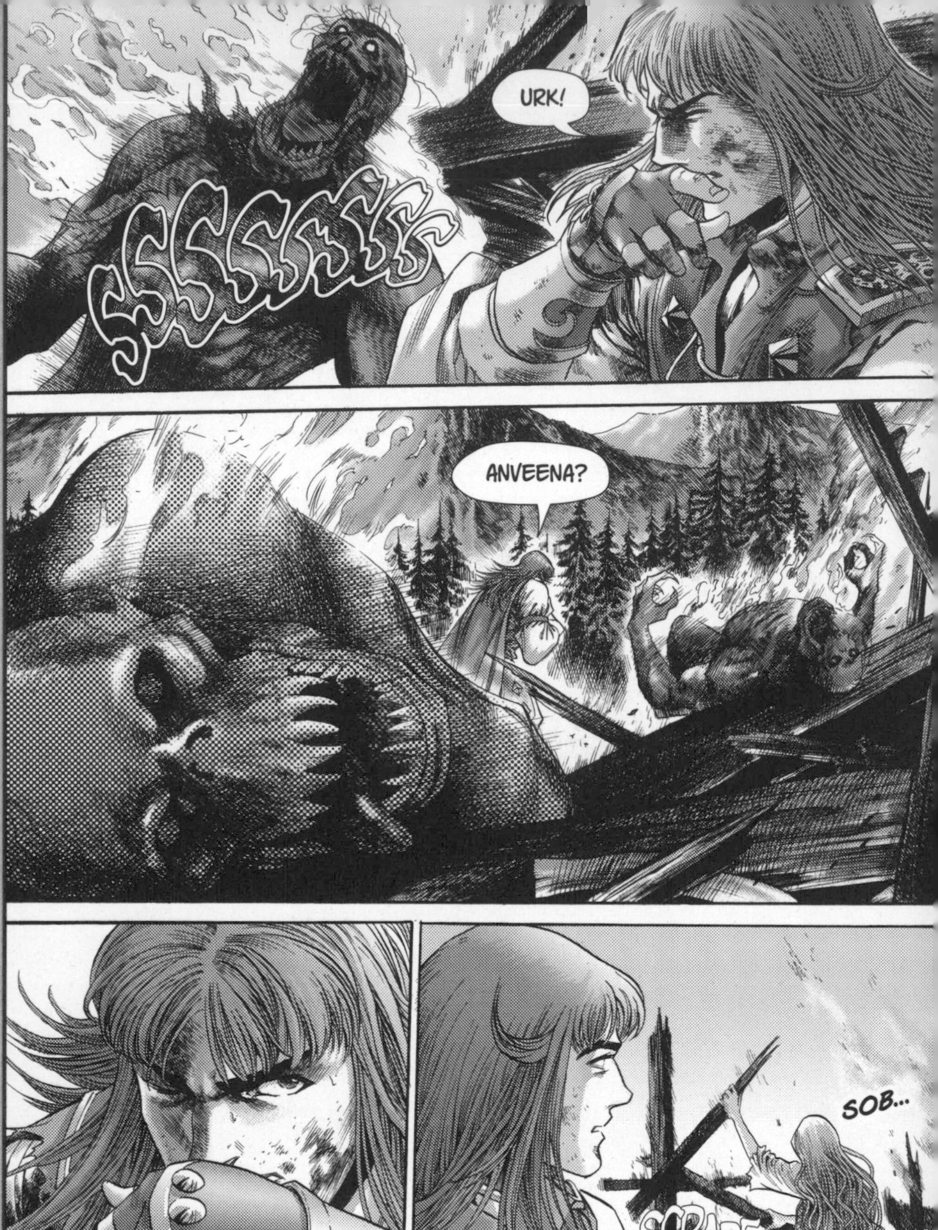
URK!
ANVEENA?
SOB...
SCRAPE
SCRAPE

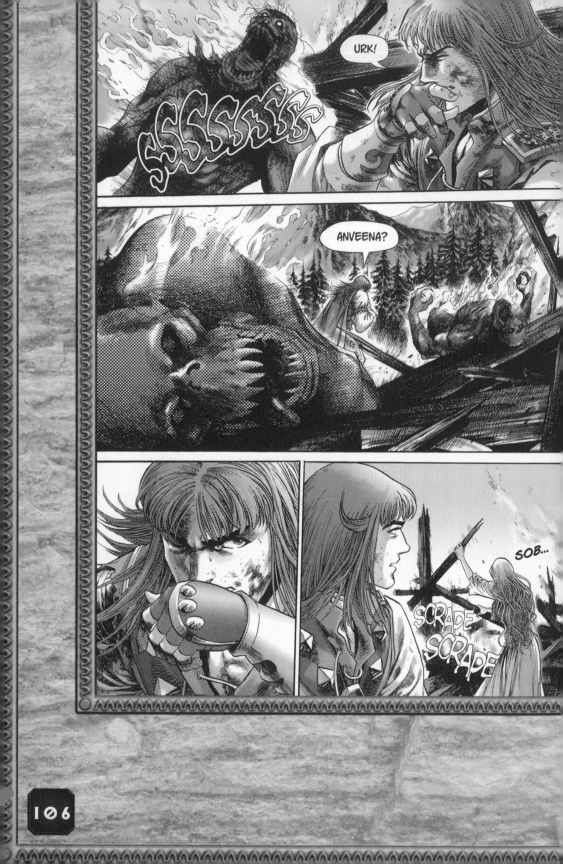

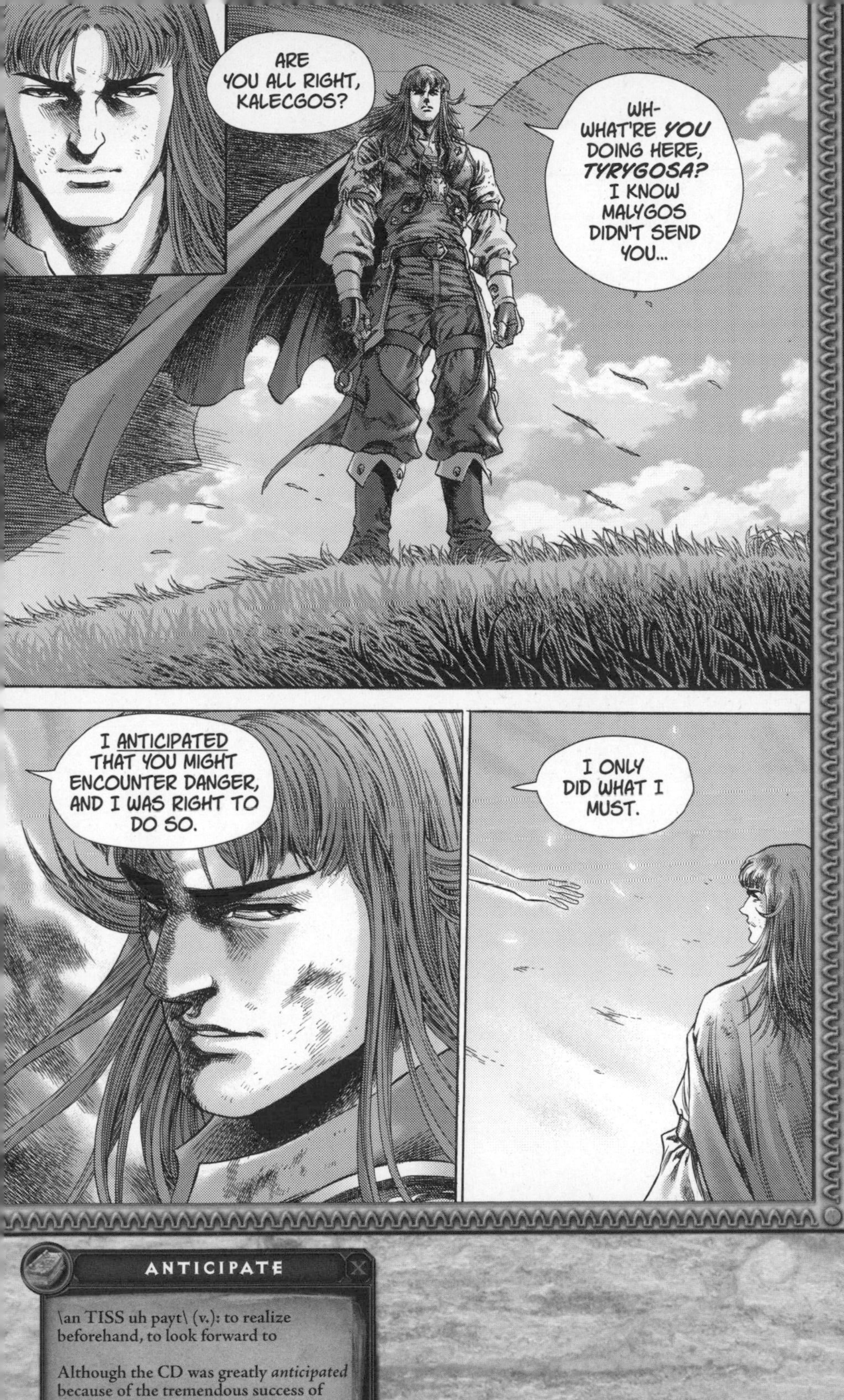
ARE YOU ALL RIGHT, KALECGOS?
WH- WHAT'RE *YOU* DOING HERE, *TYRYGOSA?* I KNOW MALYGOS DIDN'T SEND YOU...
I ANTICIPATED THAT YOU MIGHT ENCOUNTER DANGER, AND I WAS RIGHT TO DO SO.
I ONLY DID WHAT I MUST.

ANTICIPATE

\an TISS uh payt\ (v.): to realize beforehand, to look forward to

Although the CD was greatly *anticipated* because of the tremendous success of the artist's debut, it proved to be sadly disappointing.

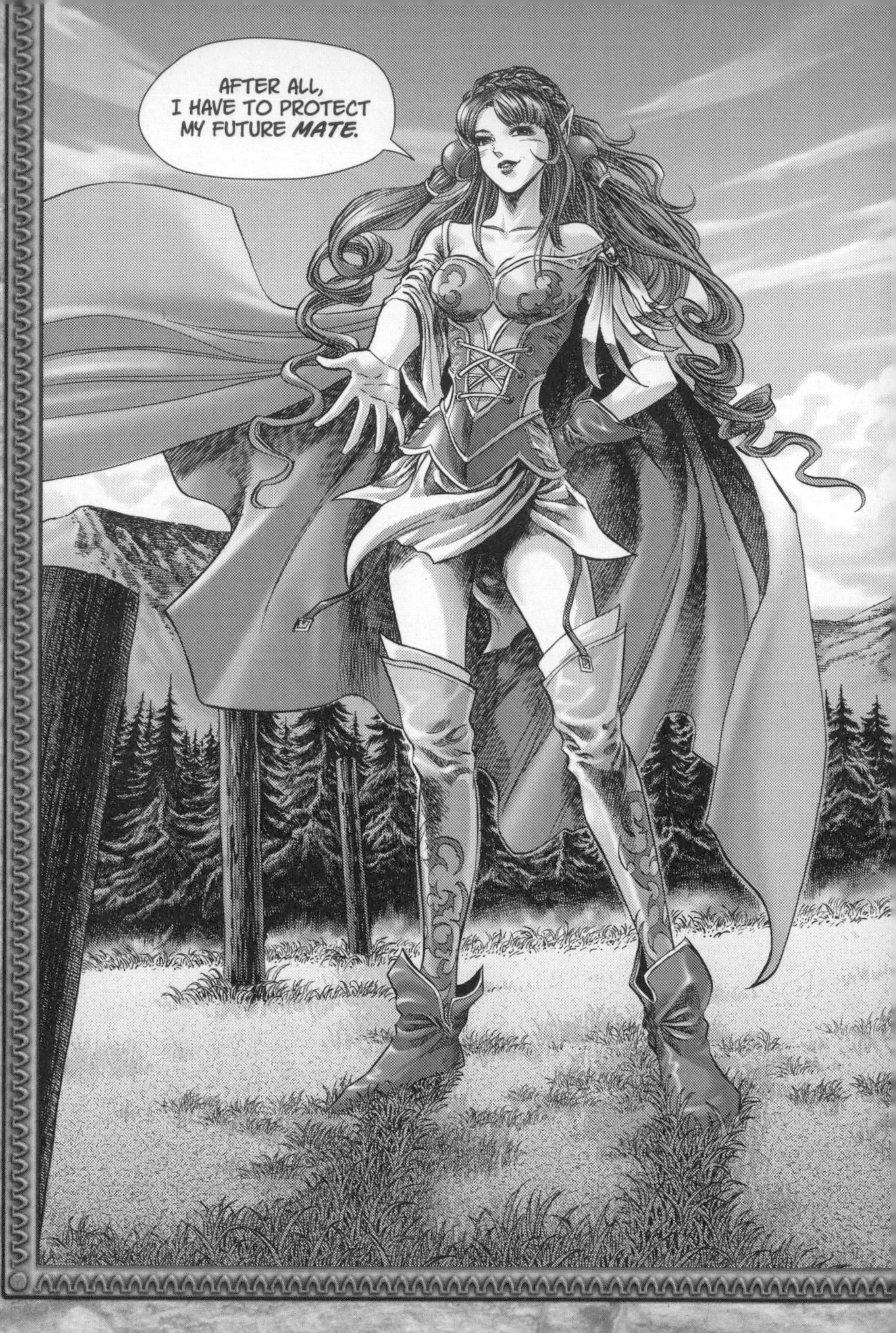
AFTER ALL, I HAVE TO PROTECT MY FUTURE ***MATE***.

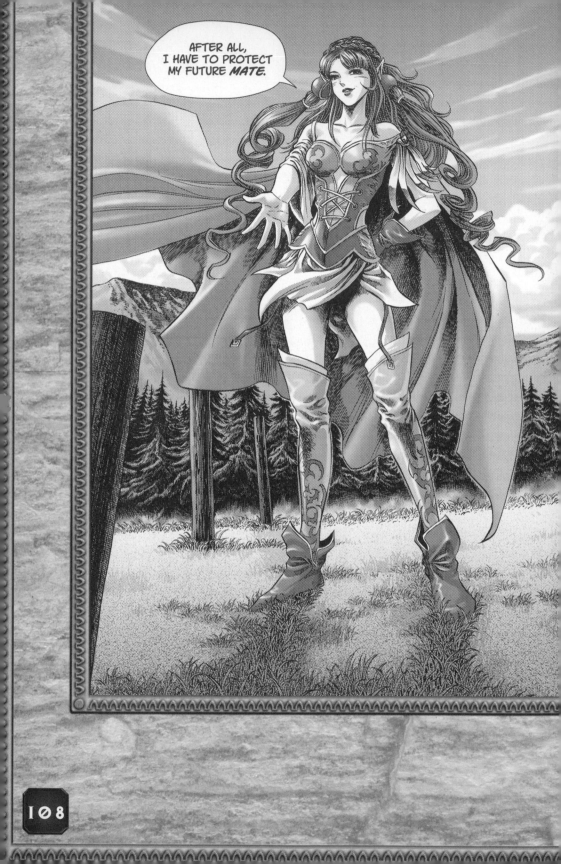

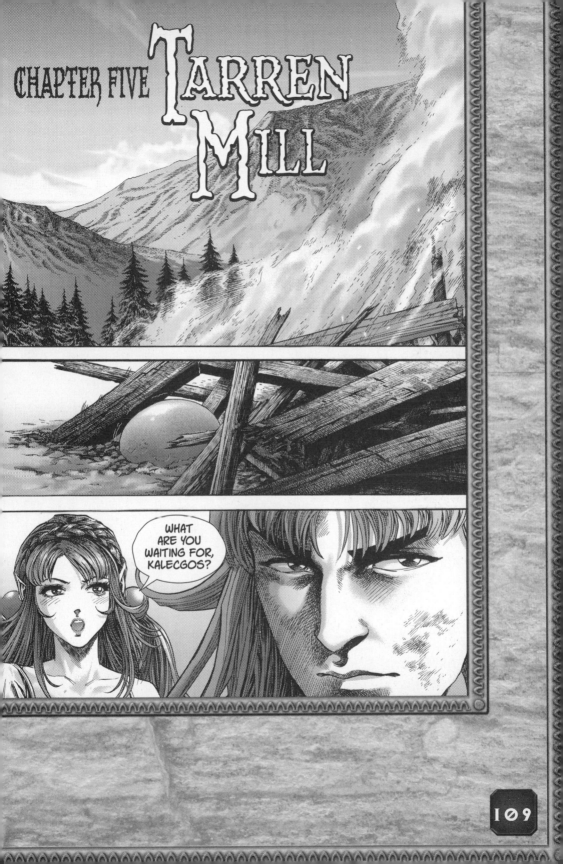

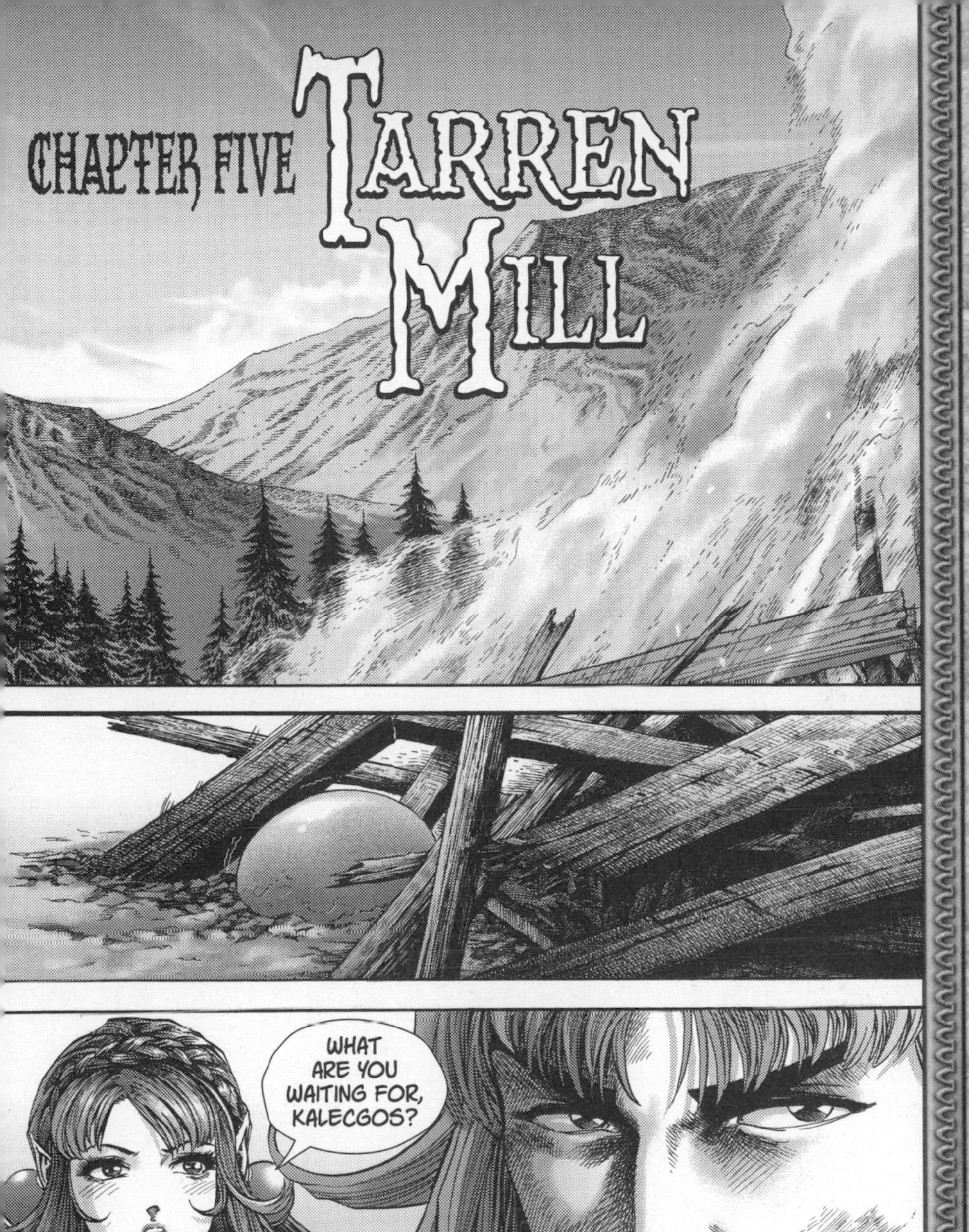
CHAPTER FIVE
TARREN MILL
WHAT ARE YOU WAITING FOR, KALECGOS?

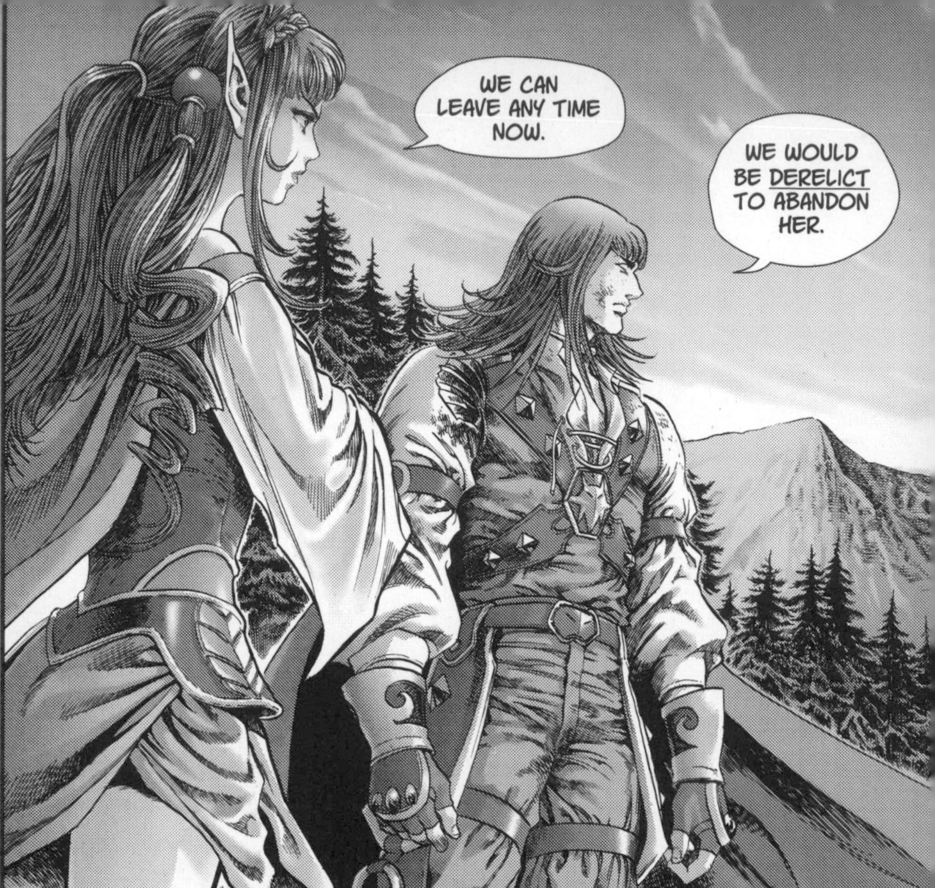
WE CAN LEAVE ANY TIME NOW.
WE WOULD BE DERELICT TO ABANDON HER.

DERELICT

\DER uh likt\ (adj.): neglectful of one's obligations; abandoned

Davey's father scolded him for being *derelict* in his household chores; the garbage hadn't been thrown out in a week.

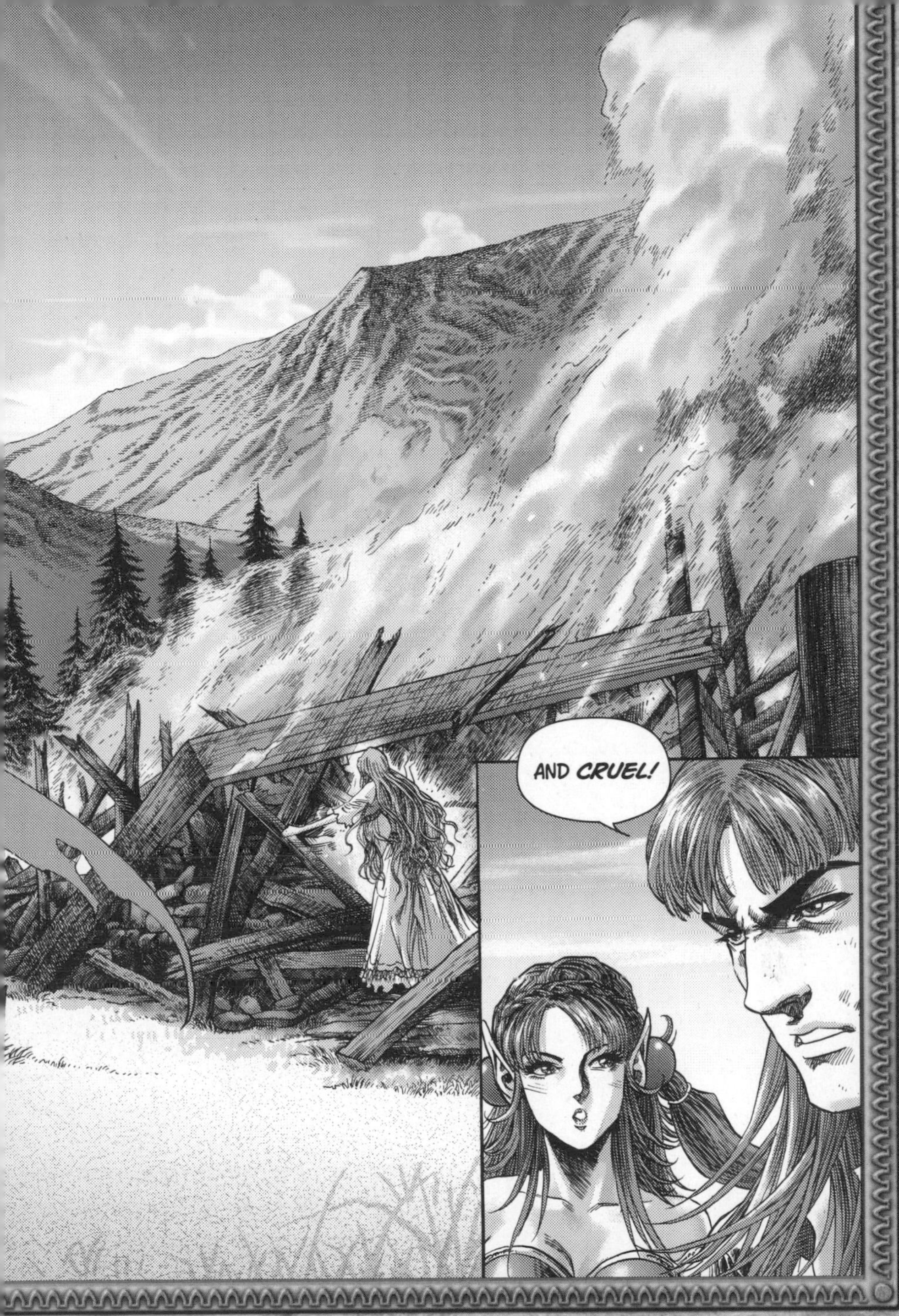
AND CRUEL!

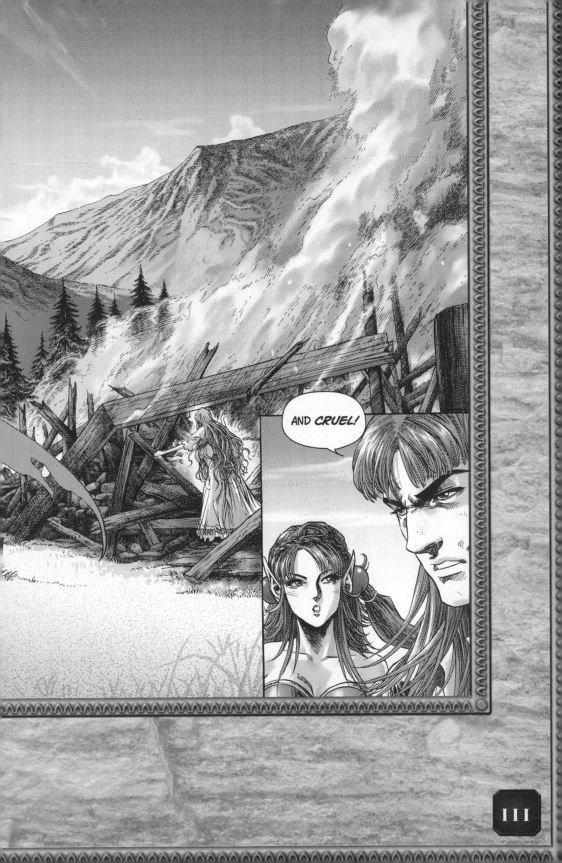

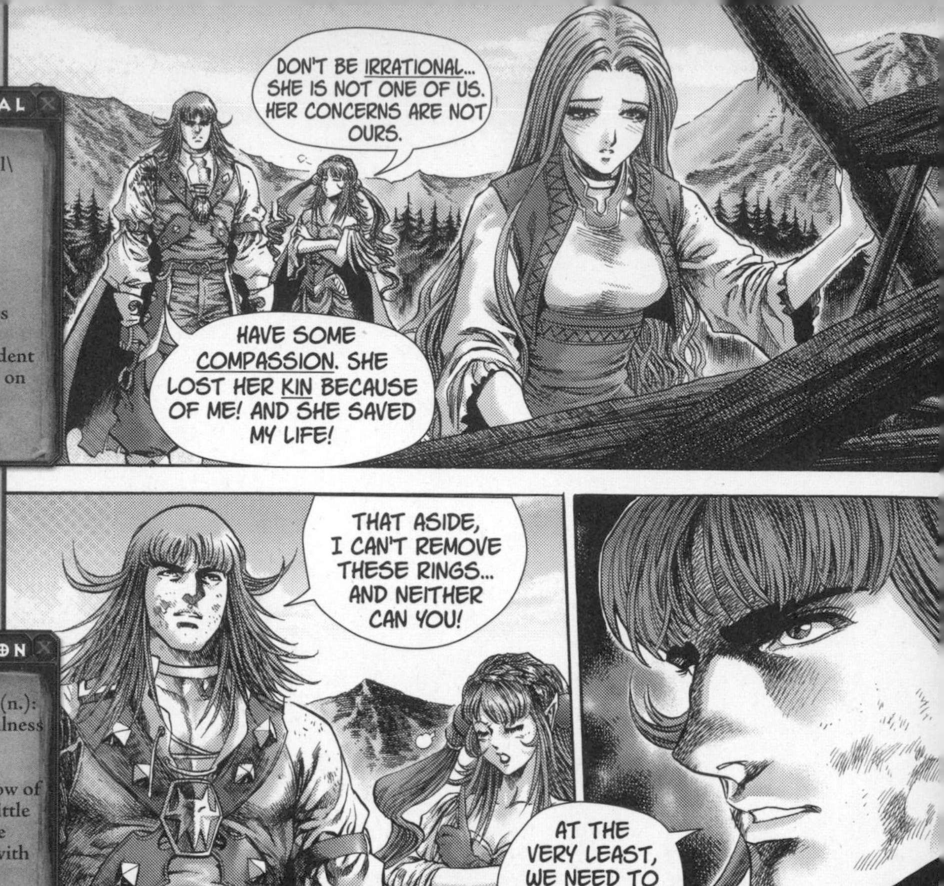
DON'T BE IRRATIONAL... SHE IS NOT ONE OF US. HER CONCERNS ARE NOT OURS.
HAVE SOME COMPASSION. SHE LOST HER KIN BECAUSE OF ME! AND SHE SAVED MY LIFE!
THAT ASIDE, I CAN'T REMOVE THESE RINGS... AND NEITHER CAN YOU!
AT THE VERY LEAST, WE NEED TO FIND SOMEONE WHO CAN!
YOU WORRY OVER NOTHING. *MALYGOS'S* DEFT HANDS SHOULD BE ABLE TO REMOVE YOURS.
BUT HE'LL NOT ALLOW A *HUMAN* TO ENTER OUR REALM.

IRRATIONAL

\ir RASH ih null\ (adj.): illogical, nonsensical, unreasonable

Rachel had an *irrational* fear of chickens, perhaps because of an unfortunate incident in her childhood on the family farm.

COMPASSION

\kum PASH in\ (n.): sympathy, helpfulness or mercy

In a touching show of *compassion*, the little girl presented the grieving widow with a flower.

KIN

\KIN\ (n.): family, relatives

Jacob went down to Egypt with his sons and all their *kin*.

DEFT

\DEFT\ (adj.): skillful, dexterous

Mario Lemieux *deftly* skated around his opponents to score the winning goal of the game.

IT WOULD BE QUITE **INDECOROUS** TO LEAVE HER ALONE LIKE THIS.

SHE'S A HUMAN. SHE'LL **SUBSIST**.

NO! WE'LL FIND SOMEONE ELSE TO **UNFETTER** HER FROM THESE!

INDECOROUS

\in DEK uh rus\ (adj.): improper, lacking good taste

The couple was embarrassed by their son's *indecorous* behavior at the dinner party.

SUBSIST

\sub SIST\ (v.): stay alive; survive

The young employee complained that there was no way to *subsist* on such a meager salary.

UNFETTER

\un FET er\ (v.): to free from restrictions

The dog owners fighting the ordinance believe they should have the right to *unfetter* their dogs occasionally, rather than keep them on leashes at all times.

113

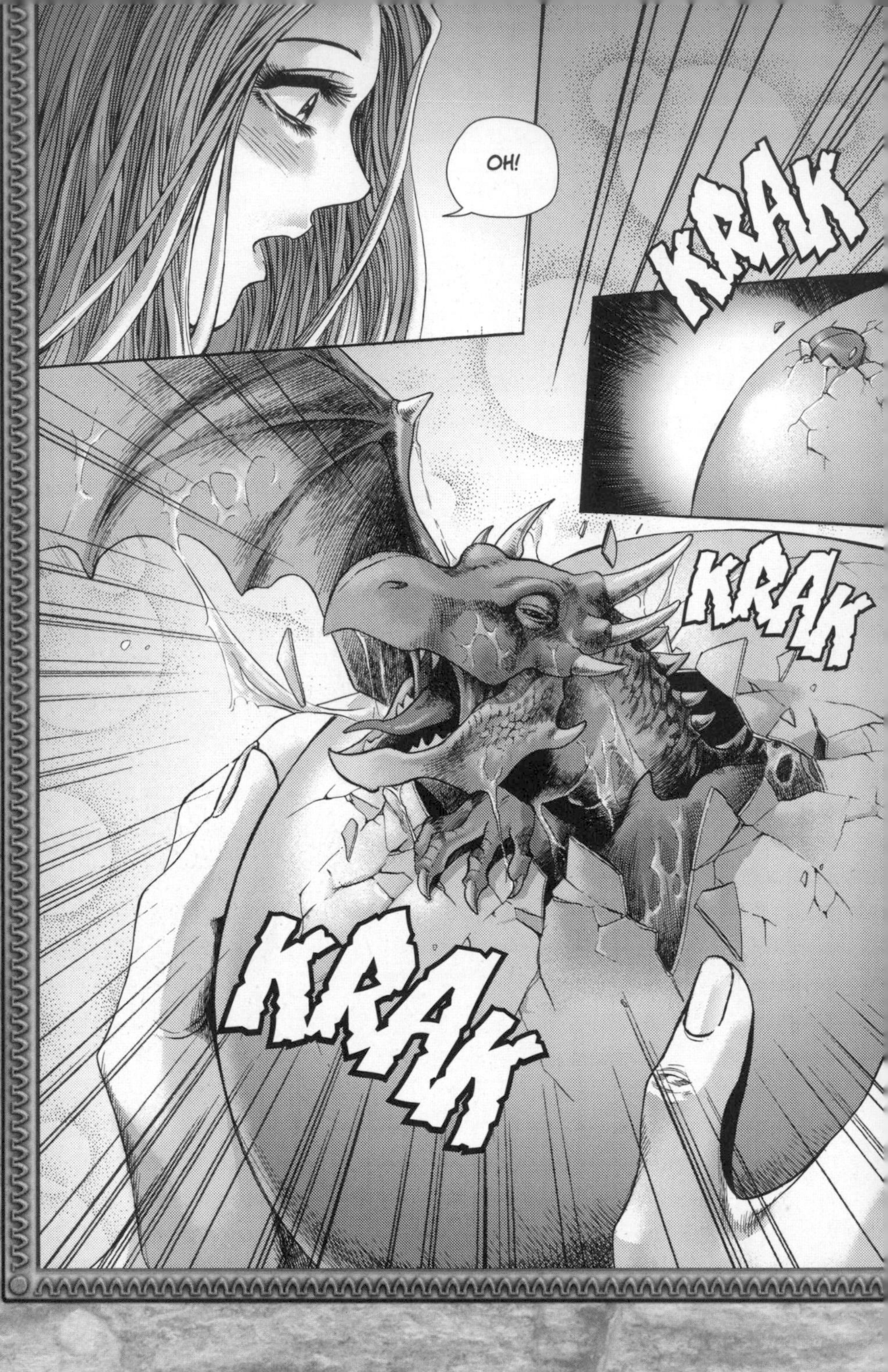
OH!
KRAK
KRAK
KRAK

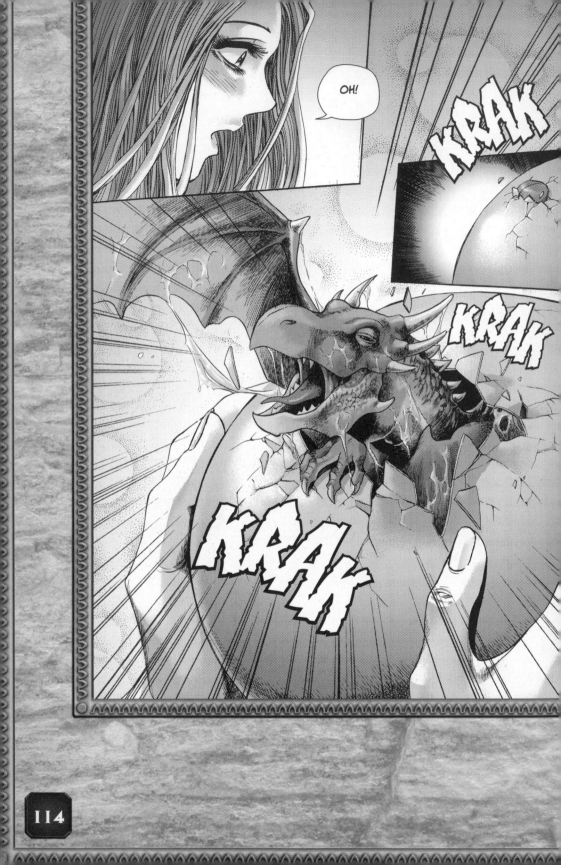

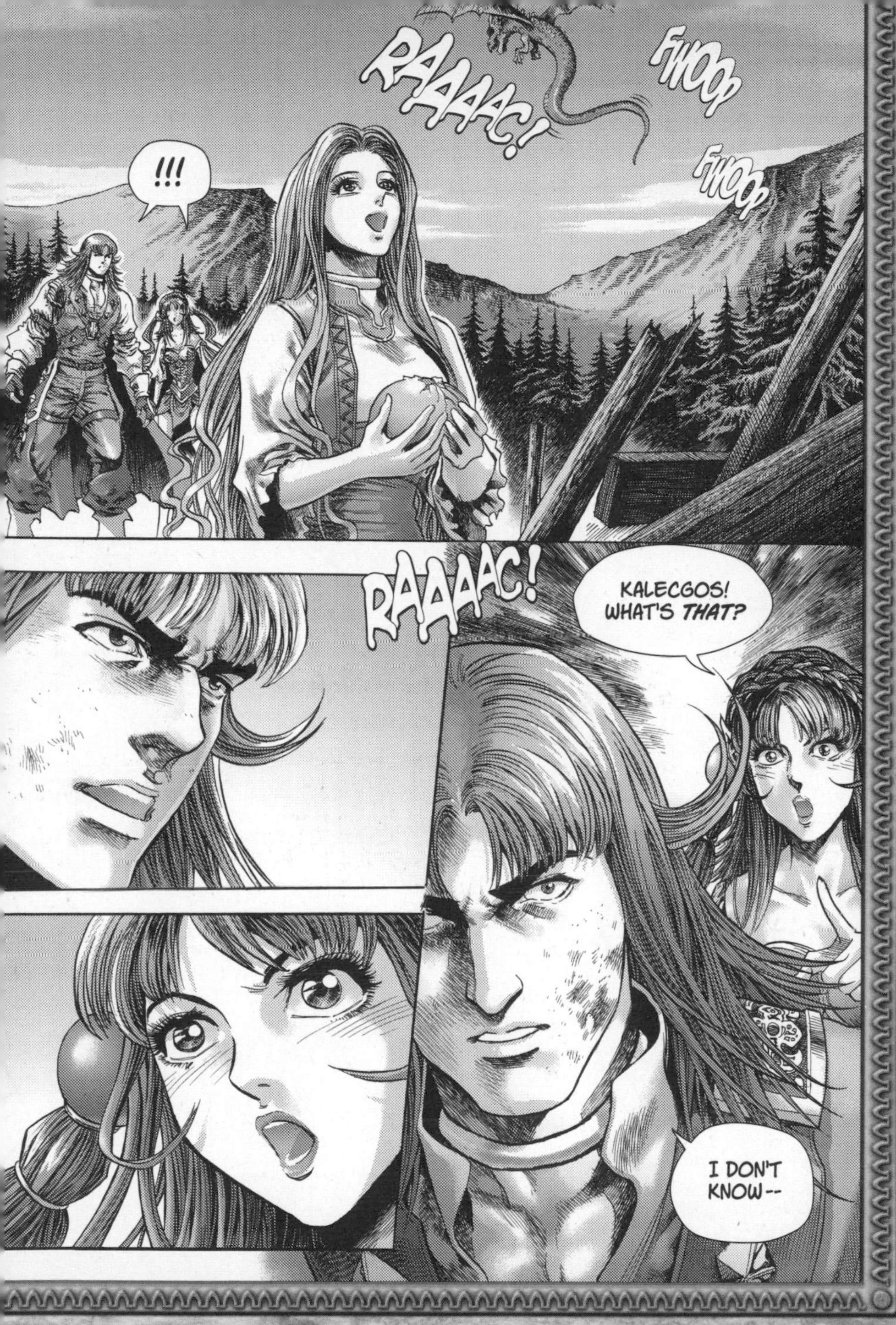
RAAAAC!
FWOOP
FWOOP
!!!
RAAAAC!
KALECGOS! WHAT'S THAT?
I DON'T KNOW--

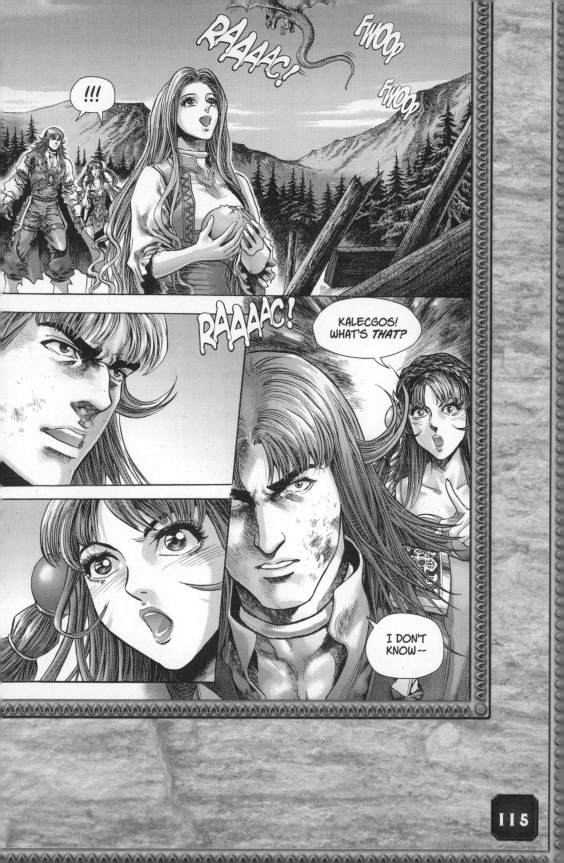

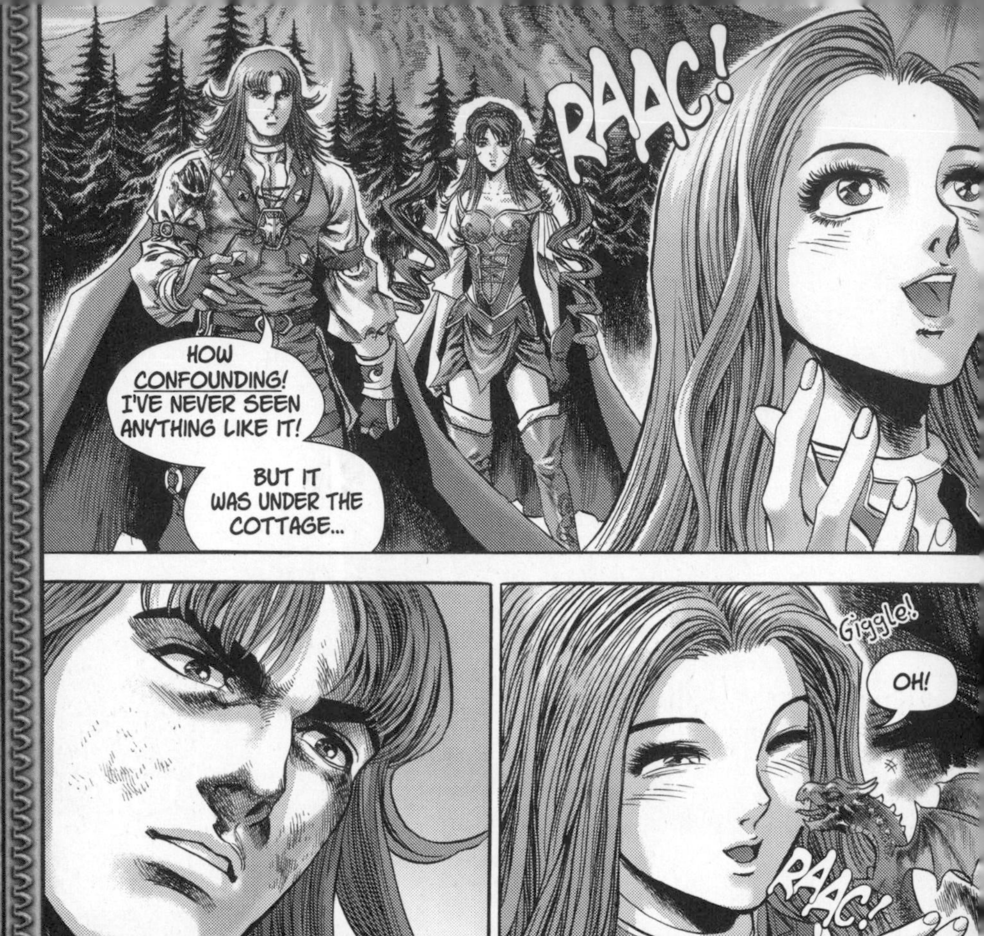
RAAC!
HOW CONFOUNDING! I'VE NEVER SEEN ANYTHING LIKE IT!
BUT IT WAS UNDER THE COTTAGE...
Giggle!
OH!
RAAC!
AND THE ELF SAID HE SENSED THE SUNWELL'S ENERGY NEAR...
SURELY YOU'RE NOT SUGGESTING THAT *THING* --

CONFOUND

\kun FOWND\ (v.): to baffle, perplex

Vince, *confounded* by the difficult algebra problems, threw his math book at the wall in utter frustration.

I DON'T KNOW... ANVEENA...

KALEC? I AM SORRY. I LOST TRACK--

ANVEENA... YOUR FAMILY... I'M SORRY... MY DEEPEST CONDOLENCES...

IT...IT IS ALL RIGHT, KALEC. YOU COULD DO NOTHING.

FORGIVE ME IF YOU FIND THIS DISCOURTEOUS ...BUT DO YOU KNOW ANYTHING ABOUT THEIR PAST?

WE HAVE LIVED HERE FOR THE DURATION OF OUR LIVES...BUT THEY HAVE SOME AFFILIATION WITH TARREN MILL. THEY HAVE A FRIEND THERE, I THINK.

WHO?

CONDOLENCE ✕

\kon DOH lens\ (n.): sympathy for a person's misfortune

After Fred's grandmother passed away we visited his house to offer our *condolences.*

DISCOURTEOUS ✕

\dis KUR tee us\ (adj.): rude

Sally's parents, disturbed by the *discourteous* manner in which their daughter's boyfriend addressed them, promptly sent him away.

DURATION ✕

\doo RAY shun\ (n.): period of time that something lasts

Doreen was seasick in her cabin for the entire *duration* of the voyage.

AFFILIATION ✕

\ah FILL ee AY shun\ (n.): an association to a group or organization

As a result of Diane's *affiliation* with the Dance Committee, she was unable to be chosen as Homecoming Queen.

117

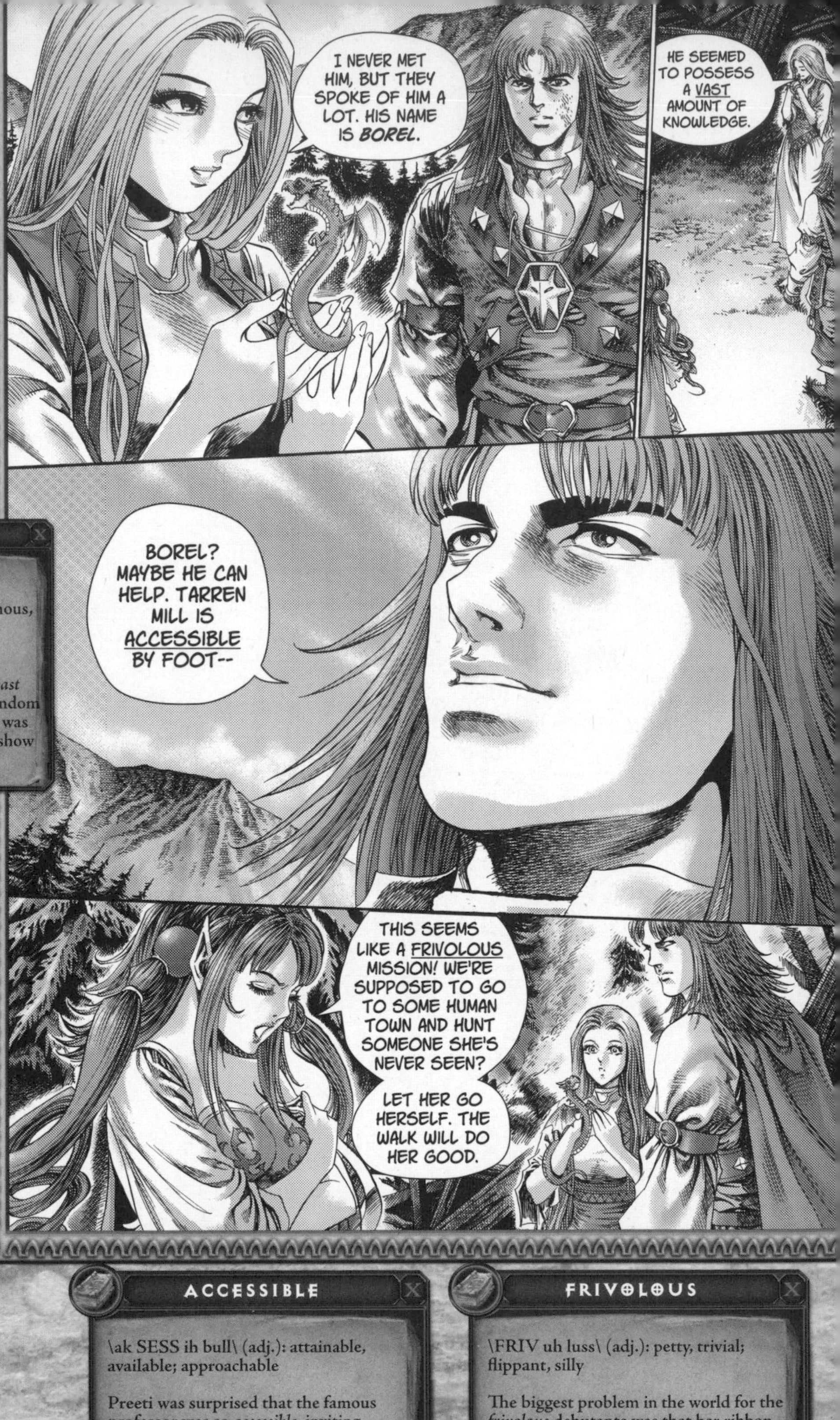
I NEVER MET HIM, BUT THEY SPOKE OF HIM A LOT. HIS NAME IS *BOREL*.
HE SEEMED TO POSSESS A VAST AMOUNT OF KNOWLEDGE.
BOREL? MAYBE HE CAN HELP. TARREN MILL IS ACCESSIBLE BY FOOT--
THIS SEEMS LIKE A FRIVOLOUS MISSION! WE'RE SUPPOSED TO GO TO SOME HUMAN TOWN AND HUNT SOMEONE SHE'S NEVER SEEN?
LET HER GO HERSELF. THE WALK WILL DO HER GOOD.

VAST

\VAST\ (adj.): immense, enormous, great in size or intensity

Because of her *vast* knowledge of random trivia, Margaret was an expert game show contestant.

ACCESSIBLE

\ak SESS ih bull\ (adj.): attainable, available; approachable

Preeti was surprised that the famous professor was so *accessible*, inviting student to visit him at all hours.

FRIVOLOUS

\FRIV uh luss\ (adj.): petty, trivial; flippant, silly

The biggest problem in the world for the *frivolous* debutante was that her ribbon was the wrong color.

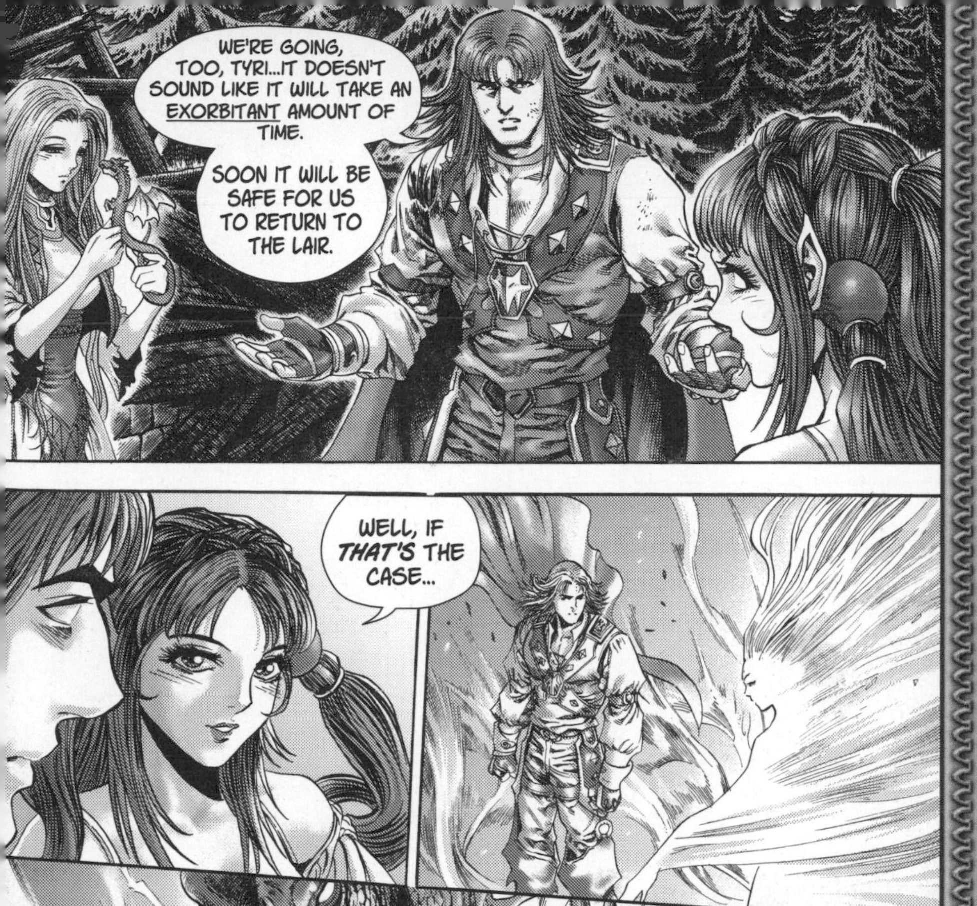
WE'RE GOING, TOO, TYRI...IT DOESN'T SOUND LIKE IT WILL TAKE AN EXORBITANT AMOUNT OF TIME.
SOON IT WILL BE SAFE FOR US TO RETURN TO THE LAIR.
WELL, IF *THAT'S* THE CASE...
...HOIST YOURSELF ON TOP AND LET'S BE AWAY FROM THIS PLACE!

EXORBITANT

\eg ZORB ih tant\ (adj.): extravagant, greater than reasonable

After freezing temperatures destroyed the harvest, shops charged *exorbitant* prices for oranges.

HOIST

\HOYST\ (v.): lift, raise

Sam backed the pickup truck to the shed and *hoisted* the wooden crate into the back.

DISPARAGE

\di SPAR ij\ (v.): to belittle, speak disrespectfully about

Gregorio loved to *disparage* his brother's dancing skills, pointing out every mistake he made on the floor.

WAIT! THAT *THING'S* NOT COMING WITH US, IS IT?

WHY DO YOU DISPARAGE HIM SO? HE'S NOT A THING! HE'S RAAC! HE'S MY FRIEND!

RAAC. HOW ORIGINAL. MAYBE IF WE FIND A DOG ON THE WAY, YOU CAN CALL HIM WOOF.

THAT WAS RUDE... THERE'S NO NEED TO TAUNT HER. PLEASE, TYRI...FOR ME?

SIGH... VERY WELL...

RUDE

\ROOD\ (adj.): crude, primitive, uncouth

Mr. Sanderson sent the boy away because of his *rude* remarks about Roger's science project.

TAUNT

\TAWNT\ (v.): to ridicule, to mock, insult

Gary sat crying in a corner of the playground because the other children had *taunted* him for wearing pink polka dot suspenders.

HOLD TIGHT!
WOOOSH
YOUR DETERMINATION IS EXEMPLARY, ANVEENA! YOU HAVE THE STRENGTH AND RESILIENCE OF ONE OF OUR KIND!
I JUST-- IT FEELS LIKE THE RIGHT THING TO DO.
AND RAAC—I CAN'T EXPLAIN, BUT WHEN I HOLD HIM, I FEEL INVIOLABLE...MORE SECURE.
HMMM...

EXEMPLARY

\egg ZEM pluh ree\ (adj.): outstanding, an example to others

His *exemplary* behavior was a model for the rest of the class.

RESILIENT

\re ZIL yent\ (adj.): quick to recover, bounce back

Luckily, Ramon was a *resilient* person, and was able to pick up the pieces and move on after losing his business.

INVIOLABLE

\in VY uh lu bul\ (adj.): safe from violation or assault

The relieved refugee, *inviolable* under the embassy's protection, finally settled into a deep sleep.

CIRCUITOUS

\sir KYOO ih tuss\
(adj.): indirect,
taking the longest
route

The cab driver took
a *circuitous* route to
the airport, making
me miss my plane.

VACANT

\VAY kent\ (adj.)—
empty, unoccupied

Although several
rooms at the motel
were *vacant*, the
owner refused to
allow the suspicious
couple to rent a room
for the night.

THAT SMOKE ON THE HORIZON! THAT MUST BE TARREN MILL!

HMMPH! GOOD!

TAKE A CIRCUITOUS ROUTE AND FIND A VACANT SPOT TO LAND IN THE WOODS! WE'LL WALK THE REST OF THE WAY!

OF COURSE! DID YOU *THINK* ME FOOLHARDY ENOUGH TO LAND IN THE *SQUARE?*

FOOLHARDY

\FOOL hard ee\ (adj.)—reckless, rash

Lisa tried in vain to dissuade Bart from
jumping over the Springfield Ravine
with a skateboard; only Homer was able
to talk his son out of the *foolhardy* act.

AH!

I HAVE NEVER SEEN SUCH A THRONG! IT IS AWE-INSPIRING!

THIS ISOLATED BACKWATER SETTLEMENT? AWE-INSPIRING?

CLATTER

CLANK

THRONG

\THRONG\ (n.): a large group of people, crowd

Glenda squeezed through the *throngs* of people trying to reach the box office before it closed.

AWE

\AW\ (n.): reverence, respect, wonder

Glenn watched in *awe* as Michael slam-dunked the basketball over Scottie's head.

ISOLATED

\IY suh lay tid\ (adj.)—solitary, singular

Though it is tempting to link the three crimes, the authorities continue to view them as *isolated* incidents.

123

THEY MUST NOT SEE ELVES OFTEN HERE. WE'RE NOT VERY INCONSPICUOUS.

I'LL NOT DEMEAN MYSELF BY TAKING A HUMAN FORM. AT LEAST ELVES ARE AESTHETICALLY PLEASING.

WELL, WITH THIS NECK RING, I'M STUCK LIKE THIS.

THAT MEANS THAT THE SOONER WE FIND THIS BOREL, THE BETTER.

BOREL?

DEMEAN

\di MEEN\ (v.)—to degrade, humiliate, humble

The editor felt that it would *demean* the newspaper to publish letters containing obscenities.

INCONSPICUOUS

\in con SPIK yoo us\ (adj.)—not easily noticeable

Jason didn't want his roommate to notice the new phone he had bought, so he placed it in as *inconspicuous* a corner as possible.

AESTHETIC

\ess THET ik\ (adj.)—pertaining to beauty or art

The museum curator, with her fine *aesthetic* sense, created an exhibit that was a joy to behold.

HE'S PRETTY **ELUSIVE**. NO ONE HERE HAS EVEN *HEARD* OF THIS *BOREL!*

I AM SORRY, KALEC!

ELUSIVE

\ee LOO siv\ (adj.)—tending to evade

Despite significant advances in theoretical physics, scientists are finding a common unifying theory for the universe to be more *elusive* than ever.

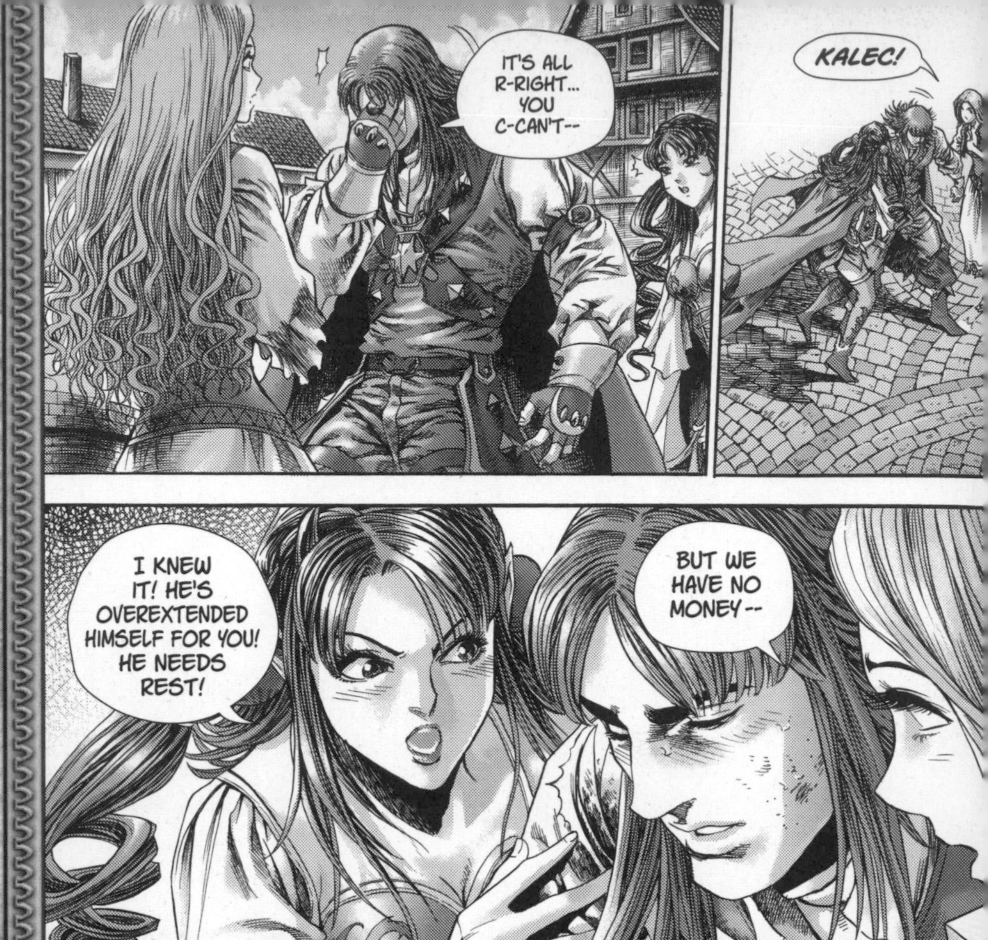
IT'S ALL R-RIGHT... YOU C-CAN'T--
KALEC!
I KNEW IT! HE'S OVEREXTENDED HIMSELF FOR YOU! HE NEEDS REST!
BUT WE HAVE NO MONEY--
A MINOR, MUNDANE PROBLEM.
AND SINCE THAT SEEMS THE ONLY PLACE, IT WILL HAVE TO SUFFICE.

MUNDANE

\mun DAYN\ (adj.): ordinary, commonplace

The plot of the thriller was completely *mundane*; as usual, the film ended with a huge explosion.

SUFFICE

\suh FIYS\ (v.): meet requirements, be capable

Although I would have liked to meet with the vice president of production, the vice president of marketing will *suffice*.

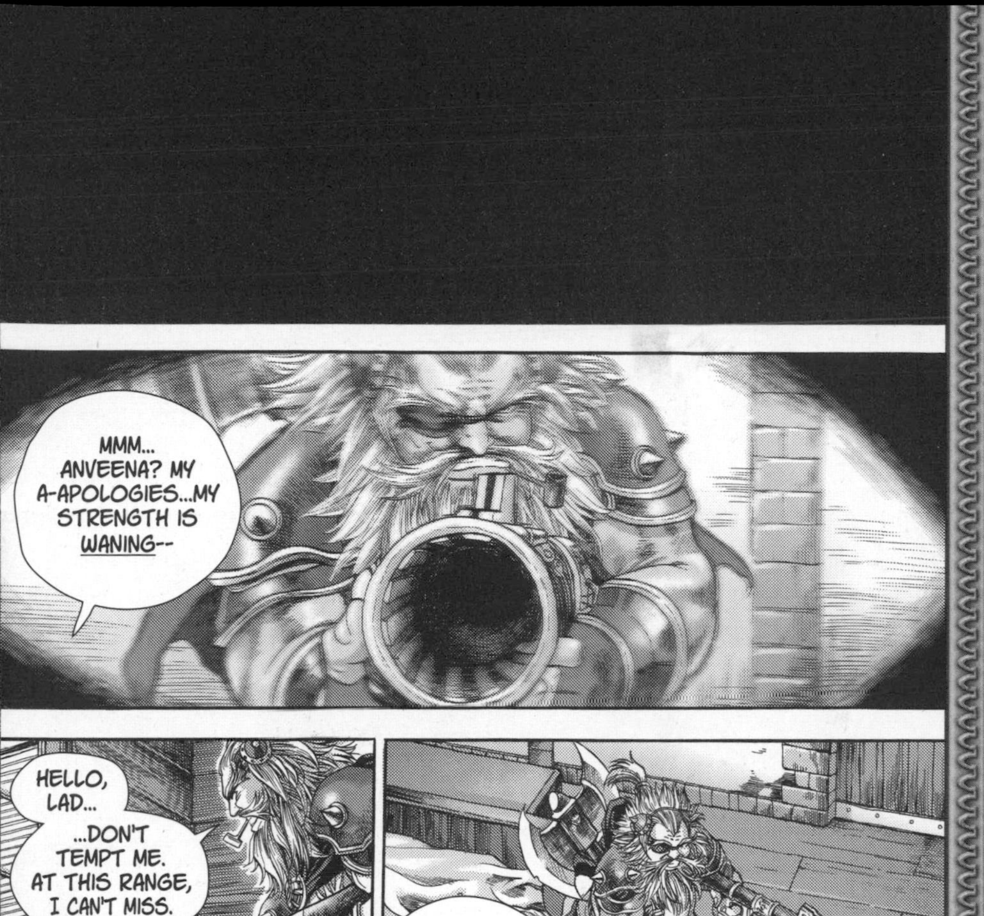
MMM... ANVEENA? MY A-APOLOGIES...MY STRENGTH IS WANING--
HELLO, LAD...
...DON'T TEMPT ME. AT THIS RANGE, I CAN'T MISS.
GET UP! THE CRYSTAL CONFIRMS THAT MY DRAGON'S NEAR...AND I'VE GOT A HUNCH VERY NEAR.

WANE

WAYN\ (v.): decline, decrease in size or intensity

The new shortstop saw his popularity begin to *wane* immediately after the serious error.

CONFIRM

\kon FIRM\ (v.): verify

Many airlines require their passengers to call a day in advance and *confirm* their reservation for their flight.

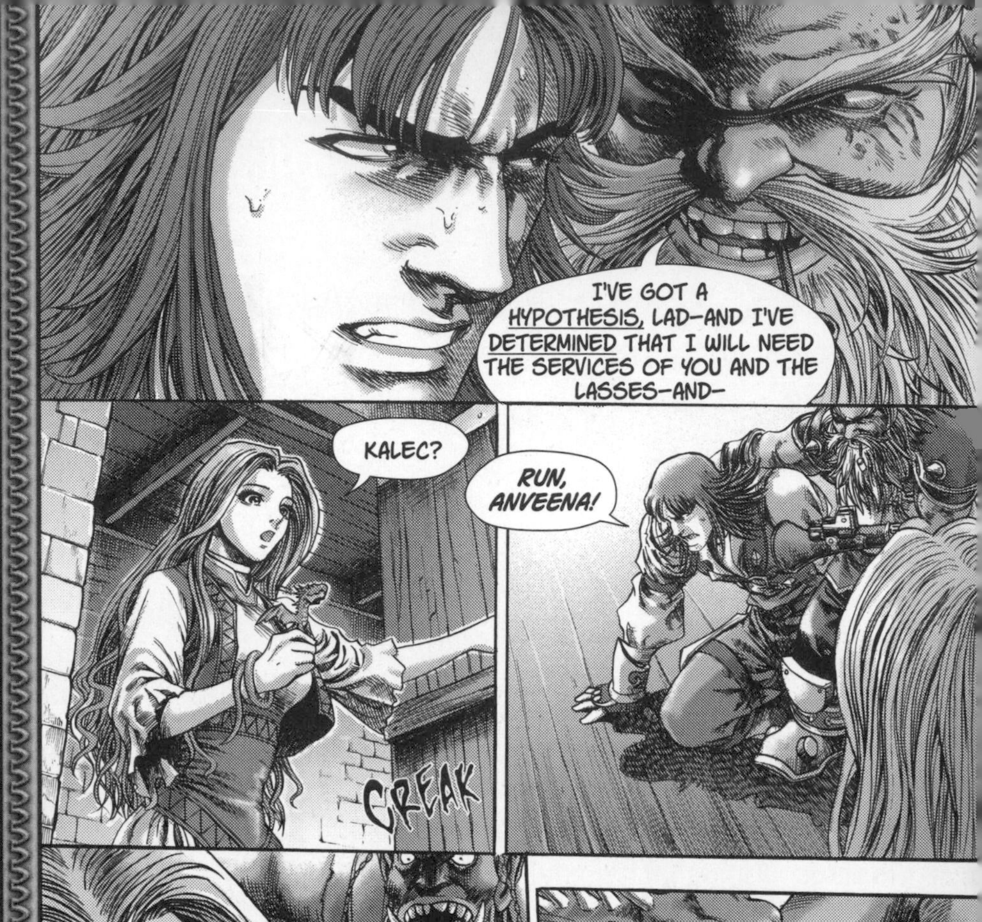
I'VE GOT A HYPOTHESIS, LAD—AND I'VE DETERMINED THAT I WILL NEED THE SERVICES OF YOU AND THE LASSES—AND—
KALEC?
RUN, ANVEENA!
CREAK
OH!
RAAAC!
YOWTCH!

HYPOTHESIS

\hi POTH a siss\ (n.): assumption, theory requiring proof

While the board found the researcher's *hypothesis* compelling, they simply couldn't adequately fund the experiment.

DETERMINE

\di TUR min\ (v.): to decide, establish

The scientists were unable to *determine* the cause of the strange ailment.

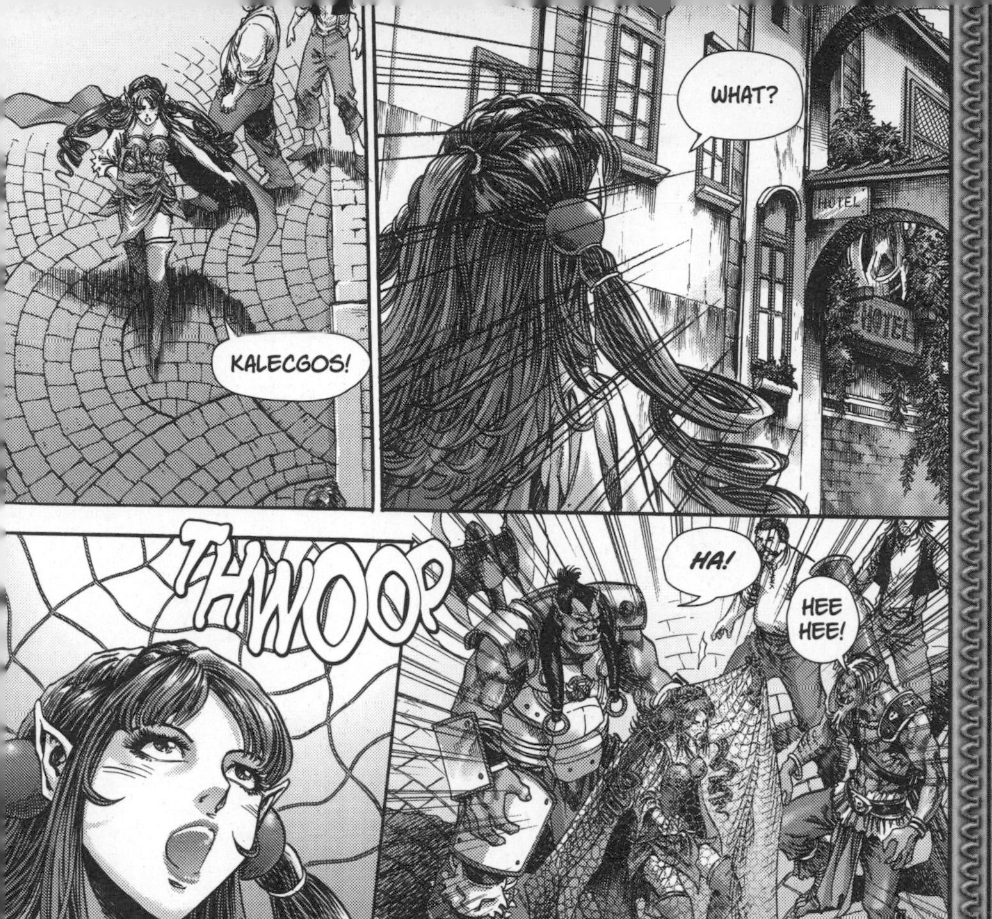
KALECGOS!
WHAT?
THWOOP
HA!
HEE HEE!
MAGIC WILL NOT SAVE YOU, FEMALE. THIS NET STIFLES INCANTATIONS.
HOTEL
HOTEL

STIFLE

\STY ful\ (v.): to smother or suffocate; suppress

Much as she longed to express her anger at the dictator, Maria *stifled* her protests for fear of being arrested.

RETAIN

\ri TAYN\ (v.): to hold, keep possession of

Britain had to give up most of its colonies, but it *retained* control over Hong Kong until the end of the twentieth century.

ESSENTIAL

\ee SEN shul\ (n.): something fundamental or indispensable

When preparing for her trip to Europe, Claudia made sure to pack her toothbrush, deodorant, and other *essentials*.

INSINUATE

\in SIN yoo ayt\ (v.): to suggest, say indirectly, imply

Feeling that an outright accusation would be tactless, Brenda instead *insinuated* that Deirdre's brother had stolen her watch.

TRANSPARENT

\trans PAR ent\ (adj.): see-through, invisible

When the glass door is cleaned, it becomes virtually *transparent*.

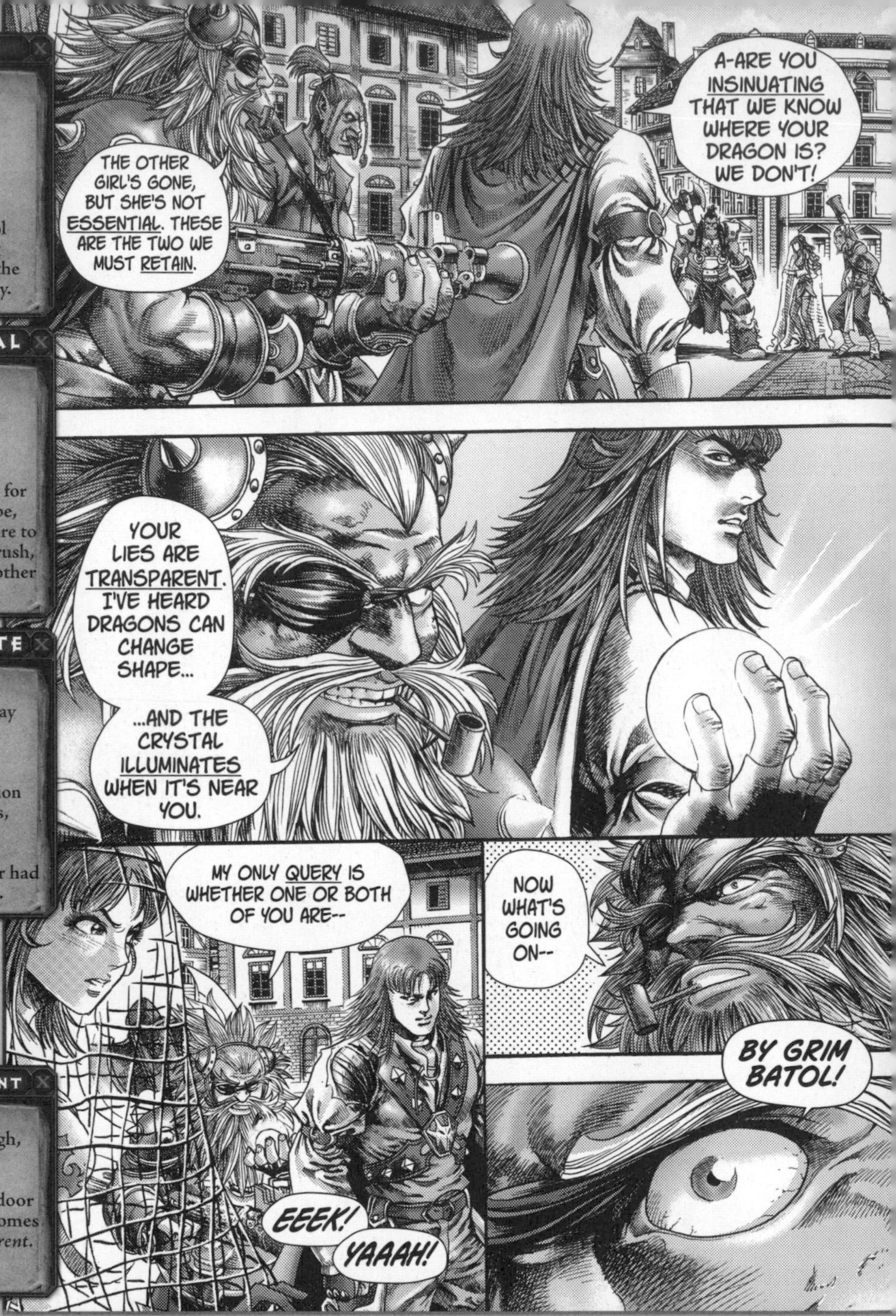
THE OTHER GIRL'S GONE, BUT SHE'S NOT ESSENTIAL. THESE ARE THE TWO WE MUST RETAIN.
A-ARE YOU INSINUATING THAT WE KNOW WHERE YOUR DRAGON IS? WE DON'T!
YOUR LIES ARE TRANSPARENT. I'VE HEARD DRAGONS CAN CHANGE SHAPE...
...AND THE CRYSTAL ILLUMINATES WHEN IT'S NEAR YOU.
MY ONLY QUERY IS WHETHER ONE OR BOTH OF YOU ARE--
EEEK!
YAAAH!
NOW WHAT'S GOING ON--
BY GRIM BATOL!

ILLUMINATE

\il LOOM ih nayt\ (v.): to fill with light

Reba switched on the light bulb to *illuminate* the corridor.

QUERY

\KWEE ree\ (n.): question

The reporter's *query* about the location of the criminal's hideout annoyed the police.

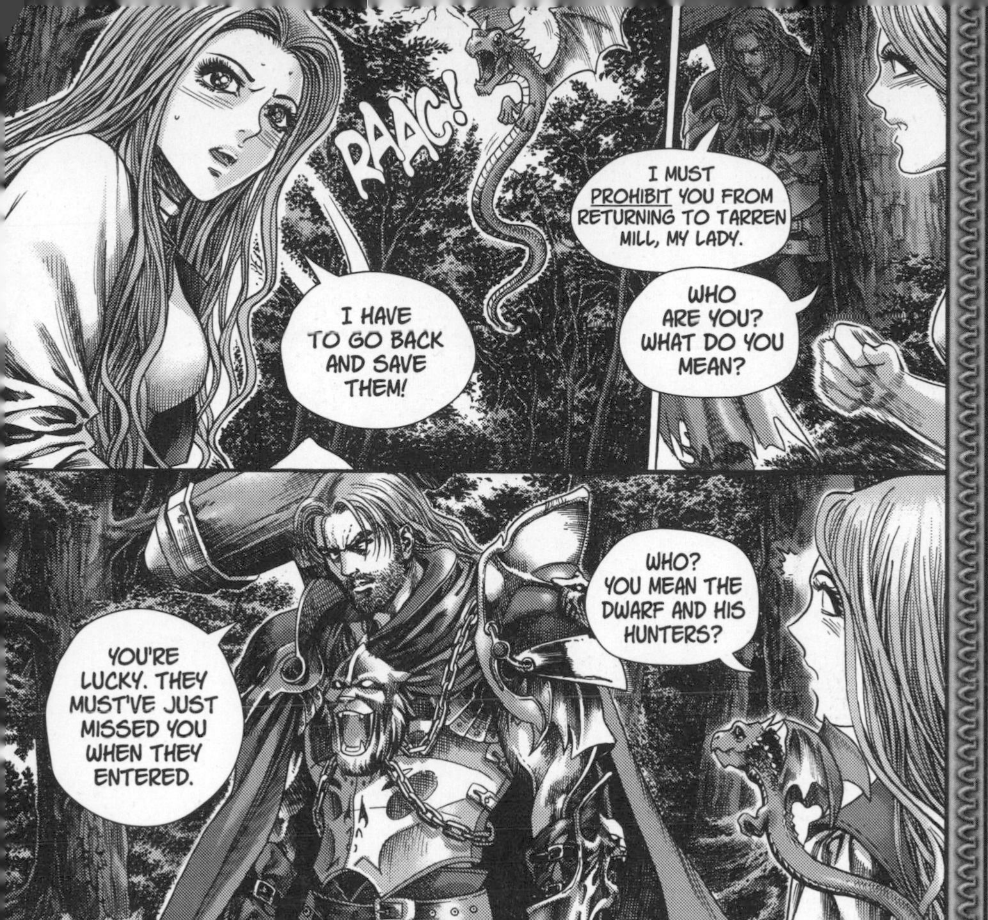
RAAC!
I HAVE TO GO BACK AND SAVE THEM!
I MUST PROHIBIT YOU FROM RETURNING TO TARREN MILL, MY LADY.
WHO ARE YOU? WHAT DO YOU MEAN?
YOU'RE LUCKY. THEY MUST'VE JUST MISSED YOU WHEN THEY ENTERED.
WHO? YOU MEAN THE DWARF AND HIS HUNTERS?
WOULD THAT IT WERE, MY LADY.
NO, THIS IS FAR, FAR MORE SERIOUS THAN A FEW BRIGANDS.

PROHIBIT

\pro HIB it\ (v.): to forbid, prevent

Marge's parents *prohibited* her from attending her senior prom because they thought dancing was immoral.

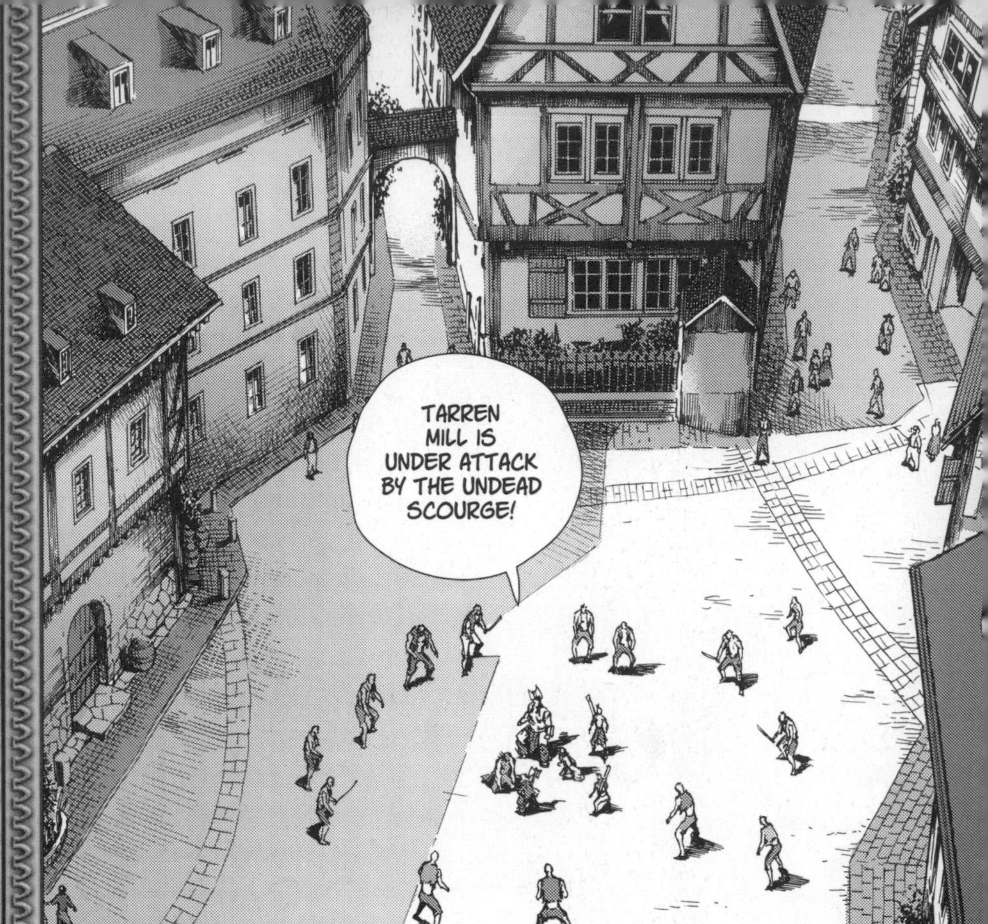
TARREN MILL IS UNDER ATTACK BY THE UNDEAD SCOURGE!

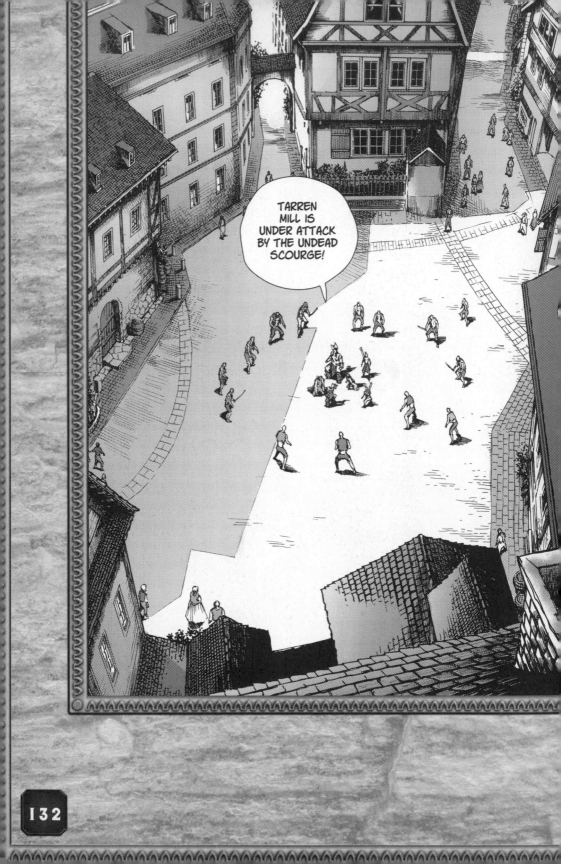

CHAPTER SIX
AGAINST THE SCOURGE

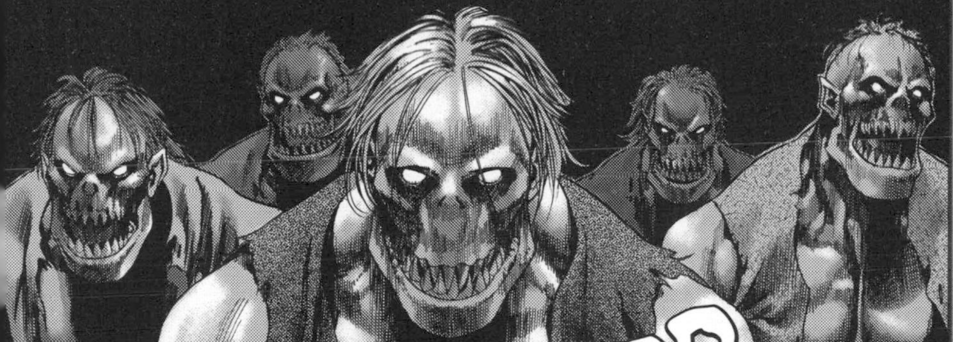
URRR

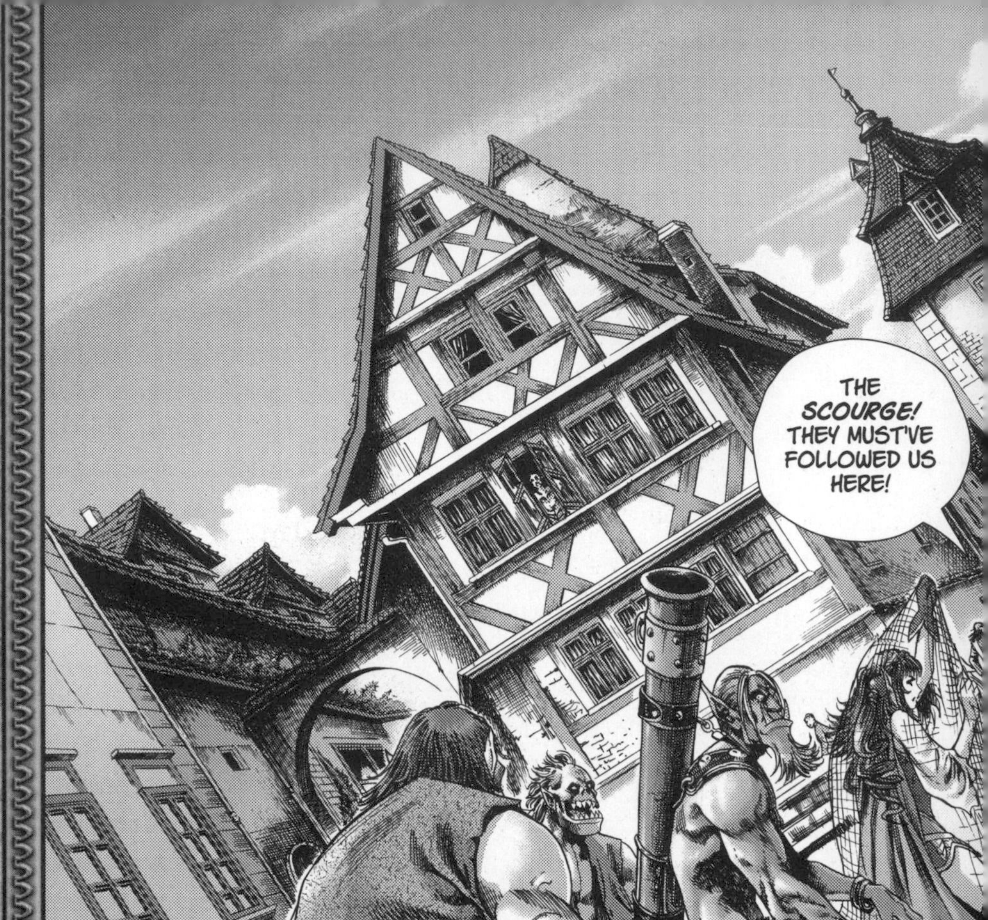
THE *SCOURGE!* THEY MUST'VE FOLLOWED US HERE!

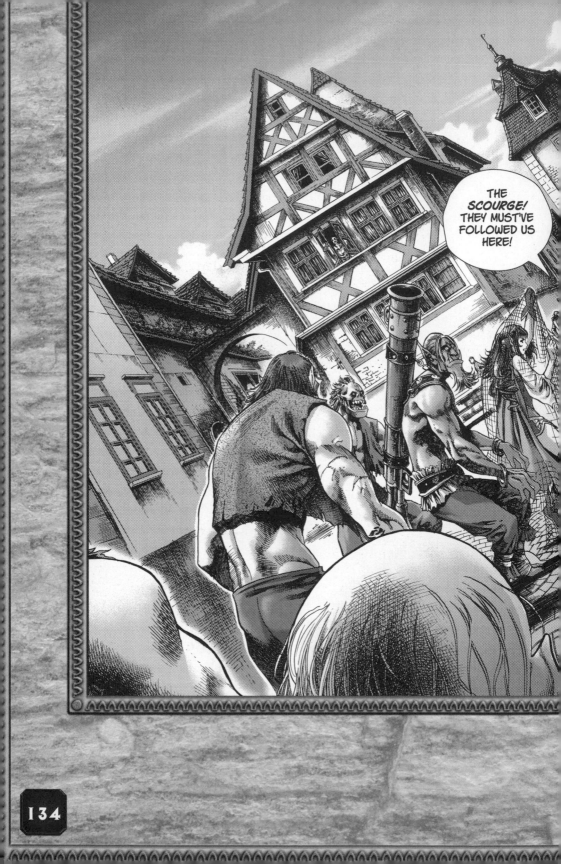

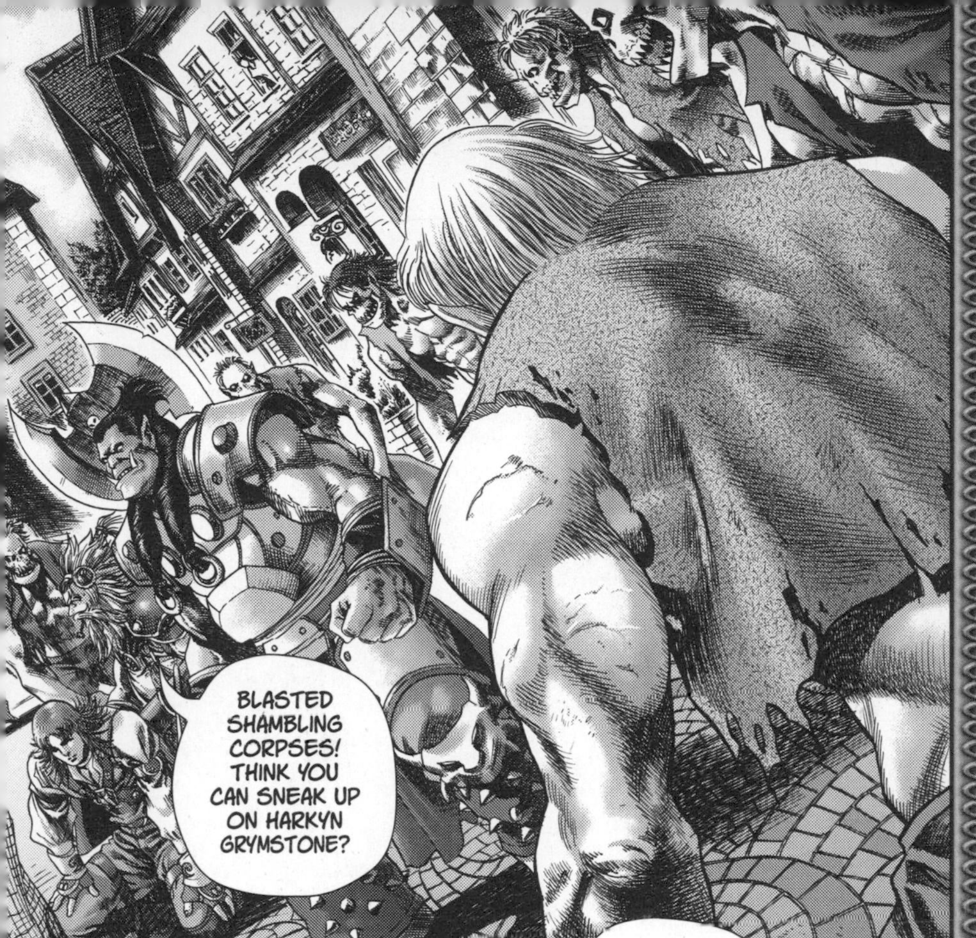
BLASTED SHAMBLING CORPSES! THINK YOU CAN SNEAK UP ON HARKYN GRYMSTONE?
I'LL BLOW YOU TO LITTLE GOBBETS OF-- EH?

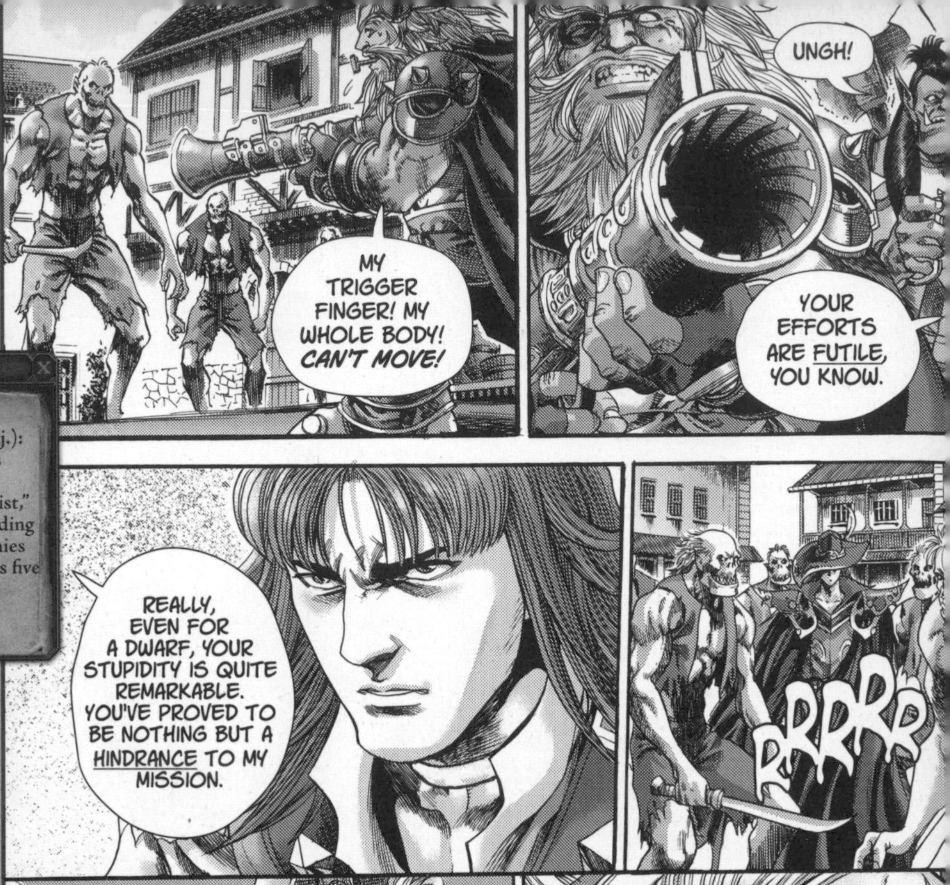
MY TRIGGER FINGER! MY WHOLE BODY! CAN'T MOVE!
UNGH!
YOUR EFFORTS ARE FUTILE, YOU KNOW.
REALLY, EVEN FOR A DWARF, YOUR STUPIDITY IS QUITE REMARKABLE. YOU'VE PROVED TO BE NOTHING BUT A HINDRANCE TO MY MISSION.
RRRRR
WHO ARE YOU TO BERATE ME SO?
YOU INCOMPETENT CREATURE! ALL YOU HAD TO DO WAS KEEP THE DRAGONS AWAY...

FUTILE

\FYOO tiyl\ (adj.): useless; hopeless

"It is *futile* to resist," claimed the invading general, "our armies outnumber yours five to one."

HINDRANCE

\HIN drens\ (n.): impediment, clog; stumbling block

Not wishing to be a *hindrance* while his mother was preparing for the party, the children packed a picnic lunch and went to the park.

BERATE

\bee RAYT\ (v.): to scold harshly

After the class's dismal performance on the exam, Professor Wilson *berated* everyone for their laziness and lack of preparation.

INCOMPETENT

\in KOM puh tent\ (adj.): unqualified, inept

Michelle's lawyer was totally *incompetent*; he didn't bother examining the witnesses or making any objections.

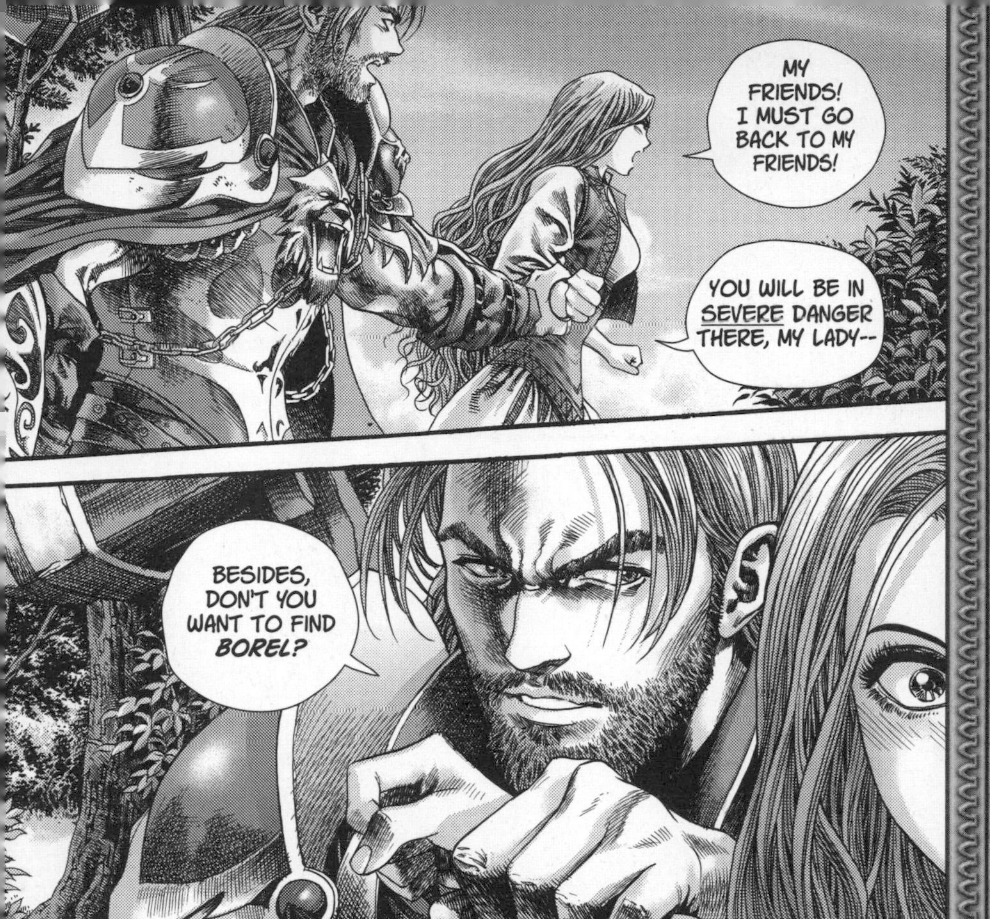
MY FRIENDS! I MUST GO BACK TO MY FRIENDS!
YOU WILL BE IN SEVERE DANGER THERE, MY LADY--
BESIDES, DON'T YOU WANT TO FIND *BOREL?*
WHAT DO *YOU* KNOW OF HIM?
COME WITH ME AND FIND OUT...
NO!
MY LADY!

SEVERE

\se VEER\ (adj.): harsh, strict, extreme

While the rest of the group went skiing, Morris stayed home with a *severe* case of the flu.

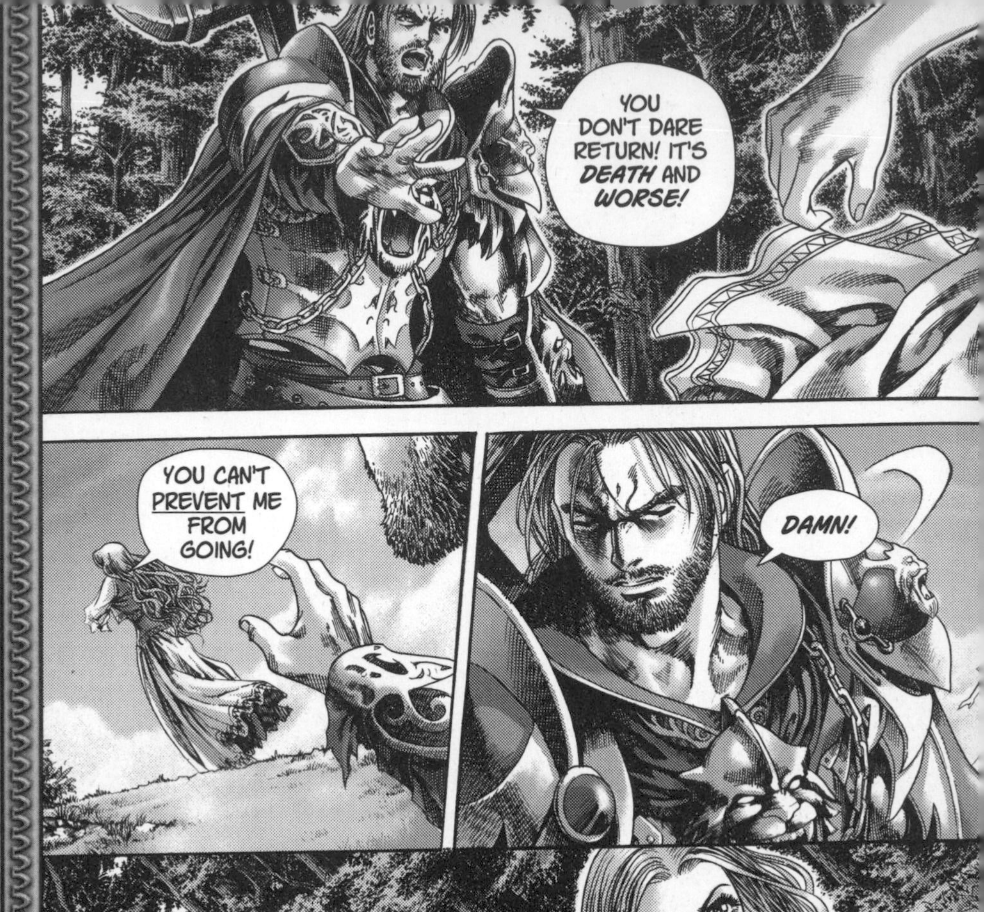
YOU DON'T DARE RETURN! IT'S *DEATH* AND *WORSE!*
YOU CAN'T PREVENT ME FROM GOING!
DAMN!
NOTHING'S WORTH THIS...

PREVENT

\pre VENT\ (v.): to keep from happening

The Panthers tried their best, but they could not *prevent* the Patriots from winning the Super Bowl again.

BUT... I AM PERPLEXED... MY EMPLOYER WAS A HUMAN! A FORMER PRINCE OF LORDAERON WHO--

AN IMAGINATIVE CASTING OF ILLUSION, MORE THAN ENOUGH TO CONVINCE A DWARF.

WHEN I FIRST BECAME COGNIZANT OF THE NEARNESS OF THE SUNWELL'S POWER, I KNEW THAT IT HAD NOT BEEN LOST...

I SENT WORD TO MY BLESSED LORD ARTHAS... WHO REMINDED ME THAT ALTHOUGH THE WIZARDS OF DALARAN MIGHT BE IN DISARRAY...

...THE DRAGONS WOULD BE DRAWN TO THE SUNWELL LIKE MOTHS TO THE FLAME.

PERPLEX

\pir PLEKS\ (v.): to confuse

Shawna had felt sure that she would beat the crowd to the sale; the sight of so many people already in the store deeply *perplexed* her.

IMAGINATIVE

\ih MAJ ih nu tiv\ (adj.): creative, clever, innovative

NASA engineers are hired to think up new and *imaginative* solutions to everyday problems.

COGNIZANT

\KOG ni zent\ (adj.): fully informed, conscious

Principal Davies kept posting signs around the school about the new dress code until he was sure that the students were *cognizant* of the changed regulations.

139

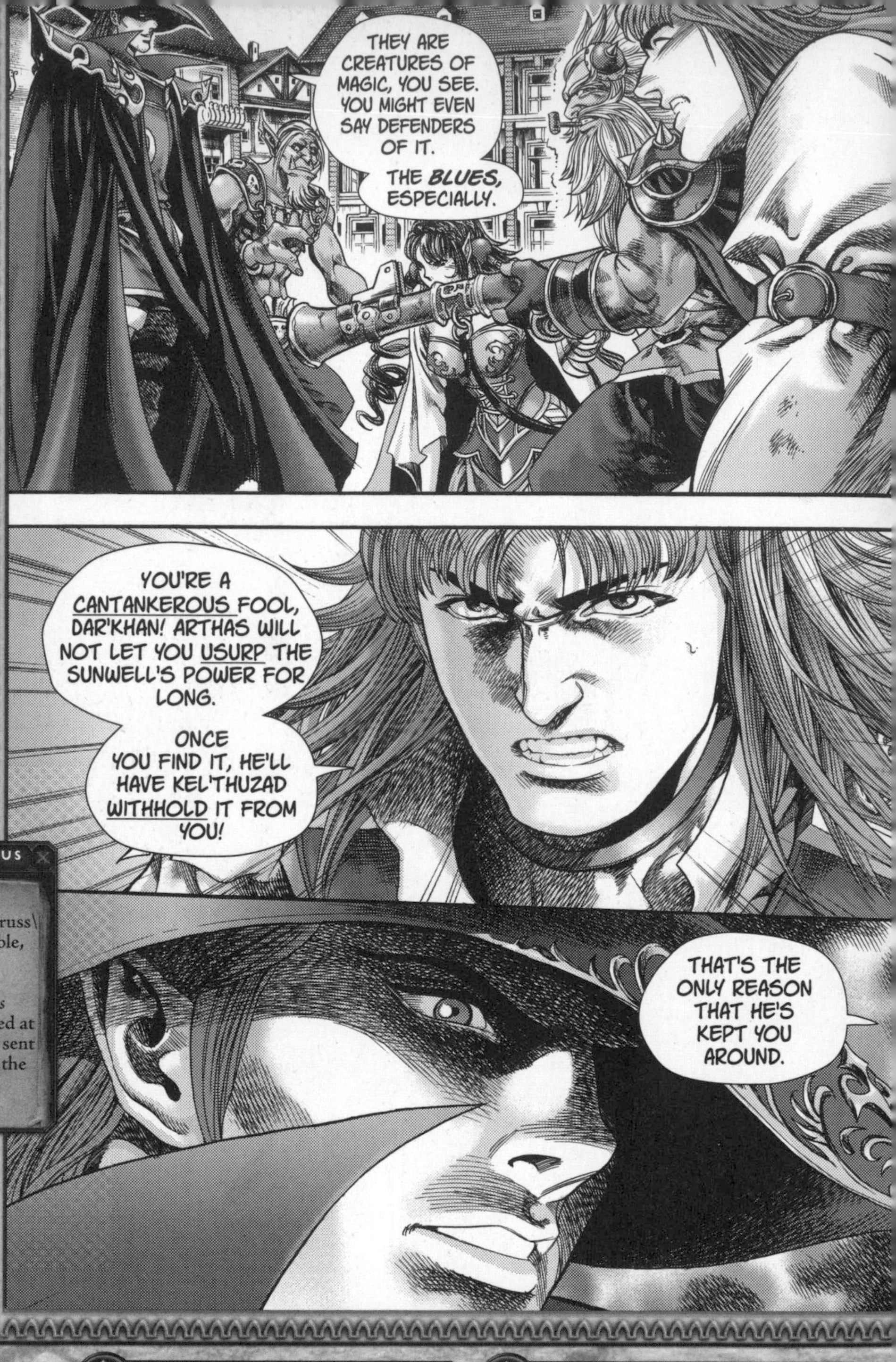
THEY ARE CREATURES OF MAGIC, YOU SEE. YOU MIGHT EVEN SAY DEFENDERS OF IT.
THE BLUES, ESPECIALLY.
YOU'RE A CANTANKEROUS FOOL, DAR'KHAN! ARTHAS WILL NOT LET YOU USURP THE SUNWELL'S POWER FOR LONG.
ONCE YOU FIND IT, HE'LL HAVE KEL'THUZAD WITHHOLD IT FROM YOU!
THAT'S THE ONLY REASON THAT HE'S KEPT YOU AROUND.

CANTANKEROUS

\kan TANK uh russ\ (adj.): disagreeable, quarrelsome

The *cantankerous* old man grumbled at the waitress and sent his soup back to the kitchen.

USURP

\yoo SURP\ (v.): to take over without right

The minister *usurped* the crown from the current king and had him imprisoned.

WITHHOLD

\with HOLD\ (v.): to restrain; keep

In order to ensure that people pay their taxes, many companies *withhold* the money from their employees' paychecks directly.

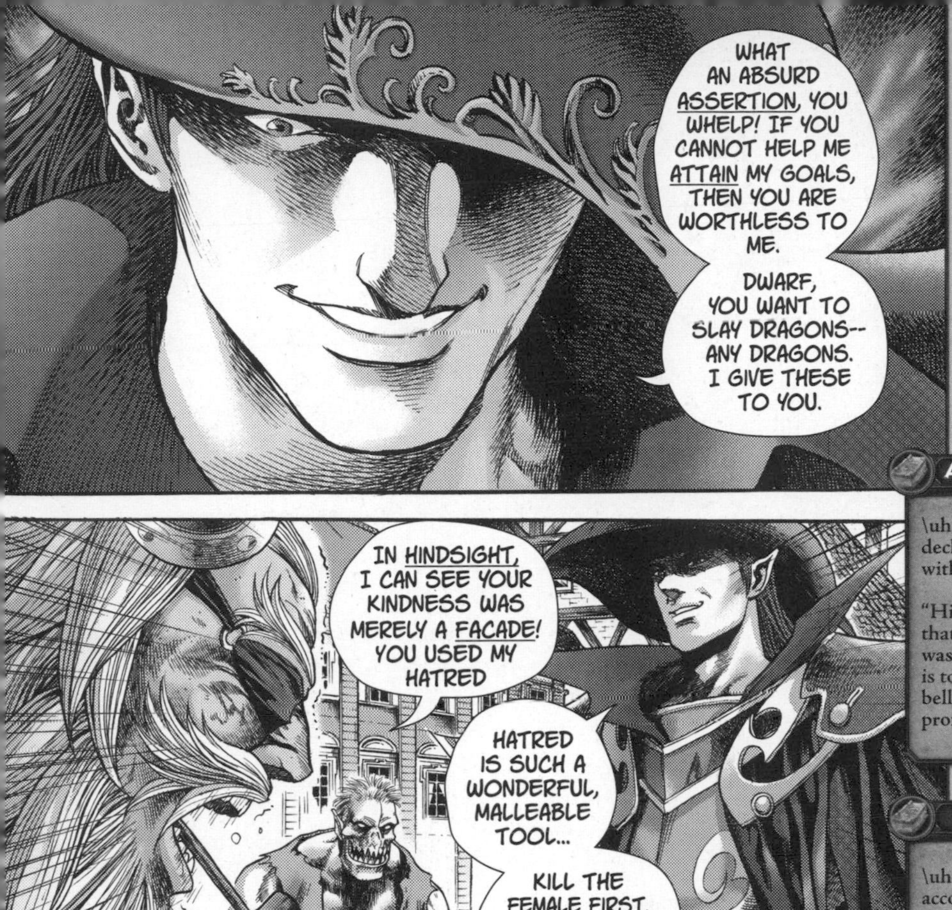
WHAT AN ABSURD ASSERTION, YOU WHELP! IF YOU CANNOT HELP ME ATTAIN MY GOALS, THEN YOU ARE WORTHLESS TO ME.
DWARF, YOU WANT TO SLAY DRAGONS-- ANY DRAGONS. I GIVE THESE TO YOU.
IN HINDSIGHT, I CAN SEE YOUR KINDNESS WAS MERELY A FACADE! YOU USED MY HATRED
HATRED IS SUCH A WONDERFUL, MALLEABLE TOOL...
KILL THE FEMALE FIRST. HE MAY REMEMBER SOMETHING, THEN.
NO! PLEASE! NO!

ASSERTION

\uh SIR shun\ (n.): declaration, usually without proof

"Hillary's *assertion* that Shakespeare was a woman is totally false!" bellowed the irate professor.

ATTAIN

\uh TAYN\ (v.): accomplish, gain

It is clear that Cleni's hard work will help him *attain* that raise he's been hoping for.

HINDSIGHT

\HIYND siyt\ (n.): perception of events after they happen

In *hindsight,* of course, I can see that lending her the car was a big mistake.

FAÇADE

\fuh SOD\ (n.): face, front; mask, superficial appearance

The criminals conducted business from a small factory in order to maintain the *façade* of respectability.

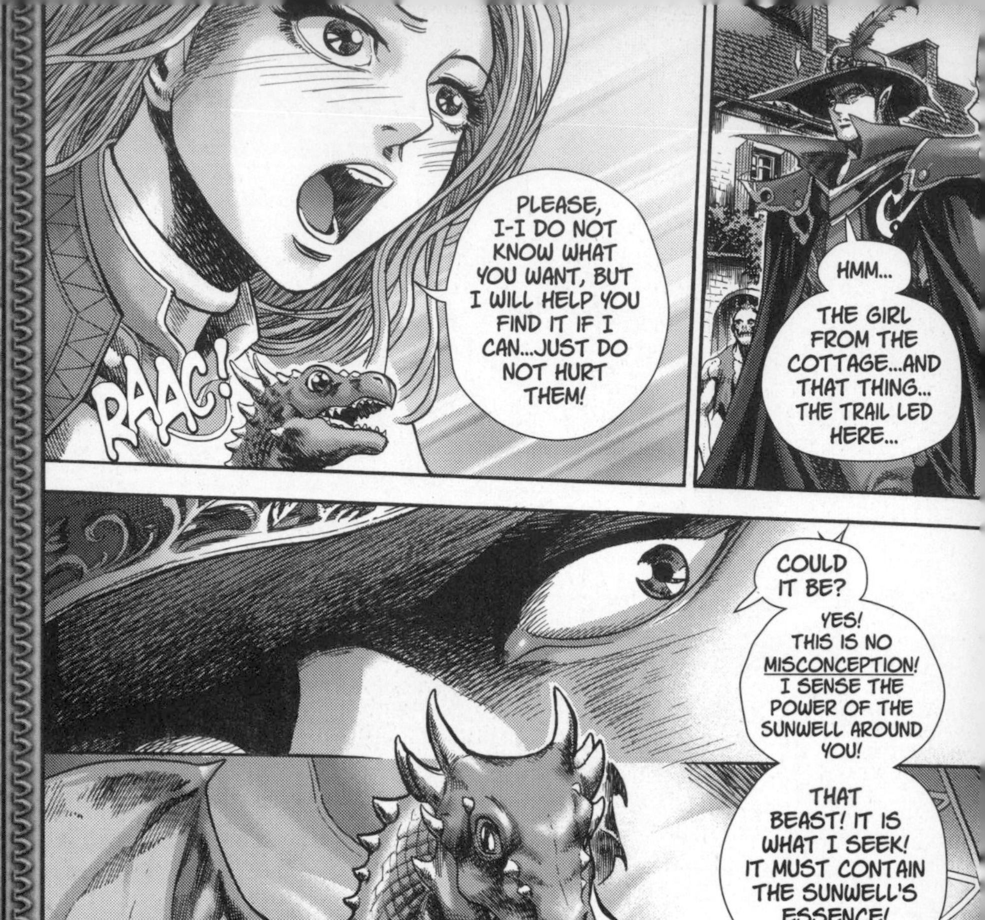
PLEASE, I-I DO NOT KNOW WHAT YOU WANT, BUT I WILL HELP YOU FIND IT IF I CAN...JUST DO NOT HURT THEM!
RAAC!
HMM...
THE GIRL FROM THE COTTAGE...AND THAT THING... THE TRAIL LED HERE...
COULD IT BE?
YES! THIS IS NO MISCONCEPTION! I SENSE THE POWER OF THE SUNWELL AROUND YOU!
THAT BEAST! IT IS WHAT I SEEK! IT MUST CONTAIN THE SUNWELL'S ESSENCE!
RAAC?
RAAC?

MISCONCEPTION

\mis kon SEP shun\ (n.): error in understanding

It is a common *misconception* that antiques are only valuable because they are old; in reality, valuable antiques are usually examples of excellent craftsmanship from their respective eras.

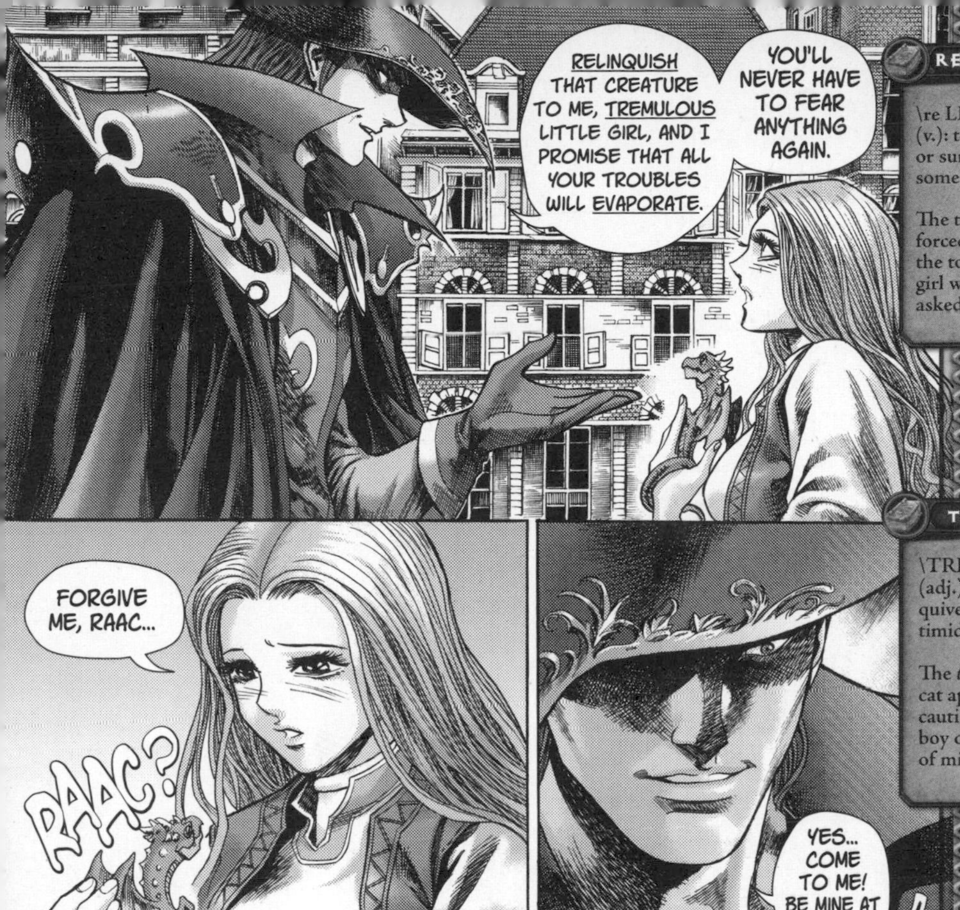
RELINQUISH THAT CREATURE TO ME, TREMULOUS LITTLE GIRL, AND I PROMISE THAT ALL YOUR TROUBLES WILL EVAPORATE.
YOU'LL NEVER HAVE TO FEAR ANYTHING AGAIN.
FORGIVE ME, RAAC...
RAAC?
YES... COME TO ME! BE MINE AT LAST!
NO, ANVEENA! HE MUSTN'T HAVE IT!
I HATE TO BE CRASS, BUT YOUR TIME IS UP... SILENCE HIM, DWARF.

RELINQUISH

\re LIN kwish\ (v.): to renounce or surrender something

The toddler was forced to *relinquish* the toy when the girl who owned it asked for it back.

TREMULOUS

\TREM yoo luss\ (adj.): trembling; quivering; fearful, timid

The *tremulous* stray cat approached cautiously as the boy offered a bowl of milk.

EVAPORATE

ee VAP uh rayt\ (v.): to vanish quickly

You need to watch the pot carefully, since the sauce will begin to burn once the water *evaporates*.

CRASS

\KRASS\ (adj.): crude, unrefined

Miss Manner watched in horror as her *crass* date belched loudly and snapped his fingers at the waiter.

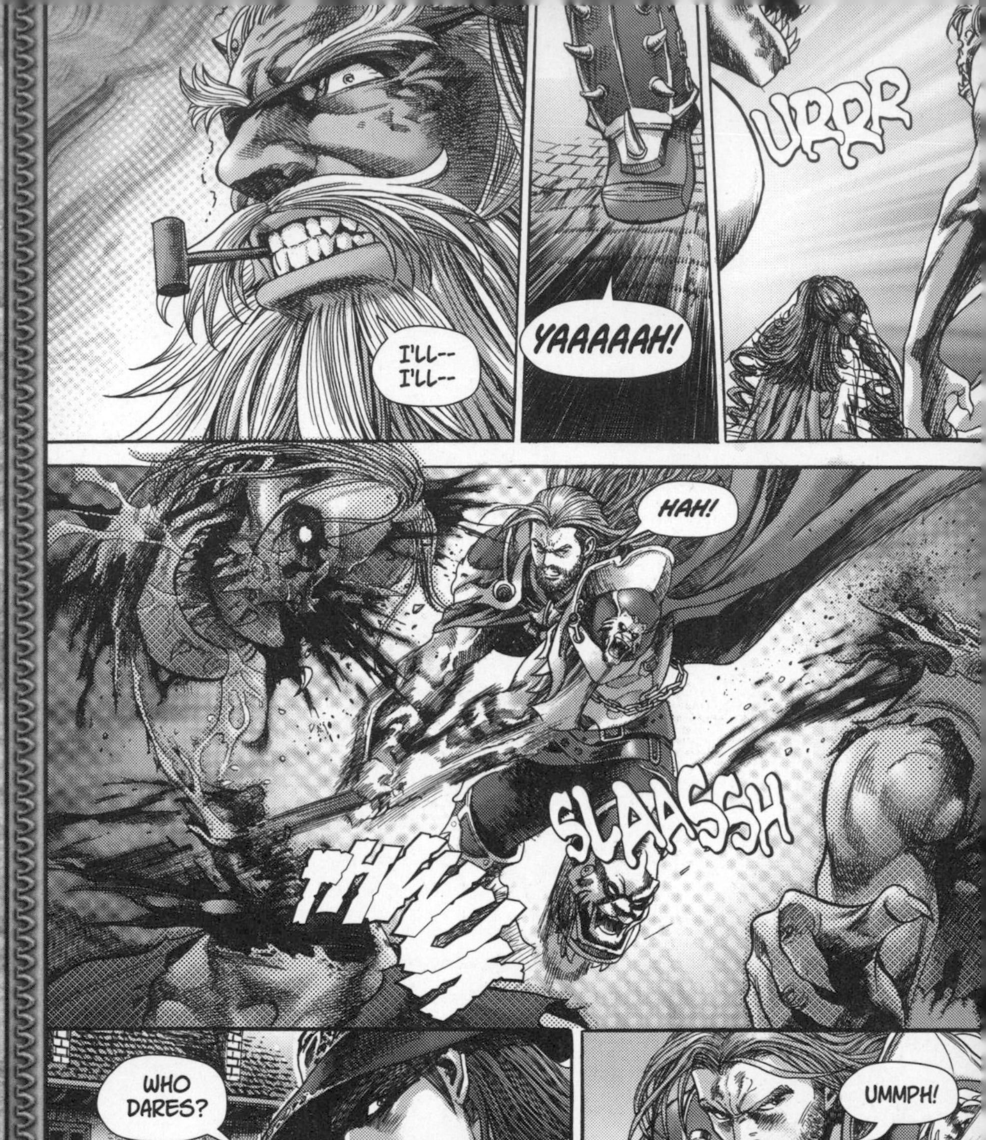
I'LL--
I'LL--
YAAAAAH!
URRR
HAH!
SLAASSH
THWUK
WHO DARES?
UMMPH!

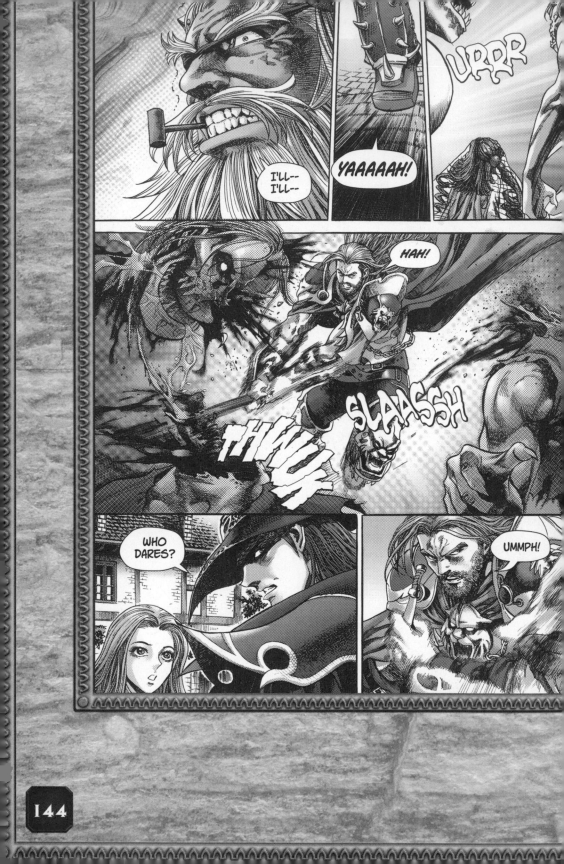

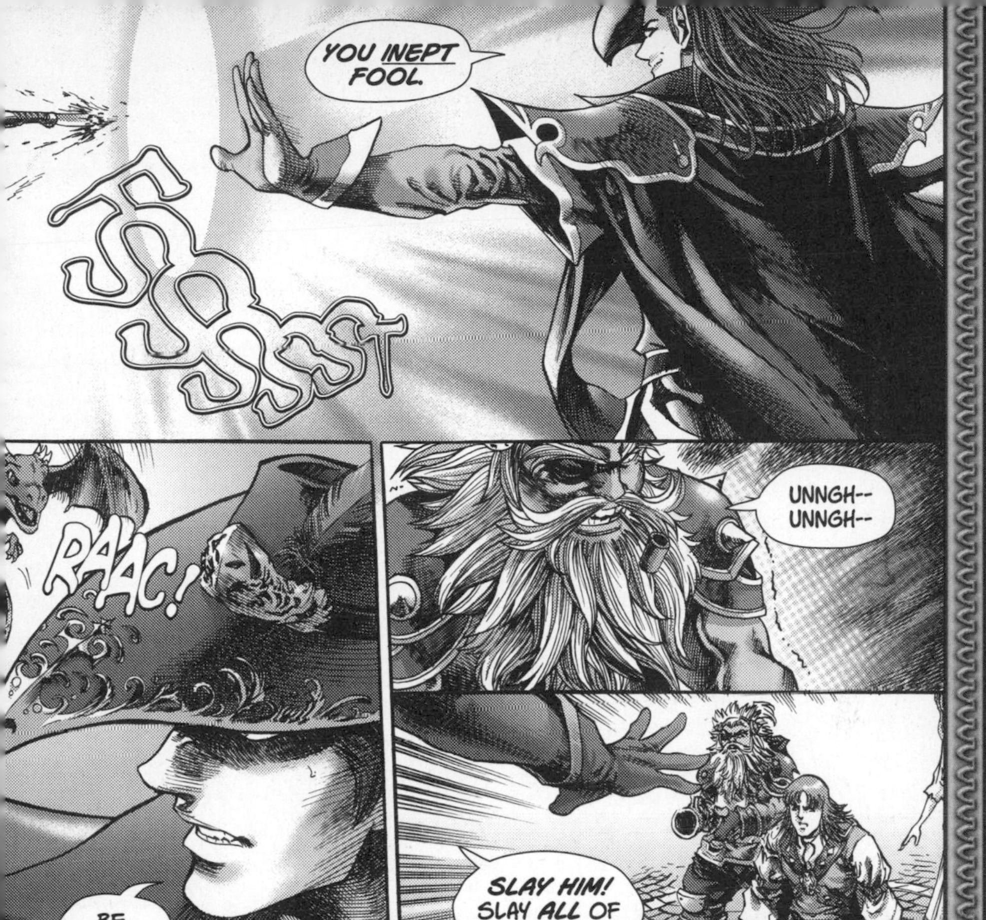
YOU INEPT FOOL.
FSSSSST
RAAC!
BE STILL!
UNNGH-- UNNGH--
SLAY HIM! SLAY ALL OF THEM!
FWOOOM

INEPT

\in EPT\ (adj.): clumsy, awkward; incapable; foolish, nonsensical

While capable of designing elegant clothing on paper, he was *inept* when it came to the real work of cutting the fabric and stitching the garments.

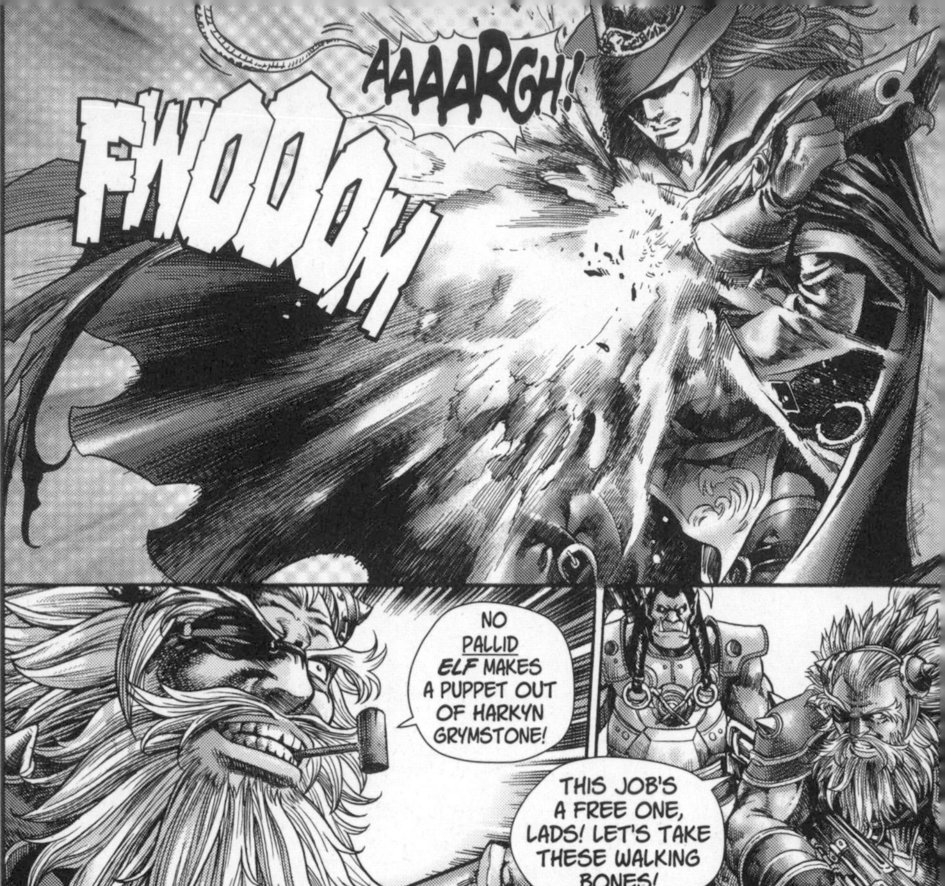
AAAARGH!
FWOOOM
NO PALLID ELF MAKES A PUPPET OUT OF HARKYN GRYMSTONE!
THIS JOB'S A FREE ONE, LADS! LET'S TAKE THESE WALKING BONES!
RRRARRR!
CRASH
URRR
HA!
SCHLOOOP

PALLID

\PAL id\ (adj.): lacking color or liveliness

After one look at her son's *pallid* complexion, Kate knew he was coming down with the same bug that his sister had contracted.

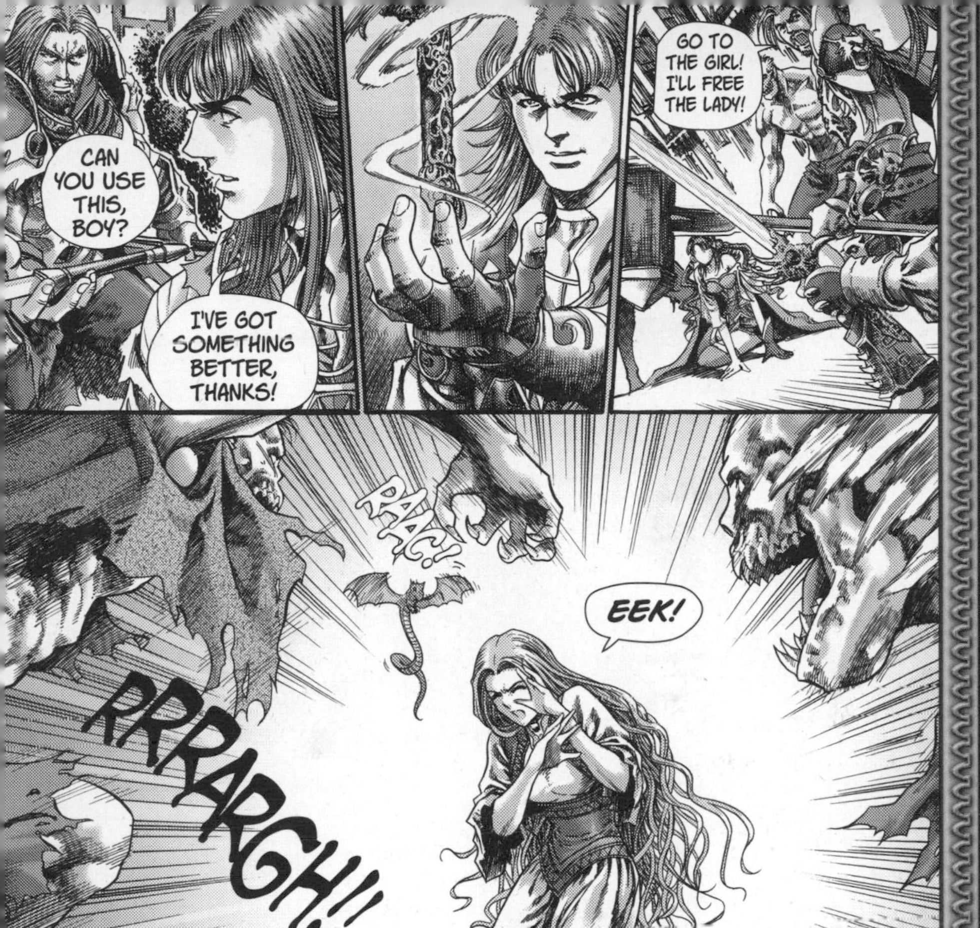
CAN YOU USE THIS, BOY?
I'VE GOT SOMETHING BETTER, THANKS!
GO TO THE GIRL! I'LL FREE THE LADY!
RAAC!!
EEK!
RRRARGH!!
SLAASSH
THWUK

HNNH --- HNNH

AHAHAH...

FOOL OF A DWARF, I AM THE PROTEGE OF THE LICH KING! I AM MORE THAN MORTAL!

PROTÉGÉ

\PRO tuh zhay\ (n.): one receiving personal direction and care from a mentor

Although David was initially a *protégé* of Pauline, he soon broke loose and developed his own style of writing.

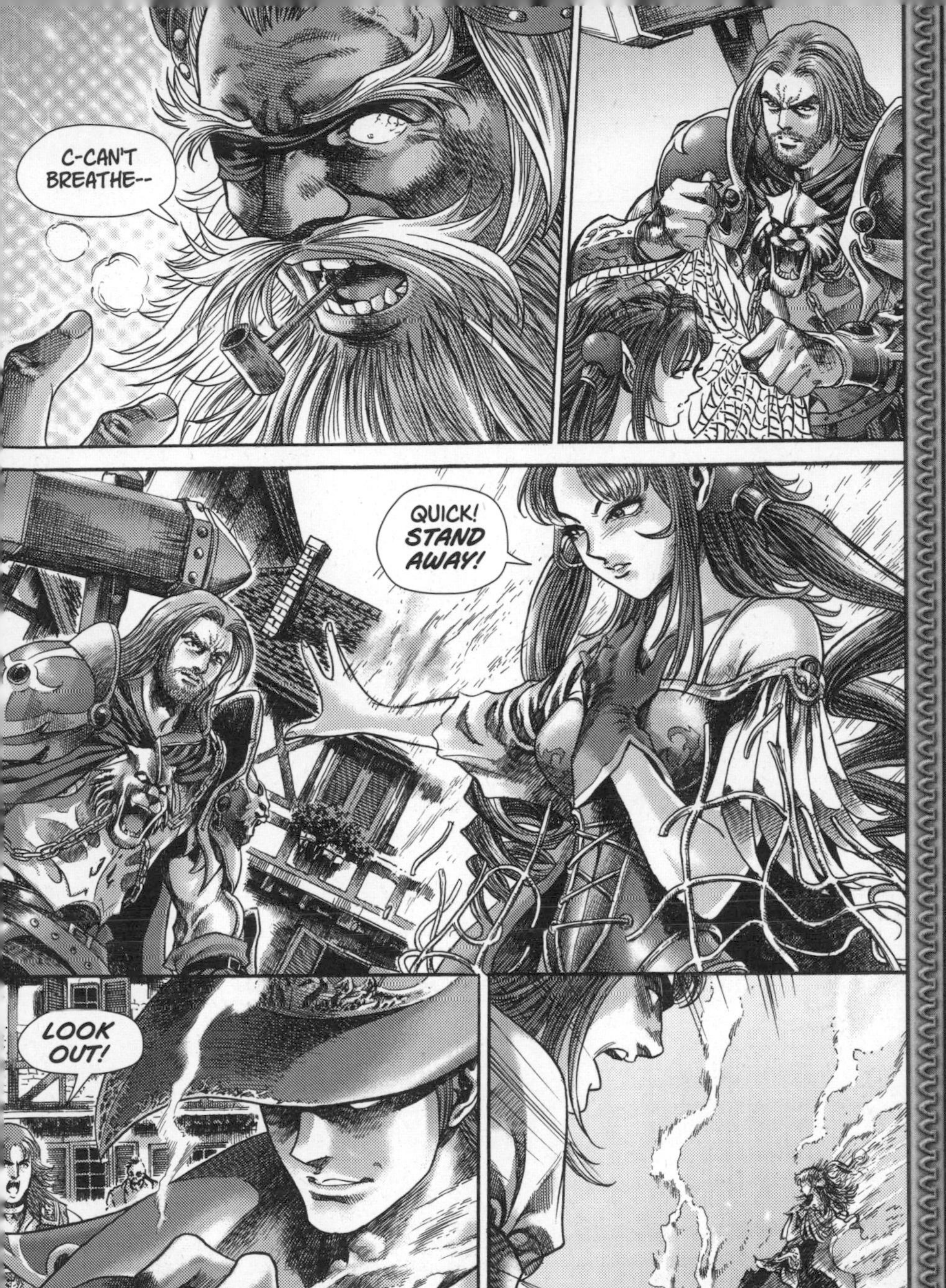
C-CAN'T BREATHE--
QUICK! STAND AWAY!
LOOK OUT!

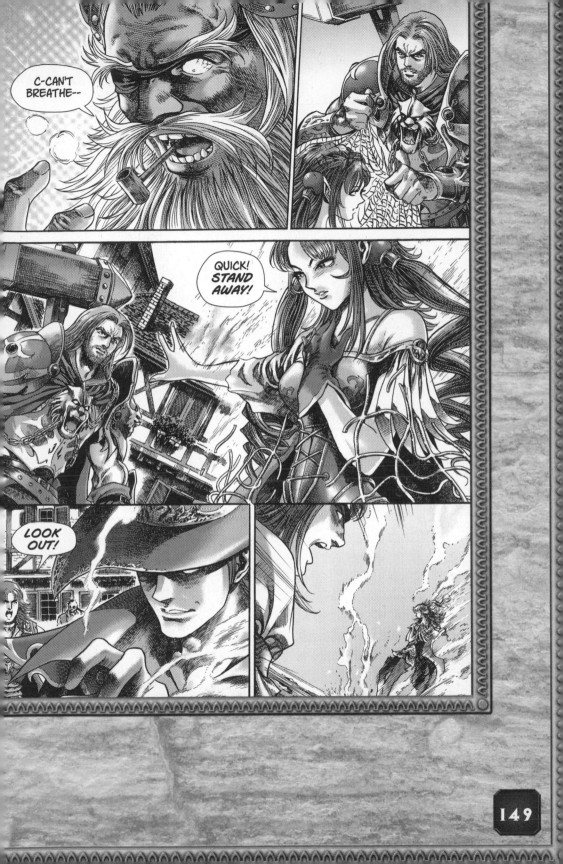

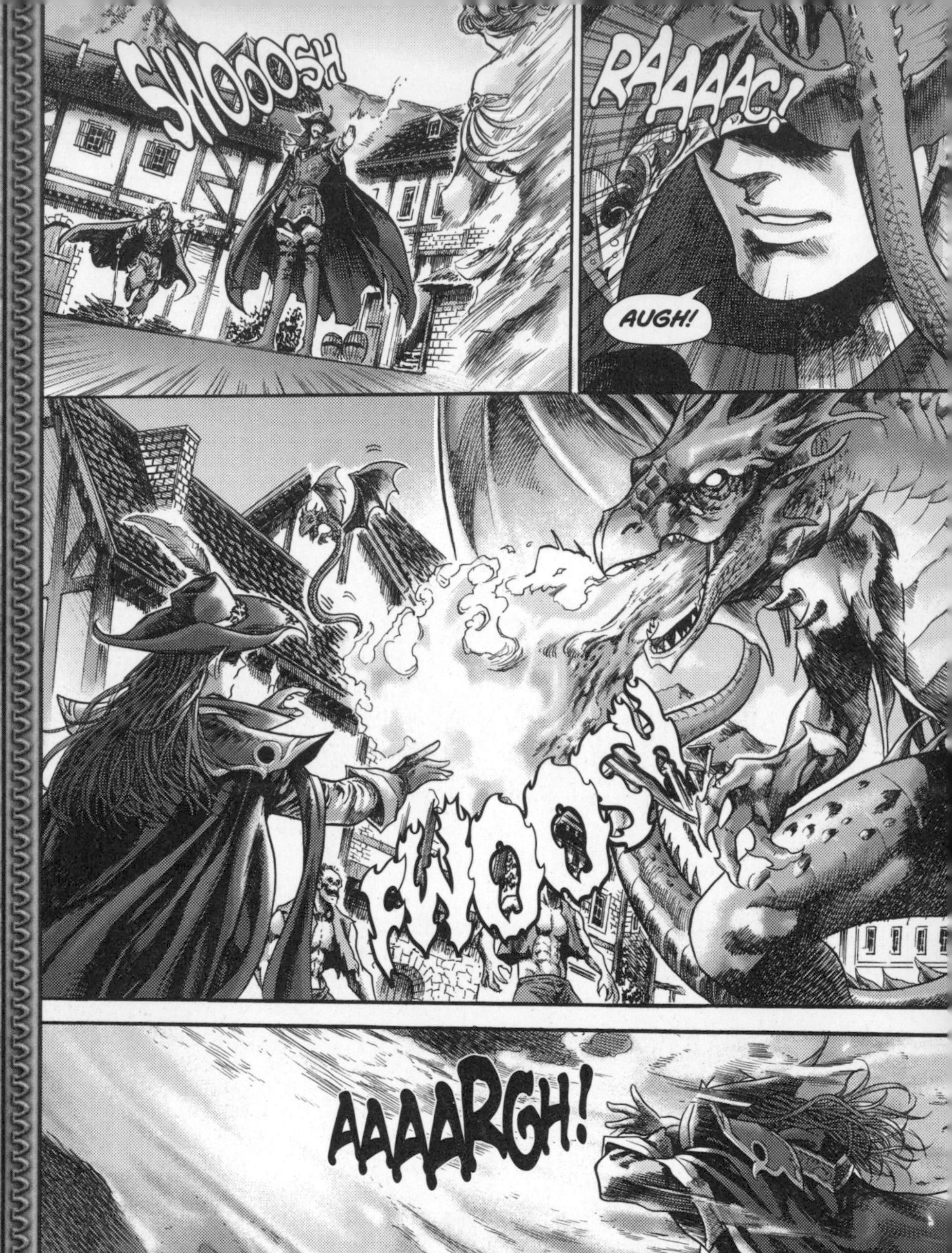
SWOOOSH
RAAAAC!
AUGH!
FWOOSH
AAAARGH!

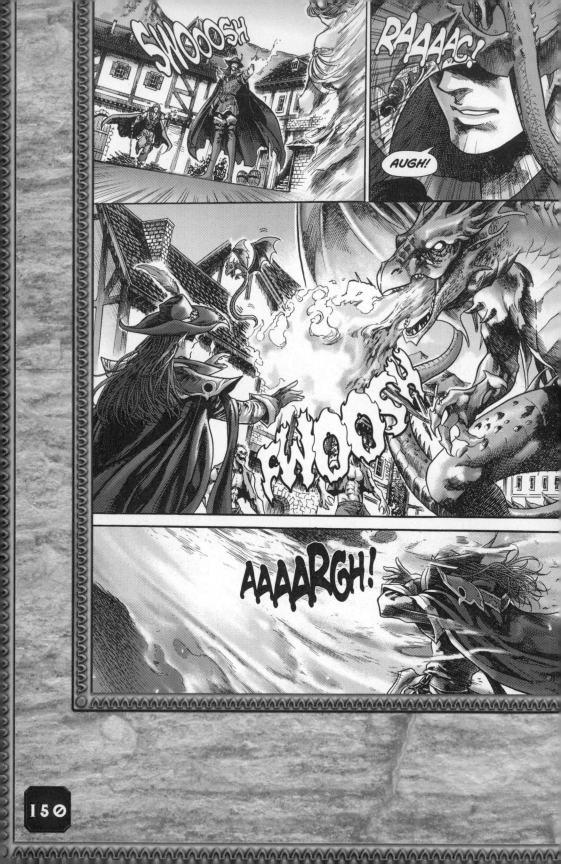

THWAM
THUD
SCHLOOOP
RRRRR

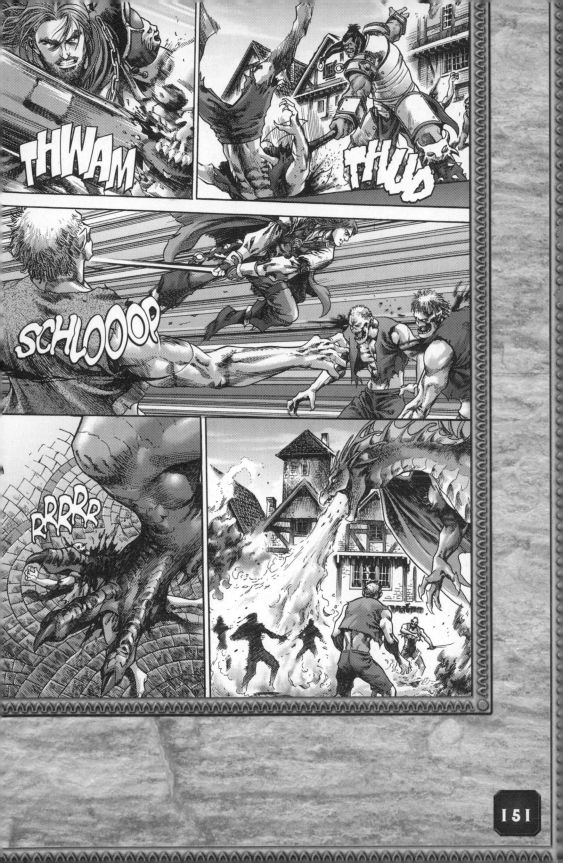

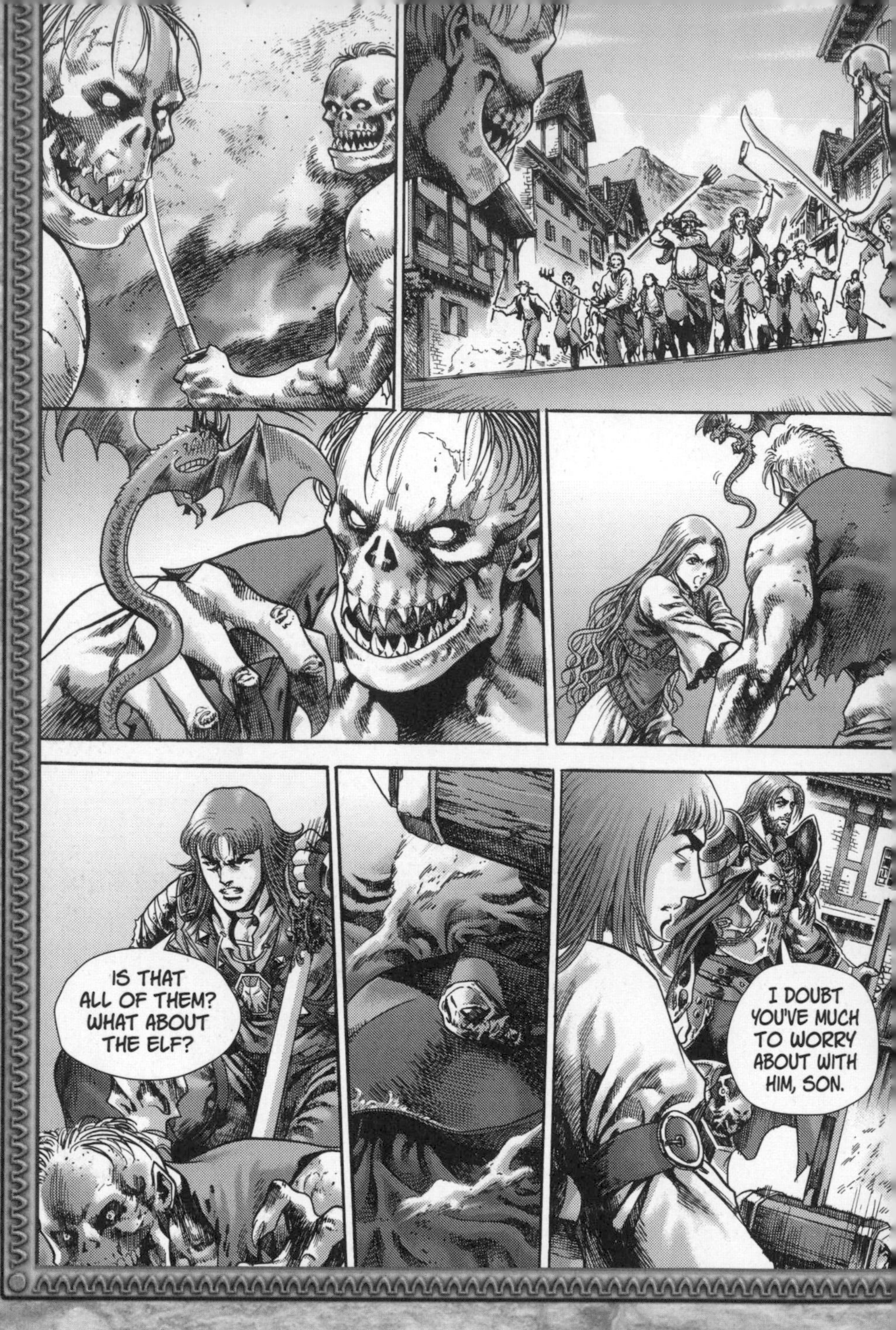
IS THAT ALL OF THEM? WHAT ABOUT THE ELF?
I DOUBT YOU'VE MUCH TO WORRY ABOUT WITH HIM, SON.

THE NEXT MORNING...

IT'S JUST AS I FEARED. ONLY THE ELF KNEW HOW TO REMOVE THESE.

I AM SORRY, KALECGOS.

IT COULDN'T BE HELPED... I CAN ONLY <u>CENSURE</u> DAR'KHAN.

BUT YOU CAN GET OUR LORD, MALYGOS, TO REMOVE YOURS.

NOT UNTIL WE CAN REMOVE ANVEENA'S, TOO. I'M NOT LEAVING HER LIKE THIS.

AND WE ALSO NEED TO FIND THIS BOREL. HE MAY KNOW SOMETHING ABOUT WHAT'S GOING ON.

CENSURE

\SEN sher\ (v.): to find fault with and condemn as wrong; blame

The president was formally *censured* by Congress for his wrongdoing.

153

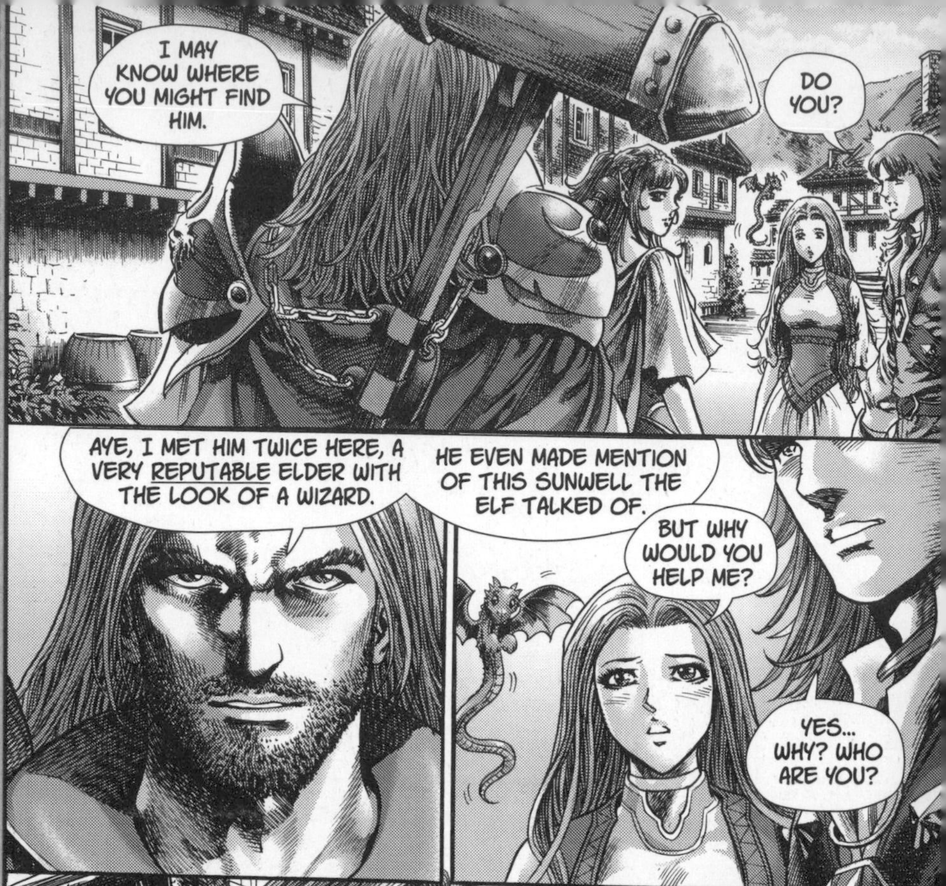
I MAY KNOW WHERE YOU MIGHT FIND HIM.
DO YOU?
AYE, I MET HIM TWICE HERE, A VERY REPUTABLE ELDER WITH THE LOOK OF A WIZARD.
HE EVEN MADE MENTION OF THIS SUNWELL THE ELF TALKED OF.
BUT WHY WOULD YOU HELP ME?
YES... WHY? WHO ARE YOU?
I WAS A PALADIN ONCE. I SWORE TO PROTECT LORDAERON. I FAILED. THIS MAY BE THE ONLY WAY TO SAVE WHAT'S LEFT.
IF THE LICH KING PROCURES THE SUNWELL, NOTHING WILL BE ABLE TO STAND AGAINST HIM.

REPUTABLE

\REH pyoo tu bul\ (adj.): honorable, respectable

Jeanie was excited to attend the lecture by the *reputable* scientist who is working on a cure for cancer.

PROCURE

\pro KYOOR\ (v.): to acquire, obtain; to get

The evidence was inadmissible in court because the police officer did not *procure* it legally.

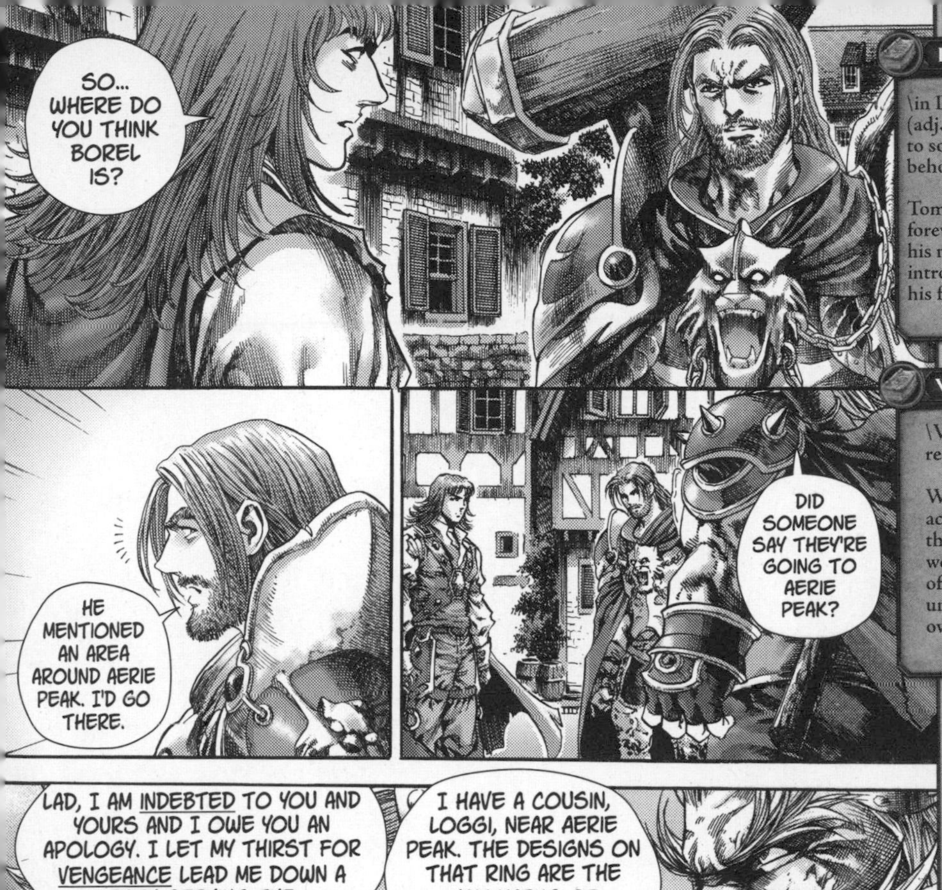
SO... WHERE DO YOU THINK BOREL IS?
HE MENTIONED AN AREA AROUND AERIE PEAK. I'D GO THERE.
DID SOMEONE SAY THEY'RE GOING TO AERIE PEAK?
LAD, I AM INDEBTED TO YOU AND YOURS AND I OWE YOU AN APOLOGY. I LET MY THIRST FOR VENGEANCE LEAD ME DOWN A PATH SERVING THE EVIL ONE.
I HAVE A COUSIN, LOGGI, NEAR AERIE PEAK. THE DESIGNS ON THAT RING ARE THE HALLMARKS OF DWARVEN WORK. HE MAY BE ABLE TO REMOVE IT.
HOW CONVENIENT—WE CAN SOLVE BOTH PROBLEMS AT ONCE...IF YOU'LL CARRY THE THREE OF US, TYRI.
FOR YOU, YES, KALECGOS.

INDEBTED

\in DET id\ (adj.): obligated to someone else, beholden

Tommy was forever *indebted* to his neighbor for introducing him to his future wife.

VENGEANCE

\VEN jinss\ (n.): retribution

While their actions against the homeowner were wrong, his act of *vengeance* was uncalled for and overdone.

HALLMARK

\HAUL mark\ (n.): specific feature, characteristic

Proper diction, a loud voice, and a compelling style are the *hallmarks* of a good public speaker.

CONVENIENT

\kon VEEN yent\ (adj.): favorable to one's comfort or needs

The hardest part about working with a big group is finding a time that is *convenient* for everyone.

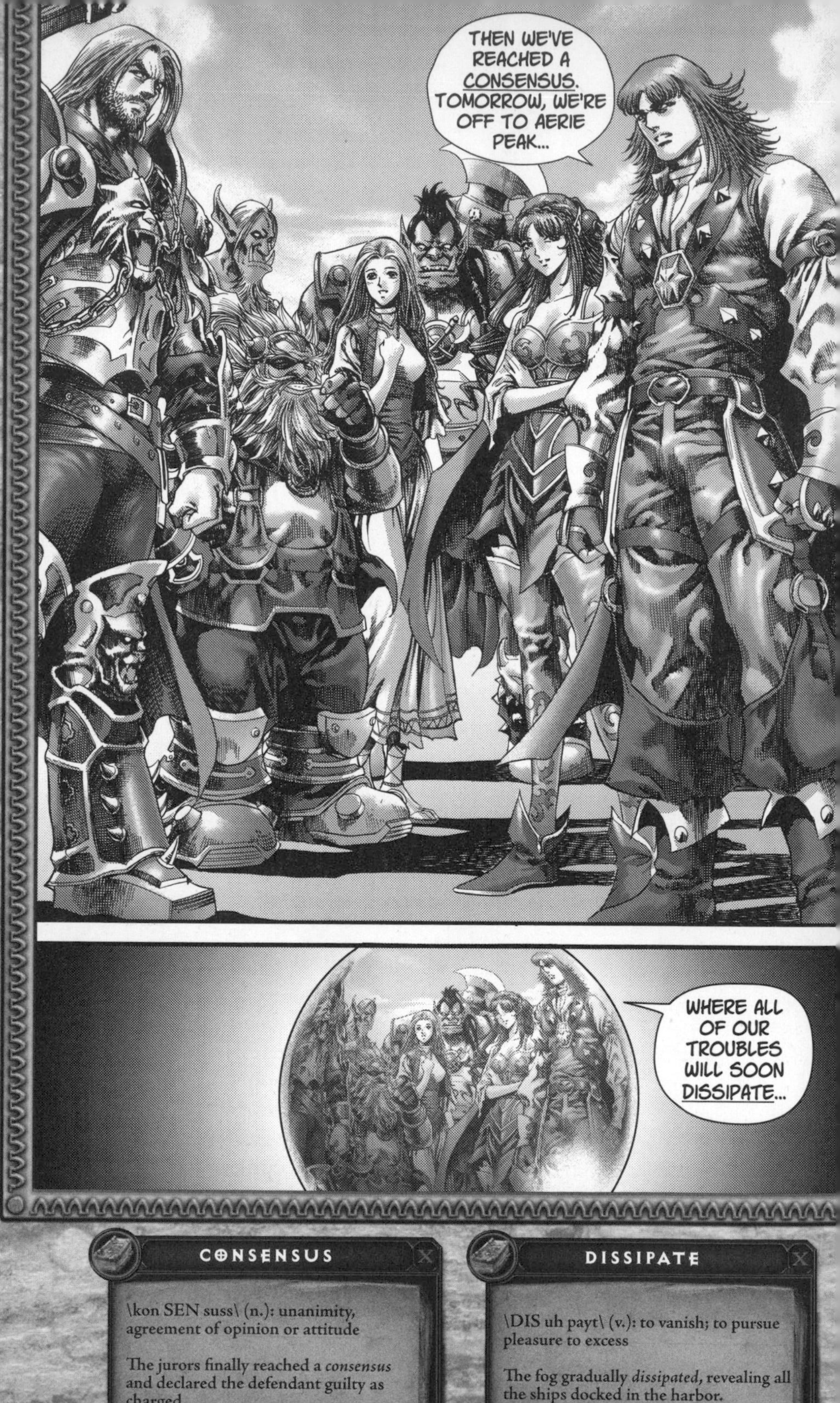
THEN WE'VE REACHED A CONSENSUS. TOMORROW, WE'RE OFF TO AERIE PEAK...
WHERE ALL OF OUR TROUBLES WILL SOON DISSIPATE...

CONSENSUS

\kon SEN suss\ (n.): unanimity, agreement of opinion or attitude

The jurors finally reached a *consensus* and declared the defendant guilty as charged.

DISSIPATE

\DIS uh payt\ (v.): to vanish; to pursue pleasure to excess

The fog gradually *dissipated*, revealing all the ships docked in the harbor.

INDEX